The Christmas Cookie Shop

Christmas Town Book 1

by

Ginny Baird

THE CHRISTMAS COOKIE SHOP
Christmas Town Book 1

Published by
Winter Wedding Press

Copyright © 2016
Ginny Baird
Trade Paperback
ISBN 978-1-942058-18-2

Edited by Martha Trachtenberg
Proofread by Sally Knapp
Cover by Dar Albert

About the Author

From the time she could talk, romance author Ginny Baird was making up stories, much to the delight—and consternation—of her family and friends. By grade school, she'd turned that inclination into a talent, whereby her teacher allowed her to write and produce plays rather than write boring book reports. Ginny continued writing throughout college, where she contributed articles to her literary campus weekly, then later pursued a career managing international projects with the U.S. State Department.

Ginny has held an assortment of jobs, including schoolteacher, freelance fashion model, and greeting card writer, and has published more than twenty works of fiction and optioned ten screenplays. She has also published short stories, nonfiction, and poetry, and admits to being a true romantic at heart.

Ginny is a *New York Times* and *USA Today* bestselling author of several books, including novellas in her Holiday Brides Series. She's a member of Romance Writers of America (RWA) and Novelists, Inc. (NINC).

When she's not writing, Ginny enjoys cooking, biking, and spending time with her family in Tidewater, Virginia. She loves hearing from her readers and welcomes visitors to her website at http://www.ginnybairdromance.com.

Books by Ginny Baird

Christmas Town Series
The Christmas Cookie Shop
A Mommy for Christmas
Only You at Christmas
The Doctor Orders Christmas

Holiday Brides Series
The Christmas Catch
The Holiday Bride
Mistletoe in Maine
Beach Blanket Santa
Baby, Be Mine

Summer Grooms Series
Must-Have Husband
My Lucky Groom
The Wedding Wish
The Getaway Groom

Romantic Ghost Stories
The Ghost Next Door (A Love Story)
The Light at the End of the Road
The House at Homecoming Cove

Romantic Comedy
Real Romance
The Sometime Bride
Santa Fe Fortune
How to Marry a Matador
Counterfeit Cowboy
The Calendar Brides
My Best Friend's Bride
The Borrowed Boyfriend
Tara (Beach Brides Book 2)
Crazy for You

Bundles
Christmas Magic:
The Complete Holiday Brides Series (Books 1 – 5)
The Holiday Brides Collection (Books 1–4)
A Summer Grooms Selection (Books 1–3)
Romantic Ghost Stories (Books 1 – 3)
Real Romance and The Sometime Bride
(Gemini Editions 1)
Santa Fe Fortune and How to Marry a Matador
(Gemini Editions 2)
My Best Friend's Bride and
The Borrowed Boyfriend
(Gemini Editions 3)
Wedding Bells Bundle

Short Story
Special Delivery
(A Valentine's Short Story)

Ginny Baird's

THE CHRISTMAS COOKIE SHOP

Chapter One

Hannah Winchester set her old clunker in park, yanked up the hand brake, and stared at the road map in front of her, comparing it to the driving directions she'd printed out from online. She thought she'd followed them precisely. Now, Hannah wondered if she'd missed a step. She appeared to be miles from civilization without any landmarks in sight. The engine heaved and chugged, sending the car lurching forward every few seconds. Hannah was definitely going to get the transmission fixed the moment she came into some money. Hopefully, that day would be *soon.*

Snow swirled around the reverberating automobile as it shuddered and bounced, sputtering beneath the loud mews coming from the back seat. The kittens were egging each other on, each one's cries meant to outmatch the other's. Jingles and Belle were entirely her seven-year-old niece's idea. Hannah's big brother, Ben, had let his daughter Lily adopt a stray kitty who'd landed on their doorstep. By the time Tulip's first vet checkup revealed she was pregnant, it was too late. Lily had become desperately attached and Ben, being the kindly single dad that he was, had indulged Lily by letting her keep the cat.

Ben had badgered his friends until he'd found homes for most of the litter. It had been Lily's idea to bestow the remaining two kittens on her Aunt Hannah. She'd tied a big red bow around each kitten's neck and given them seasonal-sounding names, saying they'd keep Hannah company in Tennessee. The last thing Hannah wanted during this trip was company for the road, or more mouths to feed on her exceedingly limited budget. But when Lily had gazed up at her with those big brown eyes set between two adorable pigtails, she'd caved. The fact that Ben had supplied a month's worth of cat food and litter, and offered to cover any future vet bills, hadn't hurt either.

Hannah caught a glimpse of the cat carrier in her rearview mirror, spying two small feline faces pressed against its slatted openings, tiny noses poking through. She had to admit the kittens were cute, even if they were raising a ruckus. Jingles was a mischievous orange tabby male that Hannah swore was part magpie, given his proclivity for stealing all things shiny. Belle was female and mostly gray, with four little white boots and a white blaze on her nose. She was far more affectionate than her brother, and had obvious ambitions of becoming a lap cat.

"Almost there!" Hannah told them, fervently hoping she was right. She'd followed her printed directions to a T, but still seemed to be in the middle of nowhere. It was hard to pinpoint her position exactly on the confusing state map, especially since she wasn't accustomed to using one. Winds gusted, slamming against the car and sending it rocking sideways. Hannah gripped the steering wheel, thinking she'd been unprepared for this weather. According to the website she'd checked in advance, the snowstorm that was destined to hit western Virginia and this portion of East Tennessee wasn't due to arrive until tomorrow. Hannah had thought she'd outrun any bad weather and be settled into her rental town house before the first snowflake fell. *Surprise!*

Hannah braced herself against the steering wheel with gloved hands until the car quit rocking, then cranked up the heat. The gas gauge indicated her tank was nearly empty. Then again, she'd filled up less than two hours ago and the gauge hadn't registered accurately for years.

Okay, she told herself, her heart racing. *Things aren't as bad as they seem.* Snow blasted against the windshield, momentarily stalling the sway of the wiper blades, and Hannah's panic spiked. *Maybe they're worse! I could be stuck here forever and freeze to death! They'll find my ice-cold body days from now, and two emaciated kittens trapped in a traveling cage!* Worrisome yowls sounded from the back seat as Hannah's pulse pounded. The pair had a point; the kittens probably wouldn't survive these conditions for long, either. Like that would be an easy situation for Ben to explain to his child. Hadn't Lily lost enough already? Hannah had to pull herself together and think clearly. Given the distance she'd covered, she should be almost to her destination. Assuming she hadn't gone off track.

The last turn she took was supposed to lead straight to the town roundabout, the one that connected with South Main Street. Hannah had been told to watch for a flagpole, the courthouse, a library, and a big town sign. But all she saw ahead of her in these near-whiteout conditions was more snow! That's when a flashing blue glimmer in her driver's side mirror caught her eye.

Thank goodness! Help has arrived. It had to be a cop figuring her for a distressed motorist. Hannah certainly couldn't get any more distressed than this.

Hannah hadn't journeyed to Tennessee for a leisurely visit. She'd inherited a business she knew absolutely nothing about, and she was determined to sell it at the first opportunity. She tried to imagine herself running a cookie shop, but just couldn't. The only picture that came to mind involved huge plumes of black smoke curling out an open doorway. Where some people had a brown thumb in the garden, Hannah wore a charred oven mitt in the kitchen. She couldn't even microwave popcorn without the bag catching fire.

Hannah spun in her seat to better view the approaching figure in dark clothing. *No, wait. It's a matching red tunic and slacks worn beneath an open field coat.* The full silhouette of a man emerged from a snowy swirl and Hannah's heart thumped. It wasn't just any outfit; it was a Santa suit. Though she'd never seen Old Saint Nick looking quite like *that*. Rather than being short and stout, he was tall and built, with an obviously solid chest and a manly jaw thinly disguised by a fake white beard. A Santa hat sat slightly askew on his head, partially covering short brown hair. He strode to her driver's side window in shiny black boots and tapped on the glass. Hannah goggled at the apparition, then lowered her window a crack.

Evergreen eyes peered in at her and Hannah caught her breath. She didn't even know eyes came in that color. They reminded her of Christmas trees: the really fresh kind, not the plastic sort that normally stood on an end table in the corner of her apartment.

"Everything okay in there? I saw that you'd pulled over. No wonder, really." Little lines crinkled around his eyes, lending them warmth beneath the wind's chill. "Given the weather." He tugged off his fake beard and stuffed it in his pocket, exposing a rugged face.

Whoa, he was a good-looking Santa. She judged him to be a few years older than her but not more than five. As if his age mattered! Hannah wasn't in Tennessee to stay and she certainly wasn't in the market for a man. She'd had enough boyfriends to last her, thank you very much. And every…single…*one* of them had let her down. *Love.* Just one more four-letter word that had been canned from her vocabulary.

The guy reached into an inside pocket and flipped open a thin leather holder, revealing a star-shaped badge. "Sheriff Carter Livingston, at your service." He had a calm confidence about him, which Hannah found soothing. Until the kittens started wailing again. The sheriff tucked away his credentials and scanned the back seat. "Not traveling alone, I see."

Hannah grimaced and spoke above their tortured cries. "Early Christmas gifts."

"Ahh."

Snow pooled in the folds of his Santa hat and stuck in tiny crystals to his eyelashes. He wiped them away with the back of his hand, squinting at her. "Where are you headed?"

"Christmas Town, Tennessee. Do you…?" Hannah stopped herself, imagining his response to the question she was about to ask. Santa, of all people, would surely know the way. "Of course, you must!" She eyed his red suit. "I mean, given your connections."

"They're stronger than you think."

"You're one of Santa's helpers?"

"I'm the real deal." The sheriff repressed a smile. "But only for today. I was filling in for a friend at the children's hospital, the next town over."

Nice looking and good-hearted too... A whole host of butterflies began winging inside her. Hannah tried her best to beat them back down. She had no business contemplating anything *at all* about the sheriff's heart. *Oops! There went another one! No!* Like whether it was good or bad—or already committed to someone. *And two more... Bad! Bad butterflies!*

"Are you all right?" The sheriff eyed her quizzically and Hannah realized she'd been batting her hands about in the air. "There's not an insect loose in there?"

"Insect?" Hannah asked feebly.

"Buzzing around inside your car." His face scrunched up in concern. "You seemed to be—"

"Oh that!" she rushed in. Hannah tucked a strand of hair behind her ear and tugged down her cap, realizing that butterflies qualified as insects. Not that she planned to say even one little word about them. "No insect! Not even a fly… Ha-ha. I was just…um…" She bit into her bottom lip, thinking fast. "Trying to fan some hot air your way… From the heater! You must be freezing out there!"

A flicker of amusement flashed across his handsome features. "I have to say, that's a first! Very considerate of you. Thanks."

Hannah steeled her resolve. She had a very specific agenda in mind and didn't need to get sidetracked by romance. By the time Hannah turned twenty-eight six months from now, she intended to have her life in order. Her dealings in Christmas Town were the first things she needed to cross off her list. She lifted the map from the console and pinched it tightly between her gloved fingers, lest her hands go crazy again. "You obviously know the area. Maybe you could point me in the right direction?"

"No need for that." He grinned and a dimple settled in the center of his chin. One very crafty butterfly broke free and spread its gigantic wings. Flapping rhythmically against her heart like a prehistoric pterodactyl or something. Hannah flattened the map against her chest, forestalling its flight.

Hannah gulped. "No?"

Carter stepped aside, gesturing grandly. "You're already here!"

Hannah stared past him through a curtain of snow. The central roundabout gradually came into focus, its gleaming flagpole towering high and disappearing into the hazy sky. Beside it, a cheery green sign draped with holly stood out against the blurred backdrop of the domed courthouse building.

Welcome to
CHRISTMAS TOWN, TENNESSEE
Where everyday dreams come true!

"What a relief!" she cried happily. By the way she was clutching that map to her chest, the poor thing must have feared she'd never make it. Naturally she'd been worried. The woman was obviously new to these parts and the elements clearly weren't cooperating.

Carter wondered what someone so young and pretty was doing in this neck of the woods. Christmas Town, Tennessee. Population: thirty-one hundred. And most of those thirty-one hundred were over the age of sixty, which was probably why Carter couldn't take his eyes off the striking brunette with warm brown eyes. Wispy raven tresses tumbled out from beneath a colorful knitted cap, framing her creamy complexion and lightly grazing her chin. She turned her eyes back on his and Carter's heart stuttered. What was wrong with his ticker today? When he'd first laid eyes on her, it had skipped a beat. Now it was slamming like a jackhammer. He pounded his chest with a fist to set it right before asking, "Long drive?"

She shook out her map and folded it, setting it aside. "I came here from Stafford, Virginia. Near Washington, DC."

"Wow. What did that take you? Seven or eight hours, I'd guess?"

"Could have been less without the weather."

"I'll bet." A blast of cold air roared through the lowered window and the woman shivered, gripping her arms by the elbows of her tattered peacoat. "My apologies," Carter said, embarrassed by his attempts to detain her. "Here I am keeping you, when what you asked for was help in getting under way."

"That's all right." Her pretty mouth drew up in a smile and heat warmed the back of his neck. "I'm new in town so I don't have many friends yet." The kittens mewed again. "Apart from those two," she said with a laugh.

"Then you're in for a treat. Everyone knows everyone in Christmas Town. It's a very friendly place."

Mirth sparked in her eyes as she lowered her window even farther and stuck out her hand. "I'm Hannah, by the way. Hannah Winchester. It's nice to meet you, Sheriff."

"Call me Carter, please." He latched on to her worn leather glove, thinking it felt soft and feminine in his calloused hand. Apart from patrolling, Carter did a whole lot of handyman work around town. All pro bono stuff to help the locals. Gave him something to do, since he'd only written one traffic ticket all year. Even then, he'd ultimately let the guy off with a warning.

"Staying in Christmas Town long?" He tried to downplay the hopefulness in his voice, but he wasn't completely successful.

She blushed and withdrew her hand. "Just passing through. I've rented a place for a month. But I might stay two, depending…"

Carter scolded himself for nearly hitting on the woman. But *nearly* wasn't doing. *Nearly* only counted in horseshoes and hand grenades… For all he knew, Hannah had a boyfriend back in Virginia. The sophisticated big-city sort, who wore a coat and tie and went into an office each day.

"I'm staying at Sisters' Row on North Main Street," she went on. "Can you tell me the best way to get there?"

Carter knew the group of three town houses that had been built by a Civil War general for his three spinster daughters. Two of the homes were occupied by locals, but the third was a rental. "Better than that," he offered jovially. "That's right on my way. Rudolph and I will take you!"

"Rudolph?" she asked with surprise.

He thumbed over his shoulder at his red pickup truck, with the portable police light flickering above the cab. "Just a little joke around here. That Ford can make it through any storm. Why don't you let me pull ahead of you and lead the way? It will be a lot easier for you to follow me than trying to make it on your own with visibility being so poor."

Hannah gave a grateful sigh as her engine heaved and groaned. Her battered sedan was ancient and it didn't appear to have been maintained. Paint peeled above the wheel hubs and rust coated the front bumper, which Carter noted was dented. "That would be terrific. Thanks!"

"Most everything's shut down today," he told her. "So there should be ample parking right in front. If not, there are spots at the Grand Hotel across the way. Already got the key?"

She nodded at an envelope on the seat beside her.

"Then I'll honk when we get there." He hesitated a moment, his gentlemanly instincts kicking in. "Would you like me to stop and help you carry your things indoors?"

She batted her eyelashes against the cold and the color in her cheeks deepened. "That's sweet of you to offer, but I'll be okay. I've only got a few bags. Plus…" She shot a glance at the noisy back seat. "All the cat stuff. But no worries. Jingles and Belle are light."

"Jingles and Belle, huh? Those two will fit right in." Carter chuckled cordially, hating to have the exchange between them end. If he had his druthers, he'd keep the charming woman engaged in conversation until his nose froze off. Which would be precisely at any second, since it had started tingling five minutes ago.

"We should probably get going," he said, lightly thumping the roof of her car. "The weather's not getting any better and dusk is settling in."

Hannah agreed and started to roll up her window before pausing. "I want to thank you." Her dark eyes sparkled. "Thank you for stopping to help me."

Carter gently tugged at the brim of his Santa hat. "All in a day's work."

Hannah laughed then asked saucily, "Santa work?"

"Ho-ho-ho," he rejoined in a deep rumble.

"You know…" She shook her finger at him with obvious admiration. "You're pretty good at that."

"Practice makes perfect."

"I thought you were only filling in?"

"You can't expect a man to reveal all his North Pole secrets in just one day."

Hannah thoughtfully twisted her lips. "No… I suppose you're right."

Carter was sorely tempted to ask Hannah about seeing her some other time, but he understood how forward and unprofessional that would appear.

"Well…" he began, still reluctant to leave.

"Well!" She beamed up at him, her expression sunny. "Hope to see you around, *Santa*."

Carter self-consciously cleared his throat. "Yeah, Hannah. You, too."

Then she sent him a megawatt smile and fully raised her window.

Carter strode back to his truck, hands shoved in his pockets and shoulders hunched against the wind. *Hannah Winchester*; the name had a musical ring to it. He also couldn't help but feel it sounded familiar. Wasn't there a Winchester family associated with Christmas Town at some point in its history? Carter had been in his appointment as Christmas Town sheriff for less than a year, but he'd been around long enough to pick up some village lore.

Founded in the early 1780s and nestled in the foothills of the Great Smoky Mountains, Christmas Town was one of the oldest towns in Tennessee. Bustling in its heyday as a stopping point for the railway that traversed the Eastern Continental Divide, the burg had suffered a steady decline, both in population and commercial potential, during the past several decades. The rail station shutting down had been a big blow. But when the bypass went in paralleling Main Street, that development had devastated the community completely.

Visitors once viewed Christmas Town as a quaint place to stop and shop, and much of the town's former enterprise came from folks simply stumbling upon it. With the construction of the new roundabout, stationed near the southern end of town, "accidental tourists" were byproducts of yesteryear. Most travelers simply took the bypass exit connecting them with the major highway.

Christmas Town's mayor, Louise Christmas, and her jolly husband Buddy, who was descended from the original Christmas family for whom the town was named, were on a mission to revitalize the ailing town. Actually, Louise was on the mission. Buddy was simply happy to assist, as were most of the other congenial townsfolk. It was Louise, in fact, who'd contacted her godson Carter in Richmond and cajoled him into running for sheriff. Carter was at loose ends after coming out of the service and tired of being a city cop, so the idea of moving to a rural area had held appeal.

Once he'd gotten to Christmas Town and set up shop, though, Carter had started to question his move. It wasn't about the town or its people, both which were terrific. It was more like Christmas Town wasn't exactly the best place for bachelors. Louise was trying to change that by inspiring more young people to move here, she'd told him later.

Carter only wished he'd better understood her success rate before his swearing-in. Not that the facts would have really swayed his decision. Carter felt called to Christmas Town and hoped to someday make a difference. He just had no idea how or when that would come about. *That's what faith is for,* Louise told him with a twinkle in her eye.

Carter yanked open the door to his truck and climbed inside, discarding his Santa hat and tossing it on top of the now-empty toy sack in the shotgun seat of his cab. His day with the kids at Mercy Central had been a blast. He'd especially loved the little ones who'd stared at him in awe and asked if he was really magic. Not quite. If he were, he wouldn't have such a disastrous track record with women, Carter thought glumly, eyeing the vehicle ahead of him.

Hannah Winchester sure was pretty. She seemed mighty nice, too. It was a shame she wasn't sticking around for more than a month or two. Of course, if she was already involved with someone, it would hardly matter anyhow. Carter cranked his ignition, deciding to ask Louise about the Winchesters. If there was anybody who knew anything—*and everything*—about Christmas Town and the people who'd lived here, it was Lou Christmas.

Hannah carefully followed Carter's taillights through the blinding snow, as they exited the roundabout at the second turn and headed north on

South Main Street. She was grateful to have the sheriff and "Rudolph" ahead of her leading the way. Wind blasted mounds of flakes across her windshield as the wiper blades struggled to keep up. Ice crunched beneath her tires, but she had little chance of skidding. Carter was taking them at a snail's pace. Her speedometer registered under ten miles per hour. The kittens seemed to have calmed themselves and had quit their whining. Perhaps they were taking their cue from Hannah, whose panic attack had passed. *Whew!* She'd made it to Christmas Town safe and sound!

She'd made a new friend as well. All right, perhaps the extra handsome Sheriff Carter Livingston wasn't quite a friend. But she had made his acquaintance, and, at his admission, this was a really friendly town. There was nothing wrong with having friends here, Hannah told herself reasonably. What did it matter that Carter was drop-dead gorgeous? She couldn't very well hold his hotness against him. What kind of woman would that make her? A beauty bigot, that's what! And Hannah always took care to treat everyone fairly.

Hannah peered through her snow-dusted windshield at the narrow street ahead of her. Glimmering lampposts held colorful Christmas decorations, their muted light shining through torrents of snow.

Carter was right about things being shut down. It was the Saturday after Thanksgiving, and the places that normally would be open this afternoon were closed because of the weather. The old-timey businesses with darkened storefronts had names like the Holly and the Ivy, All Things Christmas, Santa's Sandwich Shop, Christmas Town Drugs, and the Holiday Bank. *So, that's what Carter meant about Jingles and Belle fitting in!*

It wasn't just about the name of the town...the Christmas Spirit seemed to be infused in everything here! She laughed, then spotted Jolly Bean Java on her left and the Merry Market beside it. The Merry Market was the one store with its lights on, and it looked like a good place to pick up groceries once she'd settled in. Hannah hoped it wasn't much farther to Sisters' Row, so she could walk the distance rather than having to risk driving again.

Carter approached a cross street leading west toward a high mountain ridge, and Hannah spotted the signpost: *Santa Claus Lane.* The Christmas Cookie Shop was right on that street! Hannah couldn't help but feel excited at the prospect of seeing the place in person. She'd been able to find it online through its old rental listing, but guessed that some of the interior had been changed. On top of that, it had stood empty for a decade, so it was bound to be dusty, and maybe even cluttered with cobwebs inside.

Hannah halted at the stop sign, then cautiously followed Carter through the intersection, while snow spiraled around them, cloaking the air in a wintery haze. The Snow Globe Gallery commanded a large corner lot to her left and an enormous shuttered-down building stood kitty-corner from it across the way, where South and North Main Street joined. It was three stories tall with a covered wraparound porch and an ornate façade facing the T-intersection with Santa Claus Lane. Several empty parking places flanked it. *The Grand Hotel! Of course!*

A ceramics shop, South Pole Pottery, sat to the hotel's right, and a string of handsome Victorian homes paraded down the street to its left. Carter slowed to a stop and honked twice. Hannah glanced again to her left, spying a small group of restored town houses snuggled together behind a wrought-iron fence at the far end of the Snow Globe Gallery. All three were painted dusty rose and had dark green gingerbread trim, and each one had its porch light on. The one that shone the brightest illuminated the number she sought.

Hannah saw more historic homes situated on the other side of Sisters' Row, trailing down the street and disappearing behind curtains of snow. This was clearly the residential end of town. She honked back in thanks, then maneuvered into a curbside parking place. When she shut off her engine, Carter and Rudolph slowly pulled away. Hannah had never been so glad to have a journey end or this thrilled to have arrived at a destination safely. She turned toward the back seat. "Well, kids!"

Two sleepy-eyed kittens lifted their heads and blinked at her from inside the cat carrier.

"Looks like we're home."

Chapter Two

Hannah buttoned her coat and slid on her hat and gloves, preparing for her trip to the Merry Market. She'd gotten Belle and Jingles settled with a fresh litter box and mushy cat food, which they were lapping up eagerly from their bowls in the kitchen. The rental townhome was functional and roomy, and furnished sparsely with antiques. The two bedrooms upstairs were of equal size and shared a hall bath. Hannah had set her suitcase on the double brass bed in the rear bedroom, thinking it might best to avoid any street noise. Though she didn't imagine she'd get much of that here, you never knew. With the way things were looking in Christmas Town, Santa Claus himself might lead a parade down the avenue complete with bells and whistles! Hannah grinned at the thought of her own personal Santa, Carter Livingston, commanding a band of little children dressed as elves. *Of course, he's not really mine,* Hannah thought when her heart gave a light flutter. Misbehaving butterflies! When were they going to learn to control themselves? Precisely when Hannah did, she guessed.

Guarding her heart wasn't easy, when the darn thing had a habit of rushing headlong into relationships.

Her brother Ben claimed she'd been more in love with the concept of love than with any of her exes themselves. Hannah conceded he had half a point, but not a whole one. The truth was that she did like being in love and adored the heady feeling of falling for someone. It was just the inevitable crash of disillusionment afterward that she didn't enjoy.

Hannah sighed and glanced around the living room with its cozy, yet no-nonsense, décor. The back end of it housed a small dining room table with four chairs, set in a nook by a large bay window overlooking a brick patio and abutting a garden area. She was a little disappointed there'd be no building fires in the fireplace, which was centered against the outside wall. It had been sealed off, she guessed due to the age of the house and safety concerns. A comfy-looking love seat was backed against the wall facing the fireplace. An old oak coffee table stood on a colorful oriental rug before it, and an overstuffed armchair sat to its left. Matching end tables, fashioned from old spool cabinets, held a pair of complementary hurricane lamps on either side.

A flat-screen TV on an entertainment console was to the left of the hearth and a short bookcase, brimming with an assortment of paperback novels and hardcover nonfiction books on historical Tennessee, sat on its right. There were only two more rooms downstairs, a petite galley kitchen and a tiny half bath, but Hannah could easily work with everything here. The place was far better appointed than the small apartment she'd rented back home. Tons bigger, too. She was tempted to take turns sleeping in each of the bedrooms upstairs simply because she could!

Hannah checked the mantel clock from where she stood in the small foyer, really a brief entranceway holding a table by the door, with a mirror hanging above it in a pretty painted frame. It was five forty-five. Even if the store closed at six, she could probably still make it in time to grab a few simple provisions. She saw through the front window that the snow was still pounding down outside, but the Merry Market was just up the street. She could get there quickly if she hurried along.

Hannah slipped the key in her pocket and grabbed her purse off the entrance table, bracing herself for the cold. But when she pulled back the door, she nearly jumped out of her skin! Two strange women stood on the stoop before her.

One was short and wore a puffy black and white animal print coat with coordinating zebra-striped gloves. She appeared to be in her early sixties, but had a youthful face, offset by a sassy contemporary haircut: caramel-colored with gold highlights and white frosted tips that seemed to glint in the porch light. An ornate reindeer headband perched on her crown, its individual antlers—each bedecked in jingle bells—bouncing. She grinned broadly and the younger woman beside her, a pretty blonde around Hannah's age with bright blue eyes, did, too.

The blonde wore a puffy white ski jacket and had hair tumbling past her shoulders in waves. Her earmuffs were fluffy white balls spiked with what appeared to be bits of glittery tinsel. In her arms, she held a big wicker basket draped with a festive red-checkered covering cloth.

The shorter woman lunged at Hannah, arms outstretched. "Hannah Winchester!" *Oomph*. She yanked Hannah into a tight hug against her bony frame. "Welcome! Welcome to town!"

Hannah lightly patted her back, thinking she recognized the voice from the phone conversation she'd had when renting this place. "Mrs. Christmas?"

The woman shot back in their embrace and antler bells tinkled. "Puh-leeze!" Her grin widened as her eyes sparkled. "Call me Louise." She twisted her lips in thought. "Or Lou will do. Whichever you'd like."

Hannah grinned tightly at Louise, who was now squeezing her arms in her steely grip. The woman had the strength of a lioness! "It's, er…so nice to meet you!" She darted a glance at the blonde.

"Oh, hi!" She lifted the basket by way of greeting. "I'm Sandy."

"Sandy," Hannah replied, still stunned. "Hi!"

The kittens scampered out of the kitchen and stared out the open door, tilting their heads at the strangers. Snowflakes blasted past them, dusting the welcome mat, and each quickly shook out its fur.

"Mind if we come in?" Louise released Hannah, then answered the question herself, by barreling indoors.

Jingles and Belle hustled out of the way of the high-end fashion boots stampeding straight for them, while Lou was oblivious.

"Of course you don't. It's murder out there." Lou ripped off her gloves and laid them on the entrance table. "Chilly!" she said, glancing around. "We need to adjust the thermostat."

"No, really, it's all right!" Hannah helplessly followed her and Sandy back inside and shut the door behind her. "I like things on the cool side."

"Nonsense," protested Lou. She'd already located the thermostat on the wall near the kitchen and was adjusting the temperature. "Nobody likes it cool indoors in December. Unless maybe…" She rolled her eyes with a laugh and the jingle bells sounded again. "You're in south Florida."

"Which you definitely are not," Sandy assured Hannah with a solemn look. She stared down at the kittens, who approached her cautiously. "What have we here? What an adorable little pair."

She crouched down, balancing the basket on one knee, and extended her opposite hand, in which she gripped a shiny gold key tied to a silky green ribbon. Jingles darted for it. "Oh look, how cute!" Sandy dangled the key and the cat swatted at it. "She wants to play!"

"He."

"What?" Sandy glanced Hannah's way and Jingles seized the advantage.

"He's a boy. His name is—"

"Oh!" Sandy started in surprise at the sudden *yank* on the ribbon. Then Jingles was off! A blur of orange stripes barreling up the stairs, the key dragging from the ribbon in his mouth and whacking against each hardwood step as it hit.

"Jingles, no!"

Louise gaped at Belle, who'd begun bravely weaving herself around Louise's ankles. "What's all this?" She met Hannah's eye with obvious disapproval. "Kittens? *Two* of them?"

"No, I…"

"Heavens!" Louise gasped. "There aren't more?"

Heat seeped through her. Hannah had already booked this place when Lily gave her the kittens, and she honestly hadn't considered pets being a problem one way or another, since the rental listing said *pet friendly*. Of course, she should have asked about it. But she'd had so many other things on her mind. One thing she knew about Jingles: If Hannah didn't locate that key quickly, they might never find it. She had to move from her apartment without ever recovering that missing earring. Perhaps Jingles had swallowed it. She hoped he wouldn't try eating a key, but she wouldn't put it past him. That's all she needed now. One of the kittens choking itself to death. "Excuse me!" Hannah hurriedly dropped her purse and flew up the stairs, calling out in desperation. "I'm so sorry, Lou! I'll explain!"

Hannah reached the upstairs hall and dashed into the back bedroom she'd claimed as her own, but there was no sign of the little imp anywhere. The bathroom was probably out: not enough places to hide. So she hustled across the hall to the front bedroom, for the first time noticing that it, too, had a sealed-off fireplace. In a faraway corner near the headboard end of the bed, a skinny orange and white striped tail flicked against the carpet. Jingles was hiding under the bed! Hopefully, he still had Sandy's key with him. Hannah lowered herself to her knees slowly so as not to startle him. Suddenly, she was broiling. Her heavy coat, the hat, and gloves were all too much indoors. Particularly coupled with her rising blood pressure, not to mention the increasing temperature thanks to helpful Louise. Hannah removed her hat and gloves and softly laid them on the bed before undoing her coat buttons. Feline legs crouched, preparing to shoot farther under the bed. She'd never reach him then.

In one desperate move, Hannah lunged for the cat, slamming herself to the carpet, arms thrust forward and—*yeow! Forehead directly against a side rail holding the bedframe!* Her face dropped forward and

smacked the floor. *Ouch! Forehead first.* But she had
him pinned in her steady grasp. Hannah thought she felt
the ribbon and a key there too, but it was hard to tell for
sure above the loud pounding in her head. Boy, that
knock had smarted! Like the Dickens! She'd hit the
same spot on her forehead twice and would have a knot
the size of Mt. Everest to show for it.

Hannah cautiously raised her chin to stare under
the bed at the naughty kitten. "Gotcha!"

Jingles blinked, as if he couldn't imagine why she
sounded cross. Hadn't he done a good thing? Hiding
this precious find for safekeeping? The silky ribbon
draped past his chin, the key trailing behind it, as
Hannah pulled him out from under the bed. "Come
here, you little scamp," she said, her head throbbing.
"You've caused enough trouble for one day."

She got to her knees, then stood with Jingles in her
arms before wrestling the key away from him. He
immediately started purring, apparently liking this
game. "Hide and seek, sure," Hannah said indulgently.
"I know it was good for you…" Jingles was really
impossible to stay mad at, especially when he turned up
his motor. Still, he wasn't getting off scot-free. Jingles
was going in "kitty time-out" for the next little while,
which meant she was depositing him in the cat carrier
in the kitchen until her house guests left. *Wow, what an
introduction to Christmas Town!*

When Hannah descended the stairs, she found both
Lou and Sandy had removed their coats and were
seated in the living area. Sandy was on the couch and
she'd placed her earmuffs on the coffee table in front of
her. She appeared to be busily rearranging something
inside the wicker basket she'd set on her lap. Lou
perched on the edge of the armchair beside her, her

back held ramrod straight and still wearing her headgear. Hannah noticed Belle had jumped right up and made herself at home on Lou's lap. She was stretched out sideways, lazily licking one white paw as if there wasn't a more comfortable spot in the world. Lou, on the other hand, appeared petrified. She wasn't moving a muscle. Merely peering down at the kitten with incredulous eyes, her arms rigid at her sides while she clutched the seat cushion white-knuckled.

Hannah hurried into the kitchen carrying Jingles. "Be right back," she told the others, scuttling past them. "You stay put and out of trouble now," she whispered to the cat, before tucking him away in his cage and shutting it securely.

She paused before the threshold and inhaled a deep breath, letting it go slowly. Hannah rolled back her shoulders, then strode into the living room holding Sandy's key. "I'm sorry about that," she said, handing it over just as Sandy drew the covering cloth over her basket. "Jingles can get a little tricky that—" Hannah observed Lou's rigid form. Perhaps she was terrified of cats. Maybe she'd had an unfortunate run-in with one as a child. "Here Lou, let me take her." She lifted the purring kitten from Lou's lap and Lou sneezed vehemently. Lou shoved her hand in her jeans pocket, pulled out a tissue and sneezed again. Hannah noticed her eyes were red-rimmed. "Allergic?" she guessed weakly.

"Badly!" Lou shot to her feet in a new sneezing fit, then hightailed it into the bathroom, attempting to cover her mouth and nose with her forearms as she went—the reindeer headband jingling all the way. "Just going to pop a few allergy tablets!" she cried, nabbing her purse off the floor. *"Aaah...aahhh-choo!"*

Hannah grimaced apologetically at Sandy. "I, uh…will just run and put Belle away with her brother!"

"Jingles and Belle?" Sandy's face lit up. "How cute! Did you name them?"

"No, it was my niece, Lily. Kind of a long story…" Hannah made for the kitchen at a clip and returned briskly, after securing her second feline offender in the *pet*-itentiary. She hoped she wasn't about to get evicted already. Christmas Town was small and there were no chain hotels here. Even if there were, they probably wouldn't be any keener on cats than Louise.

Hannah glanced at the front window and the storm that raged outside. Surely, they wouldn't force her to leave tonight? "I honestly didn't think the kittens would be a problem," she told Sandy apprehensively. "The rental page said 'pet friendly.'"

Sandy kept her voice low and conspiratorial. "*Pet friendly* generally refers to dogs."

"It does?"

"Otherwise, who knows what people could bring?"

"Exotic pets?"

"Exactly!" Sandy laughed. "Think baby crocodiles or rattlesnakes."

Hannah's lips turned up in a grin. "Mice?"

"You might already have one or two." Sandy's eyes danced with mischief. "Good thing you brought cats."

Hannah sighed with relief, her laughter mingling with Sandy's.

"Did I miss a joke in here?" Lou asked, returning and straightening her headband.

"I'm so sorry, Lou," Hannah said sincerely. "I had no idea about the cats and couldn't have guessed about your allergies." She pursed her lips, then continued, "I'll look for another place tomorrow."

"Nonsense!" Lou's big eyes went round. She dabbed her nose with a tissue and sniffed. "You're not going anywhere but here."

"But Jingles and Belle—" Hannah started before Sandy cut in.

"She gave them both Christmas names. Isn't that darling?"

"Precious, yes." Lou's eyes scanned the room and she sniffed again. "Where are the little angels?"

"In their carrier in the kitchen," Hannah answered. "I call it 'kitty time-out.'"

It was Lou's turn to laugh. She pulled a fresh tissue from her pocket and dabbed her eyes. "Very well," she said, sitting back in the armchair. "Then let's get down to business!"

"We're the Christmas Town Welcoming Committee," said Sandy, her cheeks glowing with good cheer. "I'm on the Town Council and Lou, here, is our mayor."

"How nice!" Hannah glanced at the clock on the mantel. It was past six. "Quick question," she said. "The Merry Market. What time does it close?"

Sandy shook her head. "Done, I'm afraid."

"Closed at five thirty," Lou filled in.

"Five thirty?" Hannah asked limply, realizing she wouldn't have made it anyway. She really hadn't brought much in the way of food. Apart from the other half of the peanut butter and jelly sandwich she'd packed for the road.

"And they're not open tomorrow," Sandy said.

Lou nodded in agreement. "Sunday."

"Oh." Hannah felt her stomach rumble. She thought she had a granola bar in her purse. She had an apple leftover from lunch, too.

"Come here, dear." Lou leaned forward and patted the sofa cushion beside Sandy. "Why don't you have a seat and see what we brought you?"

Hannah eagerly eyed the basket, hoping its contents were edible. If not, she supposed she'd need to venture into the next town tomorrow for supplies. Assuming the weather was better. Hannah took a seat beside Sandy and the two women smiled at her encouragingly.

Sandy lifted the large basket from the coffee table and handed it to her. "Go on," she said sweetly. "Dig in!"

Hannah grinned like a little kid on her birthday. She loved opening gifts. The unexpected kind were often the best. She tossed back the red-checkered cloth and peered inside at the assortment of goodies. There were two sealed containers of something emitting steam, a wrapped loaf of banana bread, homemade biscuits, cookies, a few pears, a wedge of cheese, and a nice big bottle of wine. "Wow! I don't know what to say!"

"Say you're not a vegetarian," Lou replied. "The one container is a chicken Brunswick stew."

"No worries if you are," Sandy interrupted hastily. "The other's a vegan—gluten- and dairy-free—pumpkin bisque."

Hannah was overwhelmed with gratitude. "This was incredibly kind of both of you."

Lou smiled graciously. "The kitchen comes already stocked with coffee, tea, and some basics. Salt, pepper, sugar, baking spices, and miniature packets of nondairy creamer for your coffee or tea. Coffee filters are in the drawer below the microwave."

"Sounds like you thought of everything," Hannah said, amazed. She cradled the basket in her lap and said happily, "I can't believe you did all this for me. I can get by until Monday with what I have here."

"You may have to," Sandy told her. "The storm's not expected to let up before then."

"Is everything closed tomorrow?" Hannah asked.

"No, not everything." Lou thoughtfully studied the ceiling. "Jolly Bean Java will be open. It always is. "

"Santa's Sandwich Shop, too," Sandy added.

"And the Peppermint Bark!" Lou rejoined. "But only for lunch."

Sandy shot Hannah a wink. "Our *pet-friendly* café."

"Oh," Hannah said, picking up on the joke. "They allow dogs!"

"Quite right. Dogs. But only on the porch in nice weather." Lou was deep in thought. "There's the church, too, of course."

"But pretty much everything else will be closed," Sandy said with finality. She met Hannah's eyes with a smile. "Maybe we should meet for coffee? You'll probably be ready to get out of here sometime tomorrow. Just to stretch your legs. Even if the weather's bad."

"Coffee sounds terrific, Sandy. Thanks, I'd like that," Hannah, answered, feeling like she'd already made a new friend. Two friends, really. Lou seemed a little quirky, but she was so good-hearted.

Then it occurred to her that she might be putting Sandy out. "But if the weather is too awful, please don't feel like you need to. I'd hate for you to go to the trouble or have to drive."

"No driving necessary," Sandy said with a smile. "I live right next door."

Hannah clasped her hands to her heart. "How great!"

"And I live across the street," Lou added merrily. "The big house on the corner. Three lots down from the hotel."

"It's lovely to know I have such good neighbors."

"It's lovely to have you in town." Lou reached over and patted her hand. "Christmas Town *needs you,* Hannah. More than you know."

Needs me?

"When we heard you were moving here, the whole town was overjoyed," Sandy told her.

Moving? What? Permanently? Hannah couldn't let them think that. She had to stop them.

"The Town Council, she means," Lou corrected. "Not everyone's in on the secret."

"Secret?" Hannah asked weakly.

Lou's whole face lit up like a Christmas tree with multicolored, blinking lights. "That you've come to reopen the Christmas Cookie Shop!"

"Well, I..."

Sandy silenced her with a serious look. "To hear the locals tell it, nothing's been the same since it shut down."

Lou frowned. "The bypass didn't help much either."

"But it's all getting better now!" Sandy clasped her hands together. "Little by little, Christmas Town is coming back. First, I bought the Snow Globe Gallery. Then Carter arrived."

"His sister Olivia followed," Lou put in.

"And now you're here," Sandy said sunnily.

"That's true." Lou viewed Hannah with admiration. "Your great-grandmother, Lena, would have been so proud."

Hannah swallowed hard. The hole Lou and Sandy were digging for her just seemed to be getting deeper. It was hard to know how to climb out. "I don't want either of you to get the wrong impress—"

"Hush now," Lou said kindly. "That's just your nerves talking. Of course you can do it. And make it a success, too! All of us will help you."

Sandy nodded. "That's how things work in Christmas Town. Everyone helps everybody. You'll see."

Hannah reprised her mental image of huge black plumes of smoke curling out the cookie shop door. It wasn't just that she couldn't do it; she didn't *want to*. Hannah's head began pounding, then she recalled the beating it had taken. She raised a hand to her forehead and jerked it back with a start. "Ow!"

Sandy scrutinized her with alarm. "Gracious! Look at her forehead, Lou! It's going all black-and-blue!"

Lou blinked in incredulity and stared harder. "A big knot's forming, too!" She gawked worriedly at Hannah. "What on earth happened, dear?"

"I kind of had a run-in with the bed when I was reaching for the cat."

"That looks bad," Sandy said, hovering over her. "Probably needs ice."

"More than ice," Lou declared decidedly. "She needs a doctor!"

"No, please," Hannah protested. "It's just a little bump, really."

"Good thought," Sandy said, ignoring Hannah. "Why don't we call Kurt?"

Things were spiraling out of control here. First they thought she was staying to reopen the cookie shop. Now they were bringing in the medics? "But I don't want Kurt!"

Lou blinked at her, apparently affronted. "And what exactly is *wrong* with Kurt? He's a very fine physician. I assure you. Top-notch."

"He's also Lou's son," Sandy whispered.

"I'm sure he's very fine," Hannah rushed in, drawing a breath. "I'd just hate to trouble—"

"No trouble," Lou assured her, whipping out her cell phone. She punched a number on speed dial. In a jiffy, they were connected. "Yes, Kurt? I know. Terrible, isn't it? Yes, yes. Blizzard conditions. Thank goodness you don't have to come far… Why, to Sisters' Row, of course. It's Hannah, our new renter… Yes, that's the one. Lena's great-granddaughter… She is! Isn't that terrific?"

Hannah watched her, slack-jawed, but couldn't get her attention. Why did she have the impression Lou was avoiding looking her way on purpose?

"…a very bad bump on the head," Lou continued. "Who knows where it could lead? Concussion, maybe even amnesia!"

Hannah sighed and Sandy snickered beside her, covering her mouth with her hand. "Just let it go," she whispered softly. "Kurt's a nice guy. He won't stay here long. And," she added impishly, "Lou will never forgive him if he doesn't come. You don't want to get in the way of that."

Hannah's shoulders sagged in resignation. "No, I guess not," she whispered in return. She sat back against the sofa, examining the pretty pattern of the snowflakes in the winter landscape mounted over the fireplace. "Who's the artist?" she asked quietly, as Lou wrapped up her call.

Sandy beamed with pride and sat up a little straighter. "Like it?"

"Like it? It's gorg—" She viewed the blonde with surprise. "Wait a minute! You did that?"

Sandy glanced at the painting. "S. Claus, that's me."

"Sandy Claus?" Hannah tried to keep a straight face, but she couldn't. "Your parents didn't."

Sandy laughed and gave a nod. "Oh yes, they did," she said good-naturedly. "Not only that, I've got a brother named Nick."

Hannah grinned in return. "Bet he gets lots of comments on that."

"We were very popular kids in school." Sandy's eyes twinkled as she told her story. "Especially grade school. The other children all tried to stay on our good side. None of them were ever sure if we secretly had connections."

"Does Nick live in Christmas Town, too?"

"No, he's an architect in Bangor, Maine. My parents live up in Canada. Maritime Provinces."

"So you and Lou are not related?" Despite their differences in appearance, Hannah at first thought they might have been mother and daughter.

Sandy laughed lightly at this. "Everyone's kind of related in Christmas Town. Lou and I don't share blood, but her husband Buddy and I do. The family tie goes way back. We're something like second cousins once removed. My great-grandmother and Buddy's grandpa were sister and brother, or something like that. I had to look at it on paper to understand it."

"So what brought you to Christmas Town?"

"The Snow Globe Gallery, mostly."

"That's yours?"

"My pride and joy." She clasped Hannah's hand. "I'd love to show it to you. Maybe we can stop by after our coffee?"

"I'd like that. But isn't it closed on Sundays?"

Sandy grinned slyly. "I've got an 'in' with the owner, meaning me."

"Well, now!" Lou exclaimed, having finished her call. "That's settled. Kurt will be here in ten."

"Minutes?" Hannah asked in shock.

"Of course," Lou answered. "Best not to let things like this go on—unchecked, I mean."

Hannah stood uneasily and lifted the goody basket. "Maybe I should put things away in the kitchen before he gets here."

"Here," Sandy said, standing and addressing Hannah. "Let me help you."

"That's okay." Hannah understood they were being kind, but she badly needed a breather. "It won't take long. I'll be back in a flash!" Sandy viewed her unsurely, but sat back down. Obviously, neither she nor Lou was prepared to leave until Kurt arrived. This little town house was getting more crowded by the minute. Hannah had just set the basket on the kitchen counter when her cell rang. It was Ben calling, probably to make sure she'd arrived safely. She'd intended to phone him earlier, but had been sidetracked by...everything!

"Hey, Sis!" Ben's cheerful voice boomed through the earpiece. "Are you there yet?"

"Boy, am I ever," Hannah whispered back.

"What's that supposed to mean, and why are you whispering?"

"Hi, Aunt Hannah!" Lily called from the background. *"How are Jingles and Belle?"*

"Hi, sweetheart!" Hannah called back. "They're doing just great." She eyed the cat cage in the corner and spied the kittens curled up asleep together. They'd probably exhausted themselves by meowing for seven hours in the car. Goodness knows they'd worn Hannah out. "Keeping me lots of company." Hannah cupped her hand around the phone and spoke hoarsely. "I'll have to call you back, Ben. Now's not a good time."

"Got company?" Ben laughed like he was making a joke.

"Yes," Hannah hissed back.

"What?" He sounded thrown. "Already?"

"Not only that. The doctor's coming."

Ben's voice rose with alarm. "Doctor? What doctor?"

"Kurt Christmas, or something." Hannah shook her head and peered into the living room, before ducking back in the kitchen. Lou and Sandy seemed engaged in conversation, so hopefully they weren't listening. "Look, I've got to go. He'll be here any minute."

"Who? The doctor?"

"That's what I said, Ben!" Hannah was getting exasperated. Plus the food was growing cold, and she was hungry.

"Hannah," Ben said stonily. "I'm not hanging up until you tell me why you need a doctor."

"Is Aunt Hannah sick?" she heard Lily say. Hannah started to rub her forehead, but stopped abruptly. *Ouch, the knot is getting larger! Okay, so maybe the doctor coming is not a terrible idea.*

"I just knocked my head a little." She lowered her voice even further. "Chasing after one of the cats, but don't tell Lily."

"Don't tell me what?" the child cried. Hannah could hear Ben shooing her into the next room. "Okay, the coast is clear now," Ben said. "You can tell me the truth." His voice constricted in horror. "You didn't have a car accident?"

"Ben, no! You're getting overly excited. It's nothing, really. Let me call you back when everyone's gone."

"Everyone? You're having a *party*?"

"I'm hanging up now."

"Hannah—"

"I'll call you back."

"Promise?"

"Yes, yes! Scout's honor. Whatever!"

"You were never a scout of any kind."

"Bye, Ben! Love you! Love to Lily, too!"

She clicked off, perspiration beading her hairline. Then the doorbell rang.

Impossible! It couldn't be the doctor already. Hannah quickly stuffed some items from the basket in the fridge and left the containers of soup and stew on the stove. When she exited the kitchen, Lou was halfway to the door with Sandy trailing her. "Kurt's nothing if not prompt," Lou said, crossing the room with long brisk strides, her bedecked headband jingling. She halted suddenly and raised her hands to her head. The next instant, Lou's eyes widened. "Oh, my!" She spouted an amused laugh. "This wasn't for me, dear."

Hannah gaped as Lou swiftly removed the headband. "It's for you!" To Hannah's horror, she clomped right over and planted the ghastly thing on Hannah. *Ow!* Even the top of her head ached. "Oops, sorry!" Lou patted it in place and rearranged some of Hannah's tresses. "There. Better." Her eyes twinkled as she laid her hand on the doorknob and tugged the door open. "Merry Christmas!"

"Merry Christmas to you!" a familiar voice boomed. It wasn't the doctor at all, but a very handsome sheriff with unforgettable forest-green eyes. This time, he was wearing a uniform and he filled it out perfectly.

Hannah brought her hands to her flaming cheeks. "Carter!"

"Wait a minute," Sandy said with surprise. "You two know each other?"

"*Ye-es,* do tell…" Lou added with a sultry edge. Clearly, there was glee in her eyes.

Carter, by contrast, appeared horrified. No wonder, too. Hannah must look a wreck, what with the huge knot on her forehead and that crazy reindeer headband. "You're hurt?" His face creased with concern. "I thought it was just a fender bender?"

"A *what*?" Hannah was completely thrown, and so apparently were the other women, by the way they glanced at each other.

Lou motioned him inside and Sandy shut the door. "Don't worry," Lou said. "I've already called Kurt. He's on his way."

"I know," Carter responded. "Joy told me when I called."

"Joy's Kurt's niece," Sandy whispered to Hannah. "She helps him at the clinic."

"The clinic's open today?" Lou asked, surprised.

Carter shook his head. "I was calling Kurt about something else. His phone went straight to the answering service."

"That would be Joy," Sandy offered quietly.

"Joy told me Kurt had been summoned here. Something about a newcomer and an accident. Having met Hannah earlier today, I naturally started to worry."

"Um-hum." Lou gave a knowing nod.

Color tinged the edges of his ears. "But the car looks all right. I checked it out on the street." He regarded Hannah carefully and her pulse quickened. "You didn't try driving again? In the storm?"

"No! Of course not!"

He stepped closer and a wave of heat washed over her. "Good thing that Kurt is coming. That knot looks pretty bad. How did it happen? Did you trip carrying your things indoors? I knew I should have stopped to—"

"It was Jingles," Sandy told him. "He darted under the bed and Hannah banged her head chasing after him."

"Jingles?" Then, Carter obviously remembered. He set his hands on his lean hips and slowly shook his head. "That darn cat, huh?"

When he raised his eyes to Hannah's, her breath quickened. "Yep," she said, feeling fire in her cheeks. "He's a rascal."

Lou lifted an eyebrow at Sandy and gave a sly smile. "How very nice that you've met already. And there Sandy and I thought Hannah didn't know a soul in town."

Three raps sounded at the front door.

Sandy's tone was chipper. "She's about to meet one more!"

Chapter Three

Hannah's head was spinning so fast, she nearly tumbled over on her way to the sofa. The doctor's reflexes were excellent, though. Kurt Christmas caught her quickly, supporting her by the elbow. Hannah had to concede he was incredibly handsome. Buff and blond with chocolate-brown eyes. But it was hard to keep her eyes off the hot sheriff, worriedly standing by. He'd taken Kurt's medical bag when the other had removed his coat, and still held it, since Kurt's focus had been diverted to escorting his patient across the room. Everyone here probably assumed Hannah was dizzy from hitting her forehead. In reality, she'd been pummeled by the relentless activity. Beyond meeting friendly Sandy and effusive Louise, Carter's unexpected arrival had taken her by complete surprise. While she'd secretly hoped to see him again and had planned to casually ask Sandy about him over coffee tomorrow, Hannah had never envisioned Carter showing up now. She was in such a state! Her forehead felt as if was bulging larger each second, and the jingling on her headband was making her blooming headache worse. When she reached up to remove it with her free hand, Hannah was surprised to find it shaking in her fingers.

"Just take it easy," Kurt cautioned. "Let's get you over to the sofa, then we'll take a look."

The other faces in the room loomed closer. "You should probably check her pupils," Lou said. "You know, for signs of a concussion. And maybe give her a memory test!"

Kurt eyed Carter, motioning for him to set his medical bag on the coffee table. "Why don't you three wait in the kitchen, while I look Hannah over?" He smiled kindly at Hannah and eased her onto the couch. "No need to worry. Just going to check a few things." He glanced pointedly at Louise. "Without interruption."

Louise blanched and Carter uncomfortably cleared his throat.

"Are you sure I shouldn't stay?" he asked. "To…assist you?"

Kurt raised his brow.

"She looks a little pale," Carter said, referring to Hannah, but Lou mistook the comment as being intended toward her.

"I should say so! Given the way—"

"I think Carter was talking about Hannah, Mother," Kurt said mildly.

Sandy smirked, and Hannah pursed her lips.

"Well, fine." Lou squared her narrow shoulders. "I'll be in the kitchen then. If anyone needs me."

"Um, me too!" Sandy added, chasing after her while addressing Kurt. "Let us know if there's anything we can do."

"Maybe prepare an ice pack?" Kurt suggested. "That would be a help."

Sandy nodded and disappeared from view, as Carter shifted on his feet.

"I think I can handle this, Sheriff," Kurt told him. "Thanks."

Hannah didn't really want him around either, but she was touched that he wanted to stay. Carter was clearly concerned about her. He'd come over to check on her firsthand, hadn't he?

"Just holler if you need me." Carter tipped his hat at Hannah. "I won't go far."

The examination took all of five minutes. In that time, Hannah learned that Kurt was a bachelor who his mom, Lou, was always trying to fix up. He shared this as a warning to Hannah to stay on guard. As a new single person arriving in Christmas Town, Hannah herself would be on Lou's matchmaker list soon. That was, if she didn't have a boyfriend already.

"I've kind of sworn off boyfriends for a while," Hannah said, laughing.

"I know what you mean. I've sworn off women, too." He shot her a wink, but Hannah understood he was commiserating and not flirting. She didn't get any sort of interested vibe from Kurt. Although he was *very* nice looking, obviously well employed, and *single,* none of those little butterflies took off for her. Not that Hannah would encourage them to. They'd already gone haywire once today, thanks to a certain lawman in the next room.

While Carter was one sweet package in a Santa suit, he was pretty darn irresistible in uniform. Those tailored green slacks with black piping and complementary leather jacket outlined a rugged frame. And when he'd tipped his hat her way, Hannah had felt a familiar stirring inside. But no, she wouldn't do it! Hannah would absolutely not let her heart get carried away again, particularly given the short time frame of her intended stay in Tennessee.

Kurt dropped his stethoscope back in his bag and smiled. "Just keep up the acetaminophen every four hours, along with the ice, and you should be fine."

Hannah gingerly touched her forehead. "It's going to look awful, isn't it?"

"Your bangs cover most of the bump. Besides…" His hearty laugh rumbled. "No man's going to notice that minor mark if he's looking in your eyes." Was it her imagination, or did he lean closer? "They're really captivating."

Lou sneezed loudly in the kitchen and Hannah's cheeks heated. She hadn't thought Kurt was flirting earlier. Now, she wasn't sure. As if on cue, Carter poked his head around the doorframe to the kitchen, and Hannah wondered if he'd been listening. Perhaps they all had! "Is the coast clear to reenter?" He held up an ice pack. "I've got something for the patient." Hannah saw he'd removed his hat and jacket, exposing a form-fitting tan shirt with tapered long sleeves and a narrow green tie that matched his slacks. What was that all about? Was Carter planning to stay?
Perhaps Ben had guessed more accurately than she'd believed. This was definitely starting to feel like a party. A welcoming party, of sorts. Complete with a security officer, Hannah thought, eyeing the holstered weapon hanging below Carter's belt. Well, it was good to feel safe, wasn't it? Why then did Carter's approach send those *Danger! Danger!* signs flashing? Bright red and yellow, and on high alert.

"Here we come, too!" Sandy cried, entering the room.

Lou joined her, announcing proudly, "We started Hannah's supper on the stove."

"Supper?" Hannah viewed her with surprise, then she realized she'd turned her head too quickly. It throbbed. "Oh!"

Carter handed her the ice pack and gestured for her to apply it. "Lou's heating up the stew." The ice stung at first, but then it felt good, soothing against her swollen forehead.

"I cut some pear slices to go with the cheese," Sandy added.

"*And* we're warming a few biscuits." Lou spoke with motherly authority, addressing Hannah. "You can't neglect your starches, dear. Especially if you're planning to have any wine."

Actually, the idea hadn't occurred to her. Now that Lou mentioned it, though, a glass of that super-looking merlot sounded like a great thought. Maybe Hannah would have two glasses. Once things calmed down around here.

Lou turned her attention on Kurt. "How is she?"

"As fit as a fiddle, mostly," Kurt announced. "She might have a bump for a day or so, and probably a bit of bruising. But it's nothing that won't heal."

"I'm sorry to have troubled you," Hannah said.

"No trouble at all." Kurt slapped his knee, then stood and began gathering his things. "I hope you feel better." When he headed for his coat on the rack by the door, Hannah realized he was leaving.

"We'd better get going, too," Lou said, shooting Sandy a look.

"Quite right." Sandy's cheeks glowed. "Carter's volunteered to look after you."

"Carter?" Hannah cupped a hand to her mouth when she realized she'd nearly gasped in shock. "Oh no, really!" She peered up at him from around the edges of the ice pack. "That's not necessary. I'll be fine."

In record time, Lou and Sandy had wrestled into their coats and were following Kurt out the door. "I'll just stay a bit," Carter said. "Make sure you get your supper and are okay before I go."

"I'll check in on you in the morning, Hannah," Sandy said. "Meanwhile, if you need anything, remember I'm right next door. I've left my number on the notepad on the fridge, too."

"Mind the timer on the stove," Lou cautioned Carter. "Don't burn the biscuits."

"Thank you so much, Sandy and Lou!" Hannah called. "For everything." She craned her head and spied Kurt turning to wave. "You, too, Kurt! Thanks for coming by."

Sandy paused when she'd nearly shut the door. "Oh, Hannah," she said in a half whisper. "You might want to check on the kittens when you can. I think one of them might have vomited in the cage."

Hannah assumed her color had passed pink and gone straight to crimson by now. Of course a cat had vomited, and she could guess which one it was. The one who was always stealing things! She dropped the ice bag to a sofa cushion and made an effort to stand.

"Stay right there." Carter's kind green eyes sparkled. "You shouldn't do anything but rest for the next little bit."

"It's not that bad, really." But when Hannah stood too quickly her woozy head contradicted her, forcing her to sit back down.

Carter drew nearer, leaning over her with a worried frown. "You probably need to eat, so we can get that medicine in you. Kurt said not to take it on an empty stomach."

"But the kittens!" She glanced up at him, then grimaced and reapplied the ice pack.

"I'll take care of the little guys, and clean up their mess."

Now, that was truly going above and beyond the call. "No, Carter. Please. I can't let you—"

"How about I dust them off first and bring them to you? Which one's Belle?"

Hannah sat back, the pain in her forehead spiking. "The gray one. Jingles is the orange tabby." She smiled at him gratefully. "You're very nice to do this. I owe you one."

"No debt incurred," he said with a nod. "You need a hand and I'm happy to offer one."

Hannah wrinkled her nose. "Are you always this nice to everybody?"

Carter gave her a slow perusal and something deep inside her caught fire. It was like he was the steel and she was the flint rock, sparking under the friction of his gaze. "Nope," he finally said, after a pause. "Not *everybody*."

Then he turned and walked toward the increasingly loud mews coming from the kitchen, leaving Hannah with her heart pounding.

Carter peered into the cat carrier on the floor, bracing himself against the pungent smell. "Been having a good time in there, have you?" he asked the pair, before locating the paper towels on a mounted holder. He yanked off a big wad and dampened it, preparing to remove the kittens from the cage. Belle was backed into a corner, avoiding the spreading puddle. Jingles was sitting beside it, purring. Carter held his breath and opened the door, reaching for Jingles first. He'd soiled his two front paws, so Carter wiped them, his eye catching on something shiny in the middle of the mess. "Hey!" he called over his shoulder and out into the living room. "Are you missing an earring?"

"Does it look like a star?" Hannah yelled back.

Carter squinted at the slimy bauble, counting five points. "Yep!"

Humiliation threaded her voice. "It's mine!"

Carter chuckled and stroked the kitten under its chin. "You little scoundrel. No wonder you were doing hard time." He balanced Jingles on one knee and gingerly picked up Belle, who'd apparently managed to remain unscathed by her brother's digestive exploits. Carter chucked the paper towels in the bin with a dunk shot, then stood and held each kitten up to the light. Satisfied that they were clean enough, he carried them out to Hannah.

"Why don't you two go and sit with your mama and keep her company?" he said, depositing them beside her on the sofa one at a time. They broke into loud purrs, snuggling up against Hannah's leg and hip on one side. She stroked their furry little heads before meeting his eyes. Carter caught a whiff of her lily of the valley perfume and his heart thudded. Painful couldn't begin to describe it. It was more like muscle memory—of the worst possible kind.

"Thanks, Carter. You can just leave the rest if you want to."

"For you to deal with later? Wouldn't dream of it." At that moment, the oven timer went off. He made for the kitchen, stopping midstride. "Want some of that wine with your food? It's a local red. Fairly good vintage, too."

"Will you join me?" she asked boldly.

Boy, that was a tempting offer if he'd ever heard one. Carter was chagrined to hear himself decline. "Not tonight, I'm afraid." He patted his holster. "I'm on duty."

Hannah peered through the darkened front window and the ice crystals forming outside it. "I guess you need to keep your wits about you, especially given the weather."

"Especially that, yeah." Carter knew he was wading in deep. This was swampland territory and he'd been snared by its banks before. Still, he couldn't quell that relentless ache inside that made him want to get to know Hannah better. That was, assuming his brash buddy Kurt hadn't already moved in. He thoughtfully cocked his chin and added, "I will take a rain check, though. For some other time."

Hannah's heart beat faster, and that gargantuan butterfly resurfaced from out of nowhere, batting its enormous wings. "Great!" she said, and her lips trembled. *Oh no, not the trembling lips! It started earlier with those blasted butterflies. Now, my lips are quaking, just imagining the feel of his mouth on mine, sweet waves of heat crashing over me as he holds me in his arms...* The next things to go would be her knees!

And Hannah knew exactly what would give way after those: her heart! *Full stop.*

Hannah was glad Carter had returned to the kitchen before she'd broken out in a rapid blush. *Forget about my forehead! This ice is needed elsewhere!* She began by pressing the ice pack to the sides of her neck, then her cheeks and her collar bone, right above the V of her powder-blue pullover sweater, the frosty surface instantly cooling her scorching skin.

She wore a crisp white blouse underneath her sweater and had faded stretch jeans tucked into her favorite pair of lace-up boots. She'd gotten them at the thrift store, but they were made of real leather. All broken in and comfortable, too. Hannah supposed they were meant for hiking, but they served her well enough for everyday wear, and were especially good in the snow. She was admiring them when she felt a dribble of icy water run down her cleavage. *No, that was two dribbles. Three! An entire stream!* Hannah lifted the ice bag in horror to see it had been leaking, leaving a large wet spot on each of her breasts!

"Supper's read—" Carter stopped halfway to the couch to stare at her. "Problem?"

Hannah's head jerked up and she slapped her arms across her chest. "I...er…"

"You seem to have sprung a leak." He squinted in incredulity. "Or...two?"

"Not me!" she answered hurriedly, as Jingles scampered across her legs and Belle curled into her lap. "The ice bag! It's, uh…dripping!"

"Right." Carter quickly set the tray containing stew, pears, wine, cheese, and biscuits on the coffee table and lifted the ice pack from the soggy seat cushion. He tested the fit of its cap. "Looks like the seal came loose. I'll go grab a towel."

"And I'll just run and…change!" Hannah yelped, the instant he'd left the room. Then she scooted the kittens aside and dashed up the steps, positively mortified.

When Hannah descended the stairs, Carter was still in the kitchen. Jingles and Belle had climbed off the love seat and were darting about on the floor, chasing two of the small balls with bright feathers attached that Hannah had packed as toys. They'd batted them under the dining room table, and were each trying to grab at one with tiny cat claws extended around the legs of the chairs.

"All picked up in there," Carter said, emerging from the kitchen. He held Hannah's dangly earring in one hand. By the way its bright edges glimmered in the lamplight, he must have washed it thoroughly. Poor Carter. Hannah had put him to so much trouble—in the past hour alone.

"I couldn't find that when I was packing, thank you." She raised an accusatory eyebrow at the orange tabby. "I figured Jingles had something to do with it."

"Well, here's the hard evidence," Carter said, laying the piece of jewelry in her hand. His fingers brushed her palm just barely, and Hannah's cheeks blazed. "I refilled the ice pack and put it in the freezer," he told her. "You should try reapplying it for fifteen minutes or so, off and on. But first…" He opened his other hand and Hannah saw two tablets cradled in it. "You need to eat, and take these." He placed them on the tray by the napkin. "Doctor's orders."

Hannah glanced uncertainly at the sofa. "I feel bad eating in front of you. Why don't you join me and we can sit at the table? There's plenty of food."

"No time, I'm afraid. Got a call while you were upstairs. Motorist skidded off the road up near the bypass. I'm going out to meet the tow truck and help."

"No one's hurt, I hope?"

Carter shook his head. "Doesn't sound like it."

"Thank goodness."

"Yeah." He met her eyes. "Hannah...?"

Her chin tilted up toward his. "Yes, Carter?"

"You going to be okay here? I can always call Sandy—"

"No, please. Sandy's already done enough. So have Lou and Kurt, and..." She ducked her head with a blush. "You, *Santa*."

"Kind of funny meeting that way." When she looked up he was grinning. "Funny, but not bad—by any stretch."

"No. Not bad at all."

Hannah noticed his jacket slung over the back of the armchair and that he'd set his hat on the table by the door. Carter lifted the jacket and slipped into it, raising its zipper. "Might want to stick that bowl of stew in the microwave for a minute or two."

"I'll do that," she said brightly.

He ambled toward the door and placed the hat on his head, tapping it down. His deep voice rumbled. "Kurt's a good-looking guy."

"Kurt?" Hannah asked, flummoxed.

"Eligible bachelor, too."

"Can't say I noticed."

"No? I thought I heard the two of you talking from the kitchen—"

"Sheriff." She stopped him. "I'm not interested in *any* man right now, okay? And if I were…" Hannah swallowed hard past the lump in her throat.

"If you were…?" he said, leading.

Hannah's heart hammered and her knees felt weak. "I told you, I'm just passing through."

"Odd thing about that, Hannah." He tipped his hat her way. "Nobody in town seems to know that, but me."

Then he stepped out the door, shutting it soundly behind him.

Two hours later, Hannah clicked off her phone and stared into her half-empty glass of wine. She'd retired to her bedroom and had just finished chatting with Ben. He'd been agog at all the "trouble" she'd caused, as he not-so-gingerly put it. *Just think, Hannah. You've been there less than a day and you've already created a stir. Good thing you're not staying.* Ha-ha, Ben was so funny that way. What a jokester! One thing that hadn't left her smiling was the look on Carter's face when he'd walked out the door. Hannah wasn't sure what had gone wrong, but she feared that he'd misunderstood her. Could Carter possibly believe she'd only given him a line about "passing through" to blow him off? Nothing could be further from the truth! Hannah was desperately attracted to the handsome sheriff and she was fighting that attraction as best she could every… step…of the way.

How could she even imagine getting involved when she was here for just a month, or maybe two? Hannah had done the short-term love thing, and the long-term love thing, *and* the long-distance relationship, and none of those had worked out for her.

In fact, they'd all left her devastated. Hannah knew that wasn't what she wanted for herself *again.* What Hannah wanted was the right kind of future: one that centered on her goals. She had to get her own spiritual house in order before shacking up emotionally with anybody else. She reached down to stroke Belle in her lap and pat Jingles, who'd nestled in beside her on the fluffy down comforter. "What do you think, kitties? Isn't this a nice town?"

Jingles groggily raised his head and blinked, but Belle went right on snoozing.

Hannah set her wineglass on the nightstand, then leaned back against the headboard and sighed. "Yeah," she said softly, closing her eyes. "I think so, too."

Everyone she'd met had been so friendly. They had all gone out of their way to make Hannah feel welcomed, and like she was going to have a special place here. But Hannah wasn't in Christmas Town to stay. She was here with one express purpose: to fix up the Christmas Cookie Shop and sell it. Tomorrow, she would explain everything to Sandy over coffee, and start clearing the air.

Chapter Four

"Oh! Oh, I see." Sandy's delicate mouth turned down in a frown. "Wow, that wasn't what I expected you to tell me at all." They sat at a small table in Jolly Bean Java. It was a tiny café with only ten tables in total, plus a slim coffee bar with high metallic stools facing the counter. Heavy snow pummeled the sidewalk outside.

"I'm sorry, Sandy," Hannah said. "I thought it best to get things out in the open. There were apparently quite a few misunderstandings last night."

"Yeah, I suppose so."

"I'm not sure how anyone got the idea I was moving here permanently," Hannah said. "I mean, I never told anyone that, and the only person I talked to prior to coming here was Lou."

"Ah, Lou. She was just hopeful, I guess." Sandy's blue eyes misted. "Maybe all of us were." She briefly toyed with her coffee cup, then looked up. "*So.* Just for a month or two, huh?"

"That's the plan."

"Well, darn!" Sandy said with more emphasis than Hannah expected. She played at sounding tough but cracked a sad grin. "And there I thought I'd made a new friend."

Hannah instinctively reached out and grabbed her hand. "You have."

Sandy returned her firm squeeze, then picked up her coffee. "You know," she said, rolling her eyes toward the window. "We don't see many strangers around here. Visitors under the age of forty are hard to come by, too. I'd be lying if I said I'm not sorry to see you go."

"Nobody's going yet," Hannah said with determination. "I've got tons of work to do first."

"What's your first step?" Sandy asked her.

"I'm not sure. I haven't even seen the place."

"When are you planning on going?"

"I thought I'd stop by later this afternoon."

Sandy's face lit up. "Mind if I come with you?"

Hannah liked the sound of this. She hadn't had a close girlfriend since middle school; mainly boyfriends. Plus a lot of looking-after by her big brother. "That would be great. Sure."

"We can pop into the gallery on the way, then maybe even grab supper afterward." She sported a hopeful grin. "Santa's Sandwich Shop is not very fancy, but the food's pretty good."

"Do they have big, greasy burgers?"

"The biggest and the greasiest!"

"Milkshakes, too?"

"Made to order."

"Then I'm in!"

The two of them giggled together like companionable schoolgirls.

After a beat, Sandy asked her, "So how's the head?"

Hannah swept her bangs aside and Sandy grimaced at the sight. "Pretty black-and-blue," Hannah answered, "but healing. The ice last night helped." She decided not to mention the embarrassing ice pack disaster that had occurred in front of Carter once Sandy and Lou had gone. Hannah was still trying to forget it.

Sandy set aside her cup, her eyes twinkling with mischief. "So, what do you think of our town doctor?"

"Kurt?"

Sandy nodded coyly.

"Well, I... He's very nice."

"Nice and nice-looking, too." Sandy lowered her eyebrows. "Not only that, he's *single*."

"I'm only here for a month."

"Doesn't mean you can't have fun."

Hannah eyed Sandy over the rim of her coffee cup. "What about you?"

"What about me?"

"Why haven't you and Kurt become an item?"

"Um, because we're kind of related. Ew!"

"You said it went way back."

"It does, but still." Sandy gave a little shudder. "No, thank you. Kurt's not the guy for me. Neither is Walter."

"Walter?"

"Walt Christmas, Kurt's big brother. He's a single dad, you know. Very eligible."

"Noooo..."

"Fine."

"How old are his kids?"

"Thought you weren't interested?"

Hannah sipped from her coffee. "Asking out of curiosity."

"Noelle and Joy are seventeen."

"Twins?"

Sandy nodded.

"And Joy is…the one who helps with Kurt's answering service, right?"

Sandy smiled brightly. "Look at you. Already putting the town together."

"Not quite." Hannah drew in a breath. "Seems like there's a lot to catch up on."

"Then there's Raymond."

"Don't tell me. Another Christmas brother?"

"Third and final one, but don't worry. I won't suggest you date him. Ray's married."

Hannah sputtered a laugh.

"He and his wife Meredith have one son, Kyle."

"Wow, three sons! Lou sure had her hands full."

"Yeah, but they were all pretty well behaved. Her husband Buddy is another story."

Hannah's brow rose.

"Buddy's fun. Very affable. Just never believe what he tells you off the bat. Buddy likes to stretch the truth. And boy, he can tell some whoppers. But it's all in good fun; he always owns up to it later."

Hannah could only imagine what dinner was like at the Christmas household, with Lou at the helm. "Sounds like a pretty fun family, actually."

"Yeah, they are. World's best."

Hannah thought for a moment, putting odds and ends together. "How long have you been in Christmas Town?"

"About two years," Sandy said. "Lou let me know about the gallery going up for sale, and it was too good an opportunity to pass up."

"I can't wait to see it."

"You'll like it, I hope."

Hannah viewed her thoughtfully. Sandy was so young and pretty, with so much vivacious energy. She wondered why she didn't feel stifled in such a small town. "Have you ever regretted it? Moving here?"

Sandy answered without hesitation. "Not for a minute. Christmas Town suits me. I love the people. They're all like family." She paused, then laughed at the thought. "I guess some of them *are* family. But that's part of what makes this place special."

Hannah leaned forward. "And the social scene?"

"It's pretty dead, I'll give you that." Sandy shrugged. "But you know? I've decided not to worry. In a way, it's a relief not to have to. Nobody hits on you here."

Hannah didn't know what to say. She already felt like she'd been hit on twice in the past twenty-four hours. Then again, Kurt was only a guess. Carter was definite, though. "Not even…" she began tentatively. "Sheriff Livingston?"

"Carter? Why, no…" Her blue eyes rounded. "Hang on. Hold the phone! You're not saying that he hit on *you*?"

Hannah bit into her bottom lip. "Not sure, but I think so."

"Well, isn't this a day!" Sandy slapped the table, apparently delighted. "I didn't think old Carter had it in him."

"He's not that old, is he?"

"Figure of speech." Sandy waved a hand. "Don't think he's much over thirty. Midthirties, at most."

"And you and he never—?"

"Never crossed our minds," Sandy assured her. "Don't get me wrong. Carter is a great guy, and all right, I'll concede, he's *gorgeous*. But he's so totally serious, you know? He and I don't sync. I mean, apart from being friends. We get along just great that way." She shot Hannah an impish grin. "So, tell me. What did he say?"

Hannah suddenly felt embarrassed for mentioning it. Perhaps she'd made too much out of the comment. "Only that he'd like to have wine…sometime." She shyly lifted a shoulder. "I guess I brought it up, by asking if he wanted a glass of the merlot you and Lou gave me."

"Let me guess," Sandy said with authority. "He was 'on duty'?"

"That's what he said, but he asked for a rain check."

"Rain check?" Sandy lunged for her and gripped her arm. "Hannah," she said with a gasp. "You don't know what great news that is."

"What do you mean?"

"Sheriff Carter Livingston hasn't offered anyone 'rain checks'—or hints at dating—since coming to Christmas Town. Trust me, if he had, I would have heard about it." She rolled her eyes. "Through Lou. She's been trying to fix him up since he arrived, but he's become really skilled at dodging her schemes."

"I thought there weren't that many young people in Christmas Town?"

"Oh, there are enough. And Lou knows every *single* one. She also has plenty of friends in Johnson City, which is fairly large and not too far away. Not that a man like Carter would have trouble finding dates of his own. If he tried…" She leaned back in her chair and viewed Hannah with admiration. "You must have some kind of powerful mojo to have broken through to the sheriff. I'd take that as a very big compliment, if I were you." Then she added quickly. "Not that you don't deserve it! You probably have swarms of guys vying for your attention back home."

Swarms was probably the right word, Hannah thought solemnly, and each one of those men had left her stung. "I'm kind of taking a break from guys right now, if you want to know the truth."

"Seriously?" Sandy's lips scrunched in a disappointed frown. "Well, gosh. That's too bad," she said before playfully adding, "because you and Carter make a pretty cute couple, if you ask me…"

"You keep that up, I might just put a bug in Lou's ear to find a boyfriend for *you*."

"Don't think she hasn't tried," Sandy said lightly. "But the person who's made a real effort is Kurt."

"Kurt?" Hannah asked, taken aback.

"Matchmaking must be genetic." Sandy grinned shyly. "He's always trying to fix me up with his doctor friends. You know, from over at the hospital."

"Not a winner among them?"

"They've been all right, I guess. I mean, nice enough. Some of them fairly handsome, too. It's just that there've never been any—"

"Butterflies."

"I was going to say fireworks, but butterflies will do." Sandy thoughtfully twisted her napkin. "The problem with doctors is that they're so self-sufficient."

"Sounds better than dependent."

"I don't want dependent, silly." For a moment, she was pensive. "It's more like I need a man who *needs me*."

"Ah, *co*dependent. I see."

Sandy balled up her napkin and hurled it at Hannah.

Hannah laughed and caught it.

"The point is," Sandy continued, squaring her shoulder, "I'll know my Prince Charming when I see him, thank you. And let me tell you this…" Her eyes twinkled merrily. "He's going to be somebody who *loves* Christmas."

"That leaves Ben out," Hannah said lightly.

"Who's Ben?"

"Only my big brother and one of the top people on this planet."

"He doesn't celebrate?"

"Oh, he celebrates, yeah. On account of his daughter Lily. Otherwise, I doubt he'd even put up a…." Hannah's words fell off as guilt surged through her. She had no business talking about Ben, or bringing up his misery. While she hadn't said anything untrue about him, her comment hadn't exactly come off as flattery. Ben had been so good to Hannah, as well as to Lily and their grandparents, too. She owed him the dignity of a little privacy. "I'm sorry, Sandy. I shouldn't have mentioned… What I mean is, all of that's Ben's business, and not mine to share."

"Don't worry. Ben's secret's safe with me. We were just talking, Hannah. Woman to woman, and something I said made you think of him. I'm sure you didn't mean your brother any disrespect."

"No."

The air hung heavy as snow pounded against the windowpanes. At length, Sandy pushed back her chair and spoke in bright tones. "Come on. Let's get going and see that cookie shop of yours."

Hannah's dark mood lifted. "Can we stop by your gallery first?"

"Of course!" Sandy slipped into her coat with a grin. "Sure hope you like snow."

"I'm prepared to bundle up," Hannah said, tugging on her hat and gloves.

Sandy laughed in understanding, then nudged her. "I wasn't talking about *out there*."

Carter handed Kurt the folded-up Santa suit and hat, then passed him the pair of black boots. "Good thing we're the same size. More or less." He glanced down at his feet, then over at Kurt's. "The boots were a little tight."

"Well, thanks for suffering through the inconvenience," Kurt replied in a jovial tone. "I'm sure the kids appreciated it." It was Kurt, not Carter, who regularly donned the Santa suit each year for the children's hospital event. Only this year, an emergency in Christmas Town had demanded his attention. Della Martin's water had broken unexpectedly and she was having her baby two weeks early. Given the weather and the fact that this was Della's fourth child, Kurt judged she'd never make it to the hospital in time. It had to be a home delivery. Happily, everything came out just fine for Della and her husband Stan. They now had another healthy kid named after an herb or a spice. Their first three offspring—all girls—were Cinnamon, Clove, and Sage. They'd christened their newborn baby boy *Basil*.

"It was no inconvenience, really." Carter stroked his chin. "In fact, playing Santa came with some perks."

"Perks like rescuing a pretty damsel in distress near the roundabout?" Kurt asked, teasing. Carter had told Kurt about his and Hannah's first exchange, and now he kind of wished that he hadn't. Carter thought he'd been cagey in rehashing the story, but he must have let his interest in Hannah slip, somehow. Perhaps his admission that he'd taken a rain check on Hannah's offer of wine later last night had tipped Kurt off. Or maybe it was the thunderstruck look Carter probably wore on his face each time Hannah smiled his way. Kurt and he had been at Sisters' Row with Hannah together. It was feasible Kurt had noticed that flash of heat at his temples, or the way he'd set his lips in an extra hard line every time he'd addressed her. So much for Carter's inscrutable poker face.

"Actually, no," Carter said, deadpan. "I was talking about the kids. Sharing the joy of the season. Spreading some Christmas cheer. All that."

"Right." Kurt laid the Santa suit on a chair in his office and placed the boots on the floor. Carter had come by the clinic where Kurt was doing paperwork to return the outfit. Since it was Sunday afternoon, and a frigid one at that, nobody else was there. "Listen, buddy," he said, meeting Carter's eyes. "There's nothing wrong with being attracted to a woman. An apparently single woman—"

"Which you happen to know, because you asked her."

Kurt frowned appraisingly. "You have a problem with that, because...?"

"Because I saw her first, bro."

"Whoa!" Kurt's hands shot up. "We were *just* making conversation. Doctor to patient."

Carter indulgently shook his head. "*Captivating eyes*? That's some bedside manner."

"Unbelievable." Kurt set his jaw.

"What?"

"You were eavesdropping."

"Was not. I just overheard from the kitchen."

To his utter amazement, Kurt guffawed. Next, he strode forward and slapped Carter on the shoulder. "Poor thing, you've got it bad."

"One. I have not *got* anything but a pain-in-the-neck friend. Two. I'd appreciate it if you kept your distance."

"From Hannah?" Kurt's forehead rose in mock innocence. "Why?"

"Because she's new in town," Carter said stonily. "She doesn't need to be hassled."

"I'm not hassling, man."

"Looked pretty borderline to me."

Kurt flashed his pearly whites. "Can I help it if I have a way with the ladies?"

"That's just it. Haven't you had your share?"

Kurt recoiled.

"First, it started with my sister."

"We were sixteen, Carter. *Sixteen*."

"*You* were sixteen. Savannah was fifteen—and innocent."

"Maybe not as much as you think."

"I don't regret socking you in the jaw."

"An early effort at law enforcement?" Kurt defiantly stepped toward him. "Maybe you'd like to try again?"

Carter heaved a breath and ran a hand through his hair. How had things spiraled so out of control? With their mothers being close, Carter and Kurt had spent many childhood summers together at the shore. The two families had vacationed with one another and all of the kids had bonded, especially Carter and Kurt, as they were the closest two boys in age. It wasn't until late August of one year that Carter understood his best guy pal Kurt was also *bonding* in an amorous way with his baby sister, Savannah. Carter caught them making out under the pier and had put a quick stop to things. It hadn't just been wrong. At the time, it had seemed totally gross. Seriously? *Kurt? How could he?*

Savannah was furious at Carter for interfering, and apparently Carter's mom Janet and Lou Christmas had some kind of disagreement after that. The summer fun stopped abruptly, with each family making excuses about why they could no longer participate in the annual event. Then, all these years later, Carter reconnected with Kurt in Christmas Town and it was like no time had passed. The brotherly bond was still there. If only Kurt hadn't messed things up to begin with by going after Carter's sister.

"So," Kurt said pointedly. "How *is* Savannah?"

"Same as she was the last time you asked me. Deeply in love."

"Oh, that's right." Kurt paused as if remembering. "With some guy who's saving the planet."

"He's a heart surgeon. Pediatric," Carter said with a smug air. "Savannah finds it very endearing that he ventures around the world helping needy children."

"Glad she's happy."

"Over the moon."

"Me, too. Ecstatic." Kurt dropped into a chair, appearing glum, and Carter suddenly felt as if he'd pushed things too far. Okay, it was bad. But Kurt was right. They'd only been kids and that was years ago. That didn't excuse the way Carter was acting now as an adult.

"Listen, man. About Savannah—"

"Ancient history," Kurt assured him, looking up. "Way ancient. To tell you the truth, I'm glad things worked out for her. The high-school counselor job sounds like the perfect fit." He appeared sincere.

"I guess she got into enough trouble of her own as a teen to be able to relate."

Kurt chuckled at this. "Yeah."

"You're lucky to have all your family here in the same town."

"You've got Olivia," Kurt pointed out, mentioning Carter's older sister.

"That's true." She'd moved here last summer to take over Buddy and Louise's knickknack shop, All Things Christmas, and so far appeared satisfied with the decision. "Not that I see her much. She stays plenty busy with the store."

"And, you stay plenty busy with the law," Kurt said, even though he knew Carter spent far more time on carpentry projects than chasing down bad guys, which fortunately were in short supply around here.

"I suppose we're all finding our way."

"Not you, bud. Just look at yourself." Kurt motioned broadly. "You've landed! Sheriff of Christmas Town."

"Ha-ha."

"I wasn't trying to be funny. I meant it."

Carter sighed and took a seat in a neighboring chair. "You've done okay, too."

"I suppose." Kurt spread his hands. "Master of my domain."

"You're a good doc, don't kid yourself."

"And you're a great cop."

"Is this where we have a hug-fest and make up?"

"Sure." Kurt cracked a grin. "Until it happens."

"Until *what* does?"

"I ask Hannah out before you get up the nerve to."

Carter leveled him a look. "You wouldn't."

Kurt steepled his hands and drummed his fingertips together. "She's new in town. Bound to be lonely..."

"How's that jaw of yours feel?"

Kurt rubbed it thoughtfully. "Twitching."

Carter finally grasped where Kurt was going with this. He probably wasn't legitimately interested in Hannah. He was trying to goad Carter into becoming socially active. Goad him because he thought it would be good for him. Just as Kurt had said it would about a hundred million times. Carter found himself choking up a little. Looking after others was what Carter did. He didn't cotton to others looking after him. But Kurt was somehow different. Kurt had his ways. Beyond that, Carter understood Kurt had his back. "You really do love me," he finally said, trying to play it off.

"Yup." Kurt grinned, his features taut with emotion. After a beat, he ventured hoarsely, "I really did care for Savannah, you know…back in the day."

"I know you did," Carter said with remorse. "I'm sorry I brought it up."

"It was a diversionary tactic," Kurt guessed.

"You know me too well."

"Yeah, well, maybe you should give others a chance to know you, too. Just *ask* her, Carter. One cup of coffee… One glass of wine... It won't be the end of the world if Hannah says no."

That's where Kurt misread his hesitation. It wasn't Hannah saying no to an invitation that worried him. Carter was too tough a guy to be bruised by mere rejection. It was her potential *acceptance* of a date that scared him senseless. And Sheriff Carter Livingston wasn't afraid of much. Between those days when they'd been kids and the time he'd landed here, Carter had been down a road so dark and private that very few people knew about it. He'd buried certain secrets deep, and wasn't ready to share them with anyone, not even with Kurt.

When he'd refused to share them with Gina, that had been the end of their story. Afterward, they'd prevented him from getting close to other women, too. Carter hadn't been interested in anything beyond dating casually in what seemed like an eternity now. And yet, casual dating tended to lead to women wanting more. Clearly more than Carter was willing to give at this point in his life…maybe even ever. Something about Hannah was different, though. She didn't seem like the kind of woman who pushed. So maybe in that case, a glass of wine with her would be okay. *Just a simple outing. Harmless.* The tips of Carter's ears burned hot when he realized he'd caught himself in a lie. There was nothing harmless at all about Hannah Winchester. One look in her eyes and she'd already gotten under his skin. Made Carter want to know more about her. The places she came from and where she was going next. And, most critically, why she was so fired-up eager to get away.

Chapter Five

When Sandy slid her key into the lock and threw open the glass-paneled door, Hannah saw immediately what she'd meant about liking snow. The Snow Globe Gallery wasn't just a display space, it was an inviting wintry paradise. Impressive oil canvases lined the walls, portraying Christmas scenes or outdoor landscapes. The style seemed old-world and elegant, reminiscent of Currier and Ives, yet the subjects were contemporary and dressed in modern clothing. Even the couple taking a horse-drawn sleigh ride appeared as if they could be neighbors from down the street. The swarthy man cut a rugged form with rich dark hair and eyes. He had his arm around a pretty brunette with apple dumpling cheeks and a radiant smile. She snuggled up against him as snowflakes drifted around them, and all at once Hannah was transported. It wasn't just as if she were viewing the scene; Hannah could imagine herself *in it*. Her senses absorbed the sharp nip in the air and the cool, crisp scent of snow as billowing pines curtsied in the wintery breeze. The driver called out a command and the sturdy mare whinnied, prancing along to the tune of sleigh bells while the loving couple shared a kiss. Hannah sighed, her own lips puckering in spite of herself.

"Kind of takes you there, doesn't it?" Sandy asked happily.

Hannah gasped, snapped back to the moment where gallery lights shone around her, highlighting each masterpiece. "Wow. Yes!" Hannah had heard of paintings coming to life, but she'd never encountered anything like this. The experience had been magical.

"That's one of my favorites," Sandy said. "I call it *Winter Wedding*."

Hannah blinked at the painting, feeling sure she'd seen the couple kissing only seconds ago. But they were freeze-framed in an amorous glow, the man's mouth hovering above the woman's. Hannah saw she held something in her hand and appeared to have been offering her companion a bite. Hannah stepped closer to the painting and saw that it was a light brown heart-shaped cookie. It had a decorative edge of Christmas holly, apparently made of icing. One small piece was missing.

"It features the cookies your great-grandma used to make," Sandy continued. "Virginia Cookies. Word is they were legendary."

"Oh yeah?" Hannah asked, surprised. "Legendary how?"

Sandy's whole face brightened. "To hear Buddy tell it, they were all the rage, these Virginia Cookies of Lena's. After Lena inherited the O'Hanlon Bakery from her parents, she repurposed the store, calling it the Christmas Cookie Shop. When she introduced a special heart-shaped cookie rumored to provide its consumer with that person's heart's desire, her sales took off."

"She was a clever woman, my great-grandma," Hannah remarked. "What a great marketing strategy."

"Oh, it wasn't merely marketing. To hear some tell it around here, those cookies really had special powers."

"Well, I suppose if people *wanted* to believe."

"Trust me on this. At that time in Christmas Town's history, everybody did. World War I had just ended, and many local families had lost loved ones. The Spanish Flu epidemic that came next took even more lives. Other dark times followed, but Lena made her cookies available to all who requested them, even those who couldn't pay. Word is, she gave them away for free during the Depression and bartered them in exchange for supplies to make more during sugar rationing in the Second World War."

Hannah was suddenly sad she'd never met Lena, who'd died before Hannah was born. "She sounds like a remarkable woman."

"I'm sure it runs in the family."

"Sandy, I told you—"

"I know, I know. You're not planning to stay. Only…" She hesitated a moment, then added, "Wouldn't that be something? To see your great-grandmother's shop in business again?"

"I'm sure it will be. That's why I'm planning to sell it. So someone else can take over."

Sandy shot her a sad look. "The last people didn't do so well."

"Well, maybe the next owner will do better," Hannah said lightly. She scanned the rest of the gallery, taking in the pretty paintings, including one of a little girl in footsie pajamas poised on her tiptoes to peer into a brimming stocking hung from a mantel. A Christmas tree stood in the background, twinkling with colorful lights and brightly striped candy canes. In another portrait, a handsome dad had a boy on his shoulders. The child was reaching toward the top of a Christmas tree, preparing to crown it with the shimmery star in his grasp. "These are really marvelous," she told Sandy. "You sure have talent."

"Thanks for changing the subject." Sandy shared a knowing smile. "But I appreciate the compliment."

Hannah laughed. Then she spied something glimmering near the front of the store. As the Snow Globe Gallery stood on the corner of North Main Street and Santa Claus Lane, the shop had two street-facing windows. The one on North Main housed a display shelf containing an oversize snow globe surrounded by fake white glittery snow. Hannah drew closer to examine the details inside it. A miniature model of a red barn sat beside a cheery farmhouse with light emanating from its windows. It even appeared as if smoke curled from its red brick chimney through the constantly cascading snow. A red-and-white-striped pole spun mystically in the pine-tree-laden yard, where eight tiny reindeer were harnessed to a sleigh holding a bulging red sack in the hollow behind the driver's seat. Hannah caught her breath in wonder. "How on earth does it do that?"

"Do what?" Sandy asked her.

"Manage to look so real?"

"It's one of those things where people see what they want to see."

"But the lights—?"

"They're coming from Santa's workshop."

"Sandy…" Hannah groaned. And here Sandy had said that Buddy Christmas was the one who liked to tell tales.

Sandy shrugged mildly. "That's what I believe."

"Just like you believe in the special powers of Lena's cookies?" Hannah teased.

Sandy grinned in return. "Shall we head over to your shop?"

"Yes, let's!" After hearing Sandy's story about Lena's Virginia Cookies, she couldn't wait to see it.

Sandy took a quick glance around, then switched off the lights. Hannah could tell Sandy was proud of the gallery, and she had every right to be. It was a lovely place and Sandy's work was stunning. There was just one thing that niggled at her. The term "Virginia Cookies" didn't seem exactly right. Why Virginia, when Christmas Town was in Tennessee?

"Sandy?" Hannah asked as they made for the door. "One small question."

Sandy paused, waiting.

"Why *Virginia* Cookies?"

"Oh that! Didn't you know?" Sandy's eyes lit up. "Lena named them for her distant cousin from New York: Virginia O'Hanlon."

"Virginia…" Hannah gasped. "You mean, the child who wrote to the New York *Sun* asking if there really was a Santa Claus?"

"One and the same," Sandy replied smartly. "You *do* remember the editor's answer?"

"Yes, Virginia," Hannah mused, *"there is a Santa Claus…"* Something stirred deep within her. Hannah didn't recall the editor's reply word-for-word, but she knew he spoke of poetry and romance…and childlike faith. He'd told the inquiring little girl that just because

something couldn't be seen that didn't mean it shouldn't be believed. Hannah's heart welled with pride. Lena had taken that kernel of wisdom and spread a message of hope and renewal through her lovingly crafted cookies. *Virginia Cookies, of course!*

"Hannah?" Sandy gently touched her shoulder, and Hannah suddenly realized her face felt damp. "Hannah, are you all right?"

"I was just thinking…" Hannah lifted a glove and wiped back the single tear that had rolled down her cheek. "About what a special woman Lena was."

Sandy answered softly, "She was indeed."

"And, seriously?" Hannah laughed in disbelief. "I'm related to *that* Virginia?"

Sandy glanced her way, baiting. "You'll never believe who *I'm* related to."

Hannah scrutinized her a moment, waiting, while Sandy bit back a smile. The seconds ticked by, but Sandy held her ground.

"You're one big tease!"

"Come on!" Sandy returned. "Let's get going. We'll want to see your shop while it's still light."

Chapter Six

The Christmas Cookie Shop was just a few doors down from where the Snow Globe stood on the corner of North Main Street and Santa Claus Lane. Hannah was surprised to spy Carter's red truck parked in front of it. Sandy leaned toward the truck and spoke through the cascading snow when Carter lowered his window. "Everything all right, Sheriff?"

"Got a report from Jade Scott!" he called back through the wind's roar. "Jade said she stopped by her place across the way to pick up some books, and saw some lights on." He motioned toward the cookie shop.

"Lights?" Hannah glanced across the street to find the Elf Shelf Book Shop stationed directly opposite her store. "Couldn't be," she said, addressing Carter. "We haven't been inside."

"Not only that," Sandy told her. "The electricity's been off for at least a decade."

Carter wore a serious frown. "Where are you ladies headed now?"

"I was just going to open it." Hannah produced the key from her pocket. "Show it to Sandy."

"Mind if I come along?" He peered over Hannah's shoulder and into the darkened storefront. "Just to be sure nothing's amiss?"

"Well, I…" Hannah hesitated as heat infused her face. It was hard not to recall how affronted he'd seemed when he'd left Sisters' Row earlier. She hadn't meant to put him off; he'd been nothing but kind to her since her arrival in town. Perhaps that was part of the trouble. His kindness coupled with his good looks made it hard for Hannah to maintain her resolve to not be attracted. Maybe it was already too late.

Carter met her eyes and she grew hotter. *Yep. That horse is already out of the barn. Or the butterfly out of its box, as luck has it.* Hannah clutched a hand to her chest to still her beating heart—and prevent a mass takeoff of tiny wings.

"Won't stay long," he assured her. "Just long enough to make sure everything's okay."

Hannah self-consciously tugged down her cap, covering the bump on her forehead. "Yeah," she said. "Of course." It was silly to let Carter's appearance unnerve her. He was only doing his job. And if something funny was going on inside her store, it was certainly good to have him here.

Carter exited the truck to join Hannah and Sandy on the store's front stoop, which was protected from the elements by a slight overhang. Against the wintery backdrop, it was hard to ignore Carter's rugged appeal. He was dressed in his uniform, which brought out the deep green of his eyes, and a smattering of snow dusted the brim of his hat. He removed it briefly and shook it out as he scanned the shop's front window. It held an empty pastry case, and Hannah could spy a bakery counter lining one wall of the store behind it. There was an old cash register in place, centered before an open door leading to a darkened back room, which Hannah presumed to be the kitchen. "Looks quiet from here," Carter commented, as Hannah prepared to insert the key into the lock.

All at once, her fingers trembled, as if she were about to open the wardrobe door and enter Narnia. A sense of wonder overcame her, and it was almost as if she could detect Lena's presence beckoning her inside. This wasn't just any place she'd inherited. It was one of her family's treasures, an enterprise her great-grandmother had fully believed in—and given her heart to. Hannah couldn't imagine the passion or commitment that must have taken, and she admired Lena greatly for creating such a thriving business.

But Hannah was no businesswoman. She was even less of a baker. In fairness to the shop and her great-grandmother's memory, she'd have to pass the Christmas Cookie Shop on to someone who could do it justice.

Hannah tried for the lock with the key, but clumsily missed her mark. She got it inserted on her second try, but the lock refused to turn. She tried jiggling the key to the left and then to the right, but the mechanism wouldn't budge.

Carter's rough-hewn hand slid down her glove and Hannah's heart hammered. He was close enough for her to smell his heady scent of sandalwood and spice, his arm skimming her coat sleeve. "Allow me?"

Hannah relinquished the key, her pulse racing. "Seems stuck," she uttered, barely managing the words. Carter had never stood this close, and his proximity was intoxicating. So much so that Sandy apparently noticed the punch-drunk look on Hannah's face. She coyly lifted an eyebrow as Carter took over, and Hannah's pulse pounded in her ears. Seconds later, the deadbolt slammed open with a *clank.*

"Just needed a little muscle." Carter grinned, then stopped abruptly, trying to read Hannah's frozen expression. "Are you okay?"

She nodded and Sandy said, "She's probably just overcome by emotion."

Carter viewed them both uncertainly and twisted the doorknob. "Right." He held the door open for the ladies and a door chime tinkled, sending a merry echo through the cavernous shop. Hannah stepped inside, and wrapped her arms around herself when she felt a chill. "Pretty cold in here."

"No heat," Sandy said, entering the store behind her. Carter followed them and shut the door, which battled briefly against the wind.

"Or electricity." He unhitched a flashlight from his belt. "Precisely why I'm here."

When his deputy, Victoria Cho, was alerted to the situation, Carter could have let her cover it. Instead, he'd insisted that Victoria had the day off. She'd arranged it in advance, so she could take her five-year-old son, Bobby, to his friend Alexander's birthday party. It was Alexander's mom Jade who'd spied some movement in the cookie shop, and she'd mentioned it to Victoria a short time later. Since Jade and Wendell Scott occupied the third town house at Sisters' Row, the birthday party was fairly close by. Victoria phoned Carter, offering to pop around the corner to investigate, but Carter wouldn't hear of it. Victoria needed to stay with her son, and Carter didn't mind the short drive here from his office. Normally, on Sundays, this section of town had plenty of people milling about, out for Sunday strolls and window-shopping.

On this particular day though, Christmas Town's streets seemed like something out of a ghost town: eerily deserted with most folks hunkered down indoors. Not a bad idea with a blizzard brewing. Rather than abating, the winds seemed to be growing fiercer by the minute, as more and more snow dumped down upon them. While it wasn't quite dusk, the storm outside cast a certain gloom over the store's interior. Carter switched on his flashlight and sent its broad beams reaching across dust-covered floorboards. If someone had broken in, they sure hadn't left any tracks. Not unless they'd come in the back way.

"Doesn't look like anyone's been in here," he said, noting Hannah's awestruck look as she perused the place.

She wore that colorful knit cap again and her cheeks were pink from the cold. Her dark eyes sparkled with wonder. "I had no idea it was this big. Looks a lot smaller from the outside."

"I know," Sandy answered. "It's a pretty cool setup."

Hannah replied on a breathy sigh. "Wonderful."

Carter watched her, mesmerized, thinking she looked just like a kid on Christmas morning, someone who viewed the world with hopeful imagination, while all Carter saw were dust bunnies and cobwebs. Hannah turned his way and smiled and the heat went up on his register. Way up. Carter couldn't fight facts. He'd wanted to see Hannah again. That was why he'd refused Victoria's offer to cover for him. He'd planned to observe things from the street first, then drop by Sisters' Row afterward to share the nature of the complaint. Carter had to know if he'd experience that same spark he'd felt when he'd been with Hannah earlier. It had been so long since Carter had felt that way about a woman, he didn't completely trust his judgment anymore.

He hadn't counted on his good luck in running smack-dab into her on the street. That had thrown his plan off a little, especially since Sandy was tagging along. Not that Sandy being present seemed to make one iota of difference to his thudding heart. The darn thing appeared to have a mind of its own around Hannah. What's more, it seemed to have made up its mind. Whoever she was, and whatever she wanted, Carter had to know more about her. *Whether she's only passing through town or not...*

"Don't know what Jade saw," Sandy commented, glancing around. "But it's hard to believe it came from in here."

"Maybe we should check out the kitchen?" Carter offered.

Hannah nodded and he led the way, the flashlight out in front of him and his other hand on his holster. Carter didn't really anticipate trouble, but one never really knew. The best way to avoid it was to prepare for it in advance. "Better safe than sorry." He spoke over his shoulder as Hannah and Sandy followed closely behind him.

"It's so dark," Sandy whispered, instinctively keeping her voice down.

That was because there were no windows, other than the two narrow ones positioned above a large rack oven to the rear of the room, and those faced an alley. A butcher block island stood in the center of the room and an industrial-size refrigerator was in one corner. Beside it, two large double doors swung open to an enormous pantry housing a multitude of empty shelves. There was a heavy coating of dust on everything in here as well, and the door that led to the back alley appeared secure, with no footprints in front of it. Carter strode toward it and tested its lock, but it held steady. He turned back toward the women to find Hannah's hand on the switch plate by the door leading in from the front room. She'd apparently removed her gloves and shoved them in her pockets, and her coat was unbuttoned a notch. "Hannah, don't—!"

Just as Carter spoke, Hannah flipped up the switch and the room exploded in color with a loud *pop*. Bright twinkling lights danced around the ceiling, blinking in reds, yellows, blues, oranges, and greens. Dancing shadows cast about the room, bouncing off of countertops and appliances, skittering across the floor and the top of Carter's hat. Hannah gasped in alarm…amazement…fright! She wasn't sure which! It was stunning!

Sandy yelped and lunged for the light switch, flipping it down. The kitchen was immediately plunged into darkness, as Hannah stood there breathing hard and the scent of charred wiring lingered in the air.

Carter raised his flashlight with alarm and trained it on the light switch. "Don't move, either of you," he commanded fiercely. "I think we blew a fuse."

"I thought the power was off?" Sandy asked with confusion.

"Me, too. I just…" Hannah frowned, her knees shaking slightly. "Saw the switch, and force of habit! It was so dark in—"

Carter's face softened. "It's not your fault. You had no way to know." His beam tracked the high corners of the walls where they met the ceiling. Several strings of Christmas lights had been joined together and looped around the perimeter of the room. "Let me find the fuse box," he told them. "Looks like it's over here." He located a panel in the wall beside the refrigerator and flipped it open, throwing the master switch. "Don't know why that was on. Nothing in here is to code."

"Could a realtor have left it on?" Sandy asked. "Back when the place was for rent?"

"Who knows? The electric company was supposed to have turned things off completely. Just like the water company was supposed to cut off their supply."

He strode to the kitchen sink and tried the tap. The spigot groaned and heaved, then sputtered water in a murky stream. Carter shook his head disapprovingly. "Looks like some things fell through the cracks."

Carter shut off the water, returned to the fuse panel and shut it. "Faulty wiring can be dangerous," he told Hannah with concern. "You should have Frank Cho take a look tomorrow."

"He's the town electrician," Sandy said. "And, Victoria's husband."

"Victoria?" Hannah questioned.

"She's my deputy and a very good one," Carter explained, pulling out his phone. "Why don't we go into the other room where there's more light, and I'll give you Frank's number?"

Hannah agreed, adding her thanks.

After she'd entered Frank's number in her cell, Carter returned his phone to his pocket and zipped up his coat. "If you ladies are all set here, I guess I'll mosey along."

"We were just headed to dinner," Sandy jumped in impulsively before sending Hannah a furtive glance. "If you want to join us?"

"Nice invite, Sandy. Thank you. But—"

"Don't tell me," she teased lightly. "You're on duty?"

"Actually. Yes."

Sandy's smile was bold and bright. "Rain check?" Hannah wanted to kick her.

Carter shifted on his feet, pointedly avoiding Hannah's eyes. "Rain check. Right. That's a fine idea." He shoved his hands in his pockets and sauntered toward the door, his head hung low. But when he turned to face them, there was a devilish gleam in his eyes.

"There's just one problem," he told Sandy while she watched him, confounded. "I've already accepted one rain check this week, and I'm still waiting to make good on it."

He tipped his hat at Hannah and her skin burned hot. That was no casual look. It was the look of a man being interested in a woman, and that woman was *her*.

Hannah resisted the urge to swoon and tried to recall her laundry list of reasons she'd sworn off men. Yet the writing seemed fuzzy, one lame excuse blurring into the next. Maybe *all men* had been too broad a sweep? Perhaps *most* was better?

"Wow!" Sandy said when the door chime tinkled. "Talk about sparks!"

"Yeah," Hannah answered, purposely obtuse. "I'm calling Frank first thing tomorrow."

Sandy chided her playfully. "I wasn't talking about the store."

"You're starting to give Lou a run for her money," Hannah said. "In the matchmaking department. I thought *she* was the one to steer clear of."

"What did I do?" Seconds later Sandy chuckled. "Other than give fate a helping hand?"

"I don't need any help, thank you."

"Apparently, neither does Carter."

Hannah's voice lilted. "Seems like the man can take care of himself."

"I'm seeing a whole new side to him…" Sandy replied in low tones.

In spite of herself, Hannah reddened. "Come on! Are you hungry, or what?"

"Starved! And you?"

"Lead the way to those greasy burgers!"

Sandy nudged her, eying her pockets. "Better put those gloves back on first."

Chapter Seven

Two hours later, Hannah tugged off her gloves and laid them on the entranceway table, as Jingles and Belle curled frantically around her ankles with desperate cries. She removed her knit cap and lightly traced the knot on her forehead with her fingers, examining it in the foyer mirror. It remained tender, but the lump was getting smaller and the throbbing had subsided. The bruising still looked bad, but would go away in time. "I know, I know," she told the kittens. "I've starved you to death." They scampered into the kitchen ahead of her, mewing mercilessly until she'd filled their bowls with food and freshened their water. Hannah certainly wasn't hungry. That delicious burger and fries had filled her right up. She'd truly enjoyed Sandy's company as well. It was hard to think they'd met only yesterday. Already, they felt like fast friends.

While Sandy had broadsided her by inviting Carter to join them for dinner and teased her about their mutual attraction later, Hannah didn't really mind Sandy butting in. Sandy was the kind of woman who wanted everyone else to be happy, and Hannah understood she meant well. If only Hannah could think up the perfect match for Sandy, turnabout could be fair play. The problem was, Hannah had only been in Christmas Town a day and was just starting to know its people.

Hannah unbuttoned her coat and filled the old-fashioned teakettle with water, placing it on a gas burner. She'd have a cup of hot tea along with one of the cookies from her welcome basket, while making out her "to do" list for tomorrow. The first thing she needed to do was hit the Merry Market and pick up some groceries, she thought, mentally compiling her list as she set the tea ball on the counter, preparing to fill it. She also should buy cleaning supplies to take over to the Christmas Cookie Shop. Hannah reached for a notepad and pen that sat beside the landline telephone on the counter, and carried them to the dining room table. She was just hanging up her coat when her cell phone rang. It was Ben.

"Well, hey, big brother!"

"Hey, yourself," he answered cordially. "Just checking in and making sure today was less eventful."

Hannah settled down in a dining room chair. "If you're asking if I had another rave, the answer is no."

"Sure sounded like a houseful last night."

"I got a very warm welcome, that's for sure."

"How's the injury?"

"Doing better, thanks."

Hannah could hear Lily talking in the background. "Pumpkin sends her love." He briefly covered the mouthpiece before continuing. "And she asked about the kittens."

"Tell her I love her back, and they're doing fine." Belle appeared out of nowhere and sprang up on her lap. Hannah jumped in surprise, then smiled and stroked the cat. Belle curled into a ball against

Hannah's belly and began purring. "Keeping me really great company."

"Good. Good. I'll pass it on."

Hannah suspiciously searched, looking for Jingles, but he was nowhere in sight.

"Have you been to the shop yet?" Ben asked her.

"Just this afternoon."

"And?"

"Needs cleaning—and work. Electrical work, to be specific."

"Be careful with that. Hire a professional."

"No worries there. I know to steer clear of live wires." Hannah laughed good-naturedly, then felt her cheeks burn when she recalled the sparks that had flown back and forth between her and Carter. Had she imagined it, or had Sandy been right to spot the chemistry between them?

"So, have you met anyone interesting?"

"Interesting?"

"Yeah, you know. Like the town mayor... Or maybe...Santa Claus." Ben chuckled deeply at his own joke.

"Actually, yes."

"Yes, which?" Ben sounded intrigued. "The mayor or Old Saint Nick?"

"Both."

"Okay. How much eggnog have you had? I'm calling one of Santa's helpers and cutting you off."

"Very funny, Ben."

"I'm not the one telling tall tales."

"I'm not either," Hannah replied. "I did meet Santa on my way into town." Her heart danced when she recalled the encounter. Hannah lifted the purring fur ball and snuggled her close to her pounding chest. "He turned out to be the sheriff *dressed* as Santa, but still…"

Ben hooted. "A run-in with the law and the town doctor, all in one day!"

"You're forgetting Louise Christmas."

"Oh, right. She's the one you rented from."

"Not only that, Lou's the town mayor."

"Wow."

"Then there's Sandy…" Hannah added, her voice lilting. Of course! Why hadn't she thought of it sooner? Sandy and Ben would make such a great pair. If only Ben didn't live so far away. The teakettle whistled shrilly and Hannah gently set Belle on the floor.

"Who's Sandy?"

"I'll have to tell you later," she said, walking to the kitchen. "Better yet," Hannah said, brightening at the thought, "maybe you can come to Christmas Town!"

"Me?"

"You and Lily, too!" Hannah lifted the kettle off the stove and looked around for the tea ball she'd left on the counter.

"Not this year, Sis. I'm buried in work up to my ears. And still busy settling Grandma's estate."

"Oh, yeah." Where was that tea ball? Hannah was sure she'd left it by the sink before walking into the living area. Was her mind going already? She hadn't hit her head *that* hard yesterday.

"Plus, Lily's got her school pageant. Holiday piano recital… Lots of stuff going on before our trip to the West Coast."

Hannah's face sagged with disappointment when she recalled Ben was taking Lily to see Nancy's parents in California. "Right."

"Why don't you take lots of pictures?" Ben suggested. "Photos of the town. And your shop, of course. Lily and I would love to see them when you get home."

He was such a genius, her big brother. Hannah could even text a few pics to Ben before then. Perhaps one or two containing the image of a pretty blonde, Hannah thought sneakily. "Great thought."

But wait! Sandy wasn't interested in leaving Christmas Town. She'd just as much said so, and Ben probably wouldn't want to move here. If he did and Hannah went back to Northern Virginia, they'd be so far apart. That was, unless Hannah herself stayed in Christmas Town, which she naturally wasn't going to do. What a crazy idea! Hannah wondered briefly if the matchmaking bug was contagious, and if she'd perhaps caught a touch of it. How silly of her to think of fixing up Sandy and Ben. The concept held absolutely no merit! That's when she spied Jingles. And the tea ball! It dangled from his mouth by its chain as he darted out of the kitchen and zipped for the stairs. "Jingles! No!"

"Something tells me mischief is afoot." Ben's voice rumbled through the phone.

"Mischief is right," Hannah told him hurriedly. "I think Lily misnamed that one." Then she said her quick goodbyes and scurried for the steps, determined not to let the cat get the better of her again. She certainly planned to be much more careful diving under the bed, if that's where Jingles was headed. And Hannah was betting anything that it was.

Chapter Eight

The next morning, Hannah propped a broom and a mop against the doorframe of the Christmas Cookie Shop, while holding a brimming sack of cleaning supplies. Chilly winds danced around her, nipping at her nose and chin, but the snow had finally stopped. Snowplows had come through and sunlight bounced off the gleaming white street, reflecting in the cheery storefront windows lining Santa Claus Lane. The Christmas Cookie Shop stood on the right side of the street when one was facing the western mountains. It was two doors down from the Snow Globe Gallery, on the corner of Santa Claus Lane and North Main, and Nutcracker Sweets—a candy shop—stood between them. An interesting-looking store called Mystic Magi was to the Christmas Cookie's Shop's left and sold New Age items like crystals, incense, and essential oils.

Directly opposite Mystic Magi, a colorful red and white pole held a sign for the Candy Cane Barber Shop, which was positioned beside Yuletide Cards and Gifts on its left. On the far side of Yuletide Cards and Gifts, and precisely across the street from the Christmas Cookie Shop, the Elf Shelf Book Shop occupied a large space, easily double the size of the others. An imagining of Santa's workshop was on display in the huge front window, complete with a gnomelike Santa and several helper elves. A toy train on a track wound around a brightly decorated tree while Santa's tiny hammer beat out a happy rhythm against the miniature wagon he was nailing together. Parents with little children poured in the bookstore's front door, Hannah presumed for a regular story hour or some kind of special event. None of the other businesses were open, except for the Merry Market, which sat on the Elf Shelf Book Shop's other side, on the corner of Santa Claus Lane and South Main.

Sandy had told Hannah the market opened at eight, so she'd gotten there early to pick up groceries and other necessities. With the exception of the bookstore, which opened at nine thirty, and Jolly Bean Java, which opened at seven, most other businesses in town seemed to open at ten, including the North Pole Nursery, located in the old train depot at the far end of the street. Stands of fresh-cut Fraser firs outlined the squat building, skirting the train tracks and abutting the towering mountains. At the opposite end of Santa Claus Lane, the road ended in a T intersection bisecting North and South Main Streets.

South Main began at the roundabout that housed the courthouse and library and contained exits to the bypass and River Road. North Main led past several private homes, the Corner Church, and a few other businesses near the edge of town, where it joined a rural highway. Hannah had gotten the lay of the land from Sandy, then had begun piecing the landscape together this morning in the clear light of day.

With the storm lifted, the quaint shops and the lamppost-lined streets appeared even more enchanting than they had at dusk two days before. Hannah absorbed her spectacular surroundings, taking in the sights and sounds of the historic town. This time, her key slid easily into the lock and the door to her shop practically opened on its own. She pressed her way inside, jostling the mop and broom, then set her grocery bag on a glass pastry case. There was work to be done here, all right. A lot of it... The electrician she'd phoned, Frank Cho, was due here at eleven. But there was plenty Hannah could tackle in the meantime. She'd bought oil soap for the original hardwood floors and had purchased plenty of cleaners and dust rags. By the time Frank arrived, this front room should be gleaming. That was one good thing about the water being on. She decided she ought to poke around the place for a bathroom, too. She hadn't seen one yesterday afternoon, but she'd honestly forgotten to look. There had to be at least a modest one tucked away somewhere, and Hannah was guessing that—just like the rest of the place—it needed sprucing up.

An hour and a half later, Hannah set down her pail of suds and scanned the room with satisfaction. Polished pastry cases shone and hardwood floors gleamed beneath them. Even the tiny bathroom was spic-and-span. Hannah had located the restroom door behind the checkout counter holding the antiquated cash register. She hadn't seen it earlier because it had been hidden behind the open door leading to the kitchen. Hannah surveyed the newly polished storefront window, sparkling in the sunlight. Through it, a dark figure in a sheriff's hat hustled by. Hannah's heart thudded when she realized it was Carter heading down the street. She wondered why he hadn't stopped in to say hello, then guessed it was because he didn't know she was here. She had to have been swabbing the bathroom mirror when he'd first approached her store, and now he'd already hurried past. Hannah tried to deflect the mild disappointment surging through her. What would she and Carter have had to talk about anyway? That *rain check* of his?

Hannah's pulse raced when she recalled the slow perusal Carter had given her on his way out the door last night. She'd thought a lot about his acceptance of her offer since, and had decided to woman up and take advantage of it. So what, if she wasn't staying for long? Hadn't she only recently convinced herself of the value of making friends in Christmas Town? There was nothing wrong with her and Carter sharing a glass of wine or two. That was, assuming there was an establishment around here that sold libations after six. From what Hannah gathered, only the Peppermint Bark stayed open in the evenings—and that was just on Friday and Saturday nights.

Her phone buzzed and she pulled it from her hip pocket, answering it. Frank was calling to say he'd been delayed and was running fifteen minutes late. That would give Hannah enough time to mop the kitchen floor. She'd prop open the door to the front room to let in sunlight, and would be extra careful not to touch any light switches. Just as she'd thought that, she spied Carter striding back up the street on the opposite sidewalk. Then, he seemed to pause in thought and reverse his trek, ducking into the bookstore. Hannah shook her head, deciding to empty her bucket in the commode before starting with fresh water in the kitchen.

When she returned to the front room ten minutes later, Carter was back on the street. This time, he was— *what*? *Jaywalking*? And beelining straight across the street toward the Christmas Cookie Shop! Hannah swallowed hard and self-consciously adjusted the scarf she'd tied around her head to hold back her bangs. She was sure she looked a mess, or worse than one, with all the cleaning she'd done. Her sweatshirt and hair teemed with dust and the knees of her jeans were marred with dirt. What's more, her skin felt encrusted in grime. There were probably even cobwebs behind her ears! She was about to dart back into the bathroom to rinse her face when she spotted another attractive man approaching her store. He appeared to be in his early thirties, with an easy gait and a genuine smile. His grin was directed at Carter as the men shook hands.

Carter was relieved to see Frank Cho park his van at the Grand Hotel and head down Santa Claus Lane. That meant Frank was going to the Christmas Cookie Shop to investigate Hannah's electrical problems. Now, Carter would finally have an excuse to pop in there as well. He could claim he'd spied Frank on the street, and wanted to check in with Hannah himself to be sure she hadn't discovered any other issues. Issues, right. *Like the fact that the Christmas Town sheriff has the hots for their temporary newcomer...*

Carter was embarrassed to admit it, but he'd been walking up and down this street like a lovesick puppy dog for the past twenty minutes. Ray Christmas had noted this from his nursery, and had actually said something to Carter about it. Ray had heard from his brother Kurt that Hannah Winchester was in town. He'd also apparently learned she was pretty, and that Carter had an interest in her. Carter couldn't trust Kurt as far as he could throw him. *Thanks, pal, for your discretion.*

Ray had paused in his work while carefully realigning the new batch of Christmas trees he'd put out for sale. He'd entrusted the original job to his son, Kyle. But Kyle was only ten, and still learning the trade. Ray liked the trees grouped together by price, so families could easily pick one that fit their budget. Kyle had mixed things up a bit, and Ray was straightening them out while the boy was in school. "No sense coming down on the kid," he'd said with a soft smile. "Kyle does his best and always works hard." Ray had fair hair and dark eyes like Kurt, but his jaw seemed more angular somehow. His face was also more weathered, given that he spent much of his time outdoors. Ray was a good dad and a nice guy. Except for when he was ribbing Carter. "So!" he'd said, his eyes twinkling. "Word on the street is there's a new lady in town."

"Sounds like you've been talking to your brother."

"That, and minding my eyes."

Carter shot him a look and Ray raised both eyebrows. "Seems like those sidewalks should be smoking, given all the traffic they've endured. How the shoes feeling? Getting warm yet?"

"You, Ray, are a very funny guy."

"And you, Carter, are a really chicken sheriff."

"You're letting your imagination get the best of you."

Ray shrugged mildly. "If you say so."

Carter's face heated. "I had business on this street, if you must know."

"No doubt you did."

"Had to get my hair cut first." Carter glanced quickly at the barbershop, then at Mystic Magi across the street, which was closed mornings now, due to Della's maternity leave. "Asked Stan about Della and the new baby. Then decided to pop into the Elf Shelf and pick up a little gift." He held up the bag in his hand as evidence. It contained a gift-wrapped copy of a book his little sister, Savannah, had loved as a child, *Goodnight Moon.*

"Very thoughtful of you." Ray's lips twitched in a smile. "But that only explains one trip down the street." He paused for emphasis. "Then, back up it again. Then down—"

"Anyone ever tell you that you spend way too much time paying attention to your neighbors?"

"Nuh-uh. Most of 'em appreciate it."

"Thanks, Ray! Keep up the good work!" Carter gave him a friendly pat on the back and squinted toward the corner. "I think I see Frank's truck pulling in."

"Electrical woes?"

"Seems like. The Christmas Cookie Shop is old."

"Old, but pretty special. Everyone in town is stoked that Hannah's going to reopen it."

"I wouldn't go betting on that," Carter said.

Ray's forehead creased. "Why not?"

"Lady claims she's not sticking around."

Chapter Nine

Hannah held back the door, greeting the men on the street. Frank Cho gave a friendly smile, bomber jacket zipped up tight and thumbs hitched in his utility belt. "You must be Hannah."

"Thanks for coming by, and on such short notice."

"No problem," Frank said as Carter followed him indoors, tipping his hat Hannah's way. "Electricity's nothing to mess with."

Just as Frank spoke, Carter locked on her gaze. Seconds ticked by as winds howled across the threshold. Frank turned to her, puzzled, and Carter reached up and smoothly shut the door. Hannah noted the paper bag in his hand. Its logo read The Elf Shelf Book Shop.

"Good to see you, Sheriff." Hannah shot him a smile. "Been shopping?"

"Had some errands to run." Carter awkwardly cleared his throat. "On this street."

Frank paused in unzipping his jacket to scrutinize them both. In a flash, his face registered understanding. "I'll just go check things out, while you two get acquainted."

"Oh no, we've—"

"Met," Carter finished for her. His eyes were a thicket of pines: lush, green, and inviting. Heat warmed her cheeks as Carter removed his hat and pressed it to his chest.

"Right." Frank repressed a grin. "In that case, reacquainted." Hannah was vaguely aware of Frank turning her way. "Fuse box?"

"Kitchen," she said weakly, never taking her eyes off Carter's.

Frank clucked his tongue. "Uh-huh. Uh-*huh*."

As he trailed away, Hannah could have sworn he said, "Major power surges could be an issue."

Carter shifted his hat to the hand holding the bag. "Hannah…"

"Frank seems to have gotten the wrong impression."

"What impression is that?"

Her color deepened. "That you and I—"

"But we're not," he assured her firmly.

"No."

"Not even in the least."

Hannah shook her head.

"The only thing is…"

Hannah waited, her heart drumming.

"We could be, if you wanted."

"Could be what?"

"Going out." A sly smile crept up his lips. "You did kind of invite me."

"The rain check." The words were a breathy whisper.

"Yeah." Carter raised his free hand and lightly traced her lips with his thumb.

Hannah's pulse raced and butterflies went wild within her.

"How about that *rain check*?" His palm was on her cheek now, the heel of his hand cradling her chin. Carter took a step closer. Only his hat and the shopping bag stood between them. "Can I cash it in?"

The butterflies were soaring now, completely out of control and crashing into each other. "What day…" Hannah caught her breath. "And time?"

"Why don't we say Friday at six? I'll buy you dinner."

Hannah swallowed hard, the heat of his touch seeping into her skin. "I'll buy the wine."

"Sounds like a date."

A high shrill whistle sounded from the next room. "Will you look at this?"

Carter stepped back as Frank appeared in the doorway to the kitchen, holding a pair of frayed wires in his hands.

"This is going to take some work." He shook his head, addressing Hannah. "Serious work. The entire fuse box is shot and nothing here is to code. The wiring's all going to have to be replaced."

Hannah stared at him with dismay. "That sounds bad."

"How pricey are we talking, Frank?" Carter asked him.

Frank raked a hand through his short dark hair. "I'll have to run some numbers at the shop and get back to you." He strode toward Hannah and pulled a pen and notepad from his pocket. "Got an e-mail address?"

Hannah didn't know whether to feel elated by her exchange with Carter or bummed over Frank's bad news. At least she had a lunch date to distract her. Sandy had invited her to meet at Santa's Sandwich

Shop at one. A few friends of Sandy's would be joining them, and Hannah was excited about making new acquaintances. Everyone she'd met in town had been so friendly, but no one had quite laid out the welcome mat like Carter Livingston. Hannah hated to admit it, because she'd sworn off men and everything, but the truth of the matter was that the sheriff took her breath away.

Carter was caring, kind, and devastatingly handsome. Plus, he had a solidness about him that made Hannah believe all was right with the world. His presence made Hannah feel safe, even when his proximity threatened to undo her. But Hannah simply couldn't let herself get swept away again. This wasn't the time or place to fall for someone. Yet, when Carter was near, her heart seemed to have a will of its own.

Hannah locked up her shop and hustled through the cold toward the corner. She passed the Snow Globe Gallery, spying a sign on its door saying it was closed for lunch. Sandy had said she'd go on ahead and grab a table for the group. Hannah paused at the intersection, then crossed over to South Main, thinking she couldn't wait to meet the others. Between the hours she'd spent cleaning her store and the fresh sparks that had flown between her and Carter, she'd worked up quite an appetite.

When Hannah breezed into Santa's Sandwich Shop, she was glad she was hungry. Delicious smells wafted through the air, conjuring visions of barbequed beef, fried chicken, and crispy applewood bacon. Hannah passed a couple of women enjoying fried green tomato BLTs with thick-cut fries, and her mouth watered. The décor was cute and homey, with no-fuss red-checkered plastic placemats set on tables surrounded by customers. A curly-haired waitress hustled past her with an apology and a fresh pot of coffee as Hannah made her way toward a corner booth set for four. Sandy smiled and waved enthusiastically from her seat on one side of the table. She'd saved the spot beside her in the booth. Two women sat across from her.

The first had nutmeg-colored skin and chocolate-brown eyes. Her two-toned brown and blond pixie haircut was pulled back on one side and secured by a decorative candy cane barrette that complemented her deep red cardigan sweater. Beneath it she wore a white high turtleneck shell and slim gray slacks. Her features were fine and elegant, and a smile graced her face. "You must be—"

An arm jutted across the table. "Hannah Winchester!" Hannah stared down at the second woman with the outstretched hand and blinked.

"Why, yes. And you are…?"

"Olivia Livingston. So nice to meet you." The pretty redhead had a thick auburn braid slung forward over one shoulder. She wore a checkered flannel shirt and stretchy dark pants tucked into riding boots. When she smiled, there was a familiar twinkle in her deep green eyes.

Hannah blinked again and shook her hand. "You're Carter's sister?"

"Ooh, Carter…" The first woman shot Olivia a conspiratorial grin. "Sounds like your little brother and our town newcomer already know each other."

Hannah's cheeks steamed. "Just barely," she said, and Sandy pointedly cleared her throat.

"Jade Smith Scott," the first woman said, firmly shaking Hannah's hand. "Welcome to Christmas Town."

Hannah said how great it was to meet them both and slid into the booth. "Thanks for inviting me to come along," she told Sandy.

"The others wanted to meet you," Sandy said with a nod.

"Absolutely!" Olivia agreed. "And we hope you'll make it a regular tradition!"

"We meet for lunch each Monday," Jade explained. "The Peppermint Bark is closed today, so this is really the only other option nearby."

"Oh I... Well, thank you. Thank you so much. I'd love to join in." Hannah glanced uncertainly around the table. "That is, if the three of you don't mind?"

"Of course we don't mind." Sandy nudged her. "You're one of the crowd now."

Hannah had never been accepted so easily or with such genuine warmth. "You're very kind. Only..."

Jade and Olivia watched her expectantly.

"Didn't Sandy tell you? I'm not—"

"Let's not go spoiling the fun by talking about the future!" Sandy butted in.

"The future, yeah." Olivia blew out a hard breath, sending a loose tendril spiraling. "It's kind of depressing when you think about it."

Jade's mouth creased in a frown. "She's right. Sales were down again last month, and things aren't looking much better now."

Hannah recalled Carter saying that Jade ran the Elf Shelf Book Shop. "But I saw such a line at your place just this morning. Little kids and their parents were streaming out the door."

"For the free story hour, yes. Getting people to pay is something else."

"It's the economy," Olivia said, before addressing Hannah. "I own All Things Christmas, the curio shop on the way into town."

"Lou and Buddy used to run it," Sandy offered. "Olivia bought it when they retired."

"I've seen it," Hannah said. "It looks charming."

"Its charms don't extend beyond getting folks to window-shop, I'm afraid."

"Is business really that bad?" Hannah asked with concern.

"It's been bad since the bypass went in," Olivia told her.

"But the town is so historic," Hannah protested. "And quaint."

"Christmas Town itself isn't much of a destination vacation, I'm afraid." Jade sadly shook her head. "People used to stop and shop on their way to somewhere else, but now—"

"Chin up!" Sandy lifted her water glass at the others. "It is the holiday season. Who knows what might be in store?"

"I know one thing," Olivia rejoined merrily. "The reopening of the Christmas Cookie Shop!"

Perspiration swept Hannah's hairline. She tried to speak, but Jade plowed on ahead.

"That will most definitely help," she said, beaming at Hannah. "You don't know how much this means to all of us. People say that shop was once the heart of this town."

"It really was," Sandy put in, looking dreamy. "Especially when Lena was around and baking those special cookies."

Olivia eagerly leaned forward. "Do you have the recipe?"

Just then, the waitress appeared and they all realized with a laugh that none of them had even looked at the menu. Sandy asked for a few more minutes before introducing Hannah to their server. Liz Martin was in her midthirties and had short springy hair and amber-colored eyes. Faint laugh lines surrounded her mouth when she smiled.

"Welcome, Hannah!" she said in a sharp Southern twang. "Looks like we're all going to be needing your help. Especially us single ladies." She winked at the others. "I'm excluding you, Jade."

"Jade and her husband Wendell have a five-year-old son," Sandy added.

"Yeah, and he's as cute as a button," Olivia agreed.

"His name's Alexander." Jade preened proudly. "I have pictures on my phone."

Liz studied the group with a knowing air. "I'll come back in ten. In the meantime, coffee?"

Their group lunch flew by in a flash of good humor, shared stories, and laughter. Hannah particularly enjoyed hearing about the shenanigans Carter had gotten into as a boy with his best friend Kurt. Apparently the Christmas family and the Livingstons had vacationed together for many summers at the North Carolina Outer Banks. After seeing a photo of Alexander's first fishing adventure with his dad, Olivia told the others about how Carter and Kurt had gone down to the beach one morning at four a.m. because they'd heard the big fish got up early. They'd set up their poles, then got tired waiting. Eventually, they both nodded off to sleep, only to wake up hours later with terrible sunburns. Not wanting to admit they'd suffered for naught, they'd biked up to the fish market and purchased a big marlin to show for their efforts. They'd proudly presented it to their fathers, only to learn that marlin were deep-water fish, so it was extremely suspicious they'd caught one from the shore. Later, when the fish shop owner asked Buddy how his family had enjoyed the marlin, the whole story unraveled. *A big fish story, indeed.*

"What about you, Hannah?" Olivia asked her. "Do you have brothers and sisters?"

"Just one," Hannah answered. "A big brother, Ben."

"Where does Ben live?" Jade inquired politely.

"Back in Stafford, Virginia, where I come from." Hannah hesitated a moment, weighing how much to share. "We were raised by our grandparents. My mom died when I was pretty young, and our dad was never really around."

Sandy gently laid her hand on Hannah's. "I'm sorry, Hannah. I had no idea."

"Sounds rough," Olivia said sympathetically.

"Families come in all shapes and sizes," Jade observed. "Sounds like you and Ben were lucky to have your grandparents."

"Absolutely," Hannah said. "Grandpa Charles and Grandma Mabel were the best."

"So, they're both deceased now?" Olivia asked softly.

"My Grandpa Charles died when I was in high school. Grandma Mabel just a few weeks ago."

The other women shared their sincere condolences, before Hannah continued. "Grandma Mabel's the one who technically gave me the shop. Grandpa Charles had apparently wanted me to have it, but I was too young for the responsibility when he passed. So he asked my grandma to hold it in trust."

"Did you ever know anything about it?" Olivia wondered.

Hannah shook her head. "From the letter my grandma left, it seems my grandparents wanted me to follow my own ambitions first. Though Grandpa Charles clearly hoped I'd eventually take the business on."

"Charles was Lena's son, wasn't he?" Sandy asked.

"That's right," Hannah said. "He had one sibling, Henry. Both of them left Christmas Town after high school. My Great-uncle Hank became a newspaper reporter and my Grandpa Charles went into banking."

"Neither of them ever came back?" Jade asked.

"Henry died when I was little," Hannah answered. "I think he may have returned to Christmas Town once or twice as an adult, according to what my grandparents told me. My Grandpa Charles visited more regularly. To check on his investment."

Sandy squinted in concentration. "I think I remember meeting him when my family was staying with the Christmases one time. This was way before I moved here…back when I was a kid." She turned to Hannah. "Was your granddad tall and slender, and did he smoke a pipe?"

Hannah's heart pinged at the memory. She missed her grandfather so. Her Grandma Mabel, too… "That was Grandpa Charles, all right."

Olivia smiled sweetly and said, "He would have been so proud of you, Hannah. Just look at you! Coming back to finish what his mother, Lena, started."

Sandy kindly patted Hannah's arm. "It's all right," she whispered softly. "I'll explain to them later."

"Explain what?" Jade asked cagily.

Hannah heaved a breath, unable to maintain the pretense any longer. "I'm sorry, guys. I wish I could tell you otherwise, but the truth is…"

She stopped cold at Jade's shocked expression. Olivia beside her appeared as if she wanted to cry. "You're not staying?"

The disappointment in the others' eyes made Hannah feel like a heel. She'd barely made these friendships and already she was letting Jade and Olivia down. "To be honest," she said with a touch of shame, "I can't afford it."

Sandy viewed her with understanding. "It's okay, you don't have to go into the details."

"There aren't too many of them to add. Starting a business, even restarting one, takes capital." She eyed them all glumly. "The truth is, I'm up to my ears in old college debt and don't have a great paying job. I need to sell the shop to pay off my creditors and try to do better."

"Do you have specific plans?" Jade asked kindly.

Hannah nodded uncertainly, willing her shaky confidence to return. "I've started applying to graduate programs in social work. Investing in a master's degree is the key to a better future for me."

"Then you definitely need to do it," Olivia said.

"She's right," Jade affirmed. "Each of us owes it to ourselves to go for our dreams."

"That's true," Sandy said, her blue eyes brimming. "All of us here have followed our hearts. Haven't we, ladies?"

Jade and Olivia agreed.

"So then, that's exactly what you need to do," Sandy told Hannah decidedly, and the others quickly agreed.

"That doesn't mean you can't have lunch," Olivia said coyly.

"Now that you know the time and place," Jade added, "we'll expect you to be here."

Olivia grinned sweetly. "Every Monday at one."

"For as long as you're in town," Sandy finished for them.

For as long as I'm in town... All at once, Hannah's heart sank. If only she knew exactly how long that was going to be. For something deep inside her said…the longer she stayed in Christmas Town, the harder it was going to be to leave.

Chapter Ten

Hannah decided to spend the following day working on graduate school applications at Sisters' Row. There wasn't much left to do at the shop anyway. Until Frank's numbers came in, she wouldn't know just how big of a problem she was facing. Though Hannah had the sinking feeling it would be substantial. How on earth could she pay to fix electrical problems when she barely had enough in her checking account to cover her short stay here and financial aid application fees? She knew she could always ask Ben for a loan, but she was hesitant to request his assistance. Ben had helped her enough already, and at nearly twenty-eight, Hannah needed to stand on her own two feet.

Perhaps once she got Frank's estimate, she could deduct the cost of any repairs from the price she put on the establishment. Hannah planned to ask Buddy Christmas about that when she met with him tomorrow. Apart from being retired from All Things Christmas, Buddy also ran the sole realty company in town. He operated Christmas Town Realty from an old outbuilding behind his historic house. It once served as the icehouse on the property, but had since been converted to Buddy's office, as well as his sometime workshop. Sandy told Hannah that Buddy was good with his hands and liked to build things. Mostly, things made of wood. She'd cautioned Hannah against sitting in the real estate office, lest Hannah come away with splinters. She'd supposedly said it in jest, but Hannah had gotten the impression Sandy wasn't entirely kidding.

Someone knocked loudly at the door and Hannah stood from where she'd been working at the table. "Expecting anybody?" she asked the two kittens, as they dozed unconcernedly on the sofa. She strode to the foyer, noting by the clock that it was nearly six. She'd need to break for dinner soon, and maybe afterward she'd call Ben. So much seemed to be happening so fast, it was going to be hard for him to keep up!

"Hello! Happy Monday!" Louise Christmas stood on the stoop clutching a huge cardboard box. It far outmatched her in width and was tall enough to mask her chin. "Almost Tuesday, really. The day is wearing on."

"Lou! Hi…" Hannah stumbled backward as Lou tottered toward her, the box slipping in her gloved hands.

"Oh… Oops!" Lou shifted the box, hoisting it skyward and bumping herself on the nose. "Ow! That hurt."

Hannah gripped the big box at its sides and kicked the door shut. "Here, let me help with that." She had no idea what Lou had in the box but it was as heavy as a ton of bricks. Hannah struggled across the room, then slid the large box onto the sofa, shooing Jingles and Belle aside. Both jumped down quickly, shook out their fur, and made their way into the kitchen, shooting curious glances at Lou as they went. Just seeing them made Lou sneeze. She yanked a tissue from her coat pocket and honked her nose into it. "Ook-ooks!" she explained before Hannah could ask.

"Ook-ooks?" Hannah asked, confounded.

"Oh, sorry." Lou sniffled and tucked away her tissue. "Cookbooks! Family ones." She grinned tightly as if it should have been obvious. *"Yours."*

"What?"

Lou dusted off her gloves, then tugged them from her hands, one finger at a time. "Buddy's been keeping this box in his workshop. All this time! Can you believe it? In any case, your Grandpa Charles gave it to him for safekeeping," she finished, as if that explained everything.

Hannah stared at her waiting for more, but apparently nothing was forthcoming. Lou glanced around at the mess with disapproval. Paperwork was spread across the table beside Hannah's open laptop and empty coffee mugs were littered about. Hannah hadn't thought to pick up as she hadn't been expecting anybody.

"A tad untidy," Lou said with a shrug. "But yes, I'll stay." To Hannah's amazement, she undid and removed her coat, hanging it on the rack. "You *were* going to ask me?" she said, turning to Hannah.

"Of course!" Hannah thought fast. "Would you prefer coffee or wine?"

Lou checked her watch against the mantel clock. "A glass of wine sounds like heaven. That is…" She paused for a moment. "Unless you have eggnog?"

Hannah shook her head *no*.

"Then wine will do." Lou plunked down in the armchair and yanked off her boots, first one, and then the other. "Do you know how hard it is to get good-fitting boots these days?" she asked Hannah as she left for the kitchen.

"Pretty difficult, I'd guess?"

"You've got that part right," Lou called after her. "Things certainly aren't made like they were in the old days."

Hannah poked her head around the doorframe to spy Louise massaging her insteps.

"Built to last," Lou said, struggling back into her boots.

"That's why I like to buy things secondhand," Hannah answered, while filling their wineglasses. She returned to the living area and handed one to Lou.

"Smart girl, and thank you." Lou took a grateful sip of wine. "Very nice. What is it?"

Hannah sat on the edge of the sofa beside the box. "Why, it's the one you and Sandy—"

"Of course! Should have known it." Lou smiled pleasantly. "We both have excellent taste." Her eyes casually traveled the room, landing on Sandy's painting. "Where is she, by the way? Have you seen her?"

"Yes, just this afternoon. Why?"

"Because," Lou said with a hint of disbelief, "she hasn't been returning my calls."

"I'm sure she's just been bus—"

"About that handsome fellow over in Johnson City."

Hannah held her tongue, deciding not to say any more. Perhaps this was why Sandy had gone incommunicado. Lou was in matchmaking mode.

"He's a lawyer, did I tell you? Sandy loves professional men."

"Hmm," Hannah returned noncommittally, secretly thinking of Ben.

Lou took another sip of wine and studied Hannah worriedly. "How about you, dear? Making inroads with the sheriff?"

The swallow of wine Hannah had just taken into her mouth zinged up into her nose. She quickly covered her face with one hand, choking loudly.

"Oh my!" Lou leapt to her feet and swatted Hannah back's with dismay. Actually it was less like a swatting and more like a pounding. "I've said something to upset you!"

Hannah bounced forward as Lou beat down on her back again and again with bony fingers. "Excuse me," she said, deftly scooting away. "I'm going to grab a napkin."

"Here!" Lou halted Hannah's retreat by yanking a tissue from the box on the coffee table and shoving it in her direction.

Hannah took it and rapidly dabbed her face, as well as the front of her sweater. *Red wine. Great. Of course that will stain.* "Lou," she wheezed, still a little breathless from Lou's relentless assault. "You've got it all wrong—"

"I have, have I? But if you're not sweet on Carter... Then *that* means..." Her face lit up. "It's my Kurt, isn't it?" she asked, in delighted tones.

"Kurt? *What?*"

Lou clapped her hands together, her highlighted hair bouncing. "I can't wait to tell Buddy! He'll be so pleased!" She pumped her fists at the ceiling and shouted, "Kurt's finally over Savannah!"

Savannah?

Lou practically skipped toward the door and slipped on her coat, while Hannah watched, dumbfounded.

"Lou, please! Wait!" Hannah cried with dismay. "Kurt and I…we're not—"

"Shh…. Shh…." There was a gleam in Lou's eye. "Never fear, dear. I'll keep it on the low down."

"Down low?"

"Absolutely," Lou continued gleefully. "Your secret's safe with me. Yours and Kurt's, that is." She slipped her gloves back on, testily shaking her head. "I'm going to give that young man a piece of my mind. Keeping things from his mother." Lou regarded her half-empty glass of wine. "Ah! Can't waste it!" She crossed to it quickly and downed the rest of the glass, setting it on the coffee table. Hannah watched her, jaw unhinged. "Tasty vintage. Thank you!"

Hannah had a very bad feeling about where Lou was going with this. Like straight back to Buddy—then right over to Kurt's! By the morning it would make the town paper. "Lou, I really wish you'd listen to me…" She spoke in desperation, knowing all the while that her pleas fell on deaf ears.

Lou opened the front door, then paused thoughtfully. "How's Carter taking it? Not too hard, I hope?"

Hannah stared at her helplessly.

"He did see you first."

Lou peered out the door at some fast-moving dark clouds. "Here comes more snow. Best move along!" Before she darted out the door, she added, "Enjoy those cookbooks, Hannah. Happy reading!"

Then she slammed her way outside, leaving Hannah in a face-palm.

Hannah decided the best thing to do was get to Kurt before Lou did. She located the card he'd left her in the kitchen and dialed the number. Her call was picked up immediately by the answering service. The voice that came back at her was bubbly and young.

"Christmas Town Clinic. This is Joy speaking. May I help you?"

"Oh, hello! Yes, Joy. You're Kurt's niece, right?"

"Yep. And you must be Hannah Winchester."

Hannah wondered if the teen was clairvoyant. "But how did you—?"

"Didn't come up on my caller ID. And *everybody* comes up on my caller ID. I mean, everyone in Christmas Town." She continued without pausing. "New number, new voice, new arrival… Tadaahhh! I'm magic, see?"

"Wow, yes. Very good. Excellent, and correct."

"You must have heard I pick up the phones."

"Right on that, too."

"And that I've got a sister." Before Hannah could respond, Joy barreled ahead. "Noelle's older, but you'd never know it. I'm the mature one, though slightly more chatty. My Uncle Kurt will attest to that."

"Yes, well… That's why I'm calling actually."

"To talk to the doctor, I know. That's the only reason people call this number."

Hannah was starting to question whether they ever got through.

"Is he in?" she asked with tentative hope.

"Nope. That's why you got me. When he can't pick up his doc phone, his calls get forwarded."

"Okay. Well then, maybe you can take a message?"

"You're not feeling sick, are you? Because if it's an emergency I'm supposed to tell you to call nine-one-one."

"No, no. It's nothing like that."

"I heard about the bump! How's it healing?"

Hannah's free hand instinctively shot to her forehead. The lump beneath her bangs had subsided greatly, and was only mildly tender to the touch. "Doing a lot better, thanks," she answered, wondering why she was reporting on her medical condition to a high-schooler. "Listen, Joy—"

"I heard the sheriff came to check it out and everything!"

"Sheriff?"

"Sheriff Carter, but it's technically Sheriff Livingston. We call him Sheriff Carter on account of him being practically family and all. We being Noelle and me."

"I see."

"Word is he thought you were in a car wreck or something. Somehow got a signal crossed. I'm sure he was relieved to find it wasn't worse. Especially given what the other word is... You must be *very* smart and *very* pretty!"

"What?"

"Okay, I'm not supposed to tell you this." Joy lowered her voice in a conspiratorial fashion. "But my uncle—"

"Kurt?"

"No, Ray. He's the third brother: Ray, Walt, and Kurt! Walt is my dad."

Hannah drew a calming breath. "Joy, I don't really believe you should be—"

"Have you met my dad?"

Hannah blinked hard. "Walt? Why, no."

"Ray neither, I'd suspect. He and my Aunt Meredith run the North Pole Nursery. He's the one Sheriff Carter was talking to the other day, when Uncle Ray got wind of how Sheriff Carter feels about—"

Hannah tried to cut her off. "I'm sure they've got tons to dis—"

"You!"

"Me?" Hannah asked, confounded. But still, she had to admit, Joy had piqued her interest...

"I overheard the two of them in the kitchen," Joy confided quietly. "Uncle Ray and my dad. They thought I was upstairs, but... Anyway!" She sniggered softly. "Uncle Ray told Dad the damage was so bad he nearly had to call the fire department!"

"Damage?"

"From Sheriff Carter beating it up and down Santa Claus Lane so many times, right in front of your shop, trying to get up his nerve to—"

"Joy!" a stern male voice interrupted.

"Er...um. Uh-oh," she whispered into the phone before answering meekly, "Hi, Dad!"

It sounded like Joy had covered the mouthpiece with her hand, but Hannah could still hear Walt demanding to know who she was talking to.

"Answering service business!" she said a little more emphatically than necessary.

She quickly returned her attention to Hannah. "Sorry," she hissed into the receiver. "Gotta go." Then she announced much more loudly, clearly for her father's benefit, "I'll be sure to tell Dr. Christmas you called. Have a good day!"

The phone clicked off and Hannah sat there stunned, staring at her silent cell phone.

Chapter Eleven

Buddy Christmas set the brass-trimmed receiver down in the high cradle of his red vintage rotary telephone. "Sorry about that." He shared a mirthful grin. "North Pole business." Buddy was short and stout with big round cheeks, a snowy beard and mustache, and short silvery hair. He wore corduroy slacks and a heavy fisherman's sweater that added to his girth. Wire-rimmed spectacles perched on his nose. When he spoke, his blue eyes sparkled. "North Pole Nursery, that is," he said, and Hannah laughed at his joke. "Lou and I are ordering our trees."

"Trees?" Hannah asked curiously. "As in, more than one?"

"One for the parlor and one for the living room." Buddy jutted his chin toward the main house. "The Christmas family also donates a large one to Courthouse Square up by the roundabout." He stuck his hand across the desk to shake Hannah's. Though they'd spoken by phone several times, they were just now meeting in person. "Buddy Christmas. Nice to see you. Lou's told me all about you, Hannah."

Hannah's cheeks steamed. "I'm sure that she has."

"All good things," Buddy said with a jolly chuckle. "All good things!"

He paused with the pipe midway to his lips. Hannah noticed he hadn't filled it. She didn't detect a whiff of pipe smoke lingering in the air either. She remembered the scent from being around Grandpa Charles. Even though he'd never smoked indoors, the odor sometimes clung to his clothing, though Hannah had never found it offensive. Merely homey and warm like her grandpa.

"You can smoke if you'd like," she told Buddy. "It won't bother me."

Buddy withdrew the pipe from his mouth and studied it thoughtfully. "Truth is, I haven't lit up in years. Lou says smoking's bad for my health, so she pitched most of my pipes. Except for this one," he said with a *Ho-ho-ho,* setting it down on an ashtray.

He motioned for her to sit and Hannah glanced uncertainly around the room, recalling Sandy's admonishment. The space was more workshop than realty office, with woodworking equipment crowding the cramped space and a pair of sawhorses situated in the corner. Sawdust littered the floor, as did the occasional nail, bolt, or screw.

It looked like Buddy had been building toys. A small sleigh leaned up against a bookshelf, its paint apparently still drying, and a child's rocking horse teetered nearby. A little wooden train set resembling the one in the Elf Shelf's front window occupied the surface of a workbench.

Buddy sat behind a battered maple desk with an inlaid parquet top. It faced the only other piece of furniture in the room, a plaid armchair, partially covered by a cloth drape.

"Um, thanks! I think I'll stand."

"Suit yourself."

Buddy flipped open the laptop in front of him and started clicking its mousepad. The small portable printer beside it began to whir, spitting out pages.

"It's just that I've done a lot of sitting lately," Hannah tried to explain. "On the drive from Virginia, then at home. I mean, my rental home at Sisters' Row."

Buddy's blue eyes met hers. "What have you been up to there?"

Hannah shifted on her feet. "Grad school applications."

Buddy grumbled and refocused on his screen. "Going to be attending long-distance?"

"No, in person, actually."

"Because you're selling the shop." He said it as a matter of course and without judgment. Still, he appeared awfully distracted by something. Beyond him, snow lightly drifted outside the windows. Another light dusting had started a little over an hour ago.

"Just as we've been discussing, yes." Each time she'd spoken with Buddy, she'd made her intentions clear. Yesterday, she'd mentioned the electrical issues. Hannah was still awaiting Frank's formal estimate to see how they might use it to adjust their asking price.

"I know you say that is your plan." A smile crossed his face. "But plans change."

"Not this time, I'm afraid," Hannah said a little sadly.

Buddy lifted the pages from the printer tray. After briefly sorting through them, he handed the stack to Hannah.

"What's this?"

"A look at the competition. While there are no similar shops listed in Christmas Town, there are other properties for sale in zip codes nearby." Buddy nodded astutely. "Pays to know what you're going up against."

Hannah fanned out the papers in her hand, stunned by the immaculate storefront façades, the top-of-the-line industrial kitchens, and the high price tags. "Wow, these really are incredible. If only the Christmas Cookie Shop—"

"Perhaps someday it can be."

"With the right owner, I'm sure—"

"How do you know the right owner isn't already here?" Buddy asked, stopping her.

"Mr. Christmas, I know you'd like—"

"Please, call me Buddy."

"Buddy."

"And, it's not just me; it's Louise, too. She has her heart set on your staying, you know."

"You mean, you haven't told her I'm selling?"

"Most days, my dear wife hears what she wants to hear."

Hannah certainly could concur with that.

"But she's not alone in her thinking. From what I gather, there are other folks in Christmas Town longing for you to stick around. Take Sandy, for one…" he said, steepling his plump hands. "And she says you've already befriended Jade and Olivia, too." He leaned toward her, raising his brow. "Then, there's the little matter of a certain eligible bachelor."

"Mr. Christmas! Sorry. Buddy. Kurt's a wonderful doctor and a very charming man."

Buddy pushed back in his chair in surprise. "What's Kurt got to do with anything?"

"Well, I just thought… What I mean is... Didn't Lou say something to you?"

"About Kurt?" Buddy's laughter rumbled. "Of course she did. And of course she was wrong."

"Well, good! Then you know…" Hannah stopped abruptly, wondering how he'd figured it out. Her cheeks tinged hot when she asked, "Have you spoken to Kurt? Or, um…Walt maybe?"

"Keep going." Buddy cocked his chin to the side. "One more."

Hannah sucked in a breath. "Ray."

"Just got off the phone with him in fact."

Hannah gaped at the receiver. "It seems like there aren't many secrets around here."

Buddy thoughtfully thumped his chin with stubby fingers. "Oh, there are still a few. But the main thing is… Hannah. When people heard you were coming to Christmas Town, it was almost like learning your great-grandma was coming home. Have you had a chance to look at any of those cookbooks?"

"Not just yet," she admitted honestly. She'd meant to thumb through them, but had been too exhausted from her day of paperwork and long-winded conversation with Ben to do anything afterward but fall asleep.

"Perhaps you should. They must have been very important. Your late Grandpa Charles said that they were when he gave me the box."

This was something that had been bothering her all along. "But why did he give the books to you? Why didn't my Grandpa Charles hang on to them himself?"

"I suppose he was worried about them falling into the wrong hands."

"Surely, he didn't have concerns about my Grandma Mabel?"

"Not Mabel. Somebody else."

"Then who?" Hannah recalled the story about Charles's feud with his brother Henry, and wondered if it was Henry that Charles had been worried about. They'd apparently had some sort of falling out over an article Henry had intended to print about the Christmas Cookie Shop, before Charles had stopped him.

"I honestly couldn't say." Buddy shrugged. "But I did tell Charles I'd honor his wishes. They were Lena's wishes, after all."

"And those wishes were?"

"That her books would ultimately go to you."

"But I wasn't even alive when she passed."

"No, but your father Tanner was, and she wanted them to stay in the family. Only not, apparently, with him."

Hannah swallowed past the tender lump in her throat. When her mom's illness had intensified, her dad had walked out and never returned. Neither Hannah nor Ben even knew whether he was still alive.

"Your father wasn't a bad man," Buddy told her. "Only misguided. He had a certain difficulty in putting others first."

"I know."

"He came to see me one time, and I've always regretted that I wasn't here."

"What was it about?"

"He didn't tell Lou, but she said he had a suitcase. It had to have been around the time he left home."

Hannah's heart sank at the painful memory, and Buddy viewed her with sympathy.

"I know things were hard on all of you," he said. "Charles was particularly disappointed in his son. And while Lena didn't live to see that, she'd already had her reservations about Tanner. She worried that he took after his Uncle Hank rather than his own father, Charles.

"In any case, Lena felt she couldn't trust Tanner with the family business—or its secrets. After Charles died, the Christmas Cookie Shop would have to go to somebody else. While she had doubts about Tanner, Lena got to know and love your mother, April, very much. They became close and she hoped that someday April and Tanner would have a child, maybe even a baby girl, just as Lena had yearned to have a daughter of her own. She helped name you, you know."

Heat prickled Hannah's eyes. "No, I hadn't heard that."

"Hannah was the name Lena intended to give her own daughter. But she never had a girl, only sons."

"Henry and Charles," Hannah said softly.

"In turn, Charles only had one child, Tanner, and Henry had none."

"Then Charles's son Tanner had Ben, and…me."

Buddy nodded in agreement. "A little girl christened Hannah, meaning 'grace.' Because you see, my dear, even though your great-grandmother never knew you, somehow all those years ago she had the prescience to know that when you came along, you'd have a good heart. The right sort of heart, Hannah," Buddy said pointedly. "A heart that could open itself up to the people of Christmas Town, just as everyone here wants to embrace you."

Hannah tossed and turned in bed, unable to put her conversation with Buddy out of her mind. It was bad enough feeling guilty over not upholding her family obligation. Now she had to overcome substantial obstacles to selling, too. At Buddy's suggestion, she'd spent the afternoon researching bakeries for sale in the surrounding areas, and the competition was fierce. Hannah hadn't realized that the taxes on the shop were in arrears due to her Grandma Mabel's failure to make the payments. Mabel must not have understood she needed to handle this separately from her personal taxes, and somehow during the final phase of his illness, Grandpa Charles had failed to make this clear. The fact that this real estate holding had been in another state had only complicated matters.

Though the shop itself was paid off, it was essentially underwater when it came to its assessed value versus what was owed on it tax-wise, coupled with the hefty electrical bill from Frank. His estimate had arrived by e-mail just before dinner, and Hannah wished she hadn't looked at it then. The numbers had completely taken away her appetite. In viewing comparable properties, Hannah understood she'd have to make some serious improvements to the shop, including to its kitchen, to make it viable in the current real estate market.

Even though Hannah had heard *it takes money to make money,* the axiom didn't help one bit when Hannah had absolutely zero to give. Here she thought she'd inherited a godsend, when her late grandfather's bequest was becoming more of an albatross. And the longer she held on to it, the more expensive it would become. The tax burdens would only build upon themselves, while the shop fell into deeper and deeper disrepair.

Hannah sighed and punched her pillow, willing herself not to burst into a fit of tears. How on earth could she pay for graduate school, when it was hard enough to see how she could extract herself from this mess? She'd hoped to quickly sell the shop and turn a profit large enough to settle her former debt and also cover future educational expenses. It was a good thing she was applying for financial aid, because—obviously—Hannah was going to need it. Hannah heard a purring sound, then felt a pocket of warmth curl up beside her. She reached out to stroke Belle's fur, only to find Jingles snuggling up against her, too.

"Well, I suppose it's good to have friends in dark times," she told the kittens as shadows filled the room. Jingles nuzzled her hand, sending a cold shock against it. Hannah sat up with a start and switched on the light. *Not that!* Hannah's new Christmas barrette was clenched in the cat's tiny teeth. After Hannah had admired Jade's pretty hair ornament at lunch, Olivia had invited her to stop by All Things Christmas to pick out one of her own. It was apparently very popular—with the magpie in the house. "Thanks, Jingles," Hannah said, snatching the whimsical snowman barrette away from him and dropping it into the drawer of the bedside table.

Then she switched off the light, hoping for pleasant dreams. If Hannah was lucky, she'd forget about her dreary worries and dream about a sexy, green-eyed sheriff with a killer smile instead. Could the idle town gossip be true? Was it possible that the very handsome lawman was interested in her? Hannah had definitely gotten that impression a time or two, but then she'd feared she'd been letting her imagination get the best of her. There'd be no imagining things on Friday. She'd be seeing Carter in person. The two of them had a date. Though Hannah had tried to tell herself she wasn't ready to begin dating again, those faithful butterflies called her out in the lie. She was ready all right. Way more ready than she should be, given everything else she had going on, including her long-term plans to live elsewhere.

For now, she would focus on tomorrow. She wanted to complete her graduate school applications and work up some sales ideas to discuss with Buddy during their scheduled meeting on Friday morning. Hannah also wanted to set aside some time to leaf through Lena's cookbooks. She planned to keep them for their historic and sentimental value, and perhaps to pass on to her children one day. It was good she had a full agenda. That would keep her from becoming too nervous about her date on Friday night. She hadn't been able to reach Kurt, as they'd been playing phone tag. Hopefully, he'd already spoken to Buddy by now, and his dad had been able to disabuse him of any rumors— without starting any new ones of his own.

Chapter Twelve

The following afternoon, Hannah sat cross-legged on the floor in her living area. Jingles was under the dining room table chasing a glittery ball while Belle rested in her lap. Hannah reached around the purring fur ball to open the flap of the box she'd set beside her. Her hand had just rested on a cookbook, when her cell buzzed on the coffee table. Hannah checked it and found a text from Sandy.

Want to catch up? I can take a break around four.

The idea of an outing sounded great. Apart from seeing Buddy, she'd pretty much been holed up at Sisters' Row for the past few days. Then again, since the temperatures outdoors hovered below freezing, she'd enjoyed staying warm and dry. Hannah was about to type back when her phone rang. Hannah spoke in chipper tones, thinking it was Sandy.

"Let's do coffee at the Jolly Bean Java!"

"Coffee?" a masculine voice boomed back.

Hannah double-checked the phone, spying a number she didn't recognize on its display.

"Joy said that you'd called." He hesitated a beat. "I just wasn't prepared for the invitation."

"Oh! Um…Kurt?"

"Ye-es?"

"Oh gosh, wow. I'm sorry. I thought you were Sandy!"

"Sandy?" Her meaning apparently dawned. "Ah, I see. You're telling me not to get my hopes up?" Then he added with a devilish edge. "Even though my mom is all over us."

"Us?"

"As a couple," he teased.

Hannah gasped. "Lou got to you."

"Not really," Kurt said mildly. "I've been around long enough to handle my mom." He chuckled graciously. "As in, all of my life."

"Oh, well, good! That means you don't—?"

"Hannah," he said pleasantly. "It's not that I wouldn't be flattered, but I'm not really the type to cut in."

"I'm not sure what you mean."

"Carter and I have been friends for a long time. He's almost like a brother to me." He paused to let the weight of this sink in, before adding lightly, "Just do me one favor?"

Hannah's pulse pounded.

He said it half-jokingly, but Hannah suspected there was a lot of seriousness behind it. "Go easy on him."

Carter sailed his hat across his office, landing it on the hat rack by the door.

"Pretty good," Victoria told him smoothly. Through the window beside her, Carter could see it was still snowing outside. Then again, in Christmas Town in December, that was pretty much the rule.

"I never miss." Carter slid back his desk chair and took a seat while Victoria observed him, arms crossed in front of her. He pushed his weekly reports aside. "Waiting for something?"

"Details," she said, stone-faced. Her coal-black hair was in a tight chignon and her lightly starched uniform fit her slight figure to a tee. Victoria was a good-looking woman, and as tough as nails. She sure kept Frank in line.

"I already said thank you."

"For swapping shifts so you could have tomorrow evening off, sure." Victoria pursed her lips. "You never said why."

"Didn't think it was necessary." Carter's office was spare, yet functional. Two metal armchairs with plastic cushions sat across from his desk, and an aluminum Christmas tree stood beside a tall filing cabinet by the window. The fake tree had been Tilly's idea. Tilly was their office secretary, but she never came in on Tuesdays or Thursdays, as those were her duplicate bridge days. Since the Christmas Town Sheriff's Department didn't get much in the way of business anyhow, having Tilly only work part-time suited Carter fine.

"Need and courtesy are two different concepts, wouldn't you say?"

Carter didn't appreciate Victoria's grilling. She'd already told him the swap was no problem. Her little boy Bobby had a sleepover planned with his best bud Alexander. And Frank was certainly capable of fending for himself. Especially given his video streaming connections. Frank had secretly confessed to Carter that when Victoria was away, he sometimes watched romantic comedy films. She preferred procedural police shows with more grit and action. Likely because she didn't get much of that on the job.

"I thought I *was* being courteous," Carter countered. "I even removed my hat when I asked."

"You always remove your hat in here," Victoria returned dryly.

"Right." Carter pretended to focus on his inbox. Tilly insisted on printing his e-mails. She couldn't get her head around the concept that Carter was perfectly capable of reading and responding to them himself. So he went along with the game of reading the hard copies and hand-scribbling his replies, which Tilly later typed up as formal responses. Carter cleared his throat for Victoria's benefit. "Looks like duty calls," he said, indicating his cluttered desk with a broad sweep of his hand.

"Very pressing, I see." Victoria held her ground and slowly arched one perfectly manicured eyebrow. "Frank tells me he was over at the Christmas Cookie Shop on Monday."

"So?"

"And so were you… So was *Miss* Hannah Winchester," she said, accentuating the *Miss* part on purpose.

"Victoria." Carter huffed a breath. "If you've got something to say, just spill it."

"I want you to level with me." She set her hands on her hips, resting them above her holster. "Sheriff Carter Livingston," she asked, jutting her chin out in a challenge. "Have you got a date?"

She would ask, wouldn't she? Victoria couldn't still be getting over the fact that Carter wouldn't take out her cousin when she'd come to town. He'd legitimately had other plans, but in truth he also wasn't interested. A woman hadn't turned Carter's head in so long he'd nearly forgotten what that was like...until a striking brunette turned up at the roundabout.

Carter drummed his desk with his fingers, biding his time. "No, I'm just going to dinner," he finally said, deciding it was none of her business. And none of Walt's business... Or Ray's... Or Kurt's. He couldn't believe Kurt had called to see if he'd asked Hannah out yet. Even Buddy Christmas was in on this somehow. Carter had seen Buddy at the hardware store and Buddy made some offhand comment about Lou's mix-up. *Of course* Kurt wasn't seeing Hannah. Buddy had patted Carter's back with a wink, saying he understood the sheriff was the right man for the job.

Victoria's lips twisted in a grin. "Alone?" There were a lot of nosy people around here, and—despite her stoic demeanor—Victoria was one of the nosiest.

The phone on Tilly's desk rang loudly, giving off its shrill repetitive cry. "Don't you think you'd better get that?" he asked, staring past her and into the front room. It was Victoria's job to man the phones when Tilly wasn't here.

Victoria smirked. "Saved by the bell."

She had a desk in the anteroom set back from Tilly's, which faced the door leading to the courthouse hallway. There were only a few other offices in the building: one for county records and permits and another for motor vehicle affairs. The actual courtroom with its high domed ceiling was upstairs. The judge's chambers were in a separate room behind the bench, but they were rarely used.

The Honorable Tom Holiday spent more time on vacation with his wife Bethany than he did in court. Of course, the judge was always available when he was needed. Typically to issue drivers' licenses to teens or officiate impromptu weddings. It wasn't a bad life being a judge in Christmas Town, Carter supposed. Being sheriff wasn't too shabby either, and it was seeming less and less dismal all the time.

Carter was looking forward to his date with Hannah tomorrow more than he wanted to let on. He certainly wasn't going to share information about it with his deputy. Before she stalked away, she added, "Don't think I won't hear about it anyway. Word gets around, you know."

Boy, do I ever, Carter thought, shaking his head. It was one of things he'd come to love about Christmas Town. You never had to wonder where you stood. Because, if you ever had any doubt, one of the locals would make certain to tell you.

Hannah flipped through another page of *Marion Brown's Southern Cook Book,* published in 1951 by the University of North Carolina Press, and set it aside. Lena definitely had eclectic culinary tastes. And her tastes spanned nearly a century. There were at least three separate volumes on New Orleans Cajun cooking, a cookbook on low-country South Carolina cuisine, and even a tome called *Puerto Rican Cookery* by Carmen Aboy Valldejuli, 1975. There were two editions of Irma S. Rombauer's *The Joy of Cooking.* The first was a fifth edition from 1964, which had a classic cover she recognized from her Grandma Mabel's kitchen. There was also an earlier edition printed in 1946. Wow, that had to be a collector's item. But clearly nothing was as valuable as the surprises Hannah discovered at the bottom of the box. Below the heftier, more contemporary books published post–World War II, Hannah found an old hatbox containing a hidden treasure trove.

Jingles was interested in the secretive contents, too. He stood positioned on his hindquarters, his front paws hooked over the rim of the larger box, and Belle scampered over to join him, curiously sniffing the air. Hannah pushed the inquisitive kittens aside and lifted the lid off the hatbox, peering into it. Several parcels nestled together, each protected individually with loving care. Lena had been born in 1900, but one of her hobbies appeared to have been collecting classic cookbooks, ones considered vintage even in her day. Hannah unwrapped a copy of Fannie Merritt Farmer's *Boston Cooking-School Cook Book,* carefully concealed in parchment paper. This had to be the predecessor to the modern-day *Fannie Farmer Cookbook*. Hannah carefully cracked it open to check its copyright page, and caught her breath: 1896! Perhaps Lena had inherited it from her mother or grandmother before her.

Beneath that, Hannah found an even bigger prize concealed in a linen bag: a beautiful hardbound edition of *The Virginia Housewife* by Mary Randolph. It wasn't much bigger than a modern-day mass-market paperback and felt a bit like Grandpa Charles's family Bible to the touch. Hannah ran her hand across its grainy surface, then brought the well-worn cover to her nose, inhaling the earthy scent of antique leather. There were slightly raised, ornamental gold bands on the spine along with the gilt stamped title and author name. If the title had once appeared on the front of the book, it was no longer visible, perhaps due to the love and attention the piece had received throughout the years. Hannah very gingerly opened it and peeked inside. Copyright 1828! Hannah couldn't believe something so precious and historic had been in her family all this time.

Was this why Lena had worried over giving the books to her dad or Great-uncle Hank? Neither one had an interest in family things, and both were reputed to have perpetual money woes. Perhaps Lena feared they might have sold her special keepsakes. Given her current financial state, Hannah understood how that concept could prove tempting. She couldn't even begin to imagine what some of these older volumes might bring at auction. Even the first printings of some of the twentieth-century books had to be worth something.

The corner of a yellowed page at the rear of the book caught her eye and Hannah carefully turned to the back section, finding an old newspaper clipping tucked inside its pages. *Well, what do you know!* Hannah gingerly unfolded the September 21, 1897, newspaper clipping from the New York *Sun*. It was an editorial entitled "Is There a Santa Claus?" in which insightful editor Francis Pharcellus Church told the inquiring child, Virginia O'Hanlon, "Yes, Virginia, there is a Santa Claus."

Hannah's heart beat faster and her hands shook, the brittle newsprint trembling in her fingers, as she read the editor's fine and eloquent exposition on faith, the true meaning of the season, and, indeed, on Old Saint Nick himself.

This is really something, really and truly something.

Hannah felt moisture on her cheeks and realized she'd been crying. It was only then that she grasped how greatly she'd lost her way. It wasn't just her brother Ben who eschewed the holiday. Way down deep in her heart, Hannah had long ago given up on trusting in the magic of Christmas, as well. Now she found herself wondering if it was too late to learn to believe again.

Chapter Thirteen

Sandy reached her arm across the table and squeezed Hannah's hand. They sat by the window at Jolly Bean Java having their four o'clock coffee. "That's so exciting! A whole box of them, Hannah?"

"Yes. Buddy Christmas has been hanging on to them all this time."

"What do you mean? Since Lena passed?"

Hannah nodded.

"But why didn't your grandpa—?"

"It's kind of complicated," Hannah said, not wanting to go into the whole story. She wasn't one hundred percent certain why her Grandpa Charles hadn't entrusted the box to anyone other than Buddy Christmas, and she didn't want to cast any unwarranted aspersions on any family members.

Sandy took a sip from her mug. "What do you think they're worth?"

"I'm not sure. But the older ones, maybe a lot."

"But you'd never sell them, would you?"

"Me? Probably not." Hannah studied the snowflake pattern on the frosted windowpanes beside them before continuing. "It wouldn't seem right," she said, turning back to Sandy. "Not after Lena had kept them all that time."

Even though Hannah really needed the money, she couldn't bear to part with Lena's personal possessions that way. It was bad enough she was selling the Christmas Cookie Shop. Then again, that was a business.

"So, did you find it?" Sandy prodded with eager blue eyes. "The secret recipe?"

Hannah understood she was asking about the Virginia Cookies. "I did try looking," she confessed, "but there were so many cookbooks and so many places it could have been."

"Though they had to have been invented after the date of that article you mentioned. I mean, if they actually *were* named for *that* Virginia, like everyone in Christmas Town says."

"That editorial was published in the late 1800s, Sandy. There've been tons of years—and cookbooks printed—between then and the year that Lena died."

Sandy shared a sad frown. "I suppose you're right. It's like looking for a needle in a haystack."

"Doesn't mean I won't search again."

Sandy's face lit up. "Are you thinking of making some?"

Hannah shrugged noncommittally. "Only if I find the recipe, and at this point that's a pretty big maybe. It's not like there was a big flashing neon arrow in the box pointing to its hiding place."

Sandy laughed lightly. "I see your point." She toyed with her mug before casually saying, "You know, if you *did* find that recipe, it would be pretty cool to sell those cookies at Lena's shop again."

"Sandy…"

"I'm just saying," she teased with an impish grin. "That would be mighty sweet."

"You're mighty sweet."

"Now you're changing the subject."

"Yeah, but I'm guessing you're going to like the new one."

Sandy gave a happy gasp. "What?" She covered her mouth in a giggle. "Or should I ask, who?"

Hannah's face burned hot. "All right, I'll confess. I'm going out with Carter."

Sandy practically squealed. "Seriously? Hannah, that's great!" Then she dropped her voice. "I never really thought Kurt was the guy for you."

Here we go again. "Sandy," Hannah began suspiciously, "have you been talking to Lou?"

"Yes. She finally cornered me at the gallery. There's some nephew of a college roommate she's trying to set me up with."

"Maybe you should go for it?"

"I'd rather worry about finding my own guy, when the time comes." Her eyes misted slightly. "That time's not yet."

Hannah laid a hand on her arm and tried to tread gently. "Sandy? Did some—"

In the next instant, Sandy seemed to shake it off. "No, nothing!" she said, her face brightening. "I just don't trust Lou's judgment, that's all. Although she did produce three very handsome sons."

"I've only seen one so far, but based on him, I'd agree with you."

"No wonder you were conflicted. I'm sure it was hard to pick between them."

"Them?"

"Carter and Kurt," Sandy said, as if that were obvious.

"No, no. I'm afraid you've got it wrong. There never was any Kurt."

"You mean, Lou…?" Sandy rolled her eyes in understanding. "Ah, I get it. This was all in Lou's mind. Maybe she was hoping?"

"I'm sure she meant well."

"Lou always does." She lowered her eyebrows and grinned. "So, tell me. When does this big date happen?"

"Tomorrow night," Hannah said just as casually as she could, but her pulse was pounding to beat the band and her face felt hot.

"Tomorrow?" Sandy yelped with glee. Then she eagerly leaned forward and insisted that Hannah tell her everything.

The doorbell rang and Hannah slipped while applying her lipstick, smearing a bright red streak along the side of her cheek. *Great. That's all I need. To look like the* Bride of Chucky, she thought, remembering the camp horror flick about a murderously evil doll. She quickly nabbed some tissues from the box on the vanity top and wiped off her face. Hannah still appeared to be blushing extra hard on one side, but maybe Carter wouldn't notice. The doorbell rang again and Hannah danced toward it, humming lightly to herself to calm her nerves. No, that wasn't working, only making matters worse, when she—*oops*—nearly tripped over a cat!

Jingles scampered out of the way as Belle took sanctuary between the legs of the entryway table. "Wish me luck, guys," she whispered to them. To her astonishment, Belle let out a soft low whine. Hannah blinked and opened the door, only to find Sandy and Jade standing there in puffy coats. Neither one had zipped them, presumably because they hadn't traveled far. Hannah had learned during their Monday lunch that Jade and her family occupied the last townhome at Sisters' Row, on the far side of Sandy's.

"Sandy! Jade!"

"We wanted to wish you luck," Sandy said with a bright smile. "Here!" She handed over a bottle of wine. "For later!"

"Oh, that's very sweet."

"And this is just in case!" Jade winked, handing her a small wrapped package.

"Thanks so much." Hannah didn't dare to guess. She hoped it wasn't anything too personal.

"They're chocolate truffles from Nutcracker Sweets," Jade said.

"World's best," Sandy assured her.

"And they go really great with the wine." Jade turned quickly at the sound of tires crunching on the road. The snow had turned to sleet, falling in icy daggers slanting against the darkened sky. "Eeeek! Here he comes!"

Sandy grinned excitedly. "I hope you have the best time!"

"Me, too!" Jade latched on to Sandy's elbow, attempting to drag her away. "And you look fantastic!"

"Love the sweater dress!" Sandy agreed, side-stepping toward her door.

Hannah self-consciously smoothed the hem that hit mid-thigh above the tops of her brown leather boots. "Not too much?" she asked in a whisper.

"Perfect," Sandy said. A truck door popped open.

Jade scooted down the porch and Sandy leapt toward her door. "See ya!" Jade called before disappearing. A second later, two doors slammed shut and Hannah heard footfalls on the stoop. She looked up to see Carter approaching, looking unbelievably handsome in jeans and a sweater beneath an open field coat. His face was ruddy from the cold, but his evergreen eyes were as warm as ever. "You look incredible," he said, moving toward her.

Hannah quickly backed over the threshold, setting the wine and chocolates on her foyer table, but Carter didn't seem to notice. "Thanks!" She felt fire in her cheeks. "You do, too."

Hannah saw that he carried a tall, golf-style umbrella, but hadn't bothered to use it during the short trip from the curb. He leaned it against the porch railing when she motioned him inside. "I'll just be a minute," she told him, closing the door. "Let me grab my coat."

Jingles and Belle bounded over to greet him, and Carter stooped low to pet Belle on her head, then scratch Jingles under his chin. "How are you, you little scoundrel?" he asked the loudly purring feline. "Been up to any mischief lately?"

"Oh yeah, he has." Hannah slid on her coat and gloves, shooting Jingles a wary glance. "He stole my new barrette only yesterday."

"You bad boy," Carter teased the cat. "Haven't you had enough of the pokey, by now?" He stood with a chuckle, facing Hannah. "Which barrette? The one that you're wearing?"

Hannah brought a hand to her head, remembering she'd worn it as an accessory. The color of the snowman's crimson neck scarf went perfectly with the cranberry color of her dress. "Yes! That's the one."

"Very nice." Carter grinned down at the naughty kitten. "Maybe he thought he was getting a snow cone?"

"Jingles is quite a thief." She smiled and buttoned up her coat. "If it glitters, it's his kind of gold."

Carter laughed heartily at this. "I'll take that under advisement and make certain to watch what I leave lying around."

"Sandy lost her key."

"That's right! Your first night here." He took a moment to study her forehead. His eyes roamed over her and her heart beat faster. "You seem all healed up now. Is the tenderness gone?"

"Pretty much completely." The bruising had finally dissipated as well. Which was why Hannah had felt confident enough to pull her bangs back on one side. Besides that, the new accessory made her feel pretty. And Hannah found herself wanting to look feminine for Carter. Particularly since he was so obviously *all man.* She recalled the sultry sensation of his thumb tracing her lips, and her pulse quickened.

"I made us a reservation at the Peppermint Bark," he told her. "I hope that's all right. There's only one other spot open for dinner, and the Reindeer Pub has a fairly limited menu."

"The Reindeer Pub, huh?" Hannah asked, amused. She thought she'd seen all the establishments in town, but had somehow missed this one.

"It's at the other end of town. Out on River Road. You take your first right off of the roundabout when you're coming from this way," Carter explained. "Right between the library and the courthouse. It's a microbrewery, but they also serve sandwiches and pizza. That's about the extent of it. The Peppermint Bark has more choices, plus they sell wine…"

His eyes met hers and Hannah's cheeks warmed. "But if you'd rather go—"

"The Peppermint Bark sounds great." She smiled shyly. "Besides, I have to make good on that rain check."

"Yes." He met her eyes and didn't look away. "Hannah," he said after a beat. "About the other day…at your shop."

"What about it?"

"I hope I wasn't too… That I didn't…"

"Come on too strong?" she queried saucily.

Carter pursed his lips, waiting. "Well?"

"I said, yes, didn't I?" Hannah primly straightened her coat, but beneath it those butterflies were winging.

Carter stepped closer, near enough to touch her— but he didn't. Hannah's temperature spiked and her head felt light. When Carter spoke, his voice was hoarse. "I'm very glad that you did." She was glad, too. Oh yes, she was. More glad than he knew.

"Me, too," she offered quietly.

He angled his chin toward hers, and Hannah's lips involuntary parted. She couldn't help but lick them, finding them dry. Parched. Needy.

Carter slowly leaned forward and gave her a very soft kiss on the lips, warm and silky smooth like the faintest brush of a butterfly's wing. Hannah nearly fainted. "I think I'm ready for that glass of wine," he said huskily. "How about you?"

Hannah drew in a breath. "Yes."

An hour later, Carter and Hannah lingered over a second glass of wine while waiting for their entrees to arrive. A single candle burned softly in the center of their table, beside their half-empty bottle of cabernet sauvignon. Carter had selected a special appetizer for them to share: fried oysters with a cilantro lime sauce, and Hannah appeared to have enjoyed it immensely. She seemed to be looking forward to her pan-seared mountain trout with a butter-sage sauce and Carter knew he'd be pleased with his rib eye steak. They'd decided to split sides of creamed spinach and garlic mashed potatoes, and wait until later to see how they felt about dessert. For a restaurant in a small town, the Peppermint Bark lived large. It had a very talented chef who'd trained in New York City and liked treating the locals to the latest culinary innovations.

Carter didn't mind that the meal was leisurely. Far more than appreciating the food, he was savoring Hannah's company. She was radiant tonight. Beautifully attired in a tasteful red dress that accentuated her lovely figure. Her hair was prettily arranged, pulled back loosely on one side in that cute snowman barrette. Her big brown eyes met his and they warmed his soul.

She'd been telling him about her lunch at the Santa Sandwich Shop, and about meeting Jade and Olivia. He'd have to talk to his big sister later about telling tales out of school. Not that Carter really cared that Olivia had shared his big fish story. Hannah apparently found it funny, and he'd loved seeing the smile on her lips when she'd recounted it. And oh, what gorgeous lips she had. He probably shouldn't have kissed her at the start of their date, when the custom was to do so at the end. But Hannah had such a delectable mouth he'd been aching to claim it ever since that moment in the

Christmas Cookie Shop. Just looking at her now, sitting there in the candlelight, made him want to do it again.

"Thank you for bringing me here," she said. "This was a lovely pick."

"Thanks for the bottle of wine." He took a sip. "Great selection."

She raised her glass and clinked his. "I suppose now we're even."

Even, but not in equilibrium, Carter found himself thinking. His life had been thrown out of kilter ever since Hannah came into it. It was hard to bear the thought that she wouldn't stay. Carter caught a frown tugging at the edges of his mouth and stopped it. There wasn't time for self-pity tonight. He owed Hannah the pleasure of some decent company.

He set down his wine, deciding to change the subject. "So, tell me about those cookbooks." Before talking about her girls' lunch and meeting Carter's sister, Hannah had mentioned Lou dropping off the big box.

Hannah dabbed her mouth with her napkin. "They're pretty cool, actually. Some of them are ancient."

"Ancient?" he asked with surprise.

"More than a hundred years old."

"Amazing," Carter said, mulling this over. "Are any of value, do you think?"

"Probably," she answered. "But their real value's more sentimental, if you know what I'm saying. They're—"

"Special." The word trailed out of his lips.

Her eyes sparkled in the candlelight and a million stallions stampeded inside him.

"Yeah, very. And—apparently—really special to my Great-grandma Lena."

"I heard she made *special* cookies."

Her face brightened. "They were called Virginia Cookies. After Virginia O'Hanlon, the little girl who wrote to the editor at the New York *Sun*."

Carter seemed stunned. "*Yes, Virginia, there is a Santa Claus*. That Virginia?"

"One and the same." She leaned toward him and whispered, "They were reputed to work magic."

Carter surveyed her lovely features, thinking no spell could be as powerful as the one she was casting on him at this moment. "What kind of magic?"

A wisp of her hair fell forward, lightly grazing her cheek. He anticipated her words, before she spoke them, with tenderness and conviction and just a hint of longing. "Magic of the heart."

"Your entrees, Mister and Madam." Their server paused uncertainly, holding one dish in his hand while balancing the other across his forearm. He glanced first at Hannah, then over at Carter. "Should I...take these back to the kitchen to keep them warm?"

Carter sent Hannah a questioning look.

"No, thank you," she told the server. "It's fine." Her colored deepened. "Everything looks delicious." The waiter nodded and set down her plate before Carter's.

"Be careful with these," he cautioned. "Still a little hot to the touch."

"Wow! Will you look at this fish?" Hannah said with a tad more enthusiasm than necessary. "It looks— and smells—divine!"

Carter wondered if she'd secretly embarrassed herself with that business about the cookies. He hadn't been bothered by the discussion in the least. On the contrary, it had intrigued him. Though not half as much as the enticing look in Hannah's eyes. Could Carter dare to hope she was attracted to him as desperately as he was to her? It was more than her mind, and more than her beauty that appealed to him. There was something very organic about Hannah Winchester, something earthy and real. Hannah was not the kind of woman who would pretend to be someone she wasn't, because the fact was, she didn't need to. She was pretty spectacular just the way she was.

They each took a bite of food and approved it before their server discreetly refilled their wines and went on his way. "So!" Carter pressed on ahead. "Why don't you tell me about that recipe? The one for those magical Virginia Cookies? What's in them?"

"I have no idea." Hannah set down her fork and chewed thoughtfully for a minute. "This fish is really good. Would you like to try it?"

"Well, I…" Carter hadn't let anyone feed him since he was a little boy and his big sister Olivia crammed a steamed Brussels sprout in his mouth. Before he could protest too much, Hannah had already prepared him a forkful and had it hovering below his mouth.

"Come on," she said in mock sternness, though a smile teased the corners of her mouth. "Be a good boy. Open up."

Carter solemnly took a bite of food, rolling the tender morsel of fish in a savory sauce around on his tongue. He had to concede, it was cooked to perfection. "Hmm. Superb."

"Exactly what I thought!" Hannah nodded triumphantly, then she lasciviously eyed his steak.

Carter had never played this game. When Gina had suggested it once, he'd declined. Then again, Gina's offer had seemed polite and perfunctory. It had been hard to tell if she'd really meant it. By contrast, Hannah made this communal way of eating seem commonplace, almost necessary. He stiffly fed her a nice sliver of steak and she moaned.

"Oh…my…goodness, that is *so* good." She glanced between his plate and hers. "I honestly don't know which is better."

"Would you like to…share?"

"Oh, no," she said, apparently satisfied they'd completed some important ritual. "I'm good with what I've got. Thank you, though."

Carter took a giant swallow of wine, catching his breath while Hannah ate happily. "So you never found Lena's recipe?"

"For the Virginia Cookies?" she asked between mouthfuls. "No. Not yet."

He finally relaxed enough to tackle his own food. "Do you think it's in one of those cookbooks, maybe?"

"I plan to look again, but I'm not sure."

"It would be interesting to know what's in them."

"Very interesting, I agree."

"Hannah," Carter asked, the thought tormenting him. "Do you really have to…? What I mean is, about Lena's shop… It seems such a shame—"

A pained expression crossed her face. "I know it does."

"Then, why?"

Hannah set down her fork. "I met with Buddy Christmas this week. I got Frank's estimate as well." There was a telling seriousness in her eyes. "Things aren't looking good for the Christmas Cookie Shop."

A lump formed in his throat. "I'm sorry."

She gave a little laugh, but it was a tortured one. "If you haven't guessed, I'm not a rich woman."

Carter had surmised that, but he was far too much of a gentleman to ever mention it.

"Buddy and I are putting together a plan," she went on.

"To sell the shop?" Carter guessed.

"For me to get out without losing my shirt," she said, sounding desperate. "Carter…I'm not sure you appreciate the circumstances." Her eyes misted over. "It's not like I have a choice."

Carter reached out and took her hand. "I didn't mean to make things worse for you."

"You haven't," she said, blinking back her tears.

Carter lifted his napkin and gently wiped her cheeks. "You know, Hannah," he said warmly, "things have a way of working out in the end. Working out for the best."

Carter didn't know who he was fooling, because they hadn't always worked out that way for him. Still, he'd been compelled to help Hannah feel better.

"If you say so."

"I say so," he said, meeting her eyes. In that moment, Carter knew it wasn't only about brightening her spirits. He wanted to do everything in his power to help Hannah make her dreams come true.

Chapter Fourteen

They finished their dinners agreeing to shelve further discussions about the Christmas Cookie Shop for now. "Let's put something more pressing on the agenda." Carter waved over their waiter. "Like what we're going to order for dessert."

He had been so kind in taking care of her, Hannah had felt like a royal princess all evening. The dinner was wonderful, and Carter's presence so steadfast and reassuring. Even when she'd broken down and temporarily lost it over the cookie shop, he'd somehow been able to turn things around and make her feel better.

"I'm not sure I have room for anything else." Though when their server appeared wielding a gorgeous dessert tray, Hannah quickly changed her mind and ordered the crème brûlée with blackberries and whipped cream. "You're not getting anything?" She was surprised he could resist.

"Just coffee. Would you like some?"

"Coffee for me would be great."

Carter smiled at the waiter, who left to fill their order. "You know," he said, folding over his napkin, "you never did explain what you've got waiting for you back in Virginia. Or perhaps the more appropriate question would be, who?"

Hannah could tell he was treading lightly, and she was touched that he cared to ask. "It's not a who, Sheriff Livingston. Like I said, I've sworn off men."

"Yes." He gave her a scrutinizing look. "Why is that?"

"Why do you think?" she asked as their coffees arrived. Hannah added cream to hers, but Carter took his black.

"I think it has something to do with past experience. Negative experience, mostly."

"You're very good," she told him. "Maybe you ought to go into law enforcement."

"Reading people's part of the job."

"What about you?"

"What about me?"

"Women?" She took a slow sip of coffee, viewing him over the rim of her cup. "There's bound to have been a few."

"Maybe I should hire you as my deputy."

Hannah laughed. "I hear you already have one."

"Yes, and Victoria does a fine job."

"Victoria Cho?"

"That's the one."

"She's married to Frank, isn't she?"

"Yeah, and they've got a little boy. Bobby. Really cute kid."

"You're changing the subject."

"Am I?" His green gaze washed all over her and Hannah's heart stilled. "Ask me anything you want to know."

Hannah didn't want to be intrusive, but she couldn't help but wonder why Carter hadn't dated all this time. At least, not since coming to Christmas Town, according to Sandy.

"You've been in Christmas Town how long?"

"It will be a year this coming February."

"And yet you haven't... What I mean is..."

"You've probably been talking to Lou, or Sandy." Carter frowned. "Maybe even to Kurt, too."

Hannah's heart rose in her throat. "Carter, about Kurt..."

Carter set down his cup. "He didn't."

"Didn't what?"

"He didn't ask you out, did he?"

"Me? Why, no! Of course not."

"Well, that's something."

"Something what?"

Carter spread his broad hands on the table. "All right, Hannah," he said regretfully. "I'm going to come clean with you. I'm not proud of myself for doing it, but I asked Kurt to keep his distance."

"You...? What? From me? I don't understand."

"It was stupid of me. Juvenile." He shook his head in shame. "You're a grown woman. Naturally, you can make up your own mind."

"Carter, look at me." When he did, she continued, "What I told you before is true. I'm not interested in Kurt. I'm only sorry Lou started that crazy rumor."

"Rumor?" he asked, surprised.

"I can't believe you haven't heard it." Hannah heaved a sigh. "Apparently, everyone else in Christmas Town has."

"Well, that one slipped past me. The one that caught my ear is the other one going around."

"Which other one?" Hannah asked casually, though she thought she knew.

"The one about me and you." He carefully studied her. "What do you think? Any truth to it?"

Hannah self-consciously licked her lips. "Well, I…"

"Because I've heard the lady in question isn't interested—"

"That's not true!" Hannah blurted out before she could stop herself. A slow grin graced his lips and heat crept up her neck. "You tricked me."

"All's fair, I suppose."

Well, they clearly weren't at war, but hinting at love was jumping the gun as far as Hannah was concerned. Carter took another sip of coffee, his eyes never leaving hers.

"So, if it's not a *who* calling you back to Virginia, it must be a *what*."

Hannah nervously swallowed another bite of custard, her pulse still racing from their earlier exchange. At least the *what* was easier to answer. "Graduate school," she told him quickly. "I want to go back and get my master's degree, though not necessarily in Virginia. I'm applying to a variety of schools."

He leaned back in his chair and viewed her encouragingly. "Well, good for you. What do you plan to study?"

"Social work. I hope to work in a clinic eventually, helping families and…women." She'd been about to say battered women, but had stopped herself. An image of her and Ben cowering in the coat closet came to mind. Twelve-year-old Ben protectively had his arms around her, shushing his five-year-old trembling sister. Their dad was storming through the house, upending furniture and kicking things sideways. He'd returned from his job at the mill expecting dinner on the table, but Hannah's mom April had run out to help a neighbor with an emergency. Though her dad had never actually raised his hand to strike any of them, his temper had been terrifying.

Hannah blinked, recalling herself to the present. "In any case, that's the plan."

"You want to help people," Carter said with understanding.

"I'd hoped my bachelor's degree would be enough." Hannah shrugged sadly. "But all I was able to get with that was a mediocre administrative job that barely paid the bills."

"Where?"

"Braxton and Braxton Real Estate."

"Ah-ha! So you know something about—"

She shot him a silencing look and Carter held up his hands.

"Sorry. Off-limits. I recall." He observed her awhile, apparently thinking things through. "Is that why you need the money from your family shop? To help fund your studies?"

"Yeah, and to help pay off my old loans, too. Who knows?" Hannah shrugged hopefully. "I might get lucky! Maybe I'll get a scholarship to grad school."

"Are you applying for one?"

"More than one," Hannah said with a laugh. "As many as I can locate, in fact."

Compassion lined his face. "Then I'm sure that you'll get one, if not many."

"Thanks, Carter."

They finished their coffees in companionable silence. When the check arrived, Carter told her, "You know, I certainly understand life plans, and I find yours very admirable. I only wish…" He viewed her wistfully. "You didn't have to go."

Hannah found herself kind of wishing that, too. "I'm sure it will be hard. Everyone here"—she looked at him affectionately—"has been so kind. Welcoming from the start."

"But life calls," he said astutely.

"Yes, it does."

"Well then…" Carter reached out and took her hand, wrapping his fingers around hers. "What do you say we make the most of things while you're here?"

"I'd like that," Hannah replied, speaking from the heart.

A little while later, Carter brought his arm around her shoulder and hurried Hannah up the steps to her front door, shielding them from the miserable weather with his umbrella. Once they reached the covered stoop, he set it aside. "Would you like to come in?" she asked, gazing up at him. Carter knew if he did, he'd never want to leave.

"I've got another bottle of wine," she said, temptingly.

But the temptation that was too strong was the pull of her lips. Carter took her in his arms and said, "Next time."

Her mouth tilted up toward his. "Rain check?"

Carter's skin burned hot and his soul sparked with desire. "Oh, yeah," he said, diving into her kiss. Then he was lost to her sweet sultry sighs, to the fiery heat of her lips. Carter kissed her again, this time more deeply, and his heart and his head became unwound. She was so warm and tender. *So womanly…* Flames leapt down his back and caressed his belly, sparking lower until

Carter thought he'd be driven mad. Frozen rain slammed the porch railings, in tune to the wild pounding in his veins.

"Carter…" She was breathless, clinging to him as if he were a life raft on a turbulent sea. "I think we'd better—"

"Stop," he said, his voice gravelly.

She nodded weakly, appearing on the verge of collapse herself.

He brought a hand to her mouth and traced her lips. "You better watch yourself with those rain checks. You've got to know I'll always cash them in."

She lightly bit his thumb and Carter's heart stuttered.

"That's what I'm counting on," she said.

Chapter Fifteen

Hannah awoke groggily to her cell phone's loud refrain. She'd changed the ringtone to a Christmas tune, all in keeping with the season. Now, the second chorus of "Frosty the Snowman" was blaring from somewhere beside her bed. Hannah reached out her hand and fumbled around on the nightstand until she found it. She snatched up the phone and pressed it to her ear, squinting against the morning light. "Hello?"

"Good morning, dear! Happy Saturday!" It was Lou's jolly voice. Hannah blinked at the blurry bedroom clock, seeing it was close to noon. "Heavens. I didn't wake you?"

Hannah shifted Jingles and Belle aside and scooted into a sitting position against the headboard. "No, not at all," she fibbed, not wanting the other women to think her a slouch. "It just took me a minute to get to the phone."

"Could that be due to the late night you had?" Lou prodded cheerily.

Hannah ran her fingers through her hair, holding back her bangs. Where was that barrette? She glanced around the room, certain she'd laid it down somewhere. "Late night?" she asked lamely.

"Cat's out of the bag," Lou proclaimed. "Mildred Murdock was out to dinner at the Peppermint Bark last night with her sister and they said—"

"My goodness, Lou. It hasn't even been twenty-four hours."

"It's okay about Kurt, you know," Lou said, continuing as if she hadn't heard her. "Perfectly fine. He assures me he thinks Carter is the better fit for you, too."

Hannah's cheeks burned hot. "How nice of the town to form a consensus."

"Yes, well. That's Christmas Town for you! A very happy place. We all want what's best for everybody. Including you, Miss Hannah Winchester. Which brings me to why I'm calling."

Hannah's head pounded. "And why's that, Lou?"

"Why, to invite you to the church bazaar, that's why. Just think of all the fun you'll have, and what a lovely way for you to meet the rest of the town."

Hannah was overwhelmed just at the thought of it. She'd barely been keeping up, as it was. "That's really kind of you to think of me, but I'm sorry to say—"

"Uh, uh, uh…" Lou clucked. "Don't even bother with excuses. I haven't even told you when it is."

"When is it?" Hannah asked, thinking she needed some really strong coffee. Probably two cups.

"Tomorrow evening at five. There's a children's pageant first, then a church dinner, and an ornament-making workshop afterward. Buddy and I would love for you to be our guest."

"That's so sweet." Hannah bit into her lip, thinking hard, but any dodge she could come up with was too transparent.

"Delightful!" She could hear Lou clapping her hands. "Would you like Buddy and me to come and get you, or will you be walking over with Sandy?"

"Sandy's going?" Hannah asked, feeling immediately more hopeful about the situation. It wouldn't be nearly so bad meeting a whole passel of strangers with someone she already considered a good friend on her arm.

"Of course, dear," Lou answered. "Who do you think's in charge of the Christmas ball–painting booth?"

"Well, that's perfect then." Hannah's head was finally starting to clear. "I'll give Sandy a call later and coordinate coming with her." It occurred to Hannah that she might even be of help by offering to assist Sandy in carting over any craft supplies. "Thanks so much for thinking of me."

"No problem, dear. Ta! See you there!"

Hannah was just pouring her coffee in the kitchen when her cell phone buzzed. She saw the text was from Carter and her heart leapt with joy.

Really great time last night.
Care to try again?

Love to.

How do you feel about pizza?

Hannah's fingers shook excitedly when she typed:

Reindeer Pub?

My place.

Heat flooded her cheeks.

When?

Thursday at 7?

Hannah's pulse pounded.

I'll bring the wine.

Deal.

There was a knock at her front door and Hannah cinched the tie on her robe, walking toward it. "No one told us it was going to be a pajama party!" chirped Jade. She held a large white bag with steam escaping from its crumpled edges. Sandy stood beside her, holding two more bags. Both women wore street clothes and winter gear. The dismal weather had halted temporarily and bright sunshine lit up the tree-lined sidewalks of North Main. Yet, it was still chilly outside.

Jade lifted her bag and the heavenly scent of cinnamon wafted toward Hannah. "Hot sticky buns," Jade said.

"And I brought cherry cheese danishes," Sandy added. Only one person was needed to complete the party. Of course, she didn't live here.

"Wait for me!" Olivia called, scrambling around the corner while hauling a small cooler. "Fresh-squeezed juice and fruit salad coming!"

Hannah's face flamed. They couldn't all expect her to dish about her date with Carter. Even Olivia? His big sister? Hannah paused in her thinking, considering that perhaps Olivia was the most interested of all. "Well, this is…" *a little awkward,* she wanted to say; instead she finished with her voice lilting in a squeak, "a nice surprise."

"Girls' brunch," Olivia said sweetly. Her auburn hair was undone this morning, cascading in pretty waves past her shoulders.

"Just another tradition we forgot to mention," Sandy explained.

"Everyone takes turns hosting! Do you mind?" Jade asked, nosing past her over the threshold. "Very cute," she said, glancing around. "I like the extra touches you've added in here."

Hannah had put up a few simple holiday decorations. Some candles and a garland on the mantel and two Christmas stockings dangling from one end.

The others joined them inside as Sandy elbowed the door shut.

"Who are the stockings for?" Olivia asked, carrying her cooler to the kitchen.

"My two—"

Jingles darted across Olivia's path, nearly tripping her. "Oh! Oh my!"

"They are too darling," Jade said, bending low to greet Jingles and Belle.

"Watch the orange one," Sandy warned. "Don't tempt him with any fine jewelry."

"Or keys," Hannah said good-naturedly, her tensions starting to ease. Maybe the others weren't here to pry about her date after all. They were just including Hannah in another of their weekly rituals. How kind. The women crowded into the kitchen and began unpacking their wares as if they did this all the time.

"Dishes?" Sandy asked, turning to her.

Hannah speechlessly pointed to a cupboard.

They all worked seamlessly together, setting up a mini brunch bar on the counter before serving their individual plates. Once they were comfortably seated around the table, Sandy looked up with a grin and ventured. "So?"

Hannah blinked at her and the others, feigning ignorance. "So?"

"Come on," Jade said, grinning slyly. "You can't mean you don't want to talk about it."

Hannah gulped, feeling totally put on the spot. "I can't possibly—"

Olivia picked up her juice and her green eyes sparkled. "Please tell me that my brother was the perfect gentleman."

Hannah took a large bite of cinnamon roll, chewing slowly. After a beat, she addressed them boldly with a casual air. "Carter was…"

There was a collective gasp as the others held their breath and waited.

"Pretty perfect all right," Hannah continued impishly. "No comment on the 'gentleman' part…" Then she polished off her pastry with a grin.

"Well, well!" Sandy hooted while Jade rollicked with laughter.

Olivia viewed her with admiration. "Oh, I like you, Hannah Winchester. I like you a lot. Something tells me my brother does, too."

"Woo-hoo!" Jade whistled and Sandy catcalled before Olivia hushed them both down.

"Now ladies," she said with a staged air of dignity. "If Hannah doesn't want to talk about it, we should respect that."

"Thank you." Hannah beamed at Olivia and then at Sandy and Jade. "And thanks so much for the food. Everything is wonderful."

"Don't think you're getting off the hook that easily," Jade said.

"She's right," Olivia agreed. "Next time, you get to cook."

"Or buy," Sandy corrected. "There's no rule saying what you bring has to be homemade."

"The one who doesn't provide the brunch gets to host it," Olivia finished.

Hannah was starting to understand how this worked, and she felt honored to have been included. When she told them so, Sandy replied, "Of course! You're already one of us."

"Speaking of group events," Hannah ventured. "Maybe you can fill me in on the holiday bazaar?"

Olivia smiled broadly. "The one at the church? No problem. We all go each year."

"Alexander is in the pageant," Jade said proudly. "He and Bobby Cho are two of the wise men. And Olivia and I help with the decorations."

"And Carter?" Hannah couldn't help but hear herself say. She pursed her lips as the others stared at her. Eventually, they broke into grins.

"Carter will be working, more than likely," Olivia said. "He generally is."

"He begs off on the bazaar, so that Victoria can go," Sandy told her.

Jade nodded in agreement. "Victoria is Bobby's mom. So naturally, she wants to be there to see him perform."

"Of course. Makes sense." Hannah took a gulp of juice, which tasted delicious. "Olivia," she said, praising her, "this is incredible."

"Thanks! I like getting down to basics when I can."

"Olivia grows a garden in the summertime. Harvests her own vegetables," Sandy said before Jade chimed in, "That homemade salsa is superb."

Olivia's cheeks tinged pink. "You guys are making me blush."

Sandy laughed sweetly. "What's wrong, Olivia? Can't take a compliment?"

Olivia squared her shoulders. "Oh, I can take compliments all right." Then she added mysteriously, "Especially from the right parties."

"I can't believe Lou hasn't tried to fix you up," Jade said to Olivia.

"Oh, trust me, she has."

"Lou's the sweetest woman on earth," Sandy observed. "She's just not exactly tuned in to what our generation needs."

"Oh?" Olivia responded. "And what exactly is that?"

Sandy stared at Olivia a long while, then began grinning brightly. Before long her entire face was lit up like the sun rising over the ocean.

"What?" Olivia asked, surprised.

"Yeah," Jade wanted to know, "what is it?"

Sandy defiantly shook her head. "Nope. Not telling."

"You thought of someone for Olivia, didn't you?" Hannah asked her a few minutes later when they carried their dishes to the kitchen.

Sandy playfully rolled her eyes and whispered, "Maybe."

Chapter Sixteen

Hannah met Sandy on the stoop the next afternoon at exactly four o'clock. Sandy wanted to get to the church early to set up her table, so things would be ready to go after the pageant and dinner. The sky had darkened again and snow clouds loomed overhead.

"I thought I'd better drive," Sandy said, producing her keys. "It's only a few blocks away, but given what we've got to carry…" She motioned to the three copier paper boxes she had stacked on the porch. One was marked "paint," another "Christmas balls," and the final one "knickknacks." "Do you mind grabbing one of those?"

Hannah complied readily and they loaded the boxes in the rear of Sandy's small hatchback. "What kind of knickknacks?" Hannah asked as Sandy slammed the trunk shut.

"All sorts of fun stuff. Glitter, sequins, stickers, and appliques."

"Sounds like your station is well planned."

Sandy cranked her ignition and smiled. "I've done this before, remember? Last year, I forgot the glue, but that won't happen again."

"Thanks for letting me ride along," Hannah said, thinking the less she used her own car, the better. Given its condition, it probably didn't have too many extra miles left.

"Happy to!" Sandy adjusted her rearview mirror, glancing at Hannah. "You don't need to be nervous about it. Everyone there will love you. You already know a bunch of people, anyway. There's me and Jade."

"And Olivia," Hannah agreed.

"Lou, Buddy…and Kurt."

Hannah held up a finger. "Don't forget Frank!"

"There, you see," Sandy said kindly. "It will be almost like old home week."

Hannah didn't know about that. Her home had never contained that many people. After her dad walked out, it had been just her, Ben, and their mom. Even later, when she and her brother had moved in with Grandpa Charles and Grandma Mabel, there'd just been three of them around most of the time, with Ben away at college.

"I suppose the other Christmas brothers will be there?"

"You bet!"

"The oldest is Ray and he's married to Meredith?"

"Correct. Their son Kyle is ten. Walt should be there, too, with the twins, Joy and Noelle."

"I've spoken with Joy," Hannah said warily. "On the phone."

"She talks a lot, but is very cute. You'll like her and Noelle, too."

Hannah inhaled deeply, wondering if she could handle this.

"Yes, you can."

"Can what?"

"Oops." Sandy tightened her mittens around the steering wheel. "I…um…just got a vibe that you were feeling doubtful. It's one of my skills. My parents used to call it intuition. But I don't know." She shrugged mildly. "Sometimes intuition is just a lucky guess."

Hannah studied Sandy's profile, having an inkling that she was hiding something. "What else can you guess about?"

"Me? Oh nothing." She looked like she was bursting with a secret. "My brother Nick, though… He's another story."

"Really?"

Sandy shot Hannah a sly glance. "Nick can tell if someone's been naughty or nice."

"Get out!"

"I'm serious! Honest to goodness."

Hannah folded her arms in front of her. "And how exactly does he do that?"

"I'm not sure. It's kind of weird. He just looks at them."

"You mean, he reads their aura or something?"

"No! Nothing that crazy."

"O-kay."

"You might not believe me, but it's true." Sandy sounded a tad offended. "When we were little he could point out who was going to the principal's office *hours* before it happened. It was a game we used to play each morning on the bus. Because you see, for a time, even *I* didn't believe him. So I'd say, 'Okay Nick, you tell me who's been naughty and nice.' And then he'd go down the rows of seats telling me who had misbehaved the day before without being caught. Sooner or later, the kids were exposed for their mischievous deeds, and they wound up in detention."

"Maybe he saw them doing something?"

"That doesn't explain how he knew who had taken all the boys' street clothes from the locker room during gym class, and hidden them in the auditorium."

"Why not?"

"Nick wasn't even in school that day. He was out sick." Sandy kept talking, becoming increasingly animated with her story. "He even got it right about the bus driver being nice!"

"What did the bus driver do?" Hannah couldn't help but ask, intrigued.

"He took up a collection from parents and brought in a pretty balloon bouquet for a teacher who had broken her leg."

"So, Nick probably saw the balloons on the bus in the morning, right?"

"No. The driver delivered them later, after school. None of us kids knew about it until the next day. None of us except for Nick, that is."

"Then he must have overheard—"

"Hannah," Sandy said firmly. "You can rationalize it away if you want to. I know I used to do that. But sooner or later, you come to find that certain things can't be explained by the regular rules in this world. They're special."

"Special?" Hannah echoed, thinking of her conversation with Carter on Friday.

"Yes, indeed. Special." Sandy pulled into the parking lot of a quaint stone church with a high steeple. Things were already bustling, with folks moving boxes and carrying in covered dishes from their vehicles.

When Sandy shut off her engine, she turned to Hannah and winked. "Just like Lena's cookies."

Hannah didn't know what to think about Sandy's assertion that Nick could tell who'd been naughty or nice. Sandy clearly idolized her big brother, so maybe her mind had blown things out of proportion. Hannah knew firsthand what it was like to have a big brother you looked up to. When she'd been a kid, Hannah had pretty much worshiped Ben. He'd earned her admiration honestly, by always being there for her and providing a shoulder to lean on. Once Ben became a teen and a really popular magnet for the girls, Hannah had been particular about his dating choices. Though she'd instantly loved Nancy.

Nancy and Ben had met their first year of college, and had fallen headily in love. When Ben brought Nancy home to meet his grandparents and Hannah that first Christmas, Nancy had introduced Hannah to the old-fashioned tradition of stringing popcorn and cranberries on the outdoor trees. Nancy claimed to have always wanted a little sister of her own, and instinctively took Hannah under her wing. Hannah instantly bonded with her big brother's girlfriend and Grandpa Charles and Grandma Mabel adored her. Apart from being a caring wife, Nancy was a devoted mom to Lily. When Ben lost her, it hadn't only devastated him…it had been a tragedy for the entire family.

"Oh look!" Sandy cried, as they carted their boxes inside. "There's Ray Christmas. And Kyle!" she added, as a lanky young boy took long strides after him.

Ray walked over and graciously took Sandy's load out of her hands. "Well, hey there! Merry Christmas." Ray's features were handsome and solid, and he had the outdoorsy look of someone who spent a lot of time in the elements.

"Ray Christmas," he said, nodding at Hannah. "You must be the newcomer we've all been hearing so much about." He glanced at the boy beside him. "Kyle, where are your manners? Please help this lady with her box."

Kyle shyly retrieved the box from Hannah's grasp, his temples turning pink. "Sorry. Hi."

Hannah looked down at the boy. "Hi Kyle, nice to meet you. You, too, Ray."

"And I'm Meredith," a stately brunette offered, bustling in the door. She set a casserole dish covered with tinfoil on a table and dusted off her gloves. "Welcome, Hannah! We've heard so much about you."

Ray noisily cleared his throat. "Strictly positive reports," he added, carting the boxes away.

"On the far table, please!" Sandy instructed. "The one by the coffeepot!" She angled her head toward Hannah and confessed quietly, "By about seven thirty, I'll be needing my java."

The room was quickly taking form, being converted by its milling occupants into a lovely, colorful place. Tables were established for making everything from miniature crèches to Advent wreaths. At the far end of the room, several intriguing-looking items were arranged behind lined pieces of notebook paper with pens by them. "Silent auction," Sandy explained when she saw Hannah staring that way. "Oh look!" She raised her hand and waved to the pretty redhead who was setting up a holiday jewelry stand. "There's Olivia!"

Olivia smiled at them both, then Hannah noticed Jade arranging some brand new children's books on the long auction table. "She must be donating them from her shop," she commented to Sandy.

"Does so every year."

A darling little boy was at Jade's side trying to help out. Hannah suspected it was her son, Alexander. Ray and Meredith Christmas had brought fresh greens for the wreaths. And there came Frank Cho with a very attractive dark-haired woman Hannah took to be his wife, and a nugget of a child who looked just like a miniature Frank.

Frank gripped a box filled with candles and crowed, "Let there be light!"

People momentarily stopped their work as the room burst into laughter.

"Over here, Frank!" Meredith directed, waving merrily.

He spotted her and Victoria gently took Bobby by the shoulders, pointing him the right way.

A tall, slim man with cocoa-colored skin and thick black glasses emerged from the kitchen, hauling stacks of metal chairs under each arm. "That's Wendell," Sandy whispered to Hannah. "Jade's husband. I'll introduce the two of you in a bit."

Suddenly, Hannah felt at a loss. Everyone here seemed to be doing their part, and Hannah had shown up empty-handed. The moment she thought it, Sandy said, "Well, look who's here!"

Lou and Buddy Christmas hustled over, each giving Hannah a congenial hug. Lou was wearing a green felt elf hat with jingle bells cascading from it. Hannah silently wondered if she planned to wear it in church. "Come on, now." Lou grinned, crinkling the bag in her hand. "Have I got a job for you."

"Oh great." Hannah eyed her thankfully. "I was hoping to find a way to—"

To Hannah's astonishment, Lou yanked open the shopping bag and shoved it under Hannah's nose. Hannah peered down, spying a sea of green felt and shiny metal bells. "What do you want me to do with those?" Hannah asked meekly.

"Buddy and I thought though it would be nice for each of the helpers to wear one after dinner. We'll be needing volunteers to replenish coffee and tea for our hardworking table leaders."

Buddy gave a jolly rumble. "Santa's little helpers," he said with a wink.

"You don't mind helping out, do you dear?"

"No, of course not."

"Good!" Lou plucked a felt hat from the bag and planted it on Hannah's head. Its bells tinkled loudly and Hannah resisted a grimace. "Are you sure we can wear these in church?"

"It's a children's pageant," Lou proclaimed. "Of course."

Hannah glanced desperately at Sandy, who stealthily giggled. "I think that's a fine idea, Lou, and a great way for Hannah to meet more people. She can help give out hats!"

"Thanks, Sandy," Hannah returned sotto voce.

"Don't be such a spoilsport." Sandy twisted her lips in a grin. "You might even have fun."

The next forty-five minutes sped by with Hannah helping Lou and Buddy set up the buffet line by rearranging dishes in groupings—main courses, sides, and desserts—and setting out paper products and plastic tableware. Others came to help them locate serving

178 The Christmas Cookie Shop

utensils and drape garlands festooned with red-and-green-checkered bows from the tables. Hannah met the twins' father, Walt Christmas, in the process. Walt was a handsome man with darker hair than his brothers and stunning blue eyes. If she'd not looked carefully, Hannah might have judged Walt to be the oldest on account of his neatly trimmed beard. But closer inspection revealed a more youthful complexion than Ray's.

At six foot four, Walt was clearly the tallest of the three Christmas boys, but the other two weren't far behind him. Hannah wondered where they got their height, as both Lou and Buddy were on the shorter side. Sandy told her she chalked it up to recessive Nordic genes. Twins Noelle and Joy had obviously inherited them. Both were statuesque blondes with long straight hair and big blue eyes like their father's. Hannah only met them in passing on the way through the narthex. Frank Cho greeted her there as well, briefly introducing Hannah to his wife, Victoria.

Hannah and Sandy were about to enter the sanctuary with Jade and Wendell Scott for the pageant that was about to start when Jade's dad, the retired sheriff Caleb Smith, joined them. Lou had said that the brief retelling of the Bible story through verses and holiday hymns wouldn't take more than twenty minutes. It was all the children could stand. *And about as much as the adults can take, too*, Buddy added with a chuckle.

The children who were performing had gone on ahead to meet with the youth volunteer, Stan Martin, who had a tiny brood of his own. Three little girls nipped at his heels like puppies, each asking repeated questions, as the other costumed kids gathered around began to whine and complain. Stan was taking over for his wife Della, who'd just given birth to their first son, and he was clearly overwhelmed. Hannah saw Walt whisper something to each of his twins, and the girls calmly slipped toward the vestibule to assist Stan with crowd control.

"Hannah Winchester." A kindly older gentleman dressed as a clergyman handed her a program as she entered the sanctuary. "Welcome to Christmas Town. We're so glad that you could join us."

Hannah smiled at the gaunt man with snowy white hair and a pleasant face. "Thank you. It's an honor to be here."

"Pastor Wilson," he said with a nod of his head. "Please enjoy your stay."

Hannah's throat felt tender. He'd said it like she was merely a visitor here, but wasn't that precisely what she'd told everybody? In fact, she'd worked extra hard to drive that point home. "I'm sure I will," she told him. "It's a very special town."

He seemed to be distracted by something at her crown. That's when Hannah realized with horror that she'd forgotten to remove her elf hat. Lou had said before that Hannah could pass these out after the pageant. Naturally, she'd only been joking about wearing them in church. Ha-ha. Hannah gulped and her face burned hot. "Oh, sor—"

"*Love* it." Pastor Wilson surprised her with a grin. "Do you have more?"

The children's performance of the Christmas story was adorable and brought back so many memories for Hannah of when she was a young girl. True to Lou's prediction, the service was short and sweet, with Pastor

Wilson presiding over it in the elf hat that Hannah had retrieved for him. He was a congenial man of the cloth who seemed to take things in stride. Sandy shared that he was a widower of about six years and that a couple of ladies in the choir had vied for his attentions by trying to outdo each other in bringing him homemade soups. In the end, Pastor Wilson didn't appear interested in forming another relationship with a woman on earth. He'd been overheard more than once saying that he'd wait to meet his Margie in heaven.

Lou leaned toward Hannah at the round table where they sat with Buddy and some other parishioners. Sandy and her fellow table volunteers had excused themselves early to go man their stations. "How are you enjoying your dessert, dear? You barely got any. I hope you'll go back for more."

Hannah noticed other places clearing out quickly, as people prepared for the after-dinner festivities. "I've had more than enough. Thanks, Lou," she said, patting her belly. "The cooks did a great job."

Buddy nibbled on a brownie. "Outstanding, yes. Though I can't help but say, I miss Lena's cookies."

"She brought them to the potluck?" Hannah asked with a hint of surprise.

"Not for the potluck." Lou winked. "For the auction."

"Ah yes, that was a blessed day." Buddy laid a hand on his heart. "Back when I was a young buck." He turned to Hannah. "I bid on them, you know." His jolly round cheeks reddened as he grinned. "And won!"

"Oh, wow…really?" Hannah found this fascinating. "What year was this?"

"Why, the year we became engaged." Lou peered expectantly at Buddy.

"Nineteen-seventy…" he began confidently before hesitating. Buddy stroked his snowy beard. "Now, let's see—"

"Buddy Christmas!" Lou scolded. "I can't believe you—"

"Four?" he guessed.

"No!"

"Wait…five! Nineteen-seventy-five, that's right." He shot Lou a placating grin. "Of course, I remember, dear. That was a very busy year. We married at the end of it."

"And had Ray the next year."

"At Christmas." Buddy nodded fondly.

Lou became animated at the memories. "Walt came two years after that, and six years later we got our Kurt. He's at the hospital tonight, but normally he would be here."

Hannah had noticed Kurt wasn't around. "You have a wonderful family," Hannah said. "I know you're both very proud of them, and the grandkids, too."

Buddy lifted a chubby finger. "And it all started with your great-grandmother's cookies! They put a spell on Louise."

Lou blushed demurely. "Well, something sure worked like magic."

"Lena was a fine woman, as was her late husband, Emmet. Emmet Winchester ran the Grand Hotel, you know."

"Yes, I'd heard that." This reinforced what Sandy had told her earlier.

Lou rested her elbows on the table and leaned forward. "Speaking of Lena's Virginia Cookies, did you find the recipe for them in the box?"

Hannah shook her head. "I looked more than once. Some of the cookbooks were so old they didn't have indices, but—"

"Cookbooks?" Lou seemed thrown. "No, dear, I'm afraid you've got it wrong. The recipe was never printed."

"It was *top secret*," Buddy said in hushed tones.

"I'm sure she kept it in her recipe file," Lou said.

Hannah hadn't seen anything like that in the box and she told them so. Lou gasped at the news. "You're kidding me. It's gone?" She sent Buddy an accusatory stare.

"Don't look at me," he said defensively. "When Charles and I taped up the box it was in there." He looked at Hannah. "Right on top."

"I…uh… You say it was a collection of handwritten recipes?"

"Exactly that; all stored in a small wooden box. Most recipes were on index cards, but some were on slips of paper. There was even one recorded on a piece of brown paper bag."

Buddy eyed Lou suspiciously. "You looked? But darling, Charles asked us not—"

"I only took a peek!" Lou's face colored. "Very briefly, when you and Charles went off to grab the tape. I didn't actually *read* any of the recipes. But they were all in Lena's hand."

Lou's eyes shone excitedly as she addressed Hannah. "Lena invented most of the recipes for her shop, though the most famous was for Virginia Cookies." Her lips scrunched in a frown. "I can't believe that file went missing. Where on earth could it have gone?"

"I can check again when I get home, but…"
Hannah had been mulling this over. "Didn't you say the
boxed had been taped shut?"

"With packing tape," Buddy said. "The strong
kind."

Hannah recalled the mental picture of her opening
the box folds one panel at a time. They'd been tucked
into each other rather than being secured by tape.
"There was no tape on the box when I got it. Or, if there
was, it had been cut."

Buddy narrowed his eyes at Lou.

"Buddy Christmas," she said, slapping his arm.
"How dare you accuse *me*?"

"She's right," Hannah said reasonably. "If the box
was in your house all these years, Lou could have read
the recipes at any time. Or even copied them."

"Exactly right!" Lou said smugly, then her face
fell. "Wrong! I mean, I didn't… Wouldn't ever
dream—"

"Of course not, dear," Buddy soothed in placating
tones. "I apologize if I implied—"

"Excuse me," Hannah said, surveying the room.
More spots were being vacated at tables as youngsters
gobbled up their food and raced to get in line at the
various stations. "It looks like the activities are getting
started, and I haven't yet distributed the rest of my
hats." She'd also been assigned to help keep the table
volunteers well supplied with tea and coffee, and would
need to prepare for her task.

"Quite right!" Lou scraped back her chair. "Come
on, Buddy," she told her husband. "We have work to
do!"

Three hours later, Lou thanked Hannah with a hug outdoors. They were bundled in their coats and had just loaded Sandy's trunk. Car lights came on across the parking lot, as people cranked their ignitions and cautiously pulled away. The snow had started back up and now fell softly around them. "You were a tremendous help, Hannah. We're so glad you came."

Buddy squeezed her to his barrel chest and spoke gruffly. "Yes, indeed. See you Tuesday." He'd said he couldn't meet Monday to discuss real estate due to his commitment at the courthouse. He was helping Ray install the community Christmas tree, and that would likely take all morning. It was supposed to go up the Saturday after Thanksgiving, Buddy explained, but the severe weather had thrown things off. Then Ray had become swamped with seasonal sales and had been unable to take a break. Tomorrow was the first chance they had.

"Thanks, Buddy," she answered. "I'm looking forward to it. I've been working on ideas."

"Let us know if you find that recipe box!" Lou hollered as she headed for her car.

Sandy's face scrunched up quizzically. "Recipe box?"

"I'll explain on the way home." Hannah smiled merrily though her feet were killing her. She didn't know how many miles she'd covered tonight between those various stations and the kitchen, but it had to be a lot. Yet, she'd been glad to help out. Being there among the people of Christmas Town had made her feel useful. Almost like she belonged.

Sandy slid into the driver's seat and said wryly, "You had fun in spite of yourself."

"It was a good time," Hannah replied. "Busy, but good."

"Busy is always better in my experience," Sandy said sagely.

Hannah glanced out her window at the pretty streetlamps curtained by snow. "Yeah."

"So!" Sandy shot her an inquisitive stare. "What's all this about a recipe box?"

On the rest of the ride home, Hannah filled her in.

Chapter Seventeen

Hannah sat on the floor, resting her back against the pastry case closest to the front window. Snow thudded against the glass as bundled-up passersby scurried about their business on Santa Claus Lane. She'd been at the shop since early this morning and had searched every nook and cranny for any stowed-away items, finding none. After her conversation with Lou and Buddy at the church bazaar last night, she'd gone back through the box at home and was more convinced than ever that the missing recipe file wasn't inside it. How odd that such a thing would disappear. Surely, the legend attached to Virginia Cookies was just some sentimental old tale. Someone couldn't have believed the recipe valuable enough to have tried to steal it?

Hannah racked her brain for any reasonable explanations about where the recipe file could be. If it was in the big box to begin with, logic said somebody had to have taken it out. But who? Obviously not Buddy or Lou. Even if they'd wanted to, they'd had ample opportunity to glean any information they wanted from the file, then put it back in the larger box. And Buddy and Lou were genuine, down-to-earth people. Neither one was the conniving type. *Okay, so maybe Lou is a little sneaky*. She had peeked at the file, after all. But surely that was the extent of it. Besides, Hannah couldn't totally blame her. Had Hannah been in Lou's shoes, she might have done the same.

That could only leave two alternatives: Someone else in the Christmas family had taken it, or somebody untrustworthy had been given access to their house. Hannah dismissed the first option out of hand, not believing any of the Christmases capable of such subterfuge. And toward what end? Her grandpa had given Buddy the cookbook box for safekeeping years ago.

When Lena passed, leaving the shop to Charles, he'd been at odds with himself over what do to with it. So, rather than face that challenge, he'd let it sit empty while he tried to figure things out. To the townspeople's chagrin, that figuring took nearly nine years. Then Hannah arrived, and her grandpa changed course. He decided to rent out the shop to use as an income stream until the appropriate time came. Eventually, the Christmas Cookie Shop would go to Hannah, once she was old enough to run it.

Charles apparently never considered entrusting the property to his only child, Tanner. Irresponsible and irascible, with a hair-trigger temper, Tanner was clearly a disappointment to Charles, who never felt his son was worthy of gentle-spirited April. In some ways, Hannah suspected her grandpa felt guilty over Tanner's poor treatment of his wife, and doubly culpable when April's illness was too much for Tanner to bear. Grandpa Charles never badmouthed her dad in front of her, but she'd overheard him speaking to Grandma Mabel shortly after April's burial.

Tanner hadn't been there for the worst part of the cancer…or the chemo…or the funeral. He'd only called briefly later to ask if there was any money coming his way. Hannah and Ben later pinpointed that as the time when their grandparents completely severed their relationship with their son.

Hannah hung her head in defeat, resting her elbows on her bent knees. If the Virginia Cookie recipe was lost, she could think of nowhere else to look for it. As far as she knew, no one had taken it and tried to use it. Of course, it was a big country and an even bigger world. That sacred piece of paper could have flitted to any part of the planet by now. So the idea that she might eventually find it was pretty far-fetched.

Hannah blew out a breath, wondering what Lena would think if she could see things now. She'd probably be heartbroken that the shop she'd poured so much love into was about to pass out of the family forever.

A lump formed in Hannah's throat and for once she had an inkling of how her Grandpa Charles must have felt. Unloading this place wasn't going to be as easy as Hannah had originally imagined. In truth, it seemed more and more impossible each day.

The door chime tinkled, startling Hannah out of her reverie as a blast of snow skittered across the floor. "Hannah? Is that you?"

Hannah glanced up through moist eyes, seeing Sandy had appeared. She was dressed for the cold and carried a small cardboard container. "We missed you today at lunch—"

Lunch? Hannah smacked her forehead, remembering it was Monday and that she'd promised to meet Sandy, Olivia, and Jade at the Santa Sandwich

Shop at one. "Oh, Sandy! I'm so sorry," Hannah said, shamefaced. "I just didn't…" She glanced outdoors at the street. "What time is it anyway?"

"Why, it's after two o'clock. I was just on my way to deliver this ornament of Kyle's to Ray. It hadn't fully finished drying last…" She stopped talking and stepped closer. "Hey," she said, setting a hand on Hannah's shoulder. "Are you all right?"

Hannah shared a shaky smile. "Oh Sandy, I feel so terrible…about everything."

Sandy set her small box on the pastry case and sat on the floor beside her. "I know you do," she said, pulling her into a hug. Hannah's shoulders shook as she sobbed.

"I have to sell the shop," she cried hoarsely. "I don't have any choice."

"There, there." Sandy gently patted her back. "We all know that, Hannah. Nobody judges you."

The sad thing was that nobody else had to. For there wasn't a harsher judge of Hannah than herself. "I suppose I could ask Ben to help me." When she spoke, her voice warbled. "He's not rich, but he has reserves."

"He also has a daughter," Sandy reminded her gently. "From what you told me."

"This is not the life I wanted. I had plans…" Hannah shook her head and sniffed.

"I know you did." Sandy held her tightly. "And they're great ones. Hannah, look at me."

She blinked hard and did. "You want to help people, yeah?"

Hannah nodded, her chin trembling.

"Then you have to follow your heart. Like Jade said last week, that's what each of us needs to do." She smiled softly. "All right?"

"You're not making this any easier, you know," Hannah told her.

Sandy widened her blue eyes. "What?"

"Leaving Christmas Town."

Sandy pulled Hannah out of her funk by telling her to go home and clean herself up before meeting her later for cocktails. They went to the Reindeer Pub, so Hannah was finally introduced to River Road. The establishment was rustic yet inviting, with exposed beams in the low-hung ceiling. True to form in this town, Christmas decorations were everywhere. Hannah's senses responded to the heavenly aroma of fresh-baked bread, garlic, and onions, and her stomach rumbled. "Something smells to-die-for in here."

"It's the pizza." Sandy pointed to the end of the bar. A large pie on a metal stand was set between a couple helping themselves to thick, gooey slices, heaped with ingredients and dripping with cheese.

"Yum."

"We can order one, if you'd like."

Hannah thought of her date on Thursday and decided she'd better wait. "Another time, for sure."

The bartender delivered two cold beers in frosted mugs and they each took a sip.

"Carter lives down this way," Sandy said coyly.

"Does he?" Hannah asked, intrigued. "I thought this was a rural road."

"Oh, it's pretty rural all right. Not much out this way. Just a couple of farmhouses and Buddy's old fishing cabin—that's where Carter lives. It's not very big, but the setting is ideal and you can't beat the view."

"Of the mountains?" Hannah guessed.

"And the river."

Hannah tried to picture it in her mind, but suspected the live view would be even more stellar. "Sounds amazing."

Sandy playfully nudged her. "Maybe you'll get to see it sometime?"

Hannah took a casual sip of beer. "Sooner than you think."

Sandy squealed, then lowered her voice when a couple of guys in ice fishing gear stared their way. "Another date?"

"This Thursday."

Sandy eyed her with admiration. "Well, here's to you for venturing where no woman has gone before…" Sandy lifted her mug to Hannah's. "In Christmas Town, anyway."

"Shush. Someone will hear you."

"Nobody has any clue what we're talking about."

It was a good thing, too. The rumors were already rampant enough that Hannah and Carter were an item.

"Well, are you?" Sandy asked.

Hannah stared at her in surprise.

"An item?"

"Wait a minute…" Hannah said slowly. "I didn't say—"

"Simple intuition," Sandy said, cutting her off with a grin.

Later that night, Hannah called Ben.

"Well, hey there, stranger!" he answered. "Muffin and I were worried you'd fallen off the face of the earth."

"Is Lily in bed?"

"Unfortunately, yeah. She had her ballet recital today and she was pretty whipped. Did you know she was first swan?"

"No! How awesome. I bet she looked beautiful. I hope you recorded everything."

Ben chuckled fondly. "As if you have to ask."

"Good. I want to see the video. Can you send it to me?"

"Sure."

"So, how are things going there?"

"Oh, you know. The usual. I've gotten two new promotions at work, plus an enormous bonus and a raise. The Maserati's running fine, and I've just bought tickets for Europe. *Then,* there are all those pesky women who are after me. Let's see. There's the redhead June, and her cousin Julie—or is it, July? Hmm."

"Okay, stop!" Hannah cut him off in a fit of laughter. "You're killing me!"

She should have known she was asking for it. Ben never talked to her about his personal life. Hannah suspected that was because he didn't have much of one outside of Lily.

"I thought you wanted to know?"

"The truth, Ben. Heh."

"Lily's doing great." He took on a more serious, almost sentimental, tone. "But I'd be lying if I said we don't miss you."

"I miss you guys, too. A lot."

"So, how goes it in Christmas Town? Any more run-ins with the law?"

Hannah found herself wishing she hadn't shared that Santa story. "No, but I have seen the sheriff."

"Uh-huh," Ben said leadingly.

"And the good doctor."

"Now wait a minute—"

"And a whole bunch of other people too! Did I tell you I went to the church bazaar?"

"No, of course you didn't." He sounded about as dizzy as Hannah had felt when she'd first gotten here.

"I already knew some of the people, so it wasn't as bad as I thought. I mean, Lou was there, and Buddy, and Sandy—"

"She's your neighbor, right?"

"My *very good-looking and single* neighbor, yeah."

"Enough."

"She's *so* pretty and *so* nice, Ben. I really mean it."

"I'm sure she has slews of guys chasing after her in that case."

"Yeah, but none have caught her."

"I thought you were telling me about the church bazaar?"

"Oh right! It was too much fun. Seriously. Much more than I expected. I'd met Kurt, of course—"

"The doc?"

"Yes!" Man, he was good. No wonder he'd been smart enough to get through law school.

"So, Kurt was there."

"No!"

"Oh."

"He had some kind of thing—an emergency probably—at the hospital. But I finally met his brothers, Walt and Ray, and Ray's boy, Kyle…and Walt's twins, Noelle and Joy—"

"Whoa, slow down. I'm getting winded."

"I haven't even told you about Wendell!"

"Wendell?"

"Jade's husband."

"Have I heard about Jade?"

Hannah thought hard a moment. "Oops, sorry. Maybe not. Anyway, they have an *adorable* little boy, Alexander, who's best friends with Bobby Cho." This reminded Hannah what she wanted to talk to Ben about.

"Now you've lost me."

"Bobby Cho is five years old."

"Right. Got it," Ben said as if he were taking notes.

"His parents are Frank and Victoria. Victoria is the town deputy—"

"Ah-ha! Law enforcement. I knew it."

"Shut up. I'm trying to tell you something important."

"Yes ma'am."

"Frank Cho is an electrician!" Hannah found herself shouting.

"Wow. Explosive."

Hannah fumed.

When she didn't reply, Ben said tentatively, "Okay. Wired?"

"Ben—"

"Hannah, you've got to understand. I love you very much, Sis. But I have no idea where you're going with this. So many people in such little time."

"Just think of how I feel."

"Like you're ready to come home, I'll bet."

"Actually…" She hesitated an instant too long. "I'm feeling conflicted."

"Conflicted? I don't understand. About what?"

Hannah sighed heavily and sat on the sofa. She'd been pacing around the downstairs of her town house throughout the conversation and had finally worn herself out. She'd started in the kitchen, where she'd hoped to brew a soothing pot of herbal tea, but couldn't find that blasted tea ball. "Selling," she finally confided.

"You're joking. But, why?"

"Oh, only about a million reasons." Hannah's voice trembled.

"Hannah," Ben said kindly. "Talk to me."

And so, she did.

Chapter Eighteen

Carter strode up Santa Claus Lane toward South Main, blustery winds howling behind him. He'd patrolled this street more times than he could count during this week alone. At least this time he had something to show for it. Carter adjusted his grip on the trunk of the six-foot Fraser fir he'd purchased from Ray Christmas. It stood almost as tall as he did and was nice and full. It would look dynamite in the cabin. He had the perfect place to put it, on the far side of the woodstove, beyond the window. There were built-in bookshelves in that corner that would be blocked temporarily and he'd have to slide his leather club chair over, but Carter could live with the inconvenience in deference to the holiday.

This was the first Christmas that Carter would spend in Christmas Town and he was looking forward to it immensely. Since Hannah had said she'd be here at least a month, that meant she planned to stay through New Year's. Carter reached his truck and hauled the tree into its bed. Spindly green pine needles quickly disappeared beneath a blanket of snow. It was the powdery sort, though, so not bad for driving. Not that Rudolph couldn't handle a little ice. It was honestly his patrol car that had the most trouble with inclement weather, which was why Carter was glad he had this old Ford as a backup.

He intended to stop by All Things Christmas to pick up some ornaments for the tree and maybe a few other holiday odds and ends to scatter around his bachelor pad. Carter normally wasn't much for decorating, but everyone made the exception at Christmas, he reasoned. It just wouldn't be right for Carter to leave himself out. Plus, he really did want his place to look nice when Hannah came by. He'd spent all morning doing laundry and had even taken it upon himself to mop the hardwood floors. He'd had to call Olivia to ask what to use on them, and she'd scolded him for not tending to them previously. "What?" he'd asked in self-defense. "Isn't sweeping enough?"

Carter decided to leave his truck parked in front of the Grand Hotel and walk the short distance to Olivia's store. When he entered, he found her leafing through papers on the counter by the register. Olivia looked up with a dimpled grin. "Well, hey, little brother! To what do I owe the honor?"

"Tree ornaments." Carter shook out his coat sleeves over the sidewalk and shut the door.

"You've put up a Christmas tree?" The thought clearly delighted her.

"I'm in the process," he returned, smiling. Carter thumbed over his shoulder. "Just picked one up at the North Pole."

"Funny." She set her paperwork aside and stepped around the counter. "Well, come on," she said, motioning to him. "Let me show you where the ornaments are. I don't suspect you know."

Olivia had prepared a large display dangling from several fake trees near the back of the shop. There was even a miniature one on a table, but those weren't exactly ornaments on it. They looked like that accessory Hannah had worn in her hair during their date last Friday.

Olivia saw him staring and explained. "Those are not for trees, silly. Women wear them in their hair. They're called *barrettes*," she explained, as if he was five years old.

"I know what barrettes are."

"Sure you do."

Olivia quickly covered one side of her forehead with her hand. "What color is the one I'm wearing?"

"You're wearing a barrette?" he asked vaguely.

"Just as I thought." Olivia chuckled. "You've never noticed them, one way or another." She removed her hand, revealing a delicate candy cane barrette.

"That's simply not true. I've noticed them before, and yours is very pretty."

His sister eyed him suspiciously. "I'm curious about this." Olivia would be. She was always curious about everything, especially when it came to Carter, who she apparently still thought needed looking after. "Just when have you noticed them before?"

"Around. All right?" Her prying made him slightly agitated. He turned to the ornament display and began choosing the ones that he wanted.

Olivia picked up a wicker shopping basket and shoved it his way. He took it grumpily and began setting his selections down in it.

"I was just asking because I care," Olivia said with a little pout. After a few moments, she bowed her chin and said, "I'd also like to know who you've been cleaning for."

He turned to her, exasperated. "Olivia."

"I know, I know…" She held up her hands. "None of my business."

"Thank you." Carter went back to his work.

"The only thing is…"

He paused with a glittery star ornament hanging from his fingers. It sparkled and shone as it spun in the shop's soft light. Strings of Christmas bulbs were everywhere, their multicolored array twinkling against the walls and bouncing off the ceiling.

"I was just wondering if all this is about Hannah."

Carter slowly looked her way without saying a word.

"Because if it is…" Olivia shot him a winning grin. "I wouldn't be opposed."

Thursday night couldn't come quickly enough. Hannah was ready to get her mind off her worries for a change. She'd spent all of Tuesday with Buddy Christmas. In the morning, they'd gone to the shop to take photos for the sales listing. Then, they'd spent the afternoon going through paperwork. Lou had been an angel and carried lunch on a tray to Buddy's office: hot ham biscuits with homemade Brunswick stew. She'd even included some colorfully painted sugar cookies with Christmassy designs for dessert. But, through the entire process, Hannah's stomach felt sour. She'd filled out the realty papers, but had been unable to sign them. Buddy allowed her carry them home, telling her to take all the time that she needed to look them over.

Wednesday passed in a blur of graduate school applications, during which Hannah tried to distract herself and focus on living anywhere but in Christmas Town. While perfectly lovely, the stylized photos of the university campuses shown on their websites left Hannah feeling low. Due to her fractured family and early transitions, Hannah had never really had a true sense of home. In a short amount of time, Christmas Town already felt like that place. Ben had advised her to think things over, and not rush making a decision. He'd offered to help pay for the electrical work if she needed a float. Ben wasn't rich, but his credit was good. He could borrow the money, and Hannah could repay him in the future, once she was able. Yet Hannah didn't want to rely on Ben, not anymore.

Hannah reached for her earrings on the bed, finding one missing. Before taking her shower, she'd laid out her complete outfit, including jeans and her white V-neck sweater. She had two gorgeous pearl earrings that went with it nicely. Each dangled in a teardrop shape below a pretty, sparkly diamond. Real diamonds. They'd been a gift to her from her Grandma Mabel when she'd graduated from high school. *Oh no.*

She cried out in panic. "Jingles!" She'd shut the door to keep him out, but he must have pried it open with his little kitty paws. Belle, who'd been snoozing by her pillow sham, raised her head. "No worries," Hannah told her. "I know you're not the culprit." Then she cinched the towel around her and scooted out the door to find that mischievous orange cat.

Hannah paused halfway down the steps, thinking a moment. Then she pivoted quickly and raced right back upstairs again—and straight into the front bedroom. She could hear him purring even before she approached the bed. As quietly as she could, Hannah got down on all fours and craned her head low. It was Jingles, all right.

Sitting there like a miniature Lion King, proudly guarding his prizes. Hannah's Christmas barrette, the tea ball, and the newly missing earring rested on the carpet between his undulating paws.

A little while later, Carter helped Hannah into the passenger side of his truck. The wind was wickedly cold, but he had his heater going full tilt in the cab. He shut Hannah's door and scooted around the truck, thinking she looked prettier than ever tonight. While she'd been gorgeous all dressed up, she was somehow more stunning in a simple white sweater and jeans. The jewelry she'd added was a nice touch, too. Carter slid into the driver's seat, noting the way the dainty pearl earring played against the smooth line of Hannah's neck, just above her coat lapel. "I don't know how you do it." Hannah watched him expectantly and he found it even harder to speak. "Look more beautiful each time I see you."

Her cheeks went pink in the soft light reflected from the streetlamps. "I was just thinking the same about you."

Carter grinned, feeling pleased and hopeful about the evening ahead. "I'm glad you said you like pizza, because we're headed to pick some up. The Reindeer Pub is right on the way to my house. I hope you don't mind carry-out."

"No, that's so fantastic!" she rushed in with an enthusiasm he hadn't anticipated. She observed his expression and reined herself in. "What I mean is, I've seen their pizza and—oh my goodness—smelled it. I can't wait."

"Did you? When?"

"With Sandy," she said congenially. "We went for drinks on Monday."

"Girls' night?"

"Something like that." Hannah smiled happily, and Carter found himself wishing she always looked that way: carefree and delighted, like only good things were possible on earth. "So?" she asked, turning to him as she buckled her seatbelt. "Were you off the whole day?"

"Yeah, and good thing, too. I had lots of catching up to do."

"I know what you mean. I used to feel that way when I was..."

She appeared distant a moment, staring out the frosty windshield.

Carter reached out and lightly touched her arm. "What's wrong?"

"Nothing really." Hannah slowly shook her head and Carter saw she wore that snowman barrette again. It shimmered against her golden brown hair and offset the sparkle in her sweet brown eyes. "It's just funny how I was about to refer to my job at Braxton and Braxton."

"Like something from your past?"

"Yeah. That, exactly."

"Well, maybe it is."

She pursed her lips and waited for him to continue.

"From what you told me, you didn't like it much."

"No, that's true. When I left for the Thanksgiving holiday, I hoped I'd never have to return."

"Because of the cookie shop," he surmised. "Your inheritance?"

She shot him a desperate look. "Oh Carter, I don't know what to do."

"About the store?"

"About everything."

"I tell you what." He reached out and squeezed her hand. "Why don't we go grab that pizza and a couple of really cold beers, then we'll talk about it."

She stared gratefully in his eyes and Carter's heart warmed. "Sounds like a plan."

Chapter Nineteen

Hannah happily accepted another slice of pizza as Carter held it toward her plate. He'd given her the option of eating on the sofa by the woodstove or in the kitchen nook at the small rustic table. She'd opted for the comfy seating by the fire. A knotty pine coffee table stood before them holding two frosted beer mugs on coasters. The pizza box sat between their beers, still emitting delicious-smelling steam. The drive from the restaurant to Carter's cabin had taken less than five minutes, and when they'd picked up their order it had come straight from the oven, piping hot.

Hannah glanced around the room at the various pieces of furniture crammed together. The living area where they sat was toward the front of the house. A plaid armchair with a footstool was near the stove and a short table with a reading lamp stood beside it. The lower shelf of the table was stocked with hardcover novels, thrillers, and hardboiled mysteries by authors whose names she recognized. A window behind the table overlooked the front lawn and, Hannah imagined, the river and mountains in the daytime. It was situated beside the front door that led to the broad covered porch with a tin roof.

To the right of the stove, a leather club chair appeared to have been pushed forward in front of its side table. A fragrant Christmas tree stood in the corner, partially shielding the built-in bookshelves, and it was decorated to the hilt. "Gorgeous tree."

"Thanks," Carter said between bites of pizza. "Just put it up today."

Hannah noticed other holiday decorations scattered about, including a Christmas wreath made of twigs interspersed with holly hanging on the wall above the table in the nook. She even thought she'd spied some decorative Christmas tree towels and hot pads in the kitchen. Carter had briefly shown her the kitchen and pointed out the half bath in the hall between it and the living area when they'd first come inside. Hannah didn't see a television around, but suspected there might be one in the loft upstairs. "Your place looks really nice and put together," she told him. "Very in keeping with the season."

"This is my first Christmas here, so I thought I'd do it right."

"Really?"

"Got here in February. Right around Valentine's Day. I was the official Christmas Town lonely-heart bachelor."

"Stop it."

"I give Lou lots of credit, though. She tried her best…" His words fell off and he gave a heart-melting grin. "But failed."

"Something tells me you're a man who likes to make up his own mind."

"You got that part right." Carter set down his plate. "So tell me, what's going on with the cookie shop?"

"Nothing at the moment."

"Buddy hasn't put it up for sale?"

"I asked him to wait."

Carter's eyes lit in understanding. "This has something to do with Frank's estimate, doesn't it?"

"In part."

"What's the rest of the equation?"

"It's complicated." She frowned worriedly. "And getting more complex all the time."

Carter shook his head. "I had a feeling the bill would be steep. Rewiring's pretty costly."

"Other work needs to be done, too," Hannah said. "Either way."

"Either way, what?"

"Whether I sell it or keep it."

He stared at her in surprise, as she went on.

"The kitchen's completely antiquated. I'd need a new register, bookkeeping software—"

"Sounds like you've really thought this through." He sounded a little stunned. But, of course, he should be. The very idea that she'd consider reopening Lena's old shop was ludicrous.

Hannah started to panic. "I'd be in way over my head. I have no idea about running a business."

"Maybe one of your friends could give you some tips?" he offered helpfully. "Sandy and Jade each run their own operation. So does my sister."

That was true. Hannah hadn't considered this. "Olivia's very sweet. She called to check on me the other day when I missed lunch."

Carter viewed her with concern. "Did something happen?"

"I was at my shop and lost track of time. I'd spent all morning searching for the Virginia Cookie recipe and was feeling *so* discouraged."

"Why would you look there? I thought you said Lou gave you a whole box of cookbooks?"

"The recipe apparently isn't in a cookbook. It was handwritten—and kept very heavily guarded, according to Buddy and Louise."

"Top secret, huh?" Carter grinned and leaned forward. "Probably due to those cookies' side effects."

"I wonder why so many people believe it's true? That those cookies had magic?"

"Two explanations come to mind. The first one is simple. People believe because they want to believe." He shrugged. "The other answer is…it's true. Maybe they *were* kind of magical."

Hannah gave an incredulous laugh. "You can't mean it?"

Carter offered to clear her plate. She stood to help him, grabbing the pizza box and their empty beer bottles. She'd prepared a little surprise for Carter, hidden in her tote-size purse along with the wine.

"What's wrong with believing in magic?" he asked as Hannah followed him to the kitchen.

"Nothing's actually wrong with it," she answered. "It just doesn't make sense."

"Not everything makes sense, Hannah. Take the deepest human emotion of all." He set their dishes in the sink and turned to her. "Love."

Hannah nearly swallowed her tongue. "What's love got to do with it?"

"With your great-grandma's Virginia Cookies? Apparently, quite a lot. Just giving them as a gift could inspire all sorts of ardor, particularly when the gift was given from the heart."

"Who told you that?"

"Victoria."

"Has she been in Christmas Town long?"

"Born and raised here. And, according to her, her birth was a direct result of those Virginia Cookies. Victoria's grandpa presented a box of them to her grandma when they were courting and they fell instantly in love."

"No."

"Love at first bite." He winked and Hannah felt even warmer than before.

She set the pizza box on the counter, fanning herself with her hands. "You're throwing me off. I was trying to tell you about—"

"Another insect attack?" He viewed her worriedly.

"What?"

"When we first met, you had something buzzing around in your car."

"Oh that!"

"I've got to say, that's pretty unusual this time of year."

Then Hannah remembered she'd told him it wasn't an insect at all. She'd just been trying to fan some hot air his way. It was such a lame cover story, he must have seen right through it, and now he was teasing her.

Carter smacked his forehead as if remembering. "That's right. You were just doing the Good Samaritan thing. It was freezing and—"

"Carter!"

"Huh?"

"I'm not having an insect attack and I'm not trying to fan any of my…heat…your way." She gulped, realizing how bad that sounded.

"No?" He gave her a sultry perusal. "That's too bad. I wouldn't mind a little of your heat, darling."

Hannah flushed at the endearment and took a giant step backward. "Carter…"

"Baby, it's cold outside."

"You done now?"

"Not quite." He inched toward her.

She eyed him cautiously. "What are you doing?"

"I think you know." He pointed skyward, and she saw she'd positioned herself smack-dab under a sprig of mistletoe hanging from the doorframe dividing the living area and the kitchen. Hannah blinked, her mind drawing an enormous blank. She'd been about to tell Carter something important about the Christmas Cookie Shop, but he'd derailed her by talking about totally outlandish things like *magic* and *love*.

"I was trying to—"

His gaze simmered. "What were you trying to do?"

"I…um…talk to you about the recipe?"

"Hmm. Very special, I bet."

Carter brushed his lips over hers and she whimpered into his kiss. Tender yet commanding and branding-iron hot. "I…yeah. Ahh. Oh…Carter."

His touch trailed down her neck, settling at her nape. "Like this, do you?"

She nodded weakly and he kissed her again, tugging her up against him. His other hand was at the small of her back, pressing her closer. So close, Hannah nearly caught fire.

His husky whisper filled her ear. "When are you going to find that recipe?"

"Soon. Very soon," she said, her breath catching.

Hannah moaned when he nipped at her throat before returning his hot hungry mouth to hers.

"Will you make some for me?"

"As many as you want."

"Promise?"

"Uh-huh…"

"I could eat a whole box of them…" He rasped against her neck and goose bumps skittered across her flesh. Her legs went limp and her whole body trembled.

"Chilly?" he asked, holding her tighter.

Her pulse quickened. "Just the…opposite."

Carter deepened his kisses with adroit skill and Hannah sighed, her resolve crumbling. Reason was losing ground with sheer desire winning over. In another few minutes, they'd be upstairs in bed. "Carter," she whispered hoarsely. "You've got to— stop."

To her disappointment, he abruptly pulled back, his face flushed and his hair disheveled. There was wildfire in his eyes, but he was bringing it under control, though he was obviously struggling with the effort. He exhaled sharply and set his chin. "Okay."

What? She didn't mean… "No! I—"

"No?"

"Yes," Hannah panted heavily.

"Darling, you've got to be a little clearer than that." He viewed her perplexedly as Hannah's heart hammered. "With your signals."

She blurted out, her mind reeling, "I want to make cookies with you, really I do!" Oh boy, did she ever. He issued a low, sexy rejoinder.

"I'd like to make cookies with you, too. Very much."

"Just not…yet." When the timing was right, she couldn't wait to. But when would that time ever come? With her leaving Christmas Town forever, could Hannah really risk giving Carter such an important piece of her heart? She slumped against his chest and he strengthened his embrace. Her cheeks steamed as she stared up at him. *"Rain check?"*

A smile graced his handsome face: patient, kind, and understanding.

"You, sweetheart, can issue all the *rain checks* you want."

"Yeah?"

"Yeah."

He gave her a feather-light kiss, then warmly searched her eyes.

"Now, how about some dessert?" he offered. "I've got ice cream—"

"Chocolates!" Hannah answered brightly, her wind—and her sanity—returning.

"Chocolates?" he asked, intrigued.

"Chocolate truffles. I brought some in my purse."

"I thought that was a mighty big purse." Carter chuckled. "What else have you got in there?"

Hannah smiled happily. "A great big bottle of wine."

"Making good on one *rain check* at a time?"

"Something like that," she said, her skin burning hotter.

He smiled graciously and shot her a wink. "Fine by me."

Then he took her by the hand and led her to the sofa.

Carter got Hannah settled on the couch and added an extra log to the fire, before retrieving two wineglasses and a corkscrew from the kitchen. He didn't know why he'd gotten so carried away a moment ago. He could have eaten the woman alive. Hannah did something to him. Something no one else had ever done, not even Gina. Then again, with Gina, things were more on the surface. Hannah dug way down deep. She made him want to tell her things. Things he'd shared with nobody else. He sat beside her and accepted her outstretched bottle of wine.

"A very good year," he said, examining the label.

"It was a gift from Sandy."

Carter looked at her, thinking it was easy to want to give Hannah things. He'd give her the moon if he thought she'd take it. "Sandy and Lou keep you well supplied."

"This time, it was Sandy and Jade."

"Ah." He poured them each a glass and handed one to her. "To good friends, then."

"To good friends," she said, toasting him.

He took a swallow of wine, gathering his courage. "Hannah, about earlier…under the mistletoe—"

A soft smile played about her lips. "I didn't mind it."

"No?"

"I wasn't protesting, was I?"

"Truthfully, it was hard to tell." Carter cocked an eyebrow and Hannah laughed.

"Sorry about that. I didn't mean to send mixed signals." She set down her wine. "The fact is, I like you, Carter. I like you a lot." Color swept her cheeks. "More than that, I find you desperately attractive."

"Why do I sense a 'but' coming?"

"It's not you, it's Christmas Town. My uncertainty over what I'm going to do."

"You don't want to become involved if you're leaving."

Her expression said he'd nailed it. "I'm afraid I already *am* involved."

"Yeah—me, too." He slid a little closer to her on the sofa and draped an arm around her. "But I wouldn't change it," he said, meeting her eyes. "Would you?"

"Not for a minute."

Carter sweetly kissed her lips. "Good."

They sat for a while enjoying the warmth of the fire and the light pinging of ice against the tin roof. After a bit, Hannah picked up her wine, taking a sip.

"You really do have a beautiful cabin," she said, looking around. "Ultra cozy."

"Somehow it feels cozier with you here," he admitted hoarsely. And it was true. The cabin had never felt so much like a home until now—with Hannah in it.

Her face took on a cheery glow. "Have you always been a big fan of the holiday?"

"Christmas?"

"You've got so many decorations! It must have taken years to collect them."

Carter was embarrassed to admit he'd bought them all in one day, and specifically because of her. "Olivia was having a sale."

"Olivia?" Hannah's brown eyes sparkled. "You bought them at All Things Christmas?"

"Well, not everything of course," he said, leaving the illusion that perhaps he had decorated some previous year.

"Right. You got the tree at the North Pole, I'll bet."

"*And* the mistletoe." He nuzzled her neck and she giggled.

"You're a pretty spectacular date, you know that?"

He grinned, pleased. "Why, thanks, Hannah. You're no slouch in the dating department either."

"Here's to good dating partners." She lifted her glass and they toasted again.

Hannah reached for the candy box on the coffee table. "Shall we?" she asked as they both set down their wine. She pried back the lid and Carter recognized the logo from Nutcracker Sweets. While he'd never been in the store, the women around here seemed wild about it. His sister Olivia was a huge fan of their high-end confections.

"Don't mind if I do." Carter carefully chose a cocoa-colored morsel and popped it in his mouth. It melted almost instantly and was incredibly delicious. Meanwhile, Hannah selected a dainty white chocolate truffle and took a tiny nibble. "Mmm... *Soooo* good. Forget about flowers! The way to a woman's heart is definitely *here*."

"Duly noted," Carter said deftly. "The lady likes chocolates, not flowers."

"Oh, I wouldn't say that," Hannah amended. "There's nothing like a dozen roses."

"Color?"

"Red!" She covered her mouth, her cheeks turning crimson. "Not that I'm...er...hinting."

Carter chuckled happily and settled back on the sofa, wrapping his arms around her. "I'm glad to know what you like. I'm the sort of man who appreciates staying—"

"Informed?" she guessed, gazing up at him.

"Precisely," he said with a kiss.

Hannah snuggled up against his chest and sighed, and Carter's heart soared. *So this is what it's like: being contented with a woman.*

It struck Carter like a thunderbolt that he'd never known that feeling before. It occurred to him now that he'd been missing out. Only it was hard to imagine being this at ease with anybody else but Hannah.

"I'm sorry I interrupted you earlier," he said. "When you were trying to tell me about the recipe."

"No you're not," she answered sassily. "But I'll still tell you anyway. Lena's recipe is lost."

"Lost?"

"Okay, maybe stolen."

"That sounds like a matter for the law."

"It would be if anyone could prove it."

"What do you mean?"

"Lou and Buddy remember a file of handwritten recipes being in the box of cookbooks they gave me, but when I unpacked it, nothing like that was there."

"Seems kind of odd. Who would take a recipe file?"

She glanced up at him. "Who, indeed?"

"More importantly, why?"

"Oh, I know why," she said confidently. "Whoever took that file was looking for Lena's secret recipe."

"But, why?"

"I suppose it could be considered valuable—by someone who believed. And even if the thief didn't think the cookies were magical, they might have thought they could make money based on a marketing ploy. I mean, the cookies were legendary once upon a time."

"I've heard of people stealing lots of things, but never this." Carter appeared to mull things over. "You say you checked the box thoroughly?"

"Yes, why?"

"Well, it's odd that your grandpa left the box with Buddy rather than keeping it at home. He must have harbored some distrust or suspicion that someone might come looking for it."

"Go on."

"That tells me your grandpa wasn't a foolish man."

"No, he wasn't. He was very smart in fact."

"Smart enough to outfox a fox, I'd guess." When she stared at him, he added. "I'm thinking leaving something as precious as that recipe in the recipe file was too obvious. Your granddad likely tucked it away somewhere else. Someplace where you could find it."

Hannah ran a hand through her hair. "If only I knew where that was."

"I'd go back through that box, if I were you. Search it from top to bottom."

"I already have."

"Yes, but now your search will be more informed. You'll be looking for something that might be hidden."

"Right." She appeared as if she thought the situation was hopeless.

"I wouldn't throw in the towel on the cookie shop yet, just because you can't find that missing recipe," he said kindly. "There are lots of other things you can bake. Different ways to make the operation a success."

"You really think so?"

"I think you could probably do anything, if you put your mind to it."

She gave a sad frown. "Unfortunately, my mind and my money are two separate matters."

"I know." Carter hugged her to him, deciding he had to work on that. First though, Carter needed to know if her heart was in it. "Can I ask you a question?"

"Of course."

"If money were no object—"

"But it is."

"Humor me."

She smiled up at him and his heart melted. "All right."

"If money were no object," he said, starting again. "What would you do about the Christmas Cookie Shop?"

"If money were no object at all?" Her eyes glistened. For a long while, she didn't answer. Finally, she said, "I guess I'd take a chance. Take a chance and reopen Lena's store. I didn't think that's what I wanted to do until I came here. But once I got to Christmas Town, things started to change. *I* started changing. I know it sounds a little weird…"

"No, darling," he said, holding her tightly. "It doesn't sound weird at all." Carter knew just what Hannah meant. It wasn't only her. Christmas Town had changed him, too.

Chapter Twenty

The next morning, Carter made an appointment to meet Lou Christmas at Santa's Sandwich Shop during his lunch break to discuss calling a town meeting.

"I love the idea," Lou said, picking at the salad that had been served with her soup. "What does Hannah have to say about it?"

"Hannah doesn't know."

"Oh! No?" She considered this a moment, then broke into a grin. "A surprise? I like that."

"I didn't want to get her hopes up, until I'd fully investigated."

"You've always been a cautious man... Except when it comes to Hannah," she couldn't help adding with a titter.

"All right, it's true." Carter set down his sandwich and held up his hands. "I'll come clean with you, because I know you're dying to know..."

She was grinning like the Cheshire cat.

"The woman has gotten to me."

Lou's fork clanked to her plate. "Why, Carter," she said, beaming. "This is excellent news! So tell me, when's the wedding?"

Carter uncomfortably cleared his throat. "Let's just take this one hurdle at a time, shall we?"

She shrugged defensively and picked up her fork, stabbing into a radish. "Marriage isn't exactly like running in the Olympics, you know."

He viewed Lou surreptitiously, wondering if Buddy agreed. He was sure Buddy loved Lou, but some days that had to be a challenge. "No, but it's a commitment. A big one."

"Yes, and one that you're old enough to undertake. Listen, Carter, I've known you since…"

Uh-oh, here came the *since when you were in diapers* speech. He'd heard it at least a million times. It always started out—and ended—the same. With Lou giving him unsolicited advice. *As his godmother.*

"You simply don't let a girl like that get away from you." She finished talking and stared at him expectantly.

"Yes, yes. I hear what you're saying."

"Hear, aha! But did you listen?"

Truthfully, he'd tuned part of it out. Though Carter had gotten her not-so-subtle point. He took a sip of iced tea, deciding to ignore it. "About that town meeting… How soon do you think you can call it?"

"Let's see." She tapped her manicured fingernails against the table. "Since today's Friday, that's shot. I guess we could aim for Monday night, if we rush to get the word out."

"Hannah can't know."

"Oh, she won't," Lou said mysteriously. "I'll send the notice by Santa Mail."

Santa Mail was code for high priority e-mail in Christmas Town. While people sometimes ignored routine communications from Christmas Town Mayor

Louise Christmas, everyone always opened their Santa Mail. Particularly since the Christmas family was rumored to be in tight with the Clauses. "Ah, perfect."

Since Hannah wasn't on the town roster, she wouldn't receive a copy of the message, but every other taxpaying member of Christmas Town would. Carter needed to track down three other individuals before the Monday meeting: a real estate investor, an investment banker, and a stock option engineer. Carter didn't know of any such professionals locally, but there had to be a few in the surrounding areas. A quick phone call to Buddy Christmas should supply him with some names.

Hannah decided to give herself a break from computer work for the rest of the afternoon. She'd completed a total of six graduate school applications to date, and honestly didn't feel up to any more. It didn't help that her excitement about the prospect of an advanced degree had waned. Since admitting her secret wish to Carter, all Hannah had been able to think about was reopening the Christmas Cookie Shop. Hannah wanted to help people, but hadn't her great-grandmother provided a tremendous service to the community in her own way? She found mention of Lena's contributions in one of the local history books she'd discovered in her rental home, and eagerly devoured the story.

Lena apparently inherited the shop on Santa Claus Lane from her parents, Elizabeth and Harry O'Hanlon, who had run it as a bread-making bakery. Lena lost two brothers as well as her father to the First World War, but her betrothed, Emmet Winchester, returned. Sadly, both of Emmet's parents succumbed to the era's Spanish Flu epidemic, which also affected Lena's mother, causing her to lose her hearing, before she, too, became terminally ill a short time later.

Emmet was left to run his parents' hotel on Main Street, while Lena took charge of the O'Hanlon family business. At the encouragement of her schoolmate Eloise Christmas, Lena decided to rename the bakery and position it as a shop dedicated to producing only cookies. By the time World War I ended on November 11, 1918, several of Christmas Town's soldiers had fallen but others, including Lena's beloved Emmet, were blessedly able to come home.

Despite the tragedies that loomed around her, Lena took comfort in the joys of the season. Christmas was coming with its reassuring messages of hope and renewal. If only she could find a way to help the people of Christmas Town believe in those things as well, by somehow feeding their faith. Many had become despondent over losing loved ones due to illness and the war, and the resulting financial strain that had befallen those families.

While going through her late mother's cookbooks, Lena came across a newspaper clipping concerning a distant cousin in New York, who had written to the editor inquiring about the factual existence of Santa Claus. The editor's response so moved eighteen-year-old Lena, she became inspired to do something special for the people of Christmas Town.

She decided to bake a particular type of cookie, later reputed to have curative powers relating to matters of the heart. Upon accepting a cookie from another, one was liable to find oneself faithfully performing good deeds, fervently offering forgiveness, or feverishly falling in love. Parents bought them for their children to induce good behavior. Others gave them to those they'd wronged to foster forgiveness. But an even greater number proffered them to their objects of affection, hoping to receive sincere ardor in return.

The legend of these Virginia Cookies spread like wildfire, but—despite tremendous demand—Lena claimed she was unable to produce them more than once a year. She always made them at Christmastime and during the Advent season approaching the holiday, baking them in abundance during particular times of need. During the Great Depression, it was said she gave them out for free after bartering for ingredients with her fellow townsfolk. She made similar concessions during other periods of local or national strife, and never denied a patron who petitioned her with good intent. In the early days, her dear friend, Cordelia Claus, served as some sort of uncanny barometer in that regard, prior to relocating to the Maritime Provinces of Canada with her husband, Nicholas.

Whether or not historians judge the legend of the Virginia Cookie to ring true, Lena O'Hanlon Winchester did an undeniable service to the citizens of Christmas Town by uplifting their hearts and improving their spirits for more than sixty years. The recipe for her special cookies was never revealed. It was held to be a family secret.

Hannah shut the heavy tome, sliding it onto the coffee table. Belle lay sleeping beside her, and Jingles had finally worn himself out batting at a glittery toy by the front door. The orange tabby stretched out on his side in an uncustomary position of repose. Hannah had been impressed by her great-grandmother before, but was even more in awe of her accomplishments now.

What a unique and wonderful woman Lena was to put the happiness of others first. Hannah found herself wanting to do the same, aspiring to make that kind of difference. Was Carter's faith in her well founded? Could she really bring Lena's old business back if she tried?

Hannah had gone through the box of cookbooks again this morning. She'd searched it from top to bottom, just as Carter instructed, but still came up dry. There was no recipe stashed away for her to find. So she'd just have to devise a way to get by without it. She could start by asking for help from her friends at lunch. Hannah couldn't wait to learn what Sandy, Olivia, and Jade had done in order to open their businesses. Maybe there was something she hadn't thought of that could help her start her own. Hannah's initial question was very basic. It had to do with financing.

In the meantime, Hannah looked forward to seeing Carter again. He was working this weekend, but offered to meet her on Sunday afternoon for coffee. Rather than go to Jolly Bean Java, he suggested they connect at the bookstore. Hannah hadn't been inside, so she didn't know it housed a small café. The plan sounded ideal.

Hannah felt a cheery glow spread across her cheeks and realized she was smiling. But what woman wouldn't, after what Carter told her last night? He'd admitted to feeling involved, and said that he didn't regret it. Hannah didn't regret that part either. Not one bit. She loved everything about Sheriff Carter Livingston and ached to know more about him. She was particularly intrigued by the life he'd led before coming here. Carter was a private guy who didn't seem to share things easily. Yet Hannah had the sense he was opening up to her. If she was extra lucky tomorrow, she might learn a little more.

Carter walked in the door and Hannah's pulse raced. He was so good-looking, it was hard to believe he was hers. Almost hers. *Somewhat mine?* He grinned when he spotted her at a table and made his way through tall bookshelves and tables stocked with children's toys for sale. The selection of merchandise appeared educational and quality-made. Hannah guessed that was Jade's touch.

Carter removed his hat and set it on the table. "Been waiting long?"

"Just got here myself," Hannah said, still unbuttoning her coat.

"Good." He glanced at the chalkboard menu display behind the counter. "What's your pleasure?"

"I think I'll have cocoa today."

"Cocoa it is." He turned to walk over and place their orders.

Hannah reddened. "I didn't expect you to… What I mean is, I can get my own."

Carter peered over his shoulder. "Nonsense. Haven't you heard?" He winked and her insides fluttered. "We're an item."

According to whom? Hannah wondered. Was this more about town gossip, or the way Carter really felt? Besides, it was a little ballsy of him to say it without actually asking her if she agreed.

A few minutes later, he returned with two steaming cups in his hands.

Hannah sat up a little straighter and accepted her cocoa. "Since when are we an item?" she asked.

"Oh, I'd say…" Carter made a show of studying the ceiling. "Since about Thursday night when you said you wanted my whole box of cookies."

"Carter, shush!" She swatted his arm. "Did not!"

"Most certainly did."

Hannah dropped her voice to a whisper. "*You're* the one who said he wanted *mine*."

Carter grinned over the rim of his cup. "That sweet tooth is a killer."

"You are *so* not getting away with this."

He put on his utmost look of innocence. "Getting away with what?"

Hannah leaned forward to whisper again. "Acting like we're exclusive when—"

"*Exclusive.* Sweet. I like the sound of that."

Hannah exhaled sharply. "So, are we?"

"I sure hope so." He reached out and took her hand. "Otherwise, I'm going to drop down and die right on this very floor."

"What's wrong with my floor?" Jade asked him in mock complaining tones. "And, hi, Hannah! How are you?" She glimpsed their interlocked hands and her face lit up. "Very well, I see," she said, answering her own question.

"Jade! It's great to see you. I'm so sorry about last week, but I'm really looking forward to tomorrow."

Jade and Carter exchanged startled glances. Then, obviously, Jade remembered. "The lunch! That's right." She frowned, but seemed to be working too hard at it. "I'm sorry, Hannah, but lunch tomorrow's going to be tough. I…have a really busy day. Tons to do."

Hannah was truly disappointed, and not just because she'd intended to ask Jade business questions.

Hannah already counted Jade among her friends. "You mean, you're not going to be able to make it?"

"I'm afraid none of us can," she said, looking regretful. Why did Hannah have the suspicion it was a sham? What on earth was going on? Had Hannah offended them all that badly by missing one date?

"Oh, I…see. That's too bad." She tried not to let the hurt show in her voice.

"I'm sure you ladies will make it up. Some other time." Carter reassuringly squeezed her hand and she recalled he was hanging on to it. He shot Jade a look. "Right, Jade?"

"Oh yes, absolutely! Oh, hey!" she said, waving to one of the Christmas twins who'd walked in the door. "Here comes Noelle, arriving for her shift. I'm afraid I've got to go and fill her in on a few things." Then she was off, lickety-split, periodically peeking back in their direction.

"She was acting kind of weird," Hannah commented, when Jade was gone.

"Probably just holiday jitters. It's getting closer to Christmas, you know. Have you thought about what you want?"

Hannah hesitated. "From…?"

"In general."

"Oh. Yes. Well. Of course, if wishes were horses and beggars could ride—"

"The Christmas Cookie Shop. To reopen it and make it successful."

"It's a dream, I suppose."

"Nothing wrong with dreaming. Especially at Christmas."

"How about you?"

His green eyes sparkled. "I'd like to wake up to a stocking stuffed with rain checks."

"So we're exclusive. Just like that." She wasn't really going to fight him on it when the very thought made her heart dance and sing.

"No, I'd say it was more of a slow build." He viewed her thoughtfully. "That started at the roundabout, then avalanched when you first gave me that smile—oh, about ten seconds later."

Hannah grinned in spite of herself. "I knew when you first asked for that rain check."

"Clever of me."

"I hope it's not a habit." She hated the thought of Carter being with another woman. "With anyone else but me."

"Hannah, sweetheart. You're my first, my last, and my only."

"That's quite a statement for four o'clock."

"Maybe so, but it's true."

Hannah sensed this was her opening. "Where were you before Christmas Town?"

"Richmond, Virginia. Before that, Afghanistan."

"Military, both places?"

"Police force in Virginia, about five years." He paused to study her. "Why do I feel like I'm being interrogated?"

"Oh, sorry!" Hannah ducked her head with a blush. "I just seriously wanted to know."

"All right," he said smoothly. "So, now you do."

"What branch?" she asked casually.

He laughed in surprise. "The lady has staying power." He gave her hand a firm squeeze, then released it, gripping the brim of his hat. "I was in the Tenth Mountain Division. Army Infantry Light. ROTC at

Villanova, then various deployments…around." His face took on a dark cast and Hannah suddenly regretted broaching the subject. She hadn't meant to bring Carter down. "Some domestic. Others overseas. A few I can't talk about."

"Carter, I'm sorry," she said sincerely. "I didn't mean to pry."

"It isn't prying when you care." He shared a sad smile. "That's what Lou Christmas says, anyway."

Hannah approached things gently. "I've taken you back somewhere I shouldn't have."

He met her eyes and for the first time she saw remorse in his, like storm clouds rolling over the desert. "No place I haven't been before."

"Carter, I…" She felt useless, inept, tongue-tied. "I don't know what to say."

"Most women don't."

Uh-oh. It sounded like things were going from bad to worse. Then Carter caught her off guard with a compliment.

"That's where you're different. You're not most women. You may not know what to say now, but you will eventually. And then you'll tell me, won't you?" He leaned forward and stroked her cheek, speaking in a gravelly whisper. "Because I always want you to tell me…" His thumb lightly grazed her lips and Hannah's pulse quickened. "What you're thinking and feeling."

But how she was feeling right now was far too dangerous to share. It was like she was diving headlong, tumbling fast—into a crazy free fall, from which there was no return. "Okay."

Carter's phone buzzed and he checked the number. "Really sorry about this, but I'm going to have to go."

"Duty calls?"

"My civic duty," he said with an enigmatic smile. "Yes, it does."

He stood and tapped down his hat. "I forgot to ask, did you ever find that recipe?"

"No."

"Don't give up hope, Hannah. Not yet."

"On the Virginia Cookies?"

Carter squared his broad shoulders, shoulders big enough to take on the weight of the world. They were shoulders Hannah was starting to believe she could lean on, and ones she yearned to wrap her arms around. "On anything. Don't forget…" He shot her a wink. "Santa's coming."

Chapter Twenty-One

For the first time since arriving in Christmas Town, Hannah actually felt lonely. Everybody seemed to have other plans today. She'd been in Christmas Town three weeks now and Christmas was right around the corner, less than a week away. Before leaving Stafford, she had exchanged gifts with Ben and Lily, knowing they'd be spending the holidays apart. Hannah had committed to being in Christmas Town and Ben was taking Lily to visit Nancy's parents in San Francisco. That's where Ben and his late wife had met: at Berkeley, when they'd both been undergraduates.

While she hadn't expected to be in this position, it occurred to Hannah now that she'd need to purchase several more presents. Surely, she should get something for Sandy. For Jade and Olivia, too. And she couldn't forget Buddy and Louise Christmas. Then there was Carter...

A lump formed in Hannah's throat. She had no idea what to get him. She'd seen his cabin and it seemed well supplied. Plus, he was the sort of guy who probably purchased whatever he needed. He'd joked about wanting rain checks, but Hannah had to do better than some paper IOUs. She didn't have to decide on anything today, but she couldn't take forever to think about it either. She could try talking to Kurt, but suspected he might be clueless. Then a lightbulb went on—she could ask Victoria Cho!

Hannah tiptoed into the sheriff's office at the county courthouse, stealthily scanning the area to ensure Carter wasn't around.

"Can I help you, dear?" The elderly woman with a plump round face and springy red hair smiled pleasantly. A pair of lemon-yellow reading glasses hung on a chain around her neck. She wore a snug polyester dress with many Santas and their teams of reindeer flying off in all directions. The nameplate on her desk read *Tilly Anderson.*

Hannah glanced at the closed door behind her. "Is the sheriff in?"

Tilly's grin broadened, hot pink lipstick creasing. "Just a moment. I'll buzz him."

"No wait!" Hannah said in hushed tones. "It's actually Victoria I want to see. Victoria Cho?"

"Out on an errand, I'm afraid. But she should be back... What luck!" she said, as Victoria strode in the door. "There she is now!"

"Hi!" Hannah said, suddenly feeling foolish. Perhaps she should have prepared what she was going to say.

Victoria eyed her oddly and unzipped her coat. "It's Hannah, right?"

"Yes. That's right. Hannah Winchester. I... The sheriff and I... I mean, Carter..."

Hannah and Victoria turned to Tilly, who'd planted her elbows on her desk and rested her chin on her hands. She was watching them with interest, and very obviously listening.

"Er, do you think we could talk in the hall?"

"Sure." Victoria stripped off her coat and laid it across a chair at another desk, telling Tilly she'd return in a minute.

Tilly frowned in patent disappointment. "Well, don't take too long. Don't forget I've got plans tonight. In fact, we all—"

"Got it, Tilly!" Victoria hastily hooked an arm through Hannah's and tugged her out the door. "Sorry about that." She led Hannah around the corner and released her. "You were saying?"

Hannah rubbed the crook of her arm in mild shock. "I was just hoping to get a little information from you," she said quietly.

Victoria arched her eyebrows.

"On Carter," Hannah continued.

"I see."

"It's about his Christmas gift."

"Hang on! Are you two like…" She made a dueling pistols motion with her hands pointing them at each other. "Dating?"

A tall, distinguished gentleman in judge's robes walked by and Victoria straightened at attention. "Evening, sir!" she called as he passed by.

"Be seeing you later, Deputy Cho," he returned with a jovial wave.

Hannah felt like the only kid who hadn't been invited to the party. Then she told herself not to be silly. It was probably some law enforcement thing, or a county servant Christmas event. When the man disappeared up the polished steps, Victoria's posture relaxed.

"I was just wondering if you knew of anything that Carter would like?"

"Yeah, I do," Victoria said wryly. "Mostly he would like for me to stay out of his business."

Hannah's shoulders sagged as she deduced this was a wasted trip.

"But I do know of something he needs."

"Really?" Hannah asked, her hope returning.

"Yes," Victoria said decidedly. "A new wallet."

"A wallet?" Hannah's heart sank. That wasn't exactly groundbreaking, but what on earth had she expected?

"The one he has is very old," Victoria continued. "I'm sure it needs replacing."

"Right! Great idea! Well, thanks so much, Victoria. Sorry to have troubled you."

"No trouble. Merry Christmas."

"Thanks. To you, too."

A few hours later, Hannah dropped her shopping bags on the dining room table and slumped into a chair, feeling exhausted. She'd been by All Things Christmas to purchase a new hair barrette for Jade, and then to the Snow Globe Gallery to buy one of Sandy's pretty hand-painted tree balls for Olivia. She'd found a lovely art book featuring Currier and Ives Christmas paintings at the Elf Shelf Book Shop for Sandy, and secured a large box of fancy chocolate truffles for Buddy and Louise from Nutcracker Sweets.

After a quick trip to the pharmacy, her last stop had been at the men's shop, Santa's Suited Up!, which was located by the bank. It was there that she procured the requisite leather wallet for Carter. It wasn't the greatest present in the world, but it could serve as a backup until Hannah thought of something better.

While her feet ached from shopping, Hannah's ego hurt a little more. She'd felt summarily brushed aside by Olivia, who'd been helping other customers, and nearly out-and-out ignored by Sandy, who'd seemed to have her mind on something else entirely. At least, sweetly shy teenager Noelle Christmas had shown her some individual attention. She'd led Hannah straight to the art section of the bookstore and had offered a selection of a few choice books. Jade didn't appear to be anywhere in the store. If she was, and she'd spotted Hannah, she hadn't bothered to say hello.

Hannah wasn't sure what had been going on with the residents of Christmas Town these last few days, but everyone seemed out of sorts. She'd seen Lou leaving the Merry Market this afternoon, her arms loaded down with bags. Hannah was going to offer to help her, but Lou quickly disappeared around the corner—and out of sight. Had she only imagined it, or had Jade's husband, Wendell Scott, purposely ducked behind the pharmacy counter when he saw her enter Christmas Town Drugs to stock up on wrapping paper and ribbon? *Then,* when she'd passed Frank on her way back from the men's shop, he'd stared at her wide-eyed and said, "Hannah! What are you doing out?"

Out? Like she was one of the kittens, who'd escaped? Hannah had to steel herself to keep from bursting into tears on more than one occasion. These weren't the friendly, warmhearted people she'd come to know and love. It was almost like aliens had taken over their bodies! In all this madness, only one person seemed to have remained relatively the same. Carter. Maybe Hannah should just call him up and ask if he'd noticed it, too? At least he might have some reasonable explanation for everyone's odd behavior, so she wouldn't feel singled out.

She pulled her cell from her purse and dialed. He answered on the second ring.

"Hannah!" There seemed to be some kind of hubbub going on in the background, with lots of loud talking.

"Carter? Are you...?" She was about to say, *at a party,* but wait! Was that the sound of a gavel smacking down? "In court?"

"Yes," he asserted quickly. "Last minute thing. Couldn't be helped."

"Sounds like half the town is there."

"Not half. Not really."

"This meeting will come to order!" a shrill woman's voice shouted. *Hang on, I know that voice. Louise Christmas?*

"Sorry, sweetheart," Carter said brusquely. "Can't talk now."

"But—"

"I'll call you later, all right?"

Before she could utter *okay* he'd already clicked off.

Hannah leaned against the seat back, feeling more dejected than ever. At least Carter wasn't ignoring her completely, like some of the other folks around here. But who were all those people with him? And what kind of court held hearings at night? None of this made any sense. Hannah frowned, resisting that nasty tug on her emotions. The one that told her she'd misjudged her opportunity in Christmas Town, and misread the way its people felt about her. As if sensing her mood, the kittens scampered over. Jingles reached her first, but Belle wasn't far behind him.

Hannah studied their little faces, thinking how much bigger each of them had grown in just a month. Lily had given them to Hannah right before her trip to Christmas Town. Suddenly, Stafford seemed a million miles away. Hannah had a compelling urge to call Ben and talk to him and Lily both. Yet she knew they were on a plane and halfway across the country, headed to California. "I'll bet you're hungry, huh?"

When the cats mewed plaintively in reply, Hannah struggled her way out of her chair. "First you, then me," she said, thinking glumly that she'd scrounge something up. Afterward, she'd brew herself a pot of peppermint tea, and—since she didn't have any other plans for the evening— take one last look in that cookbook box.

Hannah lifted the kettle off the stove, but her scarf rippled in front of her, blocking her view and getting dangerously close to the burner. She'd gotten the gorgeous new acquisition at South Pole Pottery on her way home from shopping. Apart from ceramics, the store sold a variety of handcrafted items, including purses, belts, and earrings. She'd spotted the colorful teal and purple scarf interwoven with shimmery silver and gold threads on a carousel display by the checkout counter. It had a pretty beaded fringe that ended in a cascade of glimmering miniature disks that twirled and caught the light when she'd held up the scarf to examine it. Hannah had bought it on impulse, thinking she deserved to get at least one treat for herself. Particularly after such a hard day, when she'd been snubbed by virtually the entire community.

Hannah flipped the scarf back over her shoulder and set about making her tea, guarding her precious tea ball all the while. Jingles heard the light tapping of the metal ball against the ceramic pot when Hannah dropped it inside and scampered into the kitchen. "Not this time, buddy boy," she told him. "I've finally learned my lesson concerning tea balls and you."

Jingles let out a low soft whine and Hannah laughed.

"All right, you. Why don't you come and help me with my task?"

Hannah carried the teapot and a mug to the dining room table, passing the sofa where Belle was sleeping on her way. The fluffy gray fur ball was apparently too exhausted from eating to offer any assistance. "That's fine! Just lie there. Rest up for your next meal."

Hannah located the box in the corner behind the table, and Jingles followed close on her heels. "Let's set this down on a chair, shall we?"

Jingles watched intently as Hannah unfolded the flaps of the box. Unfortunately, it looked just as it had the last time she'd opened it. Hannah kept having this odd fantasy that if she really wished for it to be there, the missing recipe file might magically appear. No. Such. Luck. "Top to bottom," she mumbled to herself. She'd decided to take everything out and flip through the pages of every book one last time. Since there were quite a lot of them, this would probably take all night.

Hannah leaned forward to grab an armload of books and her scarf dangled forward, slipping off the side of her neck. The next thing she knew, the whole length of it was tumbling into the box. "Oh!" She quickly set the books down on the table and turned back around, but she wasn't fast enough. Jingles had leapt up against the side of the box and caught one end of her scarf in his mouth. "Jingles!"

The next thing Hannah knew, he was tearing across the floor carrying one end of the scarf as her beautiful new accessory unfurled itself, floating out of the box. The vision reminded Hannah of the classic magician's trick of pulling a never-ending series of handkerchiefs from a hat. *The old hat trick.* Or at least one of them. Another had to do with a white rabbit. Hannah raced after the cat and caught him midway to the stairs. "No you don't, you scamp!" Very gingerly, Hannah extracted the end of her scarf from his teeth. It was *kitty time-out* time. Again.

Hannah tucked Jingles in the carrier in the kitchen, wondering if he'd ever outgrow this. Belle had scarcely moved a muscle during the entire ordeal. She'd only lifted her head, just barely, to blink at Hannah as she'd toted Jingles to the pokey. "At least one of you is good," she'd said to Belle, thinking perhaps she should rename the pair Naughty and Nice.

Hannah headed back to the table and poured herself some tea. It had brewed fully by now and was tangy and delicious, its minty taste nipping at her tongue. She relived the image of her scarf floating out of the box, and something in Hannah's mind clicked. And then it clicked again, like a cog in a wheel that was stuck, and wouldn't move forward. Hannah set down her mug. *What is it about that scarf that matters? Scarf? Hat? Trick?* She stopped herself, realizing it wasn't the scarf; it was the box. Not just the box, the hatbox! The hatbox involved a trick! Yes, that was it!

She got to her feet and quickly cleared the upper contents of the big box, setting them on the table. Then she centered the circular green hatbox in her hands and hoisted it onto another chair. Was it possible? As tenderly as she could, Hannah plucked the antique cookbooks from their nesting places and laid them with the other items on the table. The hatbox smelled musty and was lined with patterned cloth, which appeared to be made of silk. Hannah ran her hands around the smooth circular inner walls of the box, and along its bottom.

Next, she flipped over the lid to search its lined underside. Nothing seemed amiss until she felt something different with her fingertips. *There!* Wait…and *there.* Hannah counted. She'd found barely perceptible ridges somehow sequestered beneath the material. Oddly, there were four of them. Two short and two long. She increased the pressure of her touch, tracing the object. Approximately, three by five inches… Hannah's heart raced. It had the dimensions of an index card.

Chapter Twenty-Two

Carter bid Judge Holiday good night and locked the courtroom door. It had been a productive Town Hall meeting, not to mention an extremely animated one. Every person in attendance was behind the idea of Hannah reopening the Christmas Cookie Shop. Once Louise Christmas helped them understand that the nature of the problem was financial, the vote was unanimous that the town should help solve it. It was in Christmas Town's interest to have thriving businesses here. Lena's old shop wasn't just historic; it was a town institution.

No resident of Christmas Town could deny they'd heard tell of Lena's special Virginia Cookies. Their magic was credited with inspiring the marriages of the antecedents of many folks here. When Lou asked all to stand who attributed the start of their family lineage to Lena's Virginia Cookies, Carter was astounded by the flurry of people who'd risen from the courtroom benches. He'd known about Victoria Cho and Lou and Buddy Christmas, but had had no idea there were so many others.

Carter had invited a few speakers to come and address the crowd. All were business professionals with different ideas about how the townsfolk could help. When the preferred option was voted on and selected, Buddy Christmas passed around a clipboard asking for contact information from those volunteering their assistance. He'd run out of paper six times, sending Tilly on mad dashes to the sheriff's office to grab more legal pads. On her final trip, she'd brought a whole stack. Plus two additional clipboards and extra pens.

Carter hauled the huge pile of legal pads back to his office and placed them on Tilly's desk. She'd agreed to start typing the names and information into a spreadsheet when she returned to work on Wednesday. Many folks in attendance at the meeting had come representing their families. So one name on the list could actually mean two or more people who might contribute. Others wrote down the names of friends they were sure would want to help. These were on a separate list of people that Tilly was supposed to contact once Carter drafted his letter laying out the particulars of the plan. If any of these other individuals were interested in participating, they would be added to the master spreadsheet.

Joy had raised her hand, offering to reach out to teens through social media. She was sure they'd find the group cause cool and several had part-time jobs like she and Noelle, so they might be willing to join the effort. Carter was hesitant about having kids become involved, but Buddy countered that allowing them to take initiative was a fine idea. Still, all agreed that only legal adults over the age of eighteen would be allowed to donate money. Judge Holiday had pretty much insisted on this. Carter's blood pumped harder when he realized this could really work. The whole town was coming together in such an incredible way. His step felt lighter just knowing he'd played a critical part by proposing the idea to begin with. But Carter's role wasn't over yet. There was tons left to do and he was under a tight deadline. In order to give Hannah what he wanted to for Christmas, he'd need to work fast.

It was nearly ten o'clock when Carter phoned Hannah. "I hope I'm not calling too late?"

Hannah snuggled back against her headboard. She'd been working on her laptop, happily researching basic cooking methods. Surely, things couldn't be as complicated as those cable network chefs made them out to be. After her wonderful discovery, all the tension had gone out of her. She felt elated, yet peaceful…and incredibly tired. So she planned to go to bed early and call Buddy Christmas in the morning. Her mind was made up: She wasn't selling the Christmas Cookie Shop. Against all odds, she'd find a way to make things work, even if she had to accept Ben's offer and let him cosign her loan. Her college debt would take longer to pay off than she'd hoped, but she'd settle it eventually. "No, not too late at all! How are you? How was the meeting?"

"Actually…" His tone was incredibly chipper. "A lot better than expected."

"Well, good."

"So? What have you been up to tonight?"

Hannah had considered telling him about her find, then decided to wait. She wanted to make it a surprise. "Just reading…" She shut her laptop. "Stuff."

Carter laughed. "Good stuff or bad?"

"Kind of excellent, truthfully."

"Wow. You'll have to give me the title of that book."

"You and I don't read the same things, Carter."

"How do you know?"

"I've been to your place and seen your bookshelf."

"Oh, yeah." He paused and drew in a breath. "Listen, Hannah, Christmas is right around the corner and it's just occurred to me that we haven't made plans."

"Sounds like an oversight for a couple that's *an item.*"

"My thinking precisely. Unfortunately, I'm working on Christmas Day, but I was wondering if I could take you to church on Christmas Eve? There's a midnight service, the sort with caroling and candles."

"I like that church. Pastor Wilson is awesome."

"Yeah, he is. So, that's a yes?"

"That's a definite yes," Hannah said, grinning. "Will you come to dinner first?"

"Sounds great."

Hannah had no idea what she'd be making. Hopefully, something that wasn't too complicated. Perhaps her girlfriends could supply some tips. That was, if they were still talking to her. "Carter, I need to ask you something. Do you think I said or did something to offend people?"

"What people?"

"The people of Christmas Town. Everybody's acting weird. Remember Jade and how she was behaving at the Elf Shelf? Well, Lou was acting like that, too. So were Sandy and Olivia. Then, when I saw Frank, he—"

"Hannah," Carter said, cutting her off. Then he softened his tone and said sweetly, "It's the holidays. People are stressed. Everyone's frantically trying to prepare for Christmas."

"Yeah, but shouldn't that make people happy? We're in Christmas Town, after all."

For a moment he was speechless. "Even in Christmas Town people get harried. I'm sure things will look better tomorrow."

"Tomorrow? But Christmas is at the end of the week."

"That's true. Which reminds me! You haven't been introduced to the river."

"The river? Carter, are you feeling all right? It's still below freezing outside—and it's snowing."

"Ideal conditions for River Run."

"What's River Run?"

"The area up past my cabin where people swim in the summertime, and cross-country ski in winter. It's really beautiful and isolated."

Hannah had a bad feeling about where he was going with this. She wasn't much of an athlete and had never been skiing. "I thought you were working. Duty calls?"

"I've got a bunch to do tomorrow, it's true. But Wednesday morning I should have some time. My secretary will be in and working on a project for me."

"Are you sure Tilly won't mind?"

There was silence down the line. "I didn't say her name was Tilly."

Oops. "I…er… Didn't you tell me that earlier?"

"Not that I recall."

"That's right!" she fibbed. "Must have been Victoria!"

"Victoria?"

"When I saw her at the church bazaar."

"I wish Victoria would just pull away from work for a change," he said, sounding a little disappointed.

"You know, take a mental break from the job. But she's so dedicated."

"Yes! Well, anyway—"

"So, you'll come?" he asked, before adding, "It would be a really big help to me, you know. I've been stuck indoors forever."

"I thought you walked a beat?"

"Not the same thing. Not at all."

"Well, I don't know…" Hannah would do anything to spend time with Carter. Well, almost anything. Apart from making herself out to be a fool on skis, and quite possibly breaking a leg. Finally, a decent excuse occurred to her. "What I mean is… Carter, of course you know I'd love to go skiing with you, but the truth is I didn't bring the right kind of clothes—"

"Which is why I called Olivia before talking to you!" he explained quickly. "You and she are about the same size. She said she's happy to loan you everything!"

"Everything?"

"Skis, bibs, goggles, coat. She'll drop the gear by your house tomorrow!"

"Are you sure you wouldn't prefer another coffee? I know! How about the Reindeer Pub?"

"On Wednesday *morning*?"

"Oh right. Bad idea. I just thought, since you're on your feet all the time…"

"Actually, I spend a lot of time at my desk."

"How about a stroll, then? We can start on Santa Claus Lane and—"

"No!"

Why did he have to sound so panicked about it? "I was just offering suggestions."

"I'll make you a deal," he finally said. "Just humor me and try it. If you're not having the time of your life, after an hour we'll go back to my place and drink cocoa."

"An *hour*?"

"Okay, forty-five minutes."

Why on earth is he being so difficult? "Thirty minutes."

"Done."

"Then we'll go back to your place and drink cocoa—by the fire. And it better be a big one, big and warm."

Hannah was surprised to get a call the first thing the next morning from an unknown number. "Hi, Hannah! It's Jade."

"Oh, Jade. Hello! What a nice surprise." She was puttering around in her kitchen waiting for her coffee to finish brewing, while the kittens kept winding around her ankles trying to trip her.

"I'm calling with an apology and an invitation," Jade said forcefully. "First, I wanted to say I'm sorry for how I acted the other day. When I saw you at the bookstore on Sunday, I know I seemed distracted, but I didn't mean to be rude."

"Oh no, you weren't rude. I was just wondering if…" The coffeemaker beeped, signaling it was done, and Hannah poured herself a cup. "Everything's all right?"

"All right, how?"

"Between us? Between all of us? You, me, Olivia, and Sandy?"

"Yeah, of course. That's the other reason I'm calling. Wendell and I are having Sandy and Olivia join us for the holiday and we'd like to invite you."

Hannah was so touched she wanted to cry. "You mean on Christmas?"

"Christmas Day, that's right. I'm making a big turkey with stuffing. My dad will be there, too."

"That sounds really wonderful, Jade. I'd love to come."

"Olivia told me Carter's working. Otherwise, we'd naturally include him as well. Maybe he can stop by on his break or something. Will you ask him?"

"Of course. Can I bring anything?"

"How well can you cook?"

"Uh…" Hannah choked on her coffee.

"Are you all right?"

"Yeah, fine. Sorry!" She wiped her mouth with a paper towel and set down her cup. "I don't cook very well, to tell you the truth. Actually, not at all."

"*You don't cook?* Seriously?" Why did she sound so shocked? "So it's just desserts, then?" Oh gosh, Hannah sure hoped Jade wouldn't ask her to bring something exotic like figgy pudding. She didn't even know what was in it. "You're a baker?"

"Not…technically. But I've been looking a lot of stuff up online."

"Stuff? What kind of stuff?"

"Oh, you know…" Hannah coiled a short strand of hair around her finger. "Get Behind Your Stove in Ten Easy Lessons! *Go at your own pace.*"

"Oh wow, that's a new twist."

"To what?" Hannah asked, flummoxed.

"Never mind. Doesn't really matter." Then she paused and lowered her voice. "You must be a really fast learner. Good at math? No, chemistry?"

Hannah was totally lost. "Would it be okay if I brought some wine?"

"Wine! Sure! Great!"

Hannah hung up and looked down at the cats, waiting for their breakfast. "Jade was sounding a little loopy," she said, rolling her eyes.

Perhaps Carter was right. It was all about Christmas stress.

Hannah made an appointment to see Buddy Christmas at three o'clock. At noon, Olivia knocked on her door, a bulging canvas tote hanging from her shoulder while she clutched two ski poles and a pair of boots. A set of skis leaned against the porch railing. For some reason they seemed frightfully long.

"Um…thanks for bringing these by," she said as Olivia shoved the pair of lime-green ski boots at her before handing her both poles.

"Size seven and a half. I hope they'll fit?"

Hannah was an eight. "Close enough, I'm sure," she said, clumsily accepting the equipment.

"It's so cool you and Carter are going to River Run." Her cheeks held a rosy cast. "Things are getting pretty serious then, huh?"

"Well, we *are*…exclusive," Hannah said, testing out the word. She hadn't told anybody else about her new status with Carter. Not even Sandy.

"Exclusive?" Olivia happily patted her mittens together. "Carter's never been exclusive with anybody!"

For a great-looking man like him, this was kind of hard to believe. "Never?"

"Well, there was that one girl." Olivia spoke confidentially. "Gina." She said the name with a grimace, then lowered her voice a notch. "Nobody in the family liked her."

"Oh!" The wind howled, blowing snow in the open doorway. "Would you like to come in?"

"Can't, sorry. Have to get back to the shop," she said, scooting down the steps.

"Of course."

"See you Sunday!"

"Sunday?"

Olivia scurried down the sidewalk, clutching her arms around herself for warmth.

"It's Christmas."

"Oh right, yes. At Jade's." They exchanged a final wave. "Bye!"

A little later, Lou called just to check on her and Sandy sent a text saying,

It's been a while. Let's catch up over coffee.

Hannah sat on the sofa and pulled Belle into her lap, thinking what a difference twenty-four hours made. There she was yesterday, feeling dejected. And here, today, everything had turned around. She couldn't wait to meet with Buddy and deliver the happy news. She was even more excited about telling Carter, but she wanted to do so in person. It would be better to talk to him tomorrow, after she'd made things official anyway. *Wheeee! I'm staying in Christmas Town!* Seconds later,

Hannah was seized with panic, hoping she was doing the right thing.

She shut her eyes, recalling the glorious moment she'd found her prize in the hatbox. After carefully cutting a slit into the lining on the underside of the lid with the kitchen scissors, she'd slipped her fingers beneath the silky fabric and pulled out the yellowed card. It was the secret recipe, all right. The one for her great-grandmother's famous Virginia Cookies, written in Lena's own hand. It was more than amazing that she'd found it; Hannah had taken it as a sign. Staying in Christmas Town was no longer a choice. It was her destiny.

Chapter Twenty-Three

Kurt's forehead rose in surprise. "You're taking Hannah *where* tomorrow?"

"What's wrong with River Run?" Carter asked defensively. They stood with Ray under the covered Christmas tree stand at the nursery. Carter had stopped to chat with Ray while on patrol, just as Kurt happened by. The sky was charcoal gray and it was snowing hard.

"Did you even ask her if she skis?" Ray wondered.

"I don't think she does, but she can learn."

"Looks like I'll have to prepare for another patient."

"Don't invite bad luck," Carter snapped. Then he told Ray, "Kurt's just jealous because Hannah threw him over to go out with me."

"That's not true!" Kurt retorted vehemently.

"What are you doing here, anyway?" Carter asked Kurt.

"Can't a man visit his brother?"

"Yeah, but he rarely does," Ray told Carter with a wink.

Kurt squared his shoulders. "So happens, I came to get my tree."

"You already have one," Carter observed. "I've seen it at the clinic."

"Not for the clinic, man. My house."

"You're cutting it mighty close," Carter ribbed. "I put mine up *days* ago."

Kurt stared at Ray for verification.

"It's true," he said to Kurt. "Carter bought a six-footer on Thursday."

Kurt turned to Carter. "Since when do you decorate?"

"Since…oh, I don't know…" Carter slowly stroked his chin. "I've been feeling more domestic."

"She's awfully pretty," Ray said with a grin.

"Hannah's more than pretty," Carter answered. "She's got a good head on her shoulders, too. Plus she's sweet, and generous, and—"

"Whoa, Nelly!" Kurt stopped him with a chuckle and glanced at Ray. "Sounds like our boy's been bitten by the bug."

"Just wait till she starts baking those Virginia Cookies." Ray howled a laugh. "It will be all over for our sheriff then."

The back of Carter's neck burned hot. "If you children are done having your fun, I'll just be on my way now. With my adult job."

"Good thing you're working on the right side of the law." Kurt waggled his finger. "You're being awfully cagey about keeping Hannah out of town. I'll give you credit for that."

Carter had had to steer Hannah clear of the Christmas Cookie Shop for the better part of the morning, so Buddy could bring some people in. He and Frank were meeting with an industrial kitchen contractor to kick around ideas and get a sense of budget. Some hard numbers were needed for the plan they had underway. "Thank you," Carter said, tipping his hat. "Thank you very much."

Ray smiled broadly. "Have fun at River Run!"

"And be careful!" Kurt added quickly.

Snow blasted in Hannah's face, completely covering her goggles. She tucked a pole under one arm and raised a ski glove to clear them.

Her arms hurt, her legs ached, and her feet throbbed in the too-tight boots. Even her stomach muscles felt wrecked. Boy, this was grueling. She shot a glance back at Rudolph, dismayed to see she'd traveled less than fifty feet.

Carter viewed her encouragingly from up ahead. "Keep going! You're doing great!"

Hannah smiled tightly, then repositioned her poles with a groan. It was literally one step forward and two steps back on these skis. Why did they have to make the bottoms so slick?

She trudged ahead, her battered body resisting. Thank goodness she'd bargained their adventure—as Carter called it—down to thirty minutes. She'd never last a full hour without having to be airlifted out of here. On the positive side, the landscape was stunning. The winding river snaked in front of them, frozen in small patches near its banks. Beyond it, the towering mountains were covered in white, telltale signs of green peeking through from the occasional spindly pine. Yet Carter seemed to be leading them away from this open panorama and toward a thicket of woods.

"How much farther?" she called, stealthily huffing and puffing. It wasn't like Hannah never did sports. She'd biked as a kid and played high-school volleyball, but in truth she was out of practice. Hot yoga might be good for her soul, but no way had it prepared her body for this. Thinking of all that heat made Hannah realize she was broiling beneath her insulated clothing. Sweat dribbled down her back and chest beneath the pretty, snowflake-patterned long johns Sandy had loaned her. The moment Hannah got home, everything was going in the wash.

"Just about two hundred more yards!" Carter answered. "We're going there!" He pointed to an opening in the trees that Hannah hadn't spotted before. It was apparently some sort of trailhead.

As hot as the rest of her was, the exposed skin on her face was freezing. She'd completely lost sensation in her nose and felt certain her rigid eyelashes were spiked with icicles. She shot a look back at the truck, comparing the distance she'd covered to how far she still had to go. "You mean, we haven't even started?"

Carter must have noted the panic in her voice, because he deftly turned his skis around. He glided effortlessly in her direction with long, easy strides, his poles puncturing the snow as he went. When he reached her, he planted his poles in the snow and pressed up his goggles, setting them on top of his head. His eyes looked extra green against the bleakness of the sky and his handsome face was ruddy. He surveyed her worriedly, then spoke with obvious concern.

"Not enjoying this much, are you?"

"I...er... It's—the boots! They're a little snug, that's all. Otherwise, I'm fine!"

"You, Hannah Winchester, are a very poor liar."

"What?"

He chuckled amiably and planted his hands on her shoulders. "Come on, let's get you turned around."

"Around?"

"Hold still. Stop squirming, all right?" Hannah hadn't realized she was squirming; she thought she'd been trying to help him. She teetered to and fro, trying to maintain her balance with her poles as Carter did this little dance between her skis and her torso, gentling angling her toward the truck.

"There!" he said, heaving a breath. "Ready for that cocoa?"

He might as well have asked if she was ready to win a million dollars or something. "You mean we're not going skiing after all?" Gosh, she hadn't meant it to sound that gleeful.

Carter smiled warmly. "I think you've had enough for today." Then he stayed very close beside her all...the...way...back to the truck, which took another fifteen minutes.

Hannah had never been so glad to take a hot shower in her life. After helping her out of those cursed boots, Carter led Hannah upstairs in his cabin and showed her where the full bath was. He set two plush towels in her arms and told her to take her time. He'd also pushed two ibuprofen tablets on her and handed her a glass of water, insisting that she take the medicine right away. She'd tried to say she didn't need it, but Carter held firm, saying she'd be glad later that she had. Hannah let the pounding water stream over her hair and down her aching back. If Carter did this for fun, no wonder he looked fit! Hannah hoped cross-country skiing wasn't a condition of living in Christmas Town. Olivia obviously skied, too, and who knew how many others. Surely, there were additional ways to get exercise around here in the wintertime. Though, in truth, she hadn't spotted a gym in town. Not even a yoga studio.

She stepped out of the shower, a cloud of steam escaping from behind the curtain. The bathroom was rustic but functional, like the rest of the cabin. It led to the bedroom that housed Carter's queen-size bed, set on a sturdy iron frame with a decorative headboard. There were matching bedside tables on either side of it, and an antique cherry hope chest sat to the left by a tall armoire. The other side of the room had a sweeping window overlooking the snowy field and river, with the mountains towering behind it. Hannah closed the blinds and walked to the reading chair in the corner where she'd set her small travel bag containing a change of clothing. She had one towel around her body and the other wrapped turban-style around her head, when Carter shouted from downstairs. "Marshmallows for the cocoa?"

"Uh, sure!" she called back, A giant skylight hovered above the bed. It was blanketed with snow, but she guessed it provided a spectacular view of the stars in clearer weather. Hannah envisioned herself lying under Carter's big down comforter and gazing up at those stars while snuggled in his arms, and heard herself sigh. "Be right down!" she added, quickly dressing in the shirt, sweater, and jeans she'd packed. Hannah laughed to herself when she remembered it was the same outfit she'd been wearing her first night in Christmas Town, when her ice bag had dripped and Carter had thought she'd sprung a leak.

Had that only been a month ago? In some ways her time here had flown by, but in another, really comforting way, she felt like she'd been in Christmas Town forever. Hannah was going to like living there.

She just knew it. The town suited her and she loved its people. She was growing particularly fond of its sheriff, even though she didn't especially favor his choice of outdoor sports.

Hannah bounced down the steps with a happy heart, feeling like a woman who had everything. She had a business of her own and a new challenge ahead of her. She'd also had the luck to make some great friends. Plus, she had an incredibly gorgeous boyfriend, who was intelligent, steadfast, and kind. She couldn't wait to tell Carter her news about keeping the shop. While Hannah knew she'd miss Ben and Lily, they'd all prepared themselves for being apart anyway. Hannah's former plans to attend graduate school could have taken her several hundred miles in many directions. She and Ben had discussed this and knew they'd stay close regardless. They were family and he was a supportive big brother, just as he'd supported Hannah when she'd admitted to being conflicted over selling the Christmas Cookie Shop.

"There you are." Carter turned from where he'd been nursing a saucepan on the stove, steadily beating a wire whisk into it. "You look great. The shower go okay?"

Hannah smiled and shook out her damp hair. "Better than okay. It was *restorative*." She clutched the balled-up bath towels at her side. "Where should I put these?"

Carter gestured down the hall and near the half bath. "Washer and dryer are behind those double doors over there."

Hannah nodded, a thought occurring. "Would it be okay if I tossed my ski stuff in as well?"

"Better wait for mine before starting the load." He grinned broadly and stepped away from the stove. "Care to take over?"

She stared at the appliance like it was a wild animal that might bite her. "I...um."

Confusion crossed his face. "It's just cocoa, Hannah. Not a chocolate mousse."

"Oh right!" She gave a staged laugh. "Right. I know that."

"I'll be right back." Before he headed upstairs to take his own shower, Carter said, "I was thinking we could have some popcorn with our cocoa by the woodstove. Do you mind making it up while I'm gone?"

Hannah gulped.

"It's the microwave kind," he said, indicating the bag he'd already set out on the counter. "Really easy."

Carter showered and dressed in jeans and a sweatshirt in less than five minutes flat. In one way, he didn't want to spend any more time apart from Hannah than he had to. In another, he'd felt uneasy about leaving her alone in the kitchen. She really hadn't seemed to want to take over. Though Carter had no clue why. Perhaps their outing had been harder on her than he imagined, and all she wanted to do at this point was relax—and not get put to work. But, honestly? How much work could microwaving a bag of popcorn be? *Wait a minute. Is that smoke?* The minute he thought it, the kitchen smoke alarm blared.

He dashed down the stairs, taking them two at a time. When Carter reached the kitchen, he found Hannah racing away from the open microwave. The popcorn bag tightly pinched in her fingers was flaming!

In one fell swoop, she hurled it into the kitchen sink and turned on the spigot. Water gushed forth, rapidly dousing the fire and making the bag sizzle. She scooped it up in a practiced move and ran to the trash bin in the corner, the bag dripping an icky black trail behind her. She gasped, then slammed down the trashcan pedal, hurling the popcorn bag inside.

"Well done!" Carter said as the trash can lid crashed down.

Hannah spun on her heel and her hands shot to her head. "Carter!" she cried, aghast.

He casually reached up and pressed a button above the doorframe, silencing the wailing smoke alarm. "Are you all right? What happened?"

She turned crimson. "The bag caught fire."

"I saw that. It must have been defective somehow. I'm sorry."

"Defective?" She said it like it was a new word she hadn't heard of.

"Yeah, you know. Like something went wrong at the factory. You really made a good save. I'm glad it wasn't worse."

"Yeah."

Carter heard a loud hissing sound and stared at the stove. Scorched milk was bubbling over the rim of the pot and spreading out everywhere. He lunged for the burner, rapidly killing its flame, and pulled the pot aside.

Hannah's hand cupped her mouth. He couldn't tell if she was horrified or feeling ill. Either way, she probably needed to sit down. "Here," he said gently, walking over to her. "Why don't you wait on the sofa? I'll get the popcorn and cocoa. It will just take a sec."

Hannah didn't know how she was going to live this down. Who was she kidding with this running the Christmas Cookie Shop business? Her first instinct when she'd inherited the place was the right one. But now it was too late. She'd stood right there in front of Buddy Christmas yesterday afternoon and torn the real estate listing papers up. And not just in half either. She'd ripped them into itty-bitty shreds, while Buddy watched and boomed, *Ho, ho, ho. Here's to a very merry Christmas to all of us in Christmas Town. Welcome aboard, Hannah Winchester! Welcome aboard!* She'd felt elated then. Confident. Now Hannah was just scared. What had she done? No secret family recipe could rescue her from this. She'd surely burn the cookies, too.

"How's your cocoa?" Carter asked from beside her on the sofa, and Hannah realized she'd been staring blankly down into her mug. "Not enough marshmallows?"

"No!" she said abruptly. "It's perfect."

Carter studied her carefully. "You haven't even taken a sip."

"Carter," Hannah said meekly. "I have a confession to make."

He set his mug on the coffee table.

"I can't cook."

"What's that supposed to mean?"

"It's pretty much how it sounds. You saw the evidence yourself in there." She glanced over her shoulder at the kitchen. Despite Carter cracking a window, the sour order of burnt popcorn still hung in the air.

The weight of it seemed to dawn. "You don't even bake…cookies?"

"Oh, Carter!" Hannah suddenly burst into tears. "It's not the bag that was defective! It's me!"

Carter gently removed the mug that shook in her hands and put it down beside his. "Hey now," he said smoothly, wrapping his arms around her. "You know that's not true."

Hannah sagged against his chest, confronting the dismal fact. "Yes, it is." She sniffed and he passed her a napkin. "The popcorn thing wasn't some freak accident. It happens to me all the time."

He spoke calmly, trying to soothe her. "I'm sure it's not as bad as you think."

She pulled back to stare at him, teary-eyed. "No, it's worse. I tore up the listing papers."

"When?"

"Just yesterday."

"Hannah, listen to me." A tear leaked from her eye and he wiped it back with his thumb. "This is not the end of the world, okay? It's not exactly like you're starting in the Indie 500 without ever having raced before."

"Oh yes, it is."

"Hannah," he said firmly. "Cookie baking isn't deadly." His eyes rolled back toward the kitchen. "Well, okay. Not generally."

In spite of herself, Hannah laughed. "Go on and make fun of me."

"I'm not making fun. Merely trying to make you feel better." He studied her a prolonged moment, then wrinkled his brow. "Is it working?"

"A little," she admitted honestly.

"Good." He leaned forward and kissed her forehead. "You know what I think?"

"No, what?"

"That—once you get the Christmas Cookie Shop up and running—you're going to be the best darn baker in all of Tennessee!"

Her smile trembled when she asked, "You really think so?"

"There's no thinking about it," he said confidently. "I absolutely know."

She eyed him doubtfully. "How do you know?"

"Because I know you. You're a good-hearted woman, Hannah Winchester. You're a strong person who honors her commitments. Look at how you took your niece's kittens under your wing, when you knew they'd be a burden."

"But they're not," she protested. "I love Jingles and Belle!"

"Of course you do, now. Because that's who you are. But you have to admit that—initially—you were worried about the responsibility. What person wouldn't be, coming to a strange town, and with so much uncertainty ahead?"

"I didn't know my future was uncertain when I came here."

"Didn't you?" He searched her eyes. "Because I read something different during our first exchange."

"Oh?" Hannah asked, confounded yet intrigued. "What exactly did you read?"

He tightened his embrace. "I saw a very beautiful and capable young woman, who also looked a little lost. And I'm not just talking about you finding your way to Christmas Town.

"But since you've been here, Hannah, and especially since I've gotten to know you, I've seen something different. I've seen a person who's reevaluated her life. A woman who's come into her own."

Hannah recalled finding Lena's secret recipe and relived that sense of conviction. "I have, haven't I?" she said thoughtfully. "Come into my own."

"And grad school?"

"I filled out half a dozen applications, but the truth is I never submitted one. Not *one,* Carter. Somehow I couldn't bring myself to do it."

"Everyone has a path," he told her. "A direction they're meant to go. Some of us find it later; others are lucky enough to find it sooner." He looked down at her and smiled. "You know what you sat right there and told me? Right in the very spot where you are now?"

"That I wanted to reopen Lena's shop."

"Who cares if you can't cook? That's what classes are for!"

"I've already started," she admitted sheepishly.

"Is that so?" He appeared genuinely pleased.

"Online, but still it's something." She spoke authoritatively as if reporting for an infomercial. "Ten consecutive lessons. Go at your own pace."

"There you have it! You're on your way!"

They settled back against the sofa and Hannah snuggled into the crook of his arm. "Thanks, Carter."

He handed Hannah her cocoa. "That's what boyfriends are for."

"You're a mighty good one." She took a sip of the chocolaty concoction, savoring its flavors. "You also make a mighty mean cup of cocoa."

"It's probably gone cold," he said, making to stand.

"No, please." She set her hand on his thigh. "Stay." The logs crackled softly in the woodstove as snow drifted beyond the windows. "It's so lovely out here. Peaceful."

"Yeah," he said, holding her close. "I've never had a better time playing hooky."

"When do you have to go in to work?"

"Around two. After lunch." He offered a suggestion. "Would you like to stop by Santa's Sandwich Shop on the way and grab a couple of burgers?"

Hannah sighed happily, leaning up against him. "I'd love that, yeah."

Carter was such a wonderful man, Hannah couldn't imagine being without him. He made her feel special and cared for and alive, in the most basic and marvelous sense. His appeal was like a tonic, and she knew other women must have sensed that, and been drawn to him just as desperately as Hannah found herself falling. "Carter?" she said softly. "Can you tell me about Gina?"

"Gina?" he asked with mild surprise. "But how did you—?"

"Olivia mentioned something."

"Olivia, of course. And there I thought Savannah was the blabbermouth."

"Savannah's your little sister?"

"She's the baby, yeah. And the one Kurt's in love with."

"Do you mean it?"

"Oh, I don't know. They had a thing, a very long time ago. Although it's been years, sometimes I have the sneaking suspicion Kurt hasn't entirely gotten over it."

"Where does Savannah live?"

"In Miami."

"So there's a chance—?"

Carter shook his head. "She's involved with someone else. Deeply involved. Kurt knows that."

"I see." Hannah stared out the window a while, watching the snowflakes curtsey and bow. Carter hadn't answered her question about Gina, so perhaps she should drop it. Still, once he'd said he'd always tell her what she wanted to know. And Hannah wanted to know for all the right reasons. She wanted to better understand him. "And Gina?"

Carter exhaled heavily. "Gina is an old girlfriend. We started dating in high school, senior year. Then, long-distance in college. We saw each other over breaks. Talked about the future."

"What happened?"

Carter frowned. "I got deployed. There were things I couldn't tell her. She felt I'd come back changed. In a way, I guess I had."

Hannah had a sense that she shouldn't press him. That there were things Carter would only be willing to talk about in his own good time. So rather than push, she reached up and softly stroked his cheek. "You don't have to talk about it now, if you don't want to."

"Thanks, Hannah." His voice was hoarse. "I appreciate that."

"But I'm here," she said gently. "For whenever…"

His Adam's apple rose and fell, then he pulled her to him. "I know."

After a few moments of silence, Carter asked her, "What about you? Your background? Your family? Other than your brother Ben and niece Lily, you don't talk much about them."

Hannah shared a sad smile. "That's because Ben and Lily are all I have left. My mom died when I was little and Ben was in college. We went to live with our father's parents then, my Grandpa Charles and Grandma Mabel."

"And your dad?"

Hannah set her chin. "That's a very hard subject."

Carter viewed her with compassion. "I'm sorry, Hannah."

"He wasn't around much," she continued. "He couldn't handle my mom's illness, especially when it got worse. Not that he was a model father to begin with."

Carter exhaled deeply. "I'm sorry that I brought it up, that I intruded…"

She peered up at him and saw that worry lines creased his brow. "You didn't. I wanted to tell you."

"And your other set of grandparents? Your mom's folks?"

"They died when I was a baby. My mom, April, was their only child."

"April?" Carter smiled softly. "That's a pretty name."

"Yeah."

"What was she like? Your mom?"

"Sweet. Funny. Good. She made the most amazing Christmas…" Hannah started to become animated in the telling, then her voice fell off.

"Cookies?" Carter asked.

Hannah's eyes felt moist and her heart burned fiercely. It was like she was going to combust. Burst into a ball of flames…fanned by all the hurt she felt inside.

Carter gently squeezed her shoulder. "Hannah?"

Suddenly things were coming together as Hannah worked through her heartache. Each time her Grandma Mabel led her into the kitchen, it had reminded of her mother. Dear, sweet Mom. Kind, giving—and gone. Hannah hadn't been able to focus on cooking, when her insides raged from abandonment. Baking Christmas cookies with her mom was one of the few positive memories of their time together Hannah had. When her mom became too sick to do much of anything else, she still insisted on the annual ritual of baking holiday cookies with her daughter. Until that very last Christmas…when she couldn't even get out of bed, and there were no cookies at all.

"Hey?" Carter steadied her chin in his hand. "Are you all right?"

"I think I just figured out why cooking's been such a problem for me," she said, her voice warbling. "It reminds me of my mother."

"Well, maybe that's not a bad thing, right?" he said kindly. "Maybe it's a way to honor her."

"By being the best baker I can?" she asked, getting his meaning.

When Carter nodded, Hannah smiled through her tears. Of course, that made sense. Perhaps, as a child, Hannah couldn't handle it. But now, as a grown-up, she was more determined than ever to help the Christmas Cookie Shop prosper. And the more successful it became, the more Hannah would be paying tribute to the special women in her family who had gone before her. "You know, I think you're right."

"Your mother would have been very proud of you. Lena, too. And they're not the only ones." Carter held her gaze. "I'm incredibly proud of you, too."

Chapter Twenty-Four

A few hours later, Carter passionately kissed Hannah good-bye on her doorstep. The laundered bag of Olivia's skiing apparel was at her feet and the skis and poles rested against the railing.

"Why, Sheriff Livingston!" she said, gasping for breath. "It's broad daylight! Someone will see us!"

"Hmm, yes. And what will they think?" he asked, diving in again.

Hannah laughed and pressed a palm to his chest. He'd changed into his work clothes before coming to town and his professional appearance drove her wild. "I do love a man in uniform."

He clasped his fingers around hers. "Better be just *this* man in *this* uniform," he said hungrily.

"Oh, hello!"

They abruptly broke apart to see Sandy had exited her town house. "Don't mind me," she said with a saucy air. "Just stopped home for lunch." Then she directed a comment at Hannah. "Coffee later. Don't forget!"

When she left, Hannah banged her head against Carter's chest, and burst into giggles. "I guess our secret's out."

"Sweetheart," Carter said sexily. "Our secret's been out for a while."

Hannah cheerfully stared up at him. "No point in guarding it now."

"Nope. None at all." He gave her a firm peck on the lips. "I'll call you later."

Hannah waltzed back inside, dancing from room to room, as the kittens happily followed her. It was then that it occurred to her she'd have to arrange for something more permanent, another place to stay. She also needed to secure financing for the cookie shop. With Ben being away, she'd have to wait until after the holiday to firm things up. Buddy had assured her this was fine, saying a lot of lenders would be on a limited schedule this time of year anyway.

Hannah hung up her coat and searched her computer bag for some paper. While she couldn't do anything concrete about it for a while, she was eager to sketch out some ideas for her renovation of the shop. What a glorious place it was going to be! Hannah knew she'd be taking a risk by borrowing even more money for her new venture, but she felt so energized by her convictions, she had to believe her investment would pay off. Her Grandpa Charles's bequest hadn't been any sort of accident. He'd thought about it long and hard and had determined that Hannah was up to the task. While Hannah hadn't agreed with his assessment initially, she now concurred with every fiber of her being. Hannah's future wasn't at some far-off university, it was right here in Christmas Town, Tennessee, and she was meant to follow in her great-grandmother's footsteps. *Fingers crossed that I can do an equally fine job!*

"So," Sandy said, when they met at Jolly Bean Java later. "Tell me everything. And I mean don't leave out one single detail."

"Sandy! That's positively voyeuristic."

Her cheeks glowed brightly. "All right. You don't need to go *that* far."

"And no, we haven't, by the way."

Sandy looked a bit taken aback by her frankness. "Oh! Well, okay. That's your business."

"Not that I wouldn't love to."

"Hannah…"

"The man is *so* hot."

"You know what—"

"I don't think I've ever wanted anyone this much, truly."

"Stop!"

"What?" Hannah gawked at Sandy, who was covering her ears.

"For heaven's sakes, Hannah! What's with the skylight?"

Hannah blinked hard. "You're scary."

"No, I'm not."

"Yeah, you are. But just a little bit."

"Don't worry," Sandy whispered. "It doesn't happen with everybody. Just with those I'm really close to. And not even all the time."

Hannah wasn't sure whether that should make her feel comforted or more alarmed.

"Comforted. Definitely," Sandy said and Hannah laughed.

She leaned forward and latched on to Sandy's hands. "Oh Sandy, I'm so happy."

Sandy's expression brightened. "It shows."

"You know the craziest part in all of this?" Hannah asked, still feeling giddy from her wonderful morning. Okay, the wonderful part was emotional. Physically, she felt like she'd been put in a bag and beaten with sticks.

"What's the craziest part?" Sandy wanted to know.

"I can't even cook."

Sandy shuddered like she'd been doused in cold water. "Come again?" She thumped her temples and Hannah guessed she was wondering how she'd missed that part. It was probably because Hannah didn't think much about it. One way or another.

"I can't cook!" Hannah declared loudly. Others in the café turned their way and Sandy clamped her hand over Hannah's mouth.

"Are you insane?"

Hannah mumbled and Sandy removed her hand. "What's the big deal? I'm learning."

"Learning? Since when?"

"A couple of days ago. When I… Um. Decided I needed to try."

"Hannah," Sandy rasped. "You mean you *really* don't cook? Can't bake at all?"

"Not even popcorn," Hannah replied dreamily.

Sandy's face fell dramatically. "Oh, dear."

Hannah got a sinking feeling about this. "Sandy, is there something I don't know?"

"Nope," she returned brightly. "Nothing at all." But her forehead was knitted so tightly it looked like her eyebrows were going to crash into each other. Hannah could tell Sandy's mind was racing, she just didn't know about what. If only she had the *instincts* that Sandy did.

"Sandy?" Hannah asked her. "Is everything all right?"

"Oh yeah," Sandy said, patting her hand. "It's perfect." Her smile looked strained. "I was just thinking it would be fun for all of us to get together."

"All of us who?"

"You, me, Olivia, and Jade."

"I thought we were, for Christmas."

"I mean, before that," Sandy said, sounding oddly desperate.

"O-kay. If you feel it's important?"

"Not just important." Her deep blue eyes were dead serious. "It's mission critical."

"Mission critical. Right."

The following evening, Hannah found herself in Sandy's kitchen, the other women crowding in around her.

"This is a gas oven," Sandy said. "But it's got an igniter, so you don't have to light it."

"And this is a chicken," Jade declared seriously, holding a whole bird on a roasting pan.

Olivia waved a brightly patterned pair of oven mitts in the air. "And these are—"

"Guys!" Hannah said, stopping them. "I'm not *stupid*."

"Oh... Um... Er..." They glanced uncertainly at each other.

"Okay," Sandy jumped in. "We understand. We just wanted to give you some pointers."

"Three fifty," Olivia said.

"That's right," Jade agreed. "When in doubt, go with that baking temperature."

"One hour for meats. More or less!" Sandy smiled brightly and presented Hannah with a meat thermometer. "One sixty for chicken. One forty for beef—if you want it rare."

"Here!" Jade handed over an index card. "I've written down a cheat sheet."

"Cookies are eight to ten minutes," Olivia warned very seriously. "But don't let them go beyond twelve."

"Fifteen maybe, if they're big ones," Sandy commented.

Hannah's head was spinning. "This is very sweet of you, but—"

"Sweet potatoes, yes!" Sandy grabbed for something on the counter. "We almost forgot." She shoved four ovular spuds at Hannah. "Go on! Prepare them! They're already washed, so just wrap them up after adding salt, pepper, and butter."

Olivia passed over the tinfoil, slapping the box into Hannah's palm.

"Don't forget this!" Jade said, handing her the butter dish.

When Sandy had invited her to a girls' night dinner, she didn't know this was what the rest of them had planned. "Oh, ah...great!" Sweat beaded Hannah's brow as she added salt, pepper, and butter to the sweet potatoes before wrapping them in foil. She was apparently expected to prepare roasted asparagus next.

"Don't worry," Olivia whispered sweetly. "We have your back."

"You can count on us," Jade agreed.

"No room for self-doubt!" Sandy cried. "You can do it!"

When they sat down to the elegant meal, Hannah caught her breath. She couldn't believe she was responsible for this! Well, not all of it, *obviously*. Hannah had been awarded tons of help. Still, her friends had been so supportive, they'd made her feel as if she'd done it on her own. Hannah glanced around the room, happily at home here. Sandy's place was homey and inviting and chock-full of holiday cheer.

Sandy's gorgeous Christmas-themed paintings were everywhere, and fragrant garlands were draped from the windowsills, which held holiday candles. Eight miniature reindeer pranced across the mantel and a tree, brimming with ornaments, stood in the corner. The cream-colored love seat sported a bright candy-cane pattern that picked up the cherry-red hue of two matching armchairs, which held pillows complementing the colors of the sofa fabric.

A low-slung sleigh in front of the seating group served as a glass-topped coffee table. It was dark green with ornate gold trim and sat on two glistening gold runners. Hannah had peeked down inside it on her way to the dinner table and spied brightly decorated packages tucked in its hollow. Hannah's favorite touch was the tall, wooden snowman in a top hat and scarf standing guard by the front door. He had a corncob pipe and a button nose and two eyes made out of fake coal. What's more, he was wrapped in colorful, blinking Christmas lights. From the top of his hat all the way down to the floor.

"Such a beautiful repast," Sandy said, clasping her hands together.

"Yes, gorgeous," Jade agreed, looking around at their yummy food served on very fancy tableware, which included Spode Christmas china and green crystal goblets.

"We're so proud of you for preparing this," Olivia offered sweetly.

Hannah demurred. "Well, I did have a little help."

"Nonsense!" the others cried in unison, as each insisted Hannah was born to the job.

Then Sandy uncorked the wine and they all had a marvelous dinner.

Hannah returned to her place feeling genuinely motivated. While she'd had minor assistance at Sandy's, she'd basically made the meal on her own. Cooking really wasn't so hard, once she put her mind to it. The others had provided some general instruction, and now Hannah could run with it. She eagerly logged in to her cooking course, excited about the next installment. It really was academic. Hannah just needed to pay attention and follow the steps. Timing, it seemed, was key. This especially applied to fixing things in the microwave. Hannah made a promise to herself to never burn popcorn again. If the fates were with her, she'd never burn anything ever! Okay, maybe that was a little unrealistic. But if she burned something, Hannah decided she would instantly throw it out—to avoid that noxious lingering smell.

The next evening, Hannah ran into Jade on the back side of Sisters' Row.

"Hi, Hannah. How's it going?"

Hannah shoved a large black trash bag into the dumpster and grinned. "Great! It's going just great! Thanks for the cooking lessons!"

"No problem at all," Jade said. "Glad we could help!"

Chapter Twenty-Five

Carter woke up on Friday morning totally energized. It was the day before Christmas Eve, and he'd really pulled it off! No…not him alone. It was all of Christmas Town. He recognized most of the names on Tilly's master list. There were others he'd never heard of, yet they all believed in the common cause. Joy had been busy on the phone and enlisted her sister's help with social media. For the first time in decades, teens were talking to their parents at dinner, and the conversations were positive ones. By a unanimous vote, the Town Council had opted to start a crowdfunding project on Hannah's behalf, rather than involving loans or outside investors. Since she already owned the property outright, no funds were required for its purchase, only for electrical repairs and renovations. It was decided that Hannah should be helped with paying off tax liens, too.

If everyone who'd pledged their assistance gave the bare minimum of five dollars, they'd raise fifteen thousand dollars in no time. And Carter had a hunch that many would give more. He himself had secretly contributed a tidy sum and also offered to provide some physical labor. Since he was handy with carpentry, he volunteered his time in order to keep down costs. The three Christmas brothers, who were skilled woodworkers themselves, agreed to help as well. As did their father, Buddy. In the event that the Town Council raised more than was required to bring the Christmas Cookie Shop back online, any surplus would be put into a kitty and used for future community good works. In honor of the woman who'd inspired such social activism, the fund would be established in Lena Winchester's name. As this was the last business day of the week, the deadline for making contributions was this afternoon at four. Before Tilly left work, they'd have the final numbers. Then Carter would be able to share them with Hannah in person.

Carter couldn't wait to see the look in her eyes. He hoped she would be pleased, and not feel upset that she wasn't consulted. When they'd discussed letting Hannah in on the idea at the Town Hall meeting, the consensus had been that it was better to keep the project a secret until the plan came to fruition. Besides, Lou Christmas argued, Hannah might wrongly worry that she was inconveniencing people or that she was being a burden to the community. She might even try to stop the project from going forward—out of deference to those she thought she was troubling. Carter had conceded that reasoning was sound, and still believed surprising Hannah with the gift was best. He was honored and pleased that he'd been elected to share the news with her when the time came. That time would be tomorrow night.

"Morning, Sheriff!" Tilly called brightly when he ambled in the door to his office.

"You're here mighty early."

Her grin broadened. "Stayed late last night, too."

"I know, and I appreciate that." Carter was aware she'd skipped one of her regular duplicate bridge days to work on Hannah's project and he felt heavily indebted for her efforts. "Which is why I brought you this!" He handed her a box of treats from Nutcracker Sweets, tied up with a pretty red ribbon.

Tilly squealed with glee. "For me?"

"Merry Christmas," he said, laying another package on her desk. This one was smaller and wrapped in Christmas paper.

When Victoria entered from the hall, Carter handed a similar present to her. "What's this?" she asked with surprise.

"Open it."

Victoria and Tilly both dug into their gifts, eagerly ripping the Christmas wrapping apart. Victoria's jaw dropped when she pulled out the small accessory shaped like a tiny Christmas tree with brightly colored balls and an assortment of packages at its base. "Why Carter, it's so…personal."

"It's called a barrette," he informed her as if this was news. "I know you'd never wear anything like that while in uniform, but on your days off, I thought—"

She stunned him by leaping into his arms and giving him a hug. "That was so swee—" She quickly realized what she was doing and pulled back, adopting a less emotional tone. "I mean, generous of you, Carter. Very kind." She straightened and smoothed down her hair. "Thanks."

"Well, I don't mind wearing *mine* at the office," Tilly said sassily, clipping the miniature penguin with a candy cane scarf into her springy red hair. She batted her eyelashes at the others. "How does it look?"

"Beautiful, Tilly, just like you," Carter answered and the secretary blushed.

"So!" Victoria turned to her and grinned. "How's the fund-raising going?"

Tilly clasped her hands together and shook them in the air like she was shaking a handful of coins. "Jingle, jingle, jingle!" she sang merrily. "Jingle all the way!"

Hannah printed out her certificate of completion wearing a happy grin. She'd earned the gold leaf edition for finishing her lessons in record time! It was incredible how much Hannah had learned in a few short days. All right, so maybe she'd burned through quite a few ingredients in the process and she and the folks at the Merry Market were becoming fast friends... But really! For any great achievement, don't sacrifices have to be made? And Hannah was priming herself for the achievement of her lifetime: reopening the Christmas Cookie Shop. She scanned her Great-grandmother Lena's secret recipe card one last time, then pressed it to her heart. "What do you think, kids?" she asked Jingles and Belle. "Am I ready?"

The kittens, who'd taken to hiding behind the sofa each time Hannah headed for the kitchen, dashed out of sight. "Don't worry," she told them confidently. "There will be no smoke alarms this time."

Hannah had just slid the tray of cookies in the oven when the doorbell rang. It was Lou Christmas carrying a prettily wrapped jar of jam. "Merry Christmas, Hannah!" she said, handing it over. "I wanted you to have this before the holiday. Buddy and I were going to ask you to spend it with us, but a little bird told us you already have plans."

Hannah wondered if that bird was Sandy, then decided it didn't matter. Everyone knew *everything* about everybody else in Christmas Town, and she was finally getting used to it.

"Thanks so much." Hannah stepped out of the doorway. "Please come in."

Lou obliged, handing her the gift. "It's jalapeno fig jam. Buddy added the jalapenos from his garden; they provide a nice kick."

"Sounds wonderful." Hannah lifted a large package from Nutcracker Sweets off her entrance table and handed it to Lou. "Here, this is for you. Merry Christmas."

Lou took a peek at the label. "Nutcracker Sweets! Heavens, Hannah! You'll ruin my girlish figure," she said with a titter.

"Maybe you can share it with Buddy—and the rest of your family, when they come over?"

"Terrific idea." Lou smiled sweetly. "Thank you, dear." She lifted her nose in the air, then pointed it toward the kitchen. "Something smells divine in here. What are you cooking?"

"Oh, nothing," Hannah said, trying to forestall Lou's sneaky entrance into the next room, as Lou casually inched toward the kitchen.

"Smells like gingerbread? And cloves? A hint of orange? My goodness! Those couldn't be Lena's famous Virginia—"

Hannah hastily stepped in front of her. She wanted to make them as a surprise for Carter. She couldn't have Lou blabbing it all over town, before she'd even perfected her technique. "Of course not!" she said with a lighthearted laugh. "That would have to mean I'd found the recipe!"

"Ye-es..."

Hannah watched as Lou's eyes scanned the living area, roaming over the coffee table where Hannah had laid the recipe card, facedown. "Well, anyway!" Hannah said suddenly. "Thanks for stopping by!" She took Lou gently by the shoulders and pivoted her toward the door. Lou leaned back, digging her heels into the carpet.

"I was actually thinking I'd stay. Don't you want to ask me for coffee?"

"Love to, Lou! But I'm afraid I'm out." Hannah tightened her grip and starting pushing. "Some other time."

Lou finally stopped resisting, nearly toppling forward. "Well, I...never!" She testily dusted off her fake fur collar.

Hannah yanked open the door and frigid winds whistled across the threshold.

Lou zipped up her coat.

"Thanks so much for the jam," Hannah said, carefully steering Lou outside.

The older woman appeared a little stunned. "Yes, um... And thank you for the candies." Lou blinked. "Are you sure you weren't baking—?"

"Nope!"

"Because that sure smells like—"

"Isn't that just how it is?" Hannah grinned so tightly her cheeks pinched. "This time of year, all Christmas cookies smell the same."

Then she waved good-bye and shut the door, slouching back against it with a sigh.

Lou knocked from the other side and hollered, "You're sure?"

"Yes, Lou!" Hannah called over her shoulder. "I'm sure!"

She stared down at the kittens, who were observing her curiously. "What do you think?" she whispered sneakily. "Should we go and check on the cookies?" But instead of following her to the kitchen, both cats bolted behind the couch.

Chapter Twenty-Six

Carter straightened his tie, trying to remember the last time he'd worn a civilian one. It had to have been during some formal event from his past, but at the moment none of them came to mind. He'd probably blocked them out, since he'd attended most of those with Gina. She was definitely into upscale things, including fancy clothes and cars. The disappointment was written all over her face when he bought Rudolph. Seemed like he made the right call in that regard. Rudolph was the one who'd lasted. He supposed Gina might have, too, if she'd been able to change him. But Carter didn't want to be the kind of man she wanted, and that became more apparent over time.

One of the many things Carter appreciated about Hannah was that she appeared to like him just as he was. When he'd backed off on talking about his time overseas, she hadn't acted affronted. Gina was immediately on his case, conveniently making his withdrawal about her. She had the ability to do that: turn things around, so she was always the injured party. That meant Carter was typically at fault. He wasn't ready to live with her nonsensical blame. Not when he legitimately blamed himself for enough already.

Deciding a full suit was overkill, he opted for nice pair of slacks and a blazer instead. He wouldn't be dressing up this much if he hadn't asked Hannah to church. But he had, even though Carter hadn't set foot in one in ages. But holidays were different, and Hannah seemed like the kind of girl who might like to go. Were she back home, she'd probably be attending with her brother and niece. He understood both of them were in California seeing the little girl's grandparents.

Hannah clearly valued her family as much as Carter did his. That was something they had in common. They each felt motivated to help others as well, and do some common good. Beyond that, there was the toe-curling chemistry they shared that made Carter's skin heat up just recalling Hannah's fiery kisses. He lost sight of the world when Hannah was in his arms. Lost track of everything but her… Yet, in a very telling way, she'd helped Carter find himself. He was going to tell her this tonight when he delivered the special gift he'd bought her.

Hannah hoped that it was okay that she was wearing the same red sweater dress that she'd worn on her first date with Carter. She hadn't exactly expected to be *dating* when she came to Christmas Town, or going to church either. While Hannah wasn't very religious, she found it endearing that Carter had asked her to the service. Hannah enjoyed holiday hymns and loved candlelight services. She and Ben used to go to midnight Christmas church programs with her grandparents. Before that, they'd attended the annual family service with their mom, although their dad had never joined them. Hannah's heart felt heavy at the thought that she hadn't seen her father in sixteen years, and likely wouldn't see him again. While he hadn't been an exceptional dad, he'd been the only one she'd known.

No, that was wrong. In his own big brotherly way, Ben had been like a dad to her, too. So had her Grandpa Charles. Hannah understood that families came in different shapes and sizes. Her unique configuration wasn't perfect, but it worked for her. While she missed her grandparents and Ben's late wife, Nancy, she felt blessed to have Lily and Ben in her life. Hannah couldn't wait to show the two of them around Christmas Town. She was convinced Ben and Lily would love it every bit as much as she did, and Hannah was loving it—*a lot*. She smiled to herself and put in her earrings, snatching them out of Jingles's way. He'd pounced up on her dresser and tried to grab one, but she gently shooed him aside, lifting him up and depositing him on the bed.

Carter was right about the cats. Hannah hadn't been overly thrilled when she got them. But she'd taken them in, and now—just look—naughty Jingles and sweet little Belle had become treasured members of her household. Hannah was aware she talked to them, almost like they were real people, when no one else was around. So her sage niece had been right. Apart from keeping Hannah on her toes, the active kittens were also good at keeping her company. Hannah glanced at the clock, then skipped downstairs to check the dinner in the oven. Not wanting to take chances with something new, she'd made the same meal as a few nights ago. At least *that* she had down.

As she walked through the living room, the mouth-watering scent of roasting chicken and baking sweet potatoes filled the air. She'd yet to cook the asparagus, but could slide it in the oven closer to dinnertime. It occurred to Hannah that the smells from the meal made her town house homey. It reminded her of her grandmother's house, or her own when she was small and her mom was alive. Then her mother had started getting sick and didn't feel like cooking at all for such a long while. Hannah's dad had begrudgingly brought home takeout, but by the time the food arrived it was rarely hot.

Grandma Mabel tried to remedy those unhappy memories by cooking delightful dinners for her grandchildren and making each meal an event. When April died, Ben was in his first year of college and Hannah was barely eleven. Put out by her wayward son's abandonment of his family and feeling sorry for her granddaughter, Mabel pampered Hannah mercilessly with food, but never insisted on the child helping in the kitchen.

In the beginning, she tried to teach Hannah some rudimentary things about baking. But every single recipe Hannah tried got burnt to a crisp. After Hannah dashed for her room in a violent fit of tears for the umpteenth time, her kindly grandma had said not to worry. Every member of the family had their own set of skills, and one day Hannah would identify hers. *You just focus on your studies now,* her Grandma Mabel said, and Hannah had. To the point where she went off to college without learning to cook…

At the university, Hannah had a dining hall plan. Afterward, when she was working, she generally got by on canned soup and sandwiches, and the occasional nice meal Ben threw her way. Nancy taught Ben a thing or two around the kitchen, converting him into a fairly accomplished chef. Hannah had figured that Ben got the cooking gene and that it somehow skipped her.

Now she was starting to believe perhaps she'd inherited it too. It had simply been lying dormant somewhere. All...this...time. Hannah peeked in the oven, pleased to see the chicken crowning golden brown on top, and that the potatoes were coming along. She was just removing her oven mitts when the doorbell rang.

Carter walked into Hannah's town house feeling like he was entering a dream. She'd spruced things up with a real linen tablecloth on the elegantly set table, the lights were dimmed low, and candles burned all around. The air smelled heavenly and Hannah was absolutely gorgeous in her pretty red dress. She blushed when she saw he'd brought her flowers, the dozen red roses Carter picked up at the Merry Market on his way over. "Merry Christmas."

"Thank you," she said, accepting the bouquet. "They're beautiful."

"And they match your dress," he commented happily before shutting the door behind him and giving her a kiss. Carter removed his overcoat to hang it on a hook, and Hannah viewed him with admiration. "I love the look," she said, commenting on his coat and tie.

Carter eagerly drew her into his arms. "Not half as much as I love this one."

She looked up at him and her beautiful brown eyes took his breath away.

"Ah Hannah, I could do this all day."

"Do what?"

"Just stare at you."

"Hasn't anyone ever told you staring's rude?" she teased.

"Then I'll apologize with a kiss." He brought his lips to her forehead and she giggled. "And another." He kissed her cheek. "And one more..." His mouth traveled to her neck.

"Carter." Her voice was a breathy sigh.

"Okay, I'll stop." He glanced around, noticing the house was unusually quiet. Apart from the soft melodious sound of instrumental holiday music playing in the background, there was no little pitter-patter of paws. "What happened to Jingles and Belle?"

"They're hiding," Hannah informed him.

"Hiding?"

"Behind the couch. That's where they go every time I cook."

Carter chuckled, recalling the popcorn incident, and started to remark on that. Then he thought better of it. "What is cooking, by the way? It smells delicious."

"Roast chicken and sweet potatoes, with asparagus on the side." Hannah beamed proudly. "Oops! I'd better put that in." She walked to the kitchen carrying her flowers and Carter followed behind her.

"Can I help with something?"

"There's wine on the table. Will you open it while I put these in water and tend to the food?"

"Of course." Carter was amazed by how at ease Hannah seemed in the kitchen. If he hadn't seen her in action at his house a few short days ago, he'd swear she was a natural cook. He opened the wine and poured them each a glass. "How's that cooking course coming along?" he asked from the dining area.

She stuck her head around the door jamb. "Finished!"

"Already?" He carried Hannah her wine and her smile sparkled.

"In record time, it's true. I earned the gold leaf certificate."

"Very impressive," he said, handing her a glass. "I think this deserves a toast."

She clinked his glass. "Thanks, Carter. I worked very hard for it."

"And learned a lot, it seems." He marveled at her as she lightly tossed the asparagus in olive oil like an expert and popped it in the oven. Carter noticed she'd already arranged his flowers in a vase. "Want me to put this in the living room somewhere?"

"On the coffee table would be great." She whipped off her oven gloves and deftly set the timer. Carter wondered briefly if he'd walked into the wrong house.

"You *are* Hannah Winchester?" he asked jokingly. "*The* Hannah Winchester?"

"You mean the one who can't cook?"

Carter nodded and waited on her answer.

"Yep! It's me. Only here's the thing…" she added a little impishly. "A lot has changed around here."

"A lot?" Now she had him intrigued. "What other surprises does my girlfriend have in store?"

"Nuh-uh," she said defiantly. "Not telling you yet." She tugged on his arm, turning him toward the sofa. "Why don't you go have a seat? I have a few things to clean up, then I'll join you."

Carter sat and patted his jacket pocket, where he had Hannah's presents tucked inside. He so hoped she'd like both of them. While he'd been plenty wowed by Hannah previously, he was even more impressed with her now. She'd obviously been working hard at learning to cook and honing her newfound skills. Her commitment to the task demonstrated what kind of woman she was: somebody purposeful who wasn't afraid to tackle challenges. Carter wondered silently if Hannah would still want to take him on, if she knew about his history. And yet, he ached to tell her the truth. He needed to believe that she'd care for him anyway. That she wouldn't view him as damaged goods and cast him aside. Could he trust her enough to reveal his devastating secret?

He'd been waiting to find the right moment to talk to her, but somehow the optimal time never came. Perhaps there was no "best time" for something like this. Maybe he should just do it, and unburden his soul, because if Hannah no longer wanted him afterward, he owed her the opportunity to end things before they got any more deeply involved. Carter had become so attached to Hannah in these past few weeks he could scarcely wrap his head around it. His heart, however, understood things all too clearly. By confiding in her about his past, he'd either be setting the stage for a different level of relationship with Hannah—or pushing open the door for her exit.

Hannah couldn't believe how well she was doing with everything. She could be on television! Have her own cooking show! *Hannah Winchester: Christmas Town Gourmet.* Okay, perhaps *gourmet* was stretching things a little far. *Christmas Town Cookie Maker?* Hannah didn't know how she could bear to sit through dinner without telling Carter about her discovery, but she'd decided it would be more impressive to spring the truth on him during dessert. She could give him the wallet then, too.

She carried her wine into the living room and sat on the sofa beside Carter. He looked incredibly handsome, all dressed up. Then again, Carter pretty much looked dynamite in whatever he wore—including that Santa suit. "So," she said chattily. "What have you been up to lately?"

"You mean since Wednesday?"

"Yes."

"Oh… Things!"

"Things?"

"Yeah," he said, clearing his throat. "Quite a few of them."

"Like…?" She eyed him quizzically and he adjusted his jacket.

"This and that," he said vaguely. "Around town."

"I see."

"I got Victoria a present," he added after a bit.

"How nice."

"And Tilly, too. It's my first year here as sheriff, so I figured it would be a nice gesture."

"I'm sure they appreciated it. What did you get them?"

He stared blankly at the left side of Hannah's head. "One of those things there."

She lightly fingered her hair. "You mean a barrette?"

"Barrette, right. Sorry. The word escaped me." He appeared mildly distracted, as if his mind was on something else. "I found a couple of Christmassy ones at Olivia's shop. Is that where you got yours?"

Hannah nodded. "They're very cool. I bought one for Jade." Then she slyly added, "I did a bit of Christmas shopping myself, you know."

He observed the loaded stockings hanging from the mantel. "Santa's already come for Jingles and Belle?"

"I found them some small knickknacks in the pet section at Sugar Plum Feed Supply. A couple of kitty treats, too."

"Jingles is lucky he's not getting coal."

"He has been awfully naughty, it's true."

Carter scanned the floor, then peered around the back of the sofa, where he saw a flicker of an orange tail. "Looks like he's staying out of trouble for now."

"We'll see how long that lasts," Hannah said with a laugh.

Carter took her hand. "I'm really glad I'm spending this Christmas with you. More than that, I'm happy you're staying in Christmas Town. No, happy isn't exactly strong enough."

"Overjoyed?" Hannah filled in. "Ecstatic?"

Carter grinned, but his smile was a tad melancholy. "You're one incredible woman."

"I'm glad that you think so."

"I more than think it." He brought their interlocked hands to his heart and it crinkled. *Crinkled?* "I feel it, way down in here." He tenderly kissed her hand. "I'm not sure you understand the effect you have on me. You make me want to do things, and say things…tell you…"

"Tell me what?"

Carter slowly released her hand and picked up his wine. He appeared to be gathering his nerve. Finally, his eyes met hers and he said seriously, "About my past."

There was something there; she felt it. Some kind of dark history… But no history of Carter's could be too dark for her. Just look at the kind of person he was. *Totally wonderful*. At the same time, he appeared so solemn she was a little scared about where he was going with this. Maybe she didn't need to know whatever it was…just yet.

"You don't have to tell me if you don't want—"

"But I need to." He met her eyes and his were rimmed with sadness. "Hannah, it's time."

She swallowed hard, bracing herself for anything. Was he secretly married? Or worse, did he have a family sequestered somewhere? *Two* families? More? She'd read about a man who'd done that, kept separate lives in different towns. But seriously, Carter was the Christmas Town sheriff. Where on earth would he find the time?

Hannah told herself not to be overly dramatic. Whatever it was, it couldn't really be that awful. She had a sudden sinking sensation, as another possibility dawned. Maybe it really *was* horrible, because it involved something that had occurred in combat. When Carter had been reluctant to speak of his time overseas before, Hannah had intuited something terrible had happened to him. Something he didn't often talk about. Perhaps he never talked about it. And here he was confiding in her.

Carter took a slug of wine. "It was a long time ago," he began. "But sometimes it feels a lot closer than that."

"Your deployment?" she guessed.

"One of them, yeah. I can't share any of the details."

She knew that he couldn't and understood that part. "That's all right," she replied gently. "Just tell me what you're feeling." Hannah's heart beat faster because she had the notion that he was about to. It didn't matter what he had to say, she'd be ready for it. She had to be, because of how deeply she cared for him. She could tell this was hard for Carter. Almost impossible...

"Feeling?" His mouth drew a hard line. "Hurt. Angry. Betrayed." He turned toward her and his expression was stormy. "Like it should have been me. Instead, I stayed to cover from behind. But I didn't..."

"Didn't what?"

"Cover well enough." He hung his head. "I should have gone in. I was senior, more experienced, better trained." Carter stopped talking and set down his glass, folding his face in his hands. Hannah could tell he wished he'd never started this conversation, but he had, and now they were in it. Hannah was right there with him. The harrowed look in his eyes had transported her to some unimaginable place filled with smoke and fire and unspeakable horrors.

She gently laid her hand on his arm. "Things happen in war."

"I should have insisted—"

"You probably couldn't. You probably had orders."

Carter was silent a long while before he finally spoke. "I gave the orders." He bit out the words harshly, as if he was loath to say them. "*I gave the orders that got three men killed.* The warehouse was rigged. Booby-trapped. There was intelligence on it, but we received the information too late. We walked straight into a trap. Only nine of us survived; a few soldiers, just barely." Carter's face twisted in anguish. "Can you believe I got a medal for that?"

Hannah's mind quickly put the scenario together. Carter had conducted his mission based on the information he had. If he'd gone in first, he wouldn't be sitting here now. Yet, the outcome likely would have been the same. Perhaps things would have been worse without him there to help the wounded. Carter had emerged a hero, but he still blamed himself for the losses he couldn't prevent. "For saving the others?"

"A seventy-five percent survival rate isn't exactly stellar."

A single tear slid down her cheek as she absorbed his pain. It had to have been wrenching, carrying that guilt all this time. But the tragedy wasn't intentional. Carter had done his best under trying circumstances, and sadly things had come out wrong. *Sometimes very bad things happen to the best people,* Hannah thought, her heart aching at the memory of her mother. She drew in a breath, proceeding gently. "I know that every life is precious, but you really can't hold yourself account—"

"I am accountable." His eyes bored into hers. "Can't you see? The buck stops here, Hannah. There's nobody else to blame."

"How about the enemy? The ones who laid the trap?"

Carter set his jaw and looked away.

Several minutes ticked by with the mantel clock resonating sharply.

Hannah's heart ached as she measured her words. "I'm sorry you…went through that."

"It wasn't about me." He seemed lost in a world far away, and she suspected he was remembering his fallen comrades. "Never was."

"You have to believe that none of it was your fault. You're a good man…a brave man…someone who always does what's right for others. That's why they gave you that medal, I'm sure."

She brought her arms around him in a hug and he sagged against her like a dead weight. The words scraped from his throat, raw with emotion. "I don't want you to know me like this." Carter probably thought he was exhibiting weakness, but in his confession Hannah saw strength. It had taken courage for him to share such a personal memory. She probably respected him more now than she ever had, because of what he'd endured and the heroism he'd displayed, even if he wouldn't acknowledge it.

Her lips quivered. "I'm happy to know you every way I can."

"I've never told anybody," he whispered against her hair. "Not my parents, my sisters. Kurt. Anybody."

"Then thank you for telling me," she said, her voice cracking. Hannah felt so honored…so humbled…by his stark confession, she could think of nothing else to say. All she wanted to do was hold on to this incredible man, for he was so much more than she'd imagined. Carter wasn't just the rock of this community as Christmas Town Sheriff; he was somebody honorable, deep, and real. She strengthened her embrace and held him to her. And he held her back—with a fierce, desperate tenderness she'd never known, as their hearts beat steadily together…until the kitchen timer went off.

Carter felt like he'd ruined their Christmas celebration with one blow. He could have told Hannah without losing it completely. He also could have waited until later. Why had he been driven to tell her everything tonight? He'd been stupid. Self-centered. Desperately seeking her assurance. And it was too late to take back anything now. Hannah returned from the kitchen to find him sitting on the sofa in a daze.

She sat beside him and said softly, "Dinner's ready, but I can reheat it later, if you'd rather wait."

"Hannah, I'm sor—"

She brought her fingers to his lips. "No, don't say it. Don't say you're sorry that you shared with me, because I'm not. I'm only sorry for your pain and what you went through. What you're still going through. But now that you've told me," she took his hand, "you no longer have to go through it alone."

Gratitude flooded his heart and another feeling, too. Something deeper, richer, and more profound... Hannah was so kind and caring, so loving; it made him want to love her back.

"You're very special," he said, searching her eyes. "I hope you know that."

"You're special, too." She brought her hand to his cheek and kissed him gently on the lips. "Now, are you ready for dinner or shall we wait?"

"Let's eat," he said, standing to help her. Hannah had obviously worked hard on this dinner and he wasn't about to disappoint her by letting it grow cold. Though Carter had cast a pall over the evening with his old war stories, there was hopefully still time to salvage this date. He certainly owed it to Hannah to pull himself together and try.

Hannah was pleased her meal came out so well. She was extra glad that Carter liked it. He went back for second servings—of everything! To distract him from his worries and keep the mood light, she regaled him with tales of her cooking disasters. Thankfully, her tactics appeared to be working. He really did seem entertained by her stories, and Hannah delighted in seeing that smile return to his handsome face.

His earlier confession had broken her heart. It seemed his had broken again too, as he'd relieved his horrible ordeal in its retelling. Hannah cared for Carter so much, she couldn't bear to see him unhappy. She wanted him to feel good. Which was why she'd worked so hard at making this dinner pleasant and happy. It occurred to Hannah that perhaps that was part of why Carter liked her. She was generally an optimistic kind of person, while he was more even-keeled. Not that Carter was always as serious as Sandy thought he was. Hannah could get him to laugh, couldn't she? That was actually one of her strengths.

Carter finished his last bite of chicken, then set down his fork with a chuckle. "You couldn't possibly have burned all that food!"

"But I did! Scout's honor! You'll find the evidence in the dumpster out back. Though I wouldn't look if I were you." She wrinkled up her nose. "It smells really rank."

"You're a wonderful person, and wonderfully funny."

"Funny? Oh, er… All right! If you say so. Though I don't always mean to be."

"I'm sure you don't. Like that time with the ice pack."

Hannah stood and cleared their dishes. "No fair dragging up ancient history."

"Here, let me—"

"No," she said, pushing him back down. "Stay there. Let me bring dessert!"

"Great! And when you return, I have something for you too," he said, patting his pocket.

Hannah turned and raised an eyebrow, wondering if it had to do with that crinkle.

"After dessert, of course!"

"Of course," she mused, heading to the kitchen. Hannah set the dishes in the sink and reached inside a cabinet, finding her hidden tin of Virginia Cookies. She was so excited about her surprise she couldn't stand it. What a perfect moment for these. The timing couldn't be better. They'd perk Carter right up with tidings of comfort and joy! "Do you want coffee?" she asked.

"No, thanks! Wine is good!"

Hannah carefully arranged the cookies on a platter, wondering how many were enough. What if they really did have some kind of magical powers? Would it be possible to overdose on them? She opted to be conservative and only bring out four. *No, five!* she decided, adding another one on top. *There, that looks pretty.* Each one was shaped like a heart and had a frilly white frosting border dotted with little holly leaves and red berries. Hannah had kind of cheated and made the berries out of Red Hots, but she didn't think Carter would know the difference. She'd basically followed the recipe—with only a few minor shortcuts. She'd have to remember not too think too much about them when Sandy was around. It was a good thing Carter didn't have Sandy's intuitive powers.

She paraded proudly into the dining area and set the platter before Carter. "Tadahhh!"

"How great!" he remarked. "Gingerbread! I love—"

"They're Virginia Cookies!" Hannah spouted out before she could stop herself. "My Great-grandmother Lena's top-secret recipe!"

Carter stared at her agog. "You mean—?"

"Yes! I found it!" Hannah jumped up and down on her heels like a little kid. She couldn't help it. This was so exciting. Almost like finding the recipe card all over again. "I searched the box from top to bottom just like you said! And then Jingles went in—"

"Jingles?"

"Yeah! And he pulled out my scarf—"

"Wait a minute, which scarf?"

"Oh, this really pretty purple and teal one with shiny gold and silver threads. I got it at South Pole Pottery. I wasn't going to buy it at first, but then they had this amazing sale…" His eyes were glazing over and she was losing him. "Never mind. Doesn't matter." Hannah drew in a breath. "Anyway! The card was hidden in the hatbox, underneath the lid. Concealed beneath the lining! Can you believe Grandpa Charles was that sneaky?"

"Well, no! Yes!" He shot her a smile. "Why, Hannah, that's wonderful."

Hannah suddenly felt winded and took a seat. "Yes, I know."

"How long ago was this?"

"I found it Monday."

"Monday? And you didn't say a word?"

"I couldn't." She grinned at him giddily, hoping he was as happy about it as she was. "I wanted to make it a surprise."

"Well, I am surprised. Quite a bit." He stared down at the plate. "You're very good at keeping secrets. Better than I expected."

What was that supposed to mean? "Anyway!" She shoved the plate closer to him. "Go on! Take a bite!"

Carter suddenly went really, really pale, like he'd seen the Ghost of Christmas Past, or something. Was it Hannah's imagination or did he scoot back in his chair? "I'm…um…" Why on earth was he hesitating? Did he think she was proposing *marriage*? "Not entirely sure I'm ready for dessert."

"Not sure?" she asked, thrown. "You said before that you wanted to eat my whole box of cookies?"

He looked up, tension creasing his brow. "Yes, but in a figurative sense."

"A figurative sense, I see." She snatched the platter out from under his nose, deeply hurt.

Only minutes ago, they'd been as close as two people could be: almost like two hearts beating as one. Carter had shared a devastating memory with her, and she'd been genuinely supportive. Hannah had even been foolish enough to think the cookies might help. Hoping they'd brighten his spirits. *And now, he won't even try just one?* "Wait…" He laid a hand on her arm. "I might take a tiny nibble."

Heat burned in her eyes, because he certainly didn't sound like he meant it. Nobody got a no-thank-you helping of Lena's cookies. They were far too special for that.

"A nibble's not enough," she said, her voice rising. And it really wasn't. Not after she'd toiled for hours and thrown out so many blackened batches. Only thinking of him.

"Fine." He shot her a steely gaze. "Then I won't have any."

Hannah blinked in incredulity. It was the most personal Christmas gift she'd ever made, and he might as well have tossed the entire platter back in her face. "No," she practically shouted. "I suppose that you won't!"

Thank goodness I have a back-up, Hannah thought heatedly. She hauled the cookies to the kitchen with long angry strides and returned with a mid-size package. "Here," she said, slamming it down on the table. "Maybe you'd like this better."

Carter stared at her, shell-shocked. "You want me to open it?"

"No, you don't have to!" she said furiously. But he started to rip back the paper, anyway. "I can tell you what it is… It's a—"

He flipped the lid off the box. "Wallet!" he said in terribly exaggerated tones. Like when a parent gets a horribly ugly homemade gift from a child.

What? Was he going to refuse this gift, too?

"If you don't like it, I can take it back." She lunged for it, but he stopped her. "Hannah, please don't do that," he said, his countenance softening. "I love it, really I do. I love the cookies too. Here, let me have one! No, I'll eat two of them!"

"I'm afraid it's too late," she said haughtily. "You didn't accept them with a grateful heart."

His look said: *Heartburn's what you're giving me.*

Hannah gulped, hoping she hadn't caught something from Sandy.

"Well, I got you something too," he said testily. "And you probably won't like it either."

Hannah was willing to wait and see about that. Considering how agitated he'd made her, this left her feeling magnanimous.

Carter reached under his coat and pulled out a sheaf of papers. "Here!" he said, slamming it down on the table like that explained everything.

"Where?"

"There!" He pointed heatedly. "*There* is the answer to all your worries. Read it and weep." He didn't have to be sarcastic. Hannah already felt like crying.

She picked up the pages and flipped through them, seeing hundreds and hundreds of names and email addresses on some spreadsheet. "I have no idea what this means," she said, handing it back to him.

"These are all the people who've pledged to help you."

"Help *me*? With what?"

"The Christmas Cookie Shop!"

Hannah set a hand on her hip. "I have no idea what you're talking about."

"We crowdfunded," he tried to explain.

"We, who?"

"Me! The Town Council! Everybody worked so hard to raise all that money!"

Hannah grabbed the pages back and noticed a budget on the last page. While the individual donor amounts weren't given, a total dollar sum was provided at the end—and it was substantial. Hannah's head reeled as she weakly dropped the papers to the table.

"We wanted to help, Hannah," he said feebly. "So you could reopen the cookie shop without taking out loans for its repairs and upgrade." He plaintively met her eyes. "Everyone in Christmas Town loves you and wants your business to succeed."

That's when it occurred to Hannah that Carter hadn't said that dastardly four-letter word. No wonder she'd sworn it off! Just look at the trouble it caused— even in absentia!

"*Everyone?*" Her eyebrows rose doubtfully. "Even the man who doesn't want my cookies?"

"Oh for crying out loud." He glared at her and she glared back, just as frightfully as she could.

"You know what?" he said, standing. "I think I'm done here." He pulled a small wrapped gift from his jacket pocket and laid it on the table. "This is for you," he said firmly. "If you don't like it, I can return it, too." Then, to Hannah's utter horror, he yanked on his overcoat and slammed out the door, shouting, "Merry Christmas!"

Chapter Twenty-Seven

Hannah didn't even want to get out of bed the next morning, and it was Christmas. *Christmas,* of all times! The kittens were pacing around her, mewing mournfully as they circled the quilt. *Oomph!* That must have been Jingles striding across her back. Already, he was tons heavier than his sister. Beyond stealing objects, he probably also purloined Belle's food. Hannah would need to be more careful to watch them at kitty mealtime. *Reeowww!* Which apparently was now. Hannah covered her head with a pillow and counted to ten.

"All right, already," she said, grumpily kicking the quilt aside. The kittens leapt to the floor and pounded down the stairs, certain this meant breakfast.

Hannah thumped along behind them, thinking she hadn't really wanted to go to the midnight church service anyway. And she certainly hadn't asked for any handouts. In a town where everyone knew everything about everybody, her dirty laundry was certainly flapping about in the breeze. Now, everyone in Christmas Town from the judge to the undertaker knew she was dirt-poor. Lovely.

It wasn't like Hannah ever put on airs, but she did have her pride, after all. When she'd made the decision to stay in Christmas Town, it had been an active *choice,* with Hannah willing to endure the consequences. How had everyone else here become involved? She passed by the mantel, yanking down the two kitty stockings. "Here," she said to the cats, winding their way around her legs. "Knock yourselves out." She dropped the loaded stockings to the carpet, trudging on toward the kitchen and the holy grail of coffee she sought.

Loud Christmas music boomed through the adjoining wall, telling her Sandy was already up. Hannah was tempted to call Sandy and confess her horrible misfortunes. Then she worried that Sandy might judge her as harshly as Carter had. Hannah was pretty sure she'd spotted Sandy's name on that spreadsheet. Jade, Olivia, and Lou and Buddy Christmas were there, as well. So were Frank and Victoria, Tilly and Carter… Kurt Christmas and Ray… Pastor Wilson! Oh, her head throbbed.

Hannah fumbled through the steps of making coffee, vaguely hoping yesterday hadn't happened. Maybe it was some awfully horrible nightmare, and she'd wake up from it soon. Then she spotted the full platter of Virginia Cookies on the stovetop and her stomach plummeted. She'd gone to so much trouble, and Carter hadn't even eaten one! He'd basically turned up his nose at them, and why? Because he believed in that silly superstition…? Because he feared that by taking a bite, he'd be proclaiming his undying commitment? *Give me a break!*

Hannah paced back into the living room while the coffee brewed, her gaze falling on the flowers. Pretty things meant nothing when offered from a cold heart, she thought gloomily. But how could Carter's heart be cold, when he'd made her burn so hot for him? No matter how upset she was with him, Hannah couldn't paint Carter as an unfeeling individual. He'd been hurting when he'd talked to her about his deployment. Their discussion had been deeply personal, intimate. What's more, Hannah hadn't *broken through to Carter;* he'd invited her in.

Jingles and Belle were waiting by their stockings like they were expecting her to do something. "Oh, right. Sorry." She bent low to shake the contents of each stocking out, letting them fall on the floor. Jingles instantly started batting at a ball while Belle pawed at a kitty treat container. That's when Hannah remembered she hadn't fed them. *I am such a bad mother!*

It was a good thing that Carter walked out. Even better that she didn't *love* him. Certainly a great thing that she didn't want to *marry* him and have his babies. *Ever.*

Hannah stopped walking when her heart caught in her throat. *No. No way. No, no, no, noooooo.* She wasn't ready for that! Hannah blinked hard. Was she? The coffee beeped and she went to pour herself a giant mugful, mumbling to herself as she went. Was it possible that Carter was as scared as she was? Was that why he'd totally freaked out? Okay, Hannah realized she had to accept some blame. She'd freaked a tiny bit, too. *But not as much as he did. Really!*

After feeding the kittens, Hannah carried her coffee to the dining room table. While she'd cleared the dirty dishes last night, that awkward spreadsheet and Carter's parting gift sat on it. She sank into a chair and picked up the papers, going through them again—this time more carefully. The number of individuals who'd rushed to her aid was astounding, particularly since she didn't know most of them.

When Hannah got to the part at the end about any surplus cash being put in a civic fund in Lena's honor, her eyes misted over. Whoever had put this together had minded every detail. While the Town Council oversaw the crowdfunding effort, somebody had to have proposed the initial idea. Hannah had two primary suspects: Carter and Lou, but her money was on Carter. She'd confided in him regarding her hopes for the Christmas Cookie Shop way before she'd talked with Buddy Christmas about not wanting to sell it. Only Carter knew how much this meant to her. Not just on an objective professional level, but personally.

Hannah reached for Carter's prettily wrapped box and fingered its silky ribbon. He didn't even give her a chance to open it. Then again, she and Carter weren't on the most congenial terms at the time. Hannah thought of setting the package aside, then curiosity got the best of her. She slowly pried back the wrapping paper, revealing a jewelry box. Next, she opened its lid, exposing an intricate gold chain necklace attached to a small charm. She dangled it from her hand and held it up to the light. The tiny object glittered and twirled in front of her.

It was a compass.

All at once, Hannah knew what this meant.

Carter had found his way.

She'd found her way to him, too.

And now, very tragically, they'd both lost each other.

Carter sat with his back to his desk, facing the window, as snow covered the landscape outside. It came down in heavy clumps, coating telephone wires and sticking to lampposts, covering sidewalks and blanketing the street. His office was on the north side of the courthouse building facing South Main Street. If he stared hard enough he could spy the T intersection with Santa Claus Lane. Though he couldn't see that far, he knew North Main was just beyond that. Another few hundred feet and he'd be at Hannah's front door.

He'd so looked forward to this Christmas, but what a dismal holiday it had turned out to be. He'd unloaded his personal history on Hannah, and—just as he'd feared—that had led to an explosion. As Carter couldn't fathom her being displeased about the crowdfunding, Hannah's obvious anger had to be rooted in something else. He'd revealed too much and caught her off guard, and Carter was angry at himself for doing so. Then, she'd gone to all that trouble to bake those silly cookies and he hadn't even taken a bite.

While it was true he'd agreed to try one later, Hannah had seen right through his gesture, and it was too little too late. What did it matter that those Virginia Cookies were reputed to inspire true love? Just because others had married after partaking of them, that didn't mean that Carter would hear wedding bells simply by accepting dessert. It had been a particularly special dessert, made by Hannah with supreme effort. And he'd summarily shot those efforts down. Carter was embarrassed by his bad behavior and ashamed by how he'd stormed out the door.

He never let his emotions get the better of him. So what had happened here? Had he really been so afraid of giving in to love that he'd fallen apart? Carter sighed and ran his hands through his hair, feeling horrible about everything. More than anything, he felt like a jerk for ruining Hannah's Christmas. It was Carter's first Christmas in Christmas Town, but it was Hannah's first holiday here, too.

By some slanted miracle, he'd managed to mess it up for both of them.

"Welcome, Hannah! Merry Christmas!" Wendell held back the door as Hannah entered carrying a bottle of wine and a homemade pumpkin pie. She'd made it this morning to distract herself. It was actually one of the easier things she'd made so far, and she hadn't even burned the crust. She hadn't bothered to bundle up too much for the short walk over. She'd simply slipped on her pea coat and skipped the hat and gloves. She wore jeans and a nice sweater that was Christmas red with her pearl teardrop earrings and the snowman barrette.

"Merry Christmas, Wendell," she said, giving him a peck on the cheek. She'd become fast friends with Jade, and Wendell had graciously welcomed her friendship as well. Hannah almost felt sorry for Wendell, the only male at this Christmas "hen party" including her, Jade, Olivia, and Sandy, when she remembered he had a little compatriot. Alexander scooted toward her with a big bright grin. "Hi! I'm Alexander!" He zoomed by and she realized he was carrying a toy airplane, making it soar through the air as he ran in zigzag circles throughout the downstairs.

"Merry Christmas, Alexander!" she called after him, though she suspected he didn't hear. Alexander was completely absorbed in his own world, giving sotto voce commands to his pilot from his pretend control tower. One chubby hand covered his mouth as he announced, "Coming in for a landing, over!" before gliding the plane onto the coffee table.

The layout of Jade and Wendell's place was similar to hers, but the décor was much more contemporary. The furniture was sleek and upscale and modern artwork hung on the walls. Hannah noted the minimalistic color scheme was all black and white. The only splashes of color came from the brightly decorated Christmas tree in the corner, loaded with tons of homemade ornaments, and the single Christmas stocking hanging from the mantel.

Jade's dad appeared from the kitchen and held out his hand. "Caleb Smith, good to see you again." Wendell quickly relieved Hannah of the wine and Jade bustled forward to accept the pie.

"You baked for us? How nice!"

"It's pumpkin," she said, shaking hands with Caleb and wishing him a merry Christmas. She'd completely forgotten there'd be another man in the house. How nice for the entire Scott family that Alexander's grandpa could be here. The thought made Hannah briefly miss her own, but she pushed that aside, determined to focus on the positive. She'd been so downhearted this morning, she'd almost called to cancel coming over. Then she'd decided she didn't want to let down her friends. Plus, she probably needed to get out of the house. She'd already cried through two boxes of tissues.

Jade set the pie on her kitchen counter, then leaned forward to hug Hannah's shoulders. "You all right, hon?" she whispered. "Your eyes look a little red."

Hannah pulled a tissue from her coat pocket and sniffed. "Yes, just allergies."

Jade eyed her oddly. "What are you allergic to?"

Heartache, Hannah wanted to say, but she didn't. She looked around for her intuitive friend and Carter's sister. "Where are Sandy and Olivia?"

"They'll be over any minute," Jade said, offering to take Hannah's coat. Hannah slipped out of it and Jade called to Alexander. When the little boy arrived promptly in the doorway, she asked him to take Miss Hannah's coat and put it upstairs on the bed.

"He's such a cute kid," Hannah said, smiling after him.

"Thanks! We'll keep him." Jade angled toward her and lifted the small gold charm that hung from around her neck. "Nice. Is this new?" She scrutinized Hannah's features. "Maybe a special Christmas gift?"

When she'd been getting dressed she'd somehow felt compelled to try it on. It seemed like the only bit of Carter she had left. After their horrid fight last night, Hannah didn't know when she'd see him again. If Carter happened by later, like he'd planned on doing before their falling-out, she wanted to be sure to have it on. "Um, yes. It's new," she answered without revealing any details. Fortunately for her, at that moment, the doorbell rang.

"Someone else is here," Jade said, turning her attention to the other room. "Let's go see who it is!" She dusted her hands on her apron and Hannah glanced around the kitchen, seeing a beautiful stuffed turkey sitting on the stovetop cooling. A pot of gravy simmered beside it, and covered casseroles baked in the oven. Everything smelled devine.

The group of them—Wendell, Jade, Caleb, little Alexander, and Hannah—gathered around the door to welcome their newcomer and were greeted by two. Sandy and Olivia smiled, happily holding covered dishes. A tote filled with gifts hung from each of their shoulders.

"Oh gosh! I almost forgot," Hannah said suddenly. She had presents for everyone as well. She'd even run out on Christmas Eve morning and picked up something for Alexander: a small package of miniature plastic jungle animals she'd found at Christmas Town Drugs. She wasn't sure if she needed to get something for Wendell. After some deliberation, she decided the wine should be enough. Not bothering with her coat for the short trip, Hannah slipped out the door, telling the others she'd be right back.

After a marvelous meal, the group sat around the living area enjoying some eggnog and the company. They'd also just finished opening their gifts. Hannah felt pleased that she'd chosen appropriately for her friends. Jade loved her reindeer hair barrette, Olivia adored her hand-painted Christmas tree ball, and Sandy was thrilled with her art book. Little Alexander instantly ripped open his package, then plopped down on his belly making loud animal sounds as his new toys roared and squawked at one another.

Hannah had been surprised by thoughtful gifts, too: a gorgeous scarf from Olivia, a contemporary cookbook from Jade, and a set of lovely notecards made from prints of Sandy's art. This reminded Hannah of all the thank-you notes she'd need to write. Over three thousand of them, and she intended to thank every contributor personally.

Once she'd gotten over her shock in learning about the crowdfunding project, Hannah was overwhelmed by how incredibly generous the whole town had been. She also understood that she'd be foolish to turn down the townsfolk's warmhearted gesture. After so many people had worked so hard to try to ensure her happiness, she needed to return their kindness by thanking them sincerely and graciously accepting their help. Since the topic hadn't come up yet today, perhaps the others were waiting for her to introduce it.

"These presents are really wonderful." She smiled at her friends, holding her new things in her lap. "But one of the most wonderful gifts of all"—she paused and glanced at each of their faces, including Wendell's and Caleb's, whose names were also on the list—"was learning what each of you did for me."

Olivia's cheeks glowed brightly. "Carter told you?"

When she nodded, Sandy reached over and took her hand. "We're so excited it worked out." Then she stopped and observed Hannah curiously, before lowering her voice. "Hey, is everything all right?"

Hannah blinked. "Yeah."

Sandy spotted the necklace. "Pretty! Where did you get—?" Sandy stopped, abruptly rubbing her temples. "Uh-oh."

"What's wrong, Sandy?" Jade asked her. "I hope you're not getting a headache."

"No, I'm fine." Sandy shot another glance at Hannah, then whispered to her, "Seriously, what's going on?"

"So when did he tell you?" Wendell directed his comment at Hannah.

Hannah avoided looking at Sandy, smiling at Wendell. "Just last night. I was truly humbled. Am truly humbled. That so many people would go to such trouble."

"And pull it all together in just five days!" Jade declared. "It was really a feat! And Carter's idea, you know."

A lump formed in Hannah's throat. "I thought he was behind it, but he didn't say so."

"Carter doesn't like to brag on himself," Olivia said. "Not since his big fish story days, anyway."

Everyone in the room laughed, apparently having heard the whopper of a tale. Even Alexander chortled loudly, although Hannah suspected the child was just mimicking the others.

"You deserve to see the Christmas Cookie Shop prosper." Caleb raised his eggnog.

"Here's to the Christmas Cookie Shop!" Wendell said, and they all toasted.

Olivia happily sipped from her glass. "I can't wait until it reopens. When are you making your move?"

Hannah was momentarily puzzled. Did she mean business-wise or personally?

"Personally," Sandy said and Hannah jumped.

Sandy quickly covered her mouth.

"I…um…haven't really decided," Hannah said. "But sometime after the holidays, I'll go back to Virginia and grab my stuff." She honestly didn't have a lot. Just the few odd boxes and hanging clothes she'd left at Ben's place. "I'll need to find a place to live here first."

"There's a rental down on Church Street," Caleb offered helpfully.

"Yes, that's right," Olivia said enthusiastically. "Right next to the Christmas Inn."

"That's Walt Christmas's place," Jade explained, apparently thinking that Hannah might not know. "He's the middle brother, and Joy and Noelle's dad."

"Walt's late wife, Rose, died about ten years ago," Caleb remarked with a frown. "It was a very sad case. The girls were only seven."

Hannah thought of Ben's late wife, Nancy, and the issues the family had endured in losing her. "I'm sure that must have been tough—for all of the Christmases. My brother lost his wife a few years ago, too."

"Children?" Caleb asked kindly.

"A little girl."

"I think that rental's a very good idea," Jade said, turning to her dad. "That is, unless…" She looked hopefully around the room. "We could convince Louise Christmas to convert the Sisters' Row unit to a long-term rental."

"That would be awesome," Sandy said excitedly. She grinned at Hannah. "You could stay right next door!"

"Yes." Jade smiled brightly. "To all of us."

"How about the shop?" Wendell asked her. "When will you get started with its repairs?"

"One step at a time, husband." Jade nudged him playfully. "Hannah's still adjusting to the news."

It was true; she was. Hannah hadn't even told Ben about Christmas Town's enormously generous crowdfunding gift. She planned to call him and Lily later this evening to say merry Christmas. She'd fill him in then. "I'll probably look into lining people up to come work on it after the first of the year. I have no idea how long the renovation will take."

"Are you okay to get by in the meantime?" Caleb asked with fatherly concern.

"Oh yes, I'm fine. Thank you." Hannah had checked her online bank account just yesterday morning. Since she'd forgone submitting and paying for those graduate school applications, she actually had a slightly bigger cushion than she'd expected to have at this time.

Olivia suddenly seemed to notice her gold necklace, shimmering in the Christmas tree's light. "What a gorgeous compass charm," she said, turning to Hannah. "Where on earth did you get it?"

Carter slid his credit card back into his new wallet and climbed in his truck. He shook the snow from his hat, setting it on the seat beside him. Gas and Go was the only place doing business on Christmas Day, but it wasn't technically open. The small convenience store attached to an auto mechanic's garage was closed down tight. The pumps were automatic, though. Carter didn't really need the gas. He'd had more than half a tank and could have waited, but he'd been looking for something to do to fill his time, so he'd topped off his tank.

After giving up on paperwork, he'd headed out on patrol. The office was dead quiet and none of the calls had been emergencies. He'd spoken briefly with his parents in Virginia, and his sister Savannah, who was visiting them, and they'd wished each other a merry Christmas. It was hard to believe that not long ago Carter was counting this one as his best Christmas season ever. It had certainly felt that way when he'd been with Hannah. Carter was so proud of her for her spunk and her spirit. Imagine inheriting a bakery, then deciding to get it running, without even knowing how to cook! But she was learning, it seemed. Very fast.

Guilt gnawed at him over his refusal to taste Hannah's Virginia Cookies. He should have gobbled up the ones that she'd offered, then asked for more, complimenting their deliciousness—whether or not they were any good. Carter wondered if it was it too late to make things better. He certainly owed her an apology. Not by text or phone, either. Carter needed to do it in person.

He stared down the snowy road before him. He was on North Main Street and headed toward Sisters' Row. Jade had invited him to stop by, so he could pop in briefly to offer his holiday greetings. Carter feared that could prove awkward, considering how he and Hannah had parted last night. He ran a hand through his hair and blew out a hard breath, recalling Ray's words when he'd called Carter a chicken sheriff. That had been eons ago, back when Ray's brother Kurt was prodding Carter to ask Hannah out. Well, he had, hadn't he? He'd gotten to know Hannah really well. And everything he'd feared in the beginning had come to pass.

Carter had revealed himself to Hannah in an incredibly personal way. She now knew more about him that anyone else, but Carter didn't regret that. He wanted Hannah to understand him on more than just a superficial level. More than that, he yearned to have her accept him as well. Despite his imperfections, Hannah made Carter long to do better. To be the best person he could be and the sort of man she deserved. She hadn't ever tried to change him, but Carter kept changing inside. His heart was opening up to her and now it burned to hold on.

Chapter Twenty-Eight

Hannah was helping Sandy clean up the kitchen when someone knocked at the door. "I'll get it!" Olivia called. She'd been tidying the living area, while Jade tucked Alexander in for his nap upstairs. Wendell was in the process of driving Caleb home. A few seconds later, Hannah heard Olivia crow, "Well, hey, little brother!"

A familiar voice resonated from the foyer. "Merry Christmas, Sis." Hannah envisioned them giving each other holiday hugs, as Sandy viewed her quizzically.

"Well?" Sandy asked, prodding her with her elbow. "Aren't you going to go out there?"

"Is Hannah still here?" they heard Carter ask. "I tried her bell first, but didn't get an answer."

"Yeah, she is," Sandy cried brightly.

Hannah felt herself color.

"Go on," Sandy whispered and gave her small shove. "Olivia and I won't listen."

"Oh, hi, Carter!" Sandy grinned peering into the foyer. "Merry Christmas."

He tipped his hat. "Merry Christmas to you."

"Oh, Olivia?" Sandy called cheerily. "Would you mind helping me dry the dishes?"

Olivia glanced between Carter and Hannah, who stood there red-faced, and got it immediately. "Coming!"

Hannah didn't know what to think or say. All day long, she'd been hoping to see him, and now that he was here she found herself speechless. He'd been so cruel to her last night, and very nearly ruined her Christmas. But the eyes looking at her now weren't the eyes of a vengeful man. They reflected pain and sorrow. "You're wearing the necklace," he said hoarsely. "I didn't think you'd want to—"

She instinctively raised her hand and lightly traced the charm. "It's lovely. I opened it this morning."

He slid the billfold from his pocket and displayed it. "I love this, too."

Hannah's heart still reeled from the hurtful memory of the way he'd slammed out the door. Her voice shook just a little when she answered, "I'm glad you like it."

"More than like it." He removed his hat and pressed it to his chest. "Hannah, I hope you'll forgive—"

"Let's not talk about that here, all right?" She stared at him intently, wanting him to know she understood. He was here to make amends and she was willing to listen. She needed to offer some apologies, too. But this wasn't the time or place.

His Adam's apple rose and fell. "Okay. When?"

"When do you get off?"

"Midnight."

"Then midnight it is."

"That's not too late?"

Hannah's heart stilled. "I'll wait for you."

The moment he'd gone, Sandy and Olivia rushed at her like a pair of wild dogs.

"Well, so? Huh?" Sandy's face was flushed. "Is it all good? Did you make up?"

Olivia grinned broadly. "What did he say?"

"Ladies," Hannah said in a fake haughty manner. "A little privacy, please?"

They laughed in understanding and wrapped their arms around her, shouting in unison. "Yay!" As they did, Hannah brought her hands to her rapidly beating heart.

A whole host of butterflies was winging inside it.

Hannah was a nervous wreck the rest of the day. She didn't know why, but she had the instinct that something big was coming. Maybe Sandy's abilities were rubbing off on her, after all. She spoke briefly with Ben and Lily, but they couldn't talk long as they were just sitting down to a late afternoon dinner. With the time difference in California, their Christmas celebrations were just getting started.

Ben was astounded when Hannah gave him a recap of the news concerning the crowdfunding. What a wonderful and welcoming town she was moving to. Once she'd settled in and felt ready for company, he and Lily would have to come visit. He was eager to meet the many interesting people she'd talked about, and Hannah was especially excited about the prospect of Ben meeting Sandy. Hannah had a feeling about the two of them.

To amuse herself and pass the time, Hannah played with the kittens on the floor with their new cat toys. She had to be careful when leaning toward Jingles, though. He seemed to have an attraction to her pretty new necklace, which was hardly surprising. This was one piece of jewelry he wasn't getting his kitty paws on. It would always be special to Hannah, partly because of the message behind it, but mostly because of the man who'd given it to her.

Since leaving Jade's house in the early evening, Hannah had thought a lot about Carter and the events that had transpired between them. She now understood that last night he'd probably felt raw, deeply vulnerable and exposed from the truths he'd shared with her. Despite Hannah's efforts at levity during dinner, he must have been still churning things over inside. So, when she'd presented the cookies, they'd been too much. He'd misread her overture, thinking she was hinting at permanence. Happily ever after, or something silly like that. Which Hannah definitely *wasn't* doing...

Hannah stopped shaking the stick with the brightly colored feathers on its end and the kittens stared up at her, wondering why she'd paused their game.

Maybe she *had been* doing it. Maybe happily ever after was secretly what Hannah wanted. And not just with any guy, but with Carter. Hannah gulped and dropped the kitty toy to the carpet. "Merry Christmas," she told Jingles and Belle. "You two take it from here."

Hannah got to her feet, her knees shaky and her head light. It was about more than butterflies with Carter. Hannah had experienced butterflies before. Okay, maybe it was true, not quite as big ones—and never so many all at once. But! The fact was, Carter was different. Carter was...dreamy. Hannah heard herself sigh, and pulled herself together. *No. More than dreamy... Perfect. No! Nobody's perfect. Almost perfect? Yes, that's it! And perfect for me!*

A vision returned of Carter approaching her car in a red Santa suit...then of Carter taking her in his arms at the Christmas Cookie Shop...and kissing her like wildfire on her front porch. And when he'd held her under the mistletoe, he'd said he wanted all of her cookies. That was *not* just figurative. And it was not only innuendo... Hannah gasped when she realized something important. Carter had fallen in love with her. What's more, she loved him back!

She slapped her hands to her cheeks, then raced to the kitchen, pulling the Virginia Cookie tin from a cabinet. Hannah pried her fingernail under the lid and popped it open. For an instant, she thought she saw stars! Sparkles! Fairy dust! Something really, really weird dancing around in the air. She hoped they weren't dust motes. The truth was that Hannah hadn't vacuumed since she'd gotten here. But, no! Dust motes didn't shimmer with rainbow colors like a hundred billion tiny sequins flitting around!

She stared down at the prettily arranged stack in the tin. The cookie on top seemed to be tempting her to eat it. It beamed and glowed, looking deliciously warm. Like it was straight out of the oven or something. Hannah couldn't help but reach for it. *Wait*! This wasn't right! Hannah wasn't supposed to eat the cookies, was she? Then again, it probably made sense for her to try them to see if they were any good before foisting them off on Carter. And Hannah was determined to try again.

How dare he refuse her cookies when he very clearly loved her? Hannah was feeling indignant, and that was good. It kept her from being petrified by what was clearly happening. She was going mad.

Hannah shot a glance at the front door, then peeked at the kittens playing in the living area. All right. She might as well! Hannah picked up a cookie and took a tiny nibble. It dissolved in her mouth like a sugary powder that tasted almost—magical. The flavors were both sweet *and* savory, totally unusual on her tongue. Familiar in a way, yet decidedly different. *Wow, that's good!* She took another bite, unable to resist. And then, a third—just to be sure. In a few small bites, the entire thing had disappeared. *Well, gosh*, she thought, concernedly, *that didn't last long.* Hardly long enough for her to judge the true value of the treat. She'd better try another.

The doorbell rang and Hannah viewed the empty tin on the counter in horror. Then she stared at the half-eaten cookie in her hand. She couldn't have, but she did. She'd eaten them all, every one. Okay, except for this last one. This, er…half of a last one. Hannah hastily set the half-eaten heart back in the tin and slammed on the lid, wiping the crumbs from her mouth with a napkin. "Coming!" she shouted in a panic, striding to the door.

Hannah paused to examine her reflection in the foyer mirror, horrified to spy cookie crumbs dotting her red Christmas sweater. She quickly brushed them off and opened the door.

"Hannah?"

"Carter!"

"Is there something in your hair?"

"What? Where?"

He reached up and swiped the side of her head with his glove. "Looks like glitter."

"Glitter?"

"Maybe it came from your barrette?"

"Oh, right. Right. Probably so."

She invited him in and shut the door.

Carter set his hat on the entrance table, unhitched his holster, and removed his coat and gloves. The kittens scampered over and he bent low to greet them. But Jingles was distracted, batting at a tiny red dot on the floor. Carter reached over and picked it up, pinching it between his thumb and index finger. "It looks like a Red Hot."

"Oh!" Hannah tried to reach for it, but Carter held it back, examining it more closely.

"Hey, weren't there Red Hots on those Virginia Cookies?"

"No, those were berries."

"Yes, but—"

"Why don't you come in and have a seat?" She held out her hand. "I'll take that!"

"No worries. I used to love Red Hots as a kid." To her astonishment he popped it in his mouth and rolled it around on his tongue. "Hmm. It's a Red Hot, all right. Cinnamon spicy."

"Carter," she scolded. "That was on the floor."

"Well, it hasn't been there long, has it? Probably just since last night."

"Ah...yeah. Probably!"

"Are you all right?" His brow wrinkled in concern. "I've kept you up too late. You're tired."

"Nope, not tired at all! Just the opposite really!"

He scrutinized her oddly. "Have you been drinking coffee?"

"No, why? Would you like some?"

Carter slowly shook his head. "No, thank you."

"Wine?"

He checked his watch. "Just one glass."

"I'll get it."

"I'll come help you."

"No!"

"Why not?"

"I don't want you in the kitchen."

"Hannah, I'm a little more modern than that," he said, joking.

She backed into the doorway. "I...really don't need your help, Carter. The wine's already open."

"Fantastic. I'll pour." He stepped toward her and she inched back. He took another step and she recoiled again. Eventually, the small of her back was pressed against the counter.

"Hannah," he said worriedly. "Is something going on?"

She sent a frantic glance over her shoulder at the cookie tin, then stared back at him, blinking. "I have no idea what you mean." But all around his head, she saw little red hearts, almost like paper Valentines with arrows shooting through them. One was on a lacy doily background and had words on it: *Love me!* She thought she saw cherubs, too. Loads of them. And a quivering pair of lovebirds! Hannah covered her eyes with both hands.

Carter leaned toward her and gently pried apart her fingers. "Hello?"

She gaped at him through her splayed fingers. "Um...hi."

"What on earth did you guys *do* at Jade's?"

"Nothing."

"Were you really drinking or something?"

"No!"

"Nothing stronger?" He looked disapproving.

"Carter, I..." She dropped her hands and gathered her nerve. "Did something really awful."

"Okay," he said, obviously steeling himself. "I'm ready."

"I..." Heat flooded her face and she took a deep breath. "I ate the Virginia Cookies!" It came out in a rush so fast, for a moment she wasn't certain he'd heard her. "I said—"

Carter's laughter roared through the kitchen. "Is that it? Hannah, sweetheart!" He braced her shoulders with his hands. "You scared me half to death."

"Well, maybe you should be frightened. On my behalf. They have really weird side effects."

"How many did you eat?"

"All of them."

"All?" He studied her, incredulous. "You didn't leave any for me?"

"They're kind of addicting," she said sheepishly. Hannah turned and lifted the tin, handing it to him. He frowned in concentration and popped off the lid.

"Wow," he said, looking down at the pile of crumbs. "You weren't kidding."

"There is this half of one left." She picked up the broken heart, handing it to him.

Carter took it and held it up to the light on the ceiling, flipping the cookie morsel first one way and then the other. "Looks perfectly normal to me." He scrutinized it more closely and took a couple of nibbles. "Hmm. I was right! Those *are* Red Hots! Delicious!" Carter chewed thoughtfully for a minute more, before reporting, "Hannah, this is extraordinary. These are by far the best cookies I've ever tasted—in my life! You've got yourself a big hit!" He polished the rest of it off in one big bite and licked his fingers. "I can see why you couldn't stop. Each bite only leaves you hungry for more."

"Kind of like potato chips," she agreed. "Yeah."

"Well, thanks for letting me try them."

"I'm sorry, I…er, didn't save you more."

He seemed to be looking at her in an odd way. His gaze kept shooting above her head. Then to the left… Next to the right… "That's what I get for not taking you up on it last night." He gave her a lopsided grin. "Use or lose, I suppose!"

"Use or lose!" she echoed cheerily. The next thing she knew, Carter tugged her into his arms. And— *wham!* Straight up against his chest!

"Hannah," he said hungrily. "I don't want to lose you." He was insistent. Predatory.

Normally, this would seem romantic, but at the moment, it was a little overwhelming. He was not himself somehow. "I…um…" Hannah bit into her bottom lip, thinking fast. "You won't!"

"I've wanted you forever." He groaned, gazing down at her. "Ever since that first day."

She looked up helplessly. "At the roundabout?"

"Yes! There!"

"I honestly thought you were pretty hot, too." She felt fire in her cheeks. "In that Santa suit. I wanted to rip it off of you." Hannah gasped. *What did I just say?*

"You did?" He grinned sexily. "Well, I seriously wanted your cookies."

"What?"

"All of them. And everywhere." *Wait a minute. Did he just growl?* "Under the mistletoe. On my sofa… On yours… Or! We could go upstairs." He looked oddly delirious. "Oh my darling…" Carter brought his mouth down on hers and devoured her with ravenous kisses.

Hannah's knees buckled and she thought she might faint.

"Carter...uh..." She pressed back on his shoulders, but he continued.

"Tell me you don't want me to stop," he said fiercely. Like she was pushing him right over the edge.

Oh, well. It's Christmas!

"Don't stop," she gasped and he kissed her again, ultra passionately.

Her ankles were snaking around his legs: first one...and then the other, as if they had sneaky little minds of their own. The next thing she knew, her hands slid up his muscled chest... *Gosh! Yum!* This was totally bizarre. Hannah's senses were heightened, like she could feel every little thing a thousand times better than normal, and what she was feeling was *pretty amazing.*

He grabbed her backside and lifted her up, depositing her on the counter. Hannah thought she might have purred, but wasn't one hundred percent sure. She clamped herself around him. Like a vise! Her skin was so hot she was bursting into flames. Carter must have felt the heat, too, because he yanked off his necktie and tossed it over his shoulder.

They were totally broiling now, like camels crossing the desert. Camels carrying wise men! *Huh?* Carter undid the top two buttons on his shirt and there was ardor in his eyes, but panic, too. Almost like he couldn't help what he was saying. "Hannah," he rasped loudly. "I love you!"

The words spewed uncontrollably from her mouth. "Oh Carter, I love you too!"

The Virginia Cookie tin crashed to the floor with a deafening *clank.*

Then the lid rolled out of the kitchen, clattering into the foyer. But neither one could stop. It was like some weird primal force kept pushing them forward…to the tune of—*hang on*—"Deck the Halls"?

"Kiss me again," she commanded and he complied with vigor. Visions of sugarplums danced through her head, as Carter's hands traveled all over: first down her back, then around to her front… *Oooh! Ahh!* She heard jingle bells!

Hannah's temperature spiked and her pulse raced out of control. "Bedroom," she panted madly. She didn't have to ask him twice.

Carter hoisted her off the counter, gripping her bottom in his hands. Hannah feared if they didn't hurry, they'd never make it past the sofa, which she didn't think was big enough. Though she supposed it would do in a pinch. Her legs were still wrapped around him in some kind of strange pretzel knot, with her ankles overlapping at his lower back. He had one forearm under her backside now, while the other held her close, her breasts squashed against his rock-hard chest.

He groaned and carried her toward the steps, his excitement becoming increasingly obvious between them. *Oh…my…goodness!* Hannah saw stars.

She moaned as he hauled her upstairs, with her arms looped around his neck. "Quickly!"

He must have sensed the urgency, too, because he bulldozed straight into the first bedroom he saw, which was the street-facing one on the left. Carter dumped Hannah on the bed, and yanked off her boots, catapulting them into the hall. Then he ditched his shoes and prowled over her, like a jungle beast. His evergreen gaze was primitive…passionate…fueled by desire. *Flap! Flap! Flap!* Butterflies broke free, but then they had to wrestle with the reindeer. And there were so many of them. All in competing airspace!

He unzipped her jeans and Hannah frantically shimmied out of them, her heart beating crazily out of control. Next, he rid her of her sweater and adroitly unhooked her bra.

Before she knew what was happening, she'd ripped open his shirt and buttons went *zinging* everywhere! Some smacking the bedside table...others hitting the mirror...several whacking against the floor! Hannah's face burned hot, but probably not any hotter than the rest of her. "Oops! Sorry!"

"No need!" But his need was extremely evident as it collided with her thigh. Carter pushed back on his knees and undid his belt and fly, then hurriedly tugged something from his pocket. It was a little foil packet. *How sweet! And very responsible... Just like him, actually.*

Carter quickly shucked his shirt and the T-shirt underneath. Then his broad and hairy chest was bearing down on her—and another critical part, too.

"Wait!" she cried, nearly desperate. "Panties!"

In one deft move, he reached down and tugged them off. She had to admit he was very, very good. Of course, she'd helped a tiny bit by lifting her bum.

"Hannah?" His voice was guttural, dramatic...sexy. "May I?"

This was too good to be true. Almost like a miracle. Almost like a dream. "Oh, please!" Hannah hoped she wouldn't pass out from pure pleasure. Not just yet. And—to her exceptional delight—she didn't.

Thirty minutes later, Hannah and Carter stared at the ceiling, blinking. Both lay naked under the cushy goose-down duvet covering the front bedroom's double bed.

"What just happened?" he asked, dazed.

"I don't know."

"You don't actually think those cookies…?"

"Of course not." But, secretly, Hannah wondered if it *was* the cookies.

"Me either." Carter glanced her way. "But still, something came over me. Something I can't explain."

"Yeah."

"Did you follow the recipe exactly?" When she didn't answer, he turned to her. "Hannah?"

She lifted one shoulder. "I only made a few modifications."

"Well, maybe next time you should stick to the basics."

"Do you think there should be a next time?" She beheld him worriedly. "I mean, maybe they're not safe?"

"Your great-grandmother sold them for years."

"That's true."

"Ever hear of anything terrible happening to anyone?"

"All the opposite." Hannah thoughtfully shook her head. "I must have made them too strong."

"I'll say!" Carter ran his hands through his hair and then laughed. "Wow. That was really something. I feel like I need a cold shower."

"Or a cigarette? I mean, assuming you smoked. Which—obviously—you don't."

He cracked a grin. "I love your sense of humor."

"You said you loved more than that in the kitchen," she said leadingly. "Or was that just the cookies talking?"

"No. That was me."

Carter took her in his arms and Hannah sighed in his strong embrace.

"What am I going to do?"

"Try again, I guess."

"That could get dangerous," she teased.

"Not if you're very careful about selecting your taste testers."

She smiled up at him. "Are you volunteering?"

"I certainly don't want you testing them out with anyone else. That would make me horribly jealous." He gently kissed her lips, then studied her a long while before speaking. "I'm so glad you're staying in Christmas Town, and about your reopening the cookie shop. I'm sure it will be a winner.

"And, Hannah?" he said sincerely. "I'm really sorry about how I behaved last night. First, I laid my baggage on you—"

"It wasn't baggage," she said, correcting him gently. "It was part of your history, which means it's part of who you are. And I love you, Carter Livingston. I honestly do. I thought it out and came to that conclusion long before I devoured all those cookies."

"Well, it's a relief to know you didn't decide while under the influence." He smiled warmly. "I didn't either."

"No?"

"I think I've known for a while. I was just afraid to admit it."

"To me?"

"And to myself. I've spent a long time on my own, telling myself I need to be independent."

"You are."

"Perhaps. But my understanding of that has changed. I now see that being independent isn't the same thing as being alone. With true independence you trust yourself enough to know you can stand on your own while having a partner. Someone who's independent, too, but who you can bond with…someone you can lean on while they help support you." He lovingly searched her eyes and Hannah's pulse quickened. "Don't you agree?"

"I…yes. I agree that two strong people can be even stronger together."

"We're strong people, Hannah," he told her surely. "You and I."

Hannah's heart beat faster and her cheeks burned hot. He was saying all the right words, but she owed him a few of her own. He wasn't the only one who'd behaved shamefully during their fight. "Carter," she began quietly. "About last night… I need to offer an apology, too. I'm sorry I reacted so strongly when you were trying hard to do everything right."

"Not everything—" he began, but Hannah stopped him.

"No, you might have taken a cookie, that's true," she said with feigned haughtiness. "And who knows where things might have gone from there?"

Carter cocked an eyebrow. "I have a guess."

Hannah laughed and drew the covers in around them. Then she snuggled down in his arms and spoke more seriously. "I'm really sorry I didn't appear more grateful," she said, meeting his eyes. "About the town crowdfunding and your gift. Both were such wonderful gestures. I was just…overwhelmed."

"You overwhelm me, Hannah," he said huskily. "In the best possible way."

He pulled her close and ardently kissed her. When he pulled back, he grasped the chain dangling from around her neck and stroked its charm. "Hannah Winchester," he said. "You're my compass. You were lost when I met you, but it's you who's brought me home. It's a good place—the best place, and I want to stay here…for as long as you'll let me."

"I want to stay with you, too," she admitted from the heart.

"I'm not going anywhere, I promise."

"I'm not either," she said contentedly.

A few minutes later something pounced up on the bed. They heard a loud purring, then a second furry creature bounded into the room. This one was orange. "Don't look now," she told Carter as Jingles joined them. "But I think we have company."

Carter slightly raised his head off the pillow to spy the two kittens kneading the blankets by their feet, then settled back with a laugh. "I'd better take this into protective custody," he said, cupping his palm over Hannah's compass charm. "We wouldn't want any scamps running off with it."

"No, we wouldn't."

He lowered his face to hers and spoke in low tones. "Do you think those cookies have worn off yet?"

"Not entirely."

"Want to check and see?"

"Um-hmm." She nipped at his lip and his anatomy came alive again, his body heating hers. Hannah tingled all over.

"I could get used to this," he said suggestively. "This cookie testing."

Hannah grinned, her heart light. "Yeah. Me, too."

He looked longingly in her eyes and Hannah saw a winter wonderland of possibilities. She was finally starting to believe it. Right here in Christmas Town, everyday dreams really did come true. Carter brushed his lips over hers and whispered softly. "Merry Christmas, Hannah. I love you."

"Merry Christmas," she said with a breathy sigh. "I love you, too."

Chapter Twenty-Nine

Eight weeks later, Hannah closed out the register at the Christmas Cookie Shop and counted her opening week receipts. Her sales had been amazing! If things kept going at this pace, she'd pay off her old college loans in no time and buy a brand new car. Hannah glanced happily around the front room, filled with pride. The new pastry cases she'd installed were stocked with prettily made cookies of all kinds. There were white sugar cookies cut into Christmassy shapes, peanut butter balls, snickerdoodles, wreath-shaped marshmallow treats, butterscotch bars, and even gingerbread men!

Hannah summed up her selections, excited that she'd been able to make so many varieties. And she hadn't burned a single batch. The only cookies that weren't for sale were Lena's famous Virginia Cookies. Those weren't due out until next Christmas. Besides, Hannah was still finessing the recipe…with Carter's help, she thought with a blush. She'd never had a boyfriend like him, and couldn't imagine that a better one existed. Apart from acting as a thoughtful and caring partner, he'd provided his muscle in refurbishing this shop. He and the men in the Christmas family had helped with moving equipment around, and by repairing and painting the old damaged walls and trim.

Frank Cho tweaked, and re-tweaked, his numbers in order to get the electrical costs down, allowing Hannah to purchase a wonderful new rack oven and a high-end refrigerator and freezer with the savings. The entire kitchen had been overhauled with state-of-the-art *everything,* though Hannah made sure to drape Christmas lights around the perimeter to give the area a cozy holiday glow. Frank double-checked her setup to ensure there'd be no safety concerns and the Christmas Cookie Shop passed its building inspection with flying colors.

Hannah was pleased she'd been able to revamp the shop without having to dig into all the reserves the townspeople had raised for her. There'd be a new town meeting next week to address the first allocation of Lena Winchester's Good Works Fund. Hannah had heard rumors of pretty seasonal flags being purchased for the streets' lampposts, or even something as ambitious as a Christmas Town children's playground in the works. Her gaze snagged on the old newspaper clipping of the Virginia O'Hanlon editorial that she'd framed and mounted near the front door. Lena had believed in bringing the magic of the season back to Christmas Town and now Hannah was determined to do that, too.

Just then, the door chime tinkled and a tall, slim man with salt-and-pepper hair entered. Hannah was about to apologize to the stranger, telling him she'd closed for the day, when she recognized the face. "Hello, Hannah."

An icy cold sensation settled in the pit of her stomach. "Dad." His face was weathered and worn, deep crevices etched behind his grizzled beard. From the look in his eyes and his tattered clothing, it appeared that his life had been hard. He wore an old gray coat that was missing two buttons, and clutched a small wooden box in his hands.

"I heard you'd moved to Christmas Town," he said hoarsely. "So I came here to find you."

Her throat felt raw when she asked, "But why?"

He strode to the counter she stood behind and placed the small wooden box down on it. "To give you this."

All at once, Hannah knew what it was. She lifted it slowly and pried back the lid with incredulity. A whole stash of handwritten recipes was stuffed inside. Many were smudged with fingerprints and dirty, like someone had pawed through them.

"You stole this from Buddy Christmas?" Her voice cracked harshly.

"Stole is a pretty strong word. Borrowed is more like it. He just wasn't around for me to ask."

"You took it from his workshop," Hannah surmised with a gasp. She sadly shook her head, unwilling to believe he'd been that misguided. Desperate. Or both.

"I wanted to take what was rightfully mine. As you're aware, I didn't get the shop." His tone wasn't filled with rancor, only remorse. "I thought I should have something, too. Maybe something of value."

"The recipe doesn't work that way," Hannah told him. "It doesn't respond to greed. It helps with good intentions only. Charity, forgiveness, love."

He scrutinized her a moment, then asked with surprise, "You found it?"

Hannah avoided his eyes, deciding not to answer. "I read about it in a history book."

"A history book," he said doubtfully. "Right."

When her head cleared from the shock of her father's sudden appearance, Hannah had the presence of mind to ask, "What made you come here now?"

"When I heard you'd reopened Lena's shop, I thought you might be able to use the file. Even if the special recipe isn't there, there are plenty of others. But there is one more thing…" His face registered genuine pain and—in a stunning way—Hannah almost felt sorry for him. Who was this shell of a man, and what had become of her angry, turbulent father? "I came here to apologize."

Hannah didn't know how he thought he could fix things. Not after so much time. He'd left his children and his dying wife behind when they'd needed him most. He hadn't even attended either of his parents' funerals. She wasn't even sure if her dad knew that Ben had married and had a child. And, if he didn't, Hannah decided that was Ben's business to share, not hers.

"I'm not proud of who I am or what I've done, Hannah. But I am trying to change."

Heat burned in her eyes. "And have you…changed?"

He gave her a sad, uneven smile. "I'm trying my best. One day at a time."

When he turned to go, Hannah realized he was leaving again. This time, probably forever… "Dad, wait!"

He stopped and turned slowly on his heel.

"Where are you going? I mean, is there…? Is there a place where Ben and I can reach you?"

"I've got the address of this store," he said, motioning to the ceiling above him. "I'll send you a postcard."

"A postcard. Sure," she said, not entirely believing it.

As he pulled back the door, she called out one last time.

"What is it?" he asked over his shoulder.

"I just wanted to say…" Her voice broke apart…at the pain, the heartache, and the memories…that came flooding back, despite her willing them not to. "Thank you."

Her father paused for a long while and hung his head.

"I don't deserve your thanks, but I'll take them," he said gruffly, before walking away.

Hannah was still trembling when Carter arrived ten minutes later. It was his night off and the two of them had plans, as they did almost every day now, whether Carter was working or not. "Hannah? What's wrong?" he said, rushing to her. She stood by the register, where she'd been paralyzed since her father left. How could he just breeze in, then disappear that way? Again?

Carter stepped around the counter and took her in his arms, worriedly surveying her features. "Sweetheart, what's happened? Please, talk to me."

She looked up at him, willing herself not to break down. "It's my dad."

"He was here?" he asked with alarm, and Hannah nodded. "When?"

"Just a few minutes ago."

"He didn't…" He viewed her carefully. "Hurt you?"

"No. Nothing like that." Moisture pooled in her eyes. "He came to bring back the box."

Carter blinked in momentary confusion, then quickly scanned the room, locating the small wooden recipe file on the pastry case. "He's the one who took it? You're kidding? But, why?"

"He thought he could get money out of it somehow."

"Wow, Hannah. I'm sorry." His face fell in sympathy. "So, so sorry. Seeing him must have been rough, especially after all this time. Did he say anything else?"

Hannah swallowed past the lump in her throat. "He came to apologize."

"For?"

"Just about everything, I suppose."

"What did you tell him?"

"What could I, really?"

Carter tightened his embrace. "I wish that I'd been here."

"Even if you had, it probably wouldn't have changed much."

Carter studied her kindly. "Will you see him again?"

"I honestly don't know."

Carter cradled her head against his chest and gently stroked her hair. "I know it's hard. Very, very hard," he whispered. "But time passes."

"Sometimes too quickly," she said, choking on a breath.

He squeezed her to him and kissed the top of her head.

"You know what?" he rasped quietly. "It really does."

This was it: that lightning-bolt moment when Carter grasped what he had to do and when. Hannah wasn't just the most wonderful girlfriend in the world; she was the love of his life. Despite the difficulties she'd endured growing up, she'd kept her sense of humor and had a good and tender heart. Hannah was kind, giving, sensitive, and generous to a fault. And she was the most determined woman he'd ever known. When Hannah set her mind to something, she did it! Just look at how she'd learned to cook, and in record time. Carter couldn't be more proud of her for reopening the shop, just as he couldn't imagine himself caring for anyone more.

Hannah wasn't only funny and smart; she was thoughtful and intuitive. She understood him on a level that was extremely deep and personal, and Carter wanted to work hard every day to understand and honor her. Hannah might not have had the happiest home life as a child. But he'd experienced one firsthand with his loving parents and sisters, and Carter was confident he could give one to her. Carter had felt for a while that he wanted Hannah in his future. Now, all the pieces were falling into place as to how she fit in.

Chapter Thirty

By the following week, Hannah was already feeling better about her conversation with her dad. She'd talked at length with Ben about it, as well as with Sandy and Carter, and everyone agreed she'd done the right thing in treating him kindly and leaving the door open. The future was long and family was family, although—for obvious reasons—Ben had the hardest time dealing with this part. He wasn't sure when he'd be ready to see his dad again, even if Tanner made the gesture. Though Hannah and he agreed they probably wouldn't need to face that prospect for a long time. Odds were, their dad would never even send that postcard.

Hannah lifted her pearl teardrop earrings off her dresser, moving them deftly out of Jingles's way. She was getting better at forestalling his magpie advances. It helped that Sandy had given her a pretty new jewelry box as a gift to celebrate her shop's opening. It provided a safe place to stash her valuables, including her gorgeous compass charm necklace, Hannah thought, preening a bit in the mirror. Since returning to Stafford after the holidays and retrieving her things from Ben's, Hannah now a complete wardrobe to work with. She'd missed these brown denim jeans and the ivory, cable-knit cardigan she wore with them. They went well with her black Lycra, scoop-neck T-shirt, and brown leather boots, and perfectly with her jewelry.

It was late February now, but still snowing in Christmas Town. Lou had assured her that the snow always stopped by late March each year, but Hannah was silently starting to wonder. She turned toward the bed and grabbed a few kitty toys, casting them onto the floor. Jingles jumped down off the dresser and took off after them, while Belle watched him with mild interest. The gray female kitty had perched under a chair, where she spent most of her time now in the daylight. The way the sunshine angled in the windows, it seemed to hit that spot just right, keeping it nice and warm.

Hannah was glad Lou had allowed her to continue renting this place for a while, so she wouldn't have to look for something new. Of course, the truth was she spent a whole lot of time over at Carter's cabin…under that skylight. Not that she would dare think about this around Sandy!

Hannah was so disappointed that Sandy had been gone when Ben and Lily came to town for the Christmas Cookie Shop's opening. She'd had some sort of emergency with her parents in Canada. Hannah wasn't giving up, though. She had a feeling about Sandy and Ben. She'd mentioned this to Carter and he'd roundly teased her, saying she'd already been in Christmas Town too long and was taking after Louise Christmas. But Hannah couldn't help it. She only wanted everybody to be as happy as she was.

She'd been really glad to see Ben and Carter getting along. They hadn't spent much time together, since Ben and Lily had only come for the weekend, but everyone had appeared to genuinely enjoy each other's company. And little Lily had really loved seeing the kittens again, marveling at how big they'd grown.

The doorbell rang and Hannah scurried downstairs to answer it. She found Carter on the stoop carrying a pizza box and a bright red package, tied up in a pretty satin bow. She'd been expecting the pizza from the Reindeer Pub, since they'd decided to eat in, but not the present.

"What's this?" she asked, smiling, when Carter handed her the gift.

"It occurred to me, belatedly…" he said, clearing his throat. "That I never gave you a housewarming present."

"Housewarming?" she asked, surprised.

Carter closed the door behind him, then went and set the pizza box on the dining room table, along with a bottle of red wine. He turned to her and unzipped his jacket, slipping it off. "For your shop."

Hannah grinned, pleased.

"I know it opened a few weeks ago," he continued. "But things were so busy—"

"Of course. I mean, yes. I definitely know. Please, don't apologize." Hannah was hoping he wasn't going to make her wait to open it after dinner. Not when she was totally dying to open it now. What could it be? Another piece of jewelry? A thought flashed through her mind and her pulse quickened. Romantic jewelry? The *mine forever* kind? Hannah told herself not to be silly, and not to get her hopes up.

She and Carter had been enjoying things as they were: as boyfriend and girlfriend, who did a whole lot of cookie tasting from time to time. Okay, all right, it was true. She'd fed him a *mountain-load* of Virginia

Cookies, lately. Was it possible something had finally kicked in?

Deciding she needed to be cautious, Hannah had been tinkering with Lena's recipe to achieve different levels of results. She clearly had to be careful about selling cookies to children, and something like her Red Hots edition might actually be too potent for many adults! Hannah wasn't so sure she should even put out *those*. So she decided to hold them in reserve for those certain serious couples experiencing unexpected dips in passion.

Meanwhile, she planned to offer three basic varieties of Virginia Cookies each season: the Charity Cookie, intended to inspire good works—and suitable for all ages; the Clemency Cookie, meant to foster forgiveness—likewise suited to all ages; and the Commitment Cookie—strictly for those over the age of eighteen, who were looking to bond more permanently with their special someone. She'd been really working on that last one lately. Kind of a lot, a lot, *a lot.* Hannah was sure it was coincidental she kept asking Carter for his opinion on them. That was simply the variety she'd yet to perfect!

Not that these darn things probably worked anyway. Hannah was sixty percent certain their effects were all in her head. Then, there was the other forty percent of her that wondered… The most likely thing was that the cookies achieved the things people believed they would. Sort of like self-fulfilling prophecies.

"Our pizza's getting cold," Carter commented and Hannah realized she'd been staring down at the package in her hands for several minutes. He'd already put plates on the table and poured the wine. When had he done all that?

"Oh, um… I kind of thought you wanted me to open up this present?"

"Why don't you do it after dinner?" he said mildly, before politely pulling back her chair. "I'm starved."

"Oh, well…" *Darn!* "Okay. That's fine." She smiled brightly and tried not to let her disappointment show when she left the package behind her on the entranceway table and took her seat. Carter served her two delicious slices of steaming supreme pizza, and she ate them in about two seconds flat.

"Wow," Carter said, observing her empty plate. "Hungry?"

"A little."

"Here…" He leaned toward the box. "Let me get you another piece."

"No!" Hannah worked hard to collect herself, but inside she was tingling all over…like itty- bitty champagne bubbles were bursting out of her pores. And she hadn't had one single Virginia Cookie today. Maybe it wasn't the cookies causing all those strange symptoms. Maybe it was just *her.* Hannah swallowed hard, worrying that she might be a freak destined to join the circus. That definitely would not play well with the people of Christmas Town. Carter probably wouldn't like it either. Or maybe he would? Depending on her act?

"Did you just say trapeze?" he asked her, looking concerned.

"No, I most definitely did not." Hannah primly wiped her mouth with a napkin, thinking hard. "I said it's been a *breeze* running the Christmas Cookie Shop! I mean, much more manageable than I imagined."

"You're doing a mighty fine job of it, too," he said, toasting her. He caught her eyeing his pizza. "What is it? Do you want mine?" he asked uncertainly. She supposed he thought she wanted to play that food-swap-taste game again. What a brilliant idea! She was fearful this drawn-out dinner would never end.

"I'll just take a bite," Hannah said cheerily. "If you don't mind." Fortunately, he didn't question the fact that they were eating the same thing.

"All right." Carter appeared mildly amused. "Shall I cut you a piece with my knife and fork?"

"Nope! Just hand it over."

He cautiously extended his slice, like he feared she might take off a finger, and Hannah very nearly did. Carter's hand jerked back and he stared in awe of the remnants of the piece she'd chomped into. It was bitten way down to the crust!

"Hmm, good!" she said, chewing noisily. Hannah sat back in her chair and dusted off her palms, glancing down at their plates. "How about that? Looks like we're done."

Carter burst into laughter. "Oh, my dear, sweet Hannah." A smile crept up his lips. "You really can't wait, can you?"

Hannah squirmed in her chair. "Not a minute more!"

"Okay then," he said indulgently. "Go grab your gift. Let's head on over to the sofa."

"The sofa?"

He cocked an eyebrow her way as if to say, *don't question me now, I'm in charge.* So she scampered off from the table, nabbed the package, then dashed to the sofa. All in record time.

"Impressive. Olympian!" Carter chuckled and picked up his wine, slowly sauntering over. What was he doing? Torturing her?

"You got me something really good, didn't you?" she said, bouncing up and down on the sofa cushion.

Carter stopped walking and observed her astutely. "How many Virginia Cookies have you had today?"

"None of them. Promise!"

"Well, maybe you should take a break for a while. I'm worried they're building up in your system."

"Oh right. Sorry. You might have a point." But secretly, Hannah knew that he didn't. Because the cooler Carter played this, the more certain she became that he was leading up to something huge. *Yippee!*

"Would you like your wine?"

"Nope! No wine!"

"Right, you probably don't need it," she thought she heard him mumble.

"Why, Carter Livingston," she cried impulsively. "You keep this up, I won't even saaayyyy… Um." Hannah gulped hard. "Never mind."

Carter sat down beside her and took her hand, setting his wine on the coffee table. "You know that I love you," he said. "Everything about you. Whether you're up or you're down…even when you've eaten a whole tin of Virginia Cookies." He paused, looking a bit concerned. "You haven't just now, have you?"

"Carter!" she said, exasperated. "I told you, no."

"Good, because I want you to have your wits about you tonight when I ask you this very important question…"

She eagerly met his eyes and he motioned to the package. Hannah drew in a breath and held it, untying the silky ribbon. Then she pulled back the paper and opened the box. There was a smaller felt-covered box inside. It looked like a ring box. Hannah exhaled sharply, her heart hammering harder.

"Well, go on," he said warmly. "Open it."

She did—and was dazzled by the most gorgeous diamond ring she'd ever seen! In her life! Even in her dreams! Even in the movies! Okay, maybe sometimes in Hollywood the stones were slightly larger, but those were probably fakes—and this one was pretty ample. Plus, it glistened like new-fallen snow.

The minute it did, Jingles skittered over to watch, and Belle cautiously trailed him, until they'd both positioned themselves in curious perches beside the sofa.

Carter slid off the couch and dropped down on one knee, taking her hand. "I hope this ring suits you, Hannah, because I'm asking you to be my wife." His brow crinkled sweetly. "And if it doesn't, we'll go find another. Just don't break my heart by telling me no."

No? *No?* Was he totally crazy? Like out of his mind? As if she could deny this man anything. *Ever*. He was certainly getting her cookies tonight. Tons and tons of them! He'd made her the happiest woman alive! Which was why someone had turned on the waterworks and tears were gushing down her face like Niagara Falls or something. "*You* suit me just right." She sniffed and wiped back her tears. "And the ring is beautiful."

His green eyes sparkled as he took it from the box and slid it on her finger.

"Hannah Winchester, will you marry me?"

She blubbered something in reply, but it was probably unintelligible. She could barely see him because her mascara was running so badly. Hannah hoped that wouldn't count against her. At least she'd looked all right when he got here.

He gently stroked back her tears and cradled her cheeks in his palms. "Does that mean yes?" The look in his eyes was tender, soulful...inviting. Calling Hannah to finally come home.

The biggest, most beautiful, butterfly she'd ever imagined broke into flight...fluttering gracefully toward the sun. Thousands and *thousands* of others followed. And there were big puffy clouds and a rainbow! *No, two rainbows! Three!* Hannah sniffed again, realizing she'd finally stopped crying.

"Yes," she said, throwing herself into his arms. "A billion butterflies, yes!"

Carter chuckled, catching her quickly. "Butterflies?"

"Oh, if you only knew!"

Epilogue

You are cordially invited to attend the marriage
of

Hannah Elizabeth Winchester
and
Carter Johnson Livingston

The Second Saturday of December
Next Winter
Four o'clock in the afternoon

The Corner Church
301 North Main Street
Christmas Town, Tennessee

Dinner Reception
Immediately following at
The Christmas Inn

The End

A Note from the Author

Thanks for reading *The Christmas Cookie Shop*. I hope you enjoyed it. If you did, please help other people find this book.

1. This book is lendable, so send it to a friend you think might like it so that she (or he) can discover my work too.

2. Help other people find this book: Write a review.

3. Sign up for my newsletter so you can learn about the next book as soon as it's available. Write to GinnyBairdRomance@gmail.com with "newsletter" in the subject heading.

4. Come like my Facebook page: https://www.facebook.com/GinnyBairdRomance.

5. Connect with me on Twitter: https://twitter.com/GinnyBaird.

6. Visit my website for details on other books available at multiple outlets now: http://www.ginnybairdromance.com

If you enjoyed this first book in the Christmas Town series, I hope you'll follow Sandy and Ben's story in Book 2, *A Mommy for Christmas*. A brief description follows.

A MOMMY FOR CHRISTMAS
Christmas Town Book 2

Northern Virginia attorney Ben Winchester has spent the past four years being the best single dad he could be to his eight-year-old daughter Lily. Yet, last Christmas, he was unable to give her the one thing she asked for: a mommy. Since his late-wife's death, Ben has scarcely dated at all. He's also had a hard time with the holidays. When Ben and Lily venture to Christmas Town, Tennessee for Ben's sister's December wedding, they discover a village infused with holiday joy. Upbeat Sandy Claus runs The Snow Globe Gallery...loves sleigh bells, winter and kids. She has a special way about her, and is the most caring and intuitive person Ben has ever met. When Ben finds himself falling for the beautiful blonde with big blue eyes, she hesitates about becoming involved due to some unusual family history. Despite complications that ensue, will true love prevail with Ben making his—and Lily's—fondest Christmas wishes come true?

Made in the USA
Coppell, TX
16 December 2020

45497513R00208